# Titles by Anthony Horowitz

The Alex Rider series:
*Stormbreaker*
*Point Blanc*
*Skeleton Key*
*Eagle Strike*
*Scorpia*
*Ark Angel*
*Snakehead*
*Crocodile Tears*
*Scorpia Rising*
*Russian Roulette*
*Never Say Die*
*Secret Weapon*

The Power of Five (Book One): *Raven's Gate*
The Power of Five (Book Two): *Evil Star*
The Power of Five (Book Three): *Nightrise*
The Power of Five (Book Four): *Necropolis*
The Power of Five (Book Five): *Oblivion*

*The Devil and his Boy*
*Granny*
*Groosham Grange*
*Return to Groosham Grange*
*The Switch*
*Scared to Death*

The Diamond Brothers books:
*The Falcon's Malteser*
*Public Enemy Number Two*
*South by South East*
*The French Confection*
*The Greek Who Stole Christmas*
*The Blurred Man*
*I Know What You Did Last Wednesday*

# ACCLAIM FOR ALEX RIDER:

"Explosive, thrilling, action-packed – meet Alex Rider." **Guardian**

"Horowitz is pure class, stylish but action-packed ... being James Bond in miniature is way cooler than being a wizard." **Daily Mirror**

"Horowitz will grip you with suspense, daring and cheek – and that's just the first page! ... Prepare for action scenes as fast as a movie." **The Times**

"Anthony Horowitz is the lion of children's literature." **Michael Morpurgo**

"Fast and furious." **Telegraph**

"The perfect hero ... genuine 21st century stuff." **Daily Telegraph**

"Brings new meaning to the phrase 'action-packed'." **Sunday Times**

"Every bored schoolboy's fantasy, only a thousand times funnier, slicker and more exciting ... genius." **Independent on Sunday**

ACTION
ADRENALINE
ADVENTURE

# ALEX RIDER

## SCORPIA RISING

# ANTHONY HOROWITZ

**WALKER
BOOKS**

First published 2011 by Walker Books Ltd
87 Vauxhall Walk, London SE11 5HJ

This edition published 2015

8 10 9

This book has been typeset in Officina Sans

Printed and bound by CPI Group (UK) Ltd, Croydon CR0 4YY

British Library Cataloguing in Publication Data:
a catalogue record for this book
is available from the British Library

ISBN 978-1-4063-6027-1

www.walker.co.uk

MIX
Paper from
responsible sources
FSC® C020471

*For all the readers who began this journey
and who have now reached its end*

# CONTENTS

# PART ONE: SCORPIA

# *STOLEN GODS*

The man in the black cashmere coat climbed down the steps of his private six-seater Learjet 40 and stood for a moment, his breath frosting in the chill morning air. He glanced across the tarmac as a refuelling truck rumbled past. In the distance two men in fluorescent jackets were standing talking in front of a hangar. Otherwise, he seemed to be alone. Ahead of him a sign read WELCOME TO LONDON CITY AIRPORT, and beneath it an open door beckoned, leading to immigration. He headed for it, unaware that he was being watched every step of the way.

The man was in his fifties, bald and expressionless. Inside the terminal he gave his passport to the official and watched with blank eyes as it was examined and handed back, then continued on his way. He had no luggage. There was a black limousine waiting for him outside with a grey-suited chauffeur behind the wheel. The man offered no greeting as he got in, nor did he speak as they set off, following the curve of the River Thames up towards Canning Town and on towards the centre of London itself.

His name was Zeljan Kurst and he was wanted by the police in seventeen different countries. He was the chief executive of the international criminal organization known as Scorpia and, as far as it was known, he had never been seen on the streets of London. However, MI6 had been tipped off that he was coming, and they had been waiting for him to land. The passport official was one of their secret agents. They were following him now.

"Heading west on the A13 Commercial Road towards Whitechapel. Car three take over at the next intersection."

"Car three moving into position..."

"OK. Dropping back..."

The disembodied voices bounced across the airwaves on a channel so secret that anyone trying to tune in without the necessary filters would hear only the hiss of static. It would have been easier to arrest Kurst at the airport. He could have been made to disappear in five seconds, bundled out in a crate and never seen again. But it had been decided, at the very highest level, to follow him and see where he went. For the head of Scorpia to be in England at all was remarkable. For him to be on his own, and on his way to a meeting, was beyond belief.

Zeljan Kurst was not aware that he was surrounded. He had no idea that his flight plan had been leaked by one of his own people in return for a complete change of identity and a new life in Panama. But even so, he was uneasy. Everything had told him that he shouldn't be here. When the invitation had first arrived on his desk, delivered by a series of middlemen and travelling halfway round the world and back again, he had thought about refusing. He was not an errand boy. He couldn't be summoned like a waiter in a restaurant. But then he had reconsidered.

When the fourth richest man in the world asks you to meet him, and pays you one million euros just to turn up, it might be as well to hear what he has to say.

"We're on High Holborn. Car four moving to intercept."

"Wait a minute. Wait a minute. He's turning off..."

The limousine had crossed the main road and entered a narrow street full of old-fashioned shops and cafés. The move had taken the MI6 men by surprise, and for a moment, there was panic as they struggled to catch up. Two of their cars swerved across the traffic – to a blast of horns – and plunged in after it. They were just in time to see the limousine stop and Zeljan Kurst get out.

"Car four. Where are you?" The voice was suddenly urgent. "Where is the target?"

A pause. Then: "He's entering the British Museum."

It was true. Kurst had passed through the gates and was crossing the open area in front of the famous building which rose up ahead of him, its huge pillars stretching from one side to the other. He was carrying an ebony walking stick that measured out his progress, rapping against the concrete. The MI6 men were already piling out of their own cars but they were too late. Even as they watched from the other side of the gates, Kurst disappeared into the building and they knew that if they didn't act swiftly, they would lose him for good. There was more than one way out. It was unlikely that the Scorpia man would have travelled all the way to England just to look at an exhibit. He might have gone inside deliberately to shake them off.

"He's inside the museum. Cars one, two and three, surround the building. Watch all possible exits. We need immediate backup."

Someone had taken charge. But whoever it was, his voice sounded high-pitched and uncertain. It was eleven o'clock on a bright February morning. The museum would be crowded with tourists and schoolchildren. If there was going to be any action, if they were going to arrest Zeljan Kurst, this was the last place they would want to do it.

In fact, Kurst was still unaware of his pursuers as he crossed the Great Court, a gleaming white space with a spectacular glass roof sweeping in a huge curve overhead. He skirted round the gift shops and information booths, making for the first galleries. As he went he noticed a Japanese couple, tiny and almost identical, taking photographs of each other against a twisting staircase. A bearded student with a backpack was looking at the postcards, pulling them out one at a time and studying them as if trying to find hidden codes. Tap, tap, tap. The end of the walking stick beat out its rhythm as Kurst continued on his way. He knew exactly where he was going and would arrive at the precise minute that had been agreed.

Zeljan Kurst was a large man with heavy, broad shoulders that formed a straight line on either side of an unnaturally thick neck. He was bald by choice. His head had been shaved and there was a dark grey shadow beneath the skin. His eyes, a muddy brown, showed little intelligence and he had the thick lips and small, squashed nose of a wrestler, or perhaps a bouncer at a shady nightclub. Many people had underestimated him and occasionally Kurst had found it necessary to correct them. This usually involved killing them.

He walked past the statue of a crouching naked goddess. An elderly woman in a deerstalker hat, sitting on a stool with brushes and oil paints, was making a bad copy of it on a large white canvas. Ahead of him were two stone animals – strangely shaped lions – and to one side an entire temple, more than two thousand years old, brought from south-west Turkey and reconstructed piece by piece. He barely glanced at them. He didn't like museums, although his house was furnished with rare objects that had been stolen from several of them. But that was the point. Why should something that might be worth hundreds of thousands of pounds be left to moulder in a dark room, stared at by idiot members of the general public who had little or no idea of its true value? Kurst had a simple rule in life. To enjoy something fully you had to own it. And if you couldn't buy it, then you would have to steal it.

Ahead of him two glass doors led into a final gallery. He watched as a tall, well-built black man carrying a notebook and pen walked through, then went in himself. The gallery was huge, stretching out in both directions like an airport runway. Although more than a hundred people were there, it wasn't even half full. Everything was grey: the walls, the floor, the very air. But spotlights, shining down from a ceiling five times higher than the visitors who stood beneath it, picked out the treasures that the room contained, and these shone, soft and gold.

They ran along both walls, from one end to the other, a series of marble tablets with a crowd of figures that had been brought together to form a single line. They were men and women, ancient Greeks, some sitting, others standing, some talking, some riding on horseback. Some carried musical instruments, others bundles of linen or plates and glasses for a feast. Many were incomplete. Two and a half millennia had worn away their faces, broken off arms and legs. But there was something remarkable about the details that remained. It was easy to see that these had been real people who had once lived ordinary lives until they had been frozen in this waking dream, an entire world captured in stone.

Zeljan Kurst barely glanced at them. The gallery had two raised platforms, one at each end, reached by a short flight of steps with a disabled lift – which must have been used by the man he had come to see. There he was in a wheelchair, on the far right, sitting alone, with a blanket over his knees. Kurst walked over to him.

"Mr Kurst?" The voice was dry and strangled. It came from a lizard neck.

Kurst nodded. He was a careful man and made it a rule never to speak unless there was a particular need.

"I am Ariston."

"I know who you are."

"Thank you for coming."

Yannis Ariston Xenopolos was said to be worth about thirty-five billion dollars – nearly twenty-five billion pounds. He had made this fortune from a huge shipping empire which he controlled from his offices in Athens. To this he had added an airline, Ariston Air, and a chain of hotels. And now he was dying. Kurst would have known it even without reading the stories in the newspapers.

It was obvious from the sunken cheeks, the dreadful white of the man's skin, the way he sat like a hunched-up Egyptian mummy, his body disappearing into itself. But most of all it was in his eyes. Kurst had once been the head of the Yugoslavian police force and he had always been interested in the way the prisoners had looked at him just before he executed them. He could see the same thing right here. The Greek had accepted death. All hope had gone.

"I took a considerable risk coming here." Kurst spoke with a heavy mid-European accent which somehow dragged his words down. "What is it you want?"

"I would have thought the answer would be obvious to you."

"The Elgin Marbles."

"Exactly. I wanted you to come here so that you would understand."

Ariston reached out with a hand that was more like a claw, gripping a lever on one wheel of his chair. The whole thing was battery-operated and, with a soft whirr, it spun him round so that he faced the room.

"This is one of the greatest pieces of art that the world has ever produced," he began. "Take a look at the figures, Mr Kurst. They are so beautiful that it is almost impossible to find the words to describe them. They once decorated a temple in the heart of Athens – the Parthenon, dedicated to

Athena, the goddess of wisdom. The frieze which you are examining depicts the summer festival that took place every year in honour of the goddess..."

Again the claw pressed down, turning him so that he faced a group of statues which stood behind him. First there was a horse rising as if out of water, with only its head showing. Then came a naked man, lying on his back. Then three women, all missing their heads. From the way they were arranged, it was clear that these figures had once stood in one of the pediments at each end of the Parthenon.

"The horse belonged to Helios, the sun god," Ariston explained. "Next comes Dionysus, the god of wine. The figures to his left are the goddess Demeter and her daughter—"

"I am familiar with the Elgin Marbles," Kurst interrupted. It didn't matter how much he had been paid. He hadn't come here for a lecture.

"Then you will also be aware that they were plundered. Stolen! Two hundred years ago, a British aristocrat called Lord Elgin came to Athens. He tore them off the temple and transported them back to London. Since then my country has asked many times for them to be returned. We have even built a new museum in Athens to house them. They are the glory of Greece, Mr Kurst. They are part of our heritage. They should come home."

The old man fumbled in the folds of his blanket and produced an oxygen mask, which he pressed against his face. There was the hiss of compressed air and he sucked greedily. At last he continued.

"But the British government have refused. They insist on keeping this stolen property. They will not listen to the voice of the Greek people. And so I have decided that although it will be the last thing I do in my life, I will make them listen. That is why I have contacted you and your organization. I want you to steal the sculptures and return them to Greece."

In the street outside, four more cars had pulled up next to the British Museum, spilling out fifteen more agents. With the ones who had followed Kurst from City Airport, that brought the total to twenty-three. They were fairly confident that their man was still inside the building, but with seventy-six galleries covering a floor space of a fifth of a square mile, it was going to be almost impossible to find him. And already the order had gone out. "Do not, under any circumstances, approach him while he is in a public area. This man is extremely dangerous. If he feels trapped, there's no saying what he will do. The result could be a bloodbath."

Zeljan Kurst was quite unaware of the approaching MI6 men as he considered what the Greek billionaire had just said.

"Stealing the Elgin Marbles won't help you," he said. "The British government will simply demand them back. It would be better to threaten them. Blackmail them, perhaps."

"Do whatever it takes. I don't care. You can kill half the population of this loathsome country if it will achieve what I want..." Ariston broke into a fit of coughing. Pearls of white saliva appeared at the corners of his mouth.

Kurst waited for him to recover. Then he nodded slowly. "It can be done," he said. "But it will take time. And it will be expensive."

Ariston nodded. "This work will be my legacy to the Greek people. If you agree to do it for me, I will pay you five million euros immediately, and a further fifteen million when you succeed."

"It's not enough," Kurst said.

Ariston looked at him slyly. "There was a time when you might have said that and I would have been forced to agree. But Scorpia is not what it was. There have been two failures in the space of a single year. The operation called Invisible Sword and, more recently, the business in north-west Australia." He smiled, showing grey teeth. "The very fact that you are here today shows how weak you have become."

"Scorpia has regrouped," Kurst retorted. "We have taken on new recruits. I would say we are stronger than ever. We can choose our clients, Mr Xenopolos, and we do not negotiate."

"Name your price."

"Forty million."

Ariston's eyes barely flickered. "Agreed."

"Half in advance."

"As you wish."

Kurst turned and walked away without saying another word, his cane beating the same rhythm on the floor. As he made his way back towards the entrance, his mind was already focused on the task that lay ahead. Although he would never have dreamed of saying as much, he was glad he had come here today. It was very much his desire to take on the British government once again. The failures Ariston had mentioned had both involved the British secret service.

It was fortunate that the old man hadn't heard the full story. Would he have still approached Scorpia if he had known the almost incredible truth? That both failures had involved the same fourteen-year-old boy?

In the end it was just bad luck – bad timing – that Kurst left the gallery when he did. He was about to reach the Great Court when one of the MI6 agents crossed in front of him and suddenly the two of them were face to face, only inches apart. The agent – his name was Parker – was new and inexperienced. He was unable to keep the shock out of his eyes and at that moment Kurst knew he had been recognized.

Parker had no choice. He had been given his orders, but he knew that if he obeyed them he would die. He fumbled in his jacket and pulled out his pistol, a 9mm Browning, long a favourite of the SAS. At the same time, he shouted, louder than he needed to, "Stay where you are! If you move, I'll fire." It was exactly how he had been trained. He was both exerting his authority over his target and alerting any nearby agents that his cover had been blown.

In the silence of the museum and with the ceiling so high overhead, his words echoed out. A few tourists turned to see what was happening and caught sight of the gun. The first seeds of panic were planted and instantly began to grow.

Kurst raised his hands, one of them still holding the ebony walking stick, and moved very slightly to one side. Parker followed him with his eyes and didn't see something flash through the air over Kurst's shoulder, didn't even notice it until it had buried itself in his throat.

The old woman who had been painting a copy of the kneeling goddess had followed Kurst to the door. Underneath the make-up she wasn't old at all, and her brushes might have had tufts at one end but the handles were precision-made steel and razor sharp.

Parker fell to his knees. In the last second of his life his trigger finger tightened and the gun went off, the explosion amplified by the stone walls all around. That was when the panic began for real.

The tourists screamed and scattered, some of them diving into the shops or behind the information desks. A group of primary school children who had been visiting the Egyptian mummies crouched down beside the stairs, cowering together.

An American woman standing next to them began to scream. The British Museum guards, many of them old and long retired from their real careers, remained frozen to the spot, completely unprepared for an event like this. Kurst stepped over the dead man and continued to move slowly towards the main door.

Of course he hadn't come to the museum alone. Scorpia would not have risked the life of its chief executive, even for a million euros, and its agents surrounded him on all sides. As the MI6 men closed in from every direction, still unsure what had happened but knowing that all the rules had changed, they were met by a hail of machine-gun fire. The bearded student who had been examining the postcards had reached into his backpack and drawn out a miniature machine gun with folding shoulder stock and was spraying the court with bullets. An MI6 man, halfway down the West Stairs, threw his arms back in surprise, then jerked forward and tumbled down. The American woman was still screaming. The primary school children were crying in terror. All the alarms in the building had gone off. People were running in every direction.

The Japanese man who had been photographing his wife threw his camera on the floor and it exploded with a soft woomph, releasing thick, dark green fumes into the air. In seconds Kurst had disappeared. The Great Court had become a battle zone.

Two MI6 agents slid to a halt, trying to peer through the smoke. There was a loud crack, then another, and they fell to the ground. They had been shot in the legs by the Japanese woman, who had produced a pearl-handled Nambu pistol from her handbag.

Meanwhile, holding a handkerchief across his face, Kurst had reached the main doors. There had been little security when he came in; there was none as he left. Out of the corner of his eye he saw an MI6 agent try to rush him, then fall back as he was grabbed by his personal bodyguard, the black man with the notebook whom he had registered on his way to the Elgin Marbles. The human neck makes an unmistakable sound when it is snapped, and he heard it now. The agent slumped to the ground. Kurst walked out into the fresh air.

There were people running between the pillars, tumbling down the steps and hurling themselves across the open area in front of the museum. Already the police were on their way, their sirens growing in volume as they came together from different parts of the city. Kurst's limousine was waiting for him at the gates. But there were two men moving purposefully towards him, both dressed in charcoal grey suits and sunglasses. He briefly wondered why people who worked in espionage had to make themselves look so obvious. They had become aware of the chaos inside the British Museum and were racing in. Perhaps they hadn't expected him to emerge so quickly.

Kurst lifted his walking stick. It was in fact a hollowed-out tube with a single gas-fired bullet and an electric trigger concealed just beneath the handle. The bullet had been specially modified. It wouldn't just kill a man. It would tear him in half.

He fired. The man on the left was blown off his feet, landing in a spinning, bloody ball. The second man froze for just one second. It was much too long. Moving surprisingly fast for someone of his age, Kurst swung the walking stick through the air, using it like a sword. The metal casing slammed into the agent's throat and he crumpled. Kurst ran for the car. The back door was already open and he threw himself in, slamming it behind him. There was a series of gunshots. But the car windows were bulletproof and the bodywork was armour-plated. With a screech of tyres, the limousine swung out. Another man stood in the way, his gun held commando-style, in both hands. The chauffeur accelerated. There was a thud as the man hit the bumper and he was hurled out of the way.

Two hours later, a man in a blond wig, wearing sunglasses and holding a huge bunch of flowers, boarded the Eurostar train to Paris. Zeljan Kurst hated these disguises, but it was something else he had learned in his long career. If you're trying not to be seen, it often helps to make yourself as prominent as possible. The flowers and the wig were ridiculous, but although the police and MI6 were looking for him all over London, they certainly wouldn't associate them with him.

As he settled into his pre-booked seat in first class and sipped his complimentary glass of champagne, Kurst's mind was focused on the problem he had been given. The shoot-out at the museum was already forgotten. The question was – who would be the best person to handle this quite interesting business of the Elgin Marbles? There were now twelve members of Scorpia, including him, and he mentally went over them one by one.

Levi Kroll, the former Israeli agent who, in a moment of carelessness, had shot out his own eye? Mikato, the Japanese policeman turned yakuza gangster? Dr Three? Or perhaps this might be an opportunity for their newest recruit? He had the sort of mind that would enjoy working out a problem of this complexity, along with the ruthlessness to see it through to the end.

There was a blast of a whistle and the train moved off. Kurst took out his mobile phone – encrypted, of course – and dialled a number. The train slid down the platform and picked up speed, and as they left St Pancras International, Kurst permitted himself the rare luxury of a smile. Yes. Razim was perfect. He would bring his unique talents to this new assignment. Kurst was sure of it. He had chosen exactly the right man.

# THE MEASUREMENT OF PAIN

"Thank you. Thank you. Thank you, my dear Mr Kurst. I will begin to consider the matter at once."

The man was standing on the parapet of a French fort, built at the end of the eighteenth century when Napoleon had invaded Egypt. A few new buildings had been added more recently and there were signs of further construction: scaffolding, lifting equipment and a great pile of salt which had been drawn from a nearby lake to be mixed with sand to make bricks.

There was something very strange about the compound, which stood on its own, perfectly square, surrounded by sand. It looked like a scene out of a Hollywood film – or perhaps a mirage. First, there was the outer wall, not high but several metres thick with battlements all the way round and solid guard towers rising up much further at each of the four corners. These were punctuated by narrow, slot-like windows, making it easy to look out but impossible to look in. The only way into the fort was through an arched gateway with two huge gates made of whole tree trunks bound with steel. It would have taken several men to open them if they hadn't been electrically operated.

Inside, the fort was like an army barracks with a dozen buildings neatly laid out around a central well. Water, of course, was everything in the desert. An army would be able to survive here for months – living, sleeping, exercising and drilling on the parade ground, hardly aware of the world outside. There were two accommodation blocks – one for officers, one for common soldiers – a prison block, various storerooms, an old bakehouse and a chapel. All of these had been converted, with air conditioning, hot and cold running water, every modern comfort. The old stables had been turned into a recreation room with snooker tables and a cinema screen. The armoury still contained weapons – though very different from the ones used by the forces of Napoleon.

These now included flame-throwers, hand grenades and even hand-held rocket launchers – for the man who had privately purchased the fort and redesigned it needed to be safe, and beneath the sun-baked bricks, the dusty courtyard and the ancient battlements lay some very sophisticated equipment indeed. Everything was powered by an electric generator, housed in what had once been the forge. A radio mast and three satellite dishes rose above one of the towers. CCTV cameras watched for any movement. At night infrared lights and radar scanned the area all around. These were wired up to the control room, once the bakehouse. A single chimney rose above its flat roof, leading up from what had been the bread oven. The control room was manned twenty-four hours a day, and nobody could enter or leave the fort without authorization; the main gates could only be opened from inside. It was in constant radio communication with the guards on patrol. These were local men, dressed in Bedouin style – headdresses, loose-fitting robes and sandals – with knives at their belts. They also had machine guns slung over their shoulders.

The man's name was Abdul-Aziz al-Razim but that wasn't what he called himself now. As an internationally wanted terrorist and convicted war criminal, it was better not to have any name at all. To his friends in Scorpia he was known simply as Razim. And, in truth, he had no other friends. He was unmarried. Sometimes he would spend a whole month without speaking to anyone at all. But Razim didn't mind. In fact he preferred it that way.

Razim was not an Egyptian. He had been born forty-five years ago in the town of Tikrit, in Iraq. His father was a university professor; his mother had studied Arabic literature at Cambridge University and had herself become a well-known writer and poet. Abdul-Aziz (the name means "servant of the powerful" in Arabic) was one of two children – he had an elder sister called Rima. The family had lived together in one of the oldest houses of the town, a narrow, white brick building constructed around a central courtyard packed with flowers and plants and with a fountain playing in the middle.

From the very start Razim was a difficult child. His father used to joke that he had been born in a sandstorm and that some of the sand must have got into his blood. As a baby he never smiled or gurgled but lay sullenly in his cot as if wondering how he had got there and how, perhaps, he might escape. As soon as he had learned to walk, he tried to run away. Nannies never stayed long in the household. Razim's temper tantrums drove three of them away. The fourth left with a pair of nail scissors driven into her thigh after she had told him off for teasing his sister.

At least he did well at school – indeed, his teachers thought he was a genius. He came top in every subject and by the age of twelve was fluent in three languages. It was hardly surprising that he didn't get on with the other children. Even then Razim had no friends. He was a quiet, solitary boy and he had already come to realize that there was something different about him, although he wasn't quite sure what it was. Eventually he managed to work it out. He felt no emotions. Nothing scared or upset him. Nothing made him particularly happy either. There was no food that he particularly enjoyed. It was as if the whole of life had been put under a laboratory slide and he was the scientist examining it. Every day for him was the same. He didn't feel anything.

He decided to put this to the test. His parents had bought him a pet, a scruffy mongrel, when he was small and it had always been his companion. So one day he took it down to the orchard behind their house and strangled it, just to see how he felt. It didn't bother him at all. His mother and father wondered about the missing dog and they also noticed the scratches on Razim's hands and arms, but they accepted his explanation that he had brushed against a barbed wire fence. They were both intelligent people but no parent wants to think the worst of their child, and the truth was that Razim was still doing brilliantly at school. He ate his meals with them and came with them to the mosque for prayers. He clearly didn't like his sister but he was polite to her. What more could they ask?

In the 1970s the history of Iraq changed when Saddam Hussein came to power. One of his first acts as president was to arrest sixty-eight members of his party and accuse them of treason. Twenty-two of these were executed; the other forty-six were forced to make up the firing squads. When Razim heard about this little twist of cruelty, he realized that his country had been taken over by a man who was very close to his own heart. He began to think how he might get to meet him. Could he find a way into the corridors of power?

As it happened, the opportunity arose very quickly. It was obvious to many people in Iraq that Saddam was brutal, mad and dangerous, and in the late summer of that same year, Razim's parents held a secret meeting in their house with other academics, writers and well-placed friends to discuss how they might get rid of him. How were they to know that Razim was recording the entire conversation on a digital recorder that they had given him for his fourteenth birthday? The next day, he skipped school and went instead to the local police, taking the evidence with him.

Revenge came like a desert storm. Razim's parents were arrested and shot without even the benefit of a trial. Razim never found out what happened to his seventeen-year-old sister – but nor did he care. The last he saw of her, she was being dragged screaming from the house by four laughing policemen, who threw her into the back of a van. Everyone who had attended the meeting was arrested. None of them were ever seen again.

As a reward for his loyalty the local chief of police invited Razim – now an orphan – to see him in his office above the jail near the Farouk Palace. Sitting behind his desk, with his belly rising above it, the police chief examined the boy sitting opposite him. He did not like what he saw. Razim was small for his age and very slender, more like a girl than a boy. His hair was neatly cut in a fringe and he was wearing his school uniform. But what troubled him was the boy's complete lack of expression. He had the face of a waxwork, eyes that could have been made of glass. There was no warmth or curiosity. There was nothing at all.

Even so, he tried to be polite. "You have been of great service to your country," he began. "Your parents and their friends were traitors. You were right to do what you did."

The boy didn't respond.

"What would you like to happen to you now?"

"I thought I might join the police," Razim said. "I'm sure you have lots of people you have to kill. I'd like to help."

The police chief had children of his own and this boy, whose feet barely reached the floor, sickened him. "You're too young to join the police," he said.

"I don't want to go back to school. It's boring."

"I think it would be better if you left Tikrit..."

For a brief moment, the police chief was tempted to take out his gun and shoot the child. He would have felt exactly the same had he found himself faced with a scorpion or a poisonous snake. He had to hold on to his hand to prevent it from dropping down to the holster at his belt. "We will arrange for you to be fostered," he said. "Somewhere far away."

"Don't I get a reward?"

"It will come to you. In time."

In the end Razim was sent to live with a w[...] family, distant relatives of the president, in Bag[...] The family despised him at first sight but knew [...] ter than to ask any questions, and from this moment on he began to thrive. He continued to excel at school and, at seventeen, became the youngest student to enter the College of Engineering at Amir Abaad Campus, part of the University of Tehran. By now he had changed his mind about his future. He would use his scientific skills to become a weapons designer. It was well known that Saddam Hussein was developing biological and chemical weapons. Razim himself had a keen interest in small arms. In his first term at university he won a commendation for a twenty-page essay on the Yugoslavian Zastava M70, the assault rifle which, he was told, had been used to kill his parents. His dream was that he might one day invent a new weapon which he would name after himself.

It wasn't going to happen. On Razim's eighteenth birthday he received a letter printed on official government paper. It turned out that someone high up hadn't forgotten the teenager who had once betrayed his entire family. Razim was to leave university immediately. He was being invited (and it wasn't an invitation that anyone could refuse) to join the Mukhabarat. He was to report to their offices the next day.

The Mukhabarat. Iraq's dreaded secret intelligence service. Razim read the letter with a faint twinge of something that might actually have been pleasure. He had heard the horror stories about the organization and knew that it was work to which he was ideally suited. He packed immediately and left at six the next morning. Nobody at the university even noticed he had gone.

For the next twenty years Razim discovered the pleasure of being feared. Actually, it was more than that. Anyone who met him knew that he had absolute power over their life or death and that with one snap of his fingers they might never be seen again. If he were to point to a picture or a valuable vase in a man's house, the object would be waiting at the door for him to take with him when he left. The same was true for the man's wife or children. Razim boasted that he had so many enemies he could have bathed daily in their blood. The rumour in Baghdad was that he did.

His power increased. Soon he had a house the size of a palace, filled with servants who fell silent and looked away when he came into the room. He had barely grown at all. He was still the same size and shape as a schoolboy although his hair had turned silver at a very early age, making him look both very old and very young at the same time. He wore glasses that were a little too large for his face and one of his officers had once joked that he looked like a Middle Eastern Harry Potter. Razim had enjoyed the joke. He was almost smiling as he stabbed the officer nine times with a paperknife.

And then came the Iraq War of 2003 and the invasion by the American and British forces. Unlike so many of Saddam's inner circle, Razim could see which way the wind was blowing and made plans to save himself. The night before the bombing of Baghdad, he slipped out of the country in the private eight-seater Beechjet 400 that belonged to one of the president's younger half-brothers, flying over the border into Saudi Arabia. He took with him all the treasures he could carry: works of art, diamonds, gold coins and international bonds. All of these would be easier to trade than cash.

He settled in Riyadh and waited for the war to end, which it did – as he had expected – very quickly. It was clear to him that he couldn't return to Iraq, not while it was being occupied by the British and American forces, but, using the connections he had made while he was with the Mukhabarat, he contacted the local recruiting officer for al-Qaeda and soon found himself in charge of his own extensive terrorist cell. He wasn't paid, of course, but then he didn't need to be. He was a wealthy man. Nor was he interested in religion or politics. For him, terrorism was like a jigsaw puzzle. You have an embassy and a bomb. How do you fit one into the other to create the most unforgettable picture? It was a challenge which stimulated his mind, and he helped plan more than a dozen attacks in Europe and America, carefully examining the results on the fifty-five-inch plasma screen he'd had installed in his luxurious house.

This successful period in his life came to an end when his commanding officer suggested that, to show his devotion to the Islamic cause, he might like to become a suicide bomber himself. Razim was given a belt filled with high explosive and shown how to wrap it round his stomach and set it off with a single button on his mobile. He would be smuggled into Pakistan and dropped off at a central market. From there it would be a short step to paradise.

Razim thought about all this for a few minutes, and then used the explosive to blow up his commanding officer. It was time to move again. By now the British and Americans were on his trail. Saddam had been hanged; his sons had been shot. Razim had no doubt that one or other of these fates would be waiting for him if he was ever caught – unless al-Qaeda found him first. It really was quite annoying to have so many enemies. He would just have to find another city where he could start his life again.

He chose Cairo. With a population of seven million crammed into eighty-three square miles, he would be completely invisible. He briefly considered plastic surgery. There were plenty of clinics in the backstreets of West Zamalek, a high-rise area of the city close to the Nile, and if you paid enough nobody would ask any questions. But in fact very few people knew what he looked like. He had taken great care that this should be the case, always covering his head with the traditional *ghutra* or Arab scarf. Even when he was in Western clothes, he had worn sunglasses and a baseball cap pulled down low. He decided that surgery would not be needed. He lived quietly, making sure he didn't attract any attention. And he waited for the next opportunity to reveal itself, as he was sure it would.

He still owned a penthouse in the middle of Cairo and a summer house in the Red Sea resort of Sharm el-Sheikh. But his favourite home was where he was now, this long-forgotten fort lost in more than a million square miles of sand. This was where he came to escape from the crowds. It was where he felt secure. And it was a perfect setting, too, for the series of experiments in which he was now engaged.

There was a rope bridge that crossed from one side of the fort to the other. Razim had ordered it to be installed to save him walking all the way round. He used it now, putting out both hands to steady himself as it swayed beneath his feet. The salt pile was right beneath him and he watched as one of the guards emptied a wheelbarrow, adding to the heap. Razim had insisted that the new building should be done in the traditional Berber style, mixing salt with sand. It was slow, but it felt right.

Everything was quiet. The desert had settled for the night. He reached the other end of the bridge and walked along the opposite parapet until he came to a stone staircase which led back down to ground level. He took it. A second guard stood respectfully to attention as he passed by.

Razim still didn't know how Scorpia had managed to track him down. At first it had worried him. If they could find him, then any one of the world's intelligence agencies might follow. But he had soon realized that Scorpia was an organization like no other. After all, by and large the police and security services do not threaten murder or violence to get the information they want. And in the end he was glad that they had decided to seek him out. They were offering exactly the sort of work that interested him, along with the promise of enormous sums of money. The two of them really were made for each other.

Take this new assignment, the first he would handle as project leader. It was already a fascinating challenge: how to return the Elgin Marbles to Greece. Like Zeljan Kurst, Razim had already dismissed the idea of stealing them, although that would surely have been easy enough. When was the last time anyone had checked security at the British Museum? Many of the roofs were made of glass and the security staff, low paid and lazy, could be either bribed or replaced. But that wouldn't work. If the Marbles were ever to be seen in public again, then they would have to be returned legally, with the full cooperation of the

British government. So what it came down to was a question of leverage. How could Scorpia persuade them to do something that they had always refused to do before?

He took out a packet of cigarettes and lit one. He smoked Black Devils, manufactured in China and sold by the long-established firm of Heupink & Bloemen in the Netherlands. He had the packets specially modified so they no longer warned him that he would quite probably die of cancer. Razim didn't really care when he died – or how. But he didn't like being bossed around by governments. He sucked in, letting the sweet, slightly vanilla taste of the tobacco roll over his tongue.

Small clouds of dust rose around his feet as he crossed the courtyard. The beam of a spotlight swept the ground just ahead. Still smoking, he went into a circular building with a domed roof and a tower. This had once been a chapel. Razim had found faded pictures of various saints on some of the walls and there had even been a stained-glass window – the only glass in the entire place. Perhaps French soldiers had come here once to pray that they would soon be sent home. Razim had smashed the window and painted over the frescoes. They were of no interest to him. He had, of course, never believed in God.

The interior was brightly lit and kept at a pleasant temperature by a sophisticated air conditioning system. The walls were now all white and specially thick, to keep out the heat. There were machines everywhere: computers, television monitors, different-sized boxes with dials and gauges. In the middle of all this, trapped in a pool of brilliant light, a man sat in a leather dentist's chair, tied to it by soft cords around his ankles and wrists. He was wearing only boxer shorts. Dozens of wires had been attached to him – to his head, his chest, his pulse, his abdomen – held in place by sticky tape. By a happy coincidence, the man was French. He was about thirty years old and he was trying not to look afraid. He was failing.

Razim knew his name. It was Luc Fontaine and he worked for the DGSE, the French intelligence agency dealing in external security. The man was, in other words, a secret agent, a spy. Razim had always known that foreign investigators would come looking for him and he therefore kept a careful watch for them. This one had got closer than many. He had been picked up asking questions in the central market – or souk – knocked out and then brought here. He was still pretending to be a tourist, but only half-heartedly. By now he knew that he was in the hands of a man who did not make mistakes.

There was a trolley draped with a white cloth next to the dentist's chair. Razim wheeled it round and uncovered it to reveal a series of knives lined up in neat rows, each one a different shape and size, gleaming in the harsh light. There were other instruments too: swabs and silver bowls, hypodermic syringes, vials containing liquids that were colourless but somehow didn't look like water. Fontaine saw this. He tried not to show any emotion. But his naked skin crawled.

Razim pulled up a stool and sat down. He drew on the cigarette. The tip glowed.

"What do you want?" Fontaine asked. He spoke in French. His voice was hoarse.

Razim didn't answer.

"I'm not going to tell you anything." The secret agent had dropped the pretence that he was a tourist. He knew there was no longer any point in it.

"And I am not going to ask you anything," Razim replied. His French was excellent. It was one of the languages he had learned at school. "You have no information that I wish to know."

"Then why am I here?" The young man flexed his arms, the muscles bulging, but the cords held fast.

"I will tell you." Razim tapped ash into one of the bowls. "I have been many things in my life," he said, "but when I set out I was an engineer. That is how I was trained. Science, in its many varieties, has always been an interest of mine. And you should be glad that you are here with me tonight, Luc. Do you mind if I call you Luc? I am pursuing a project that will be of great benefit to the world and fate has chosen you to help me."

"My people know I'm here."

"Nobody knows you are here. Even you do not

know where you are. Please try not to interrupt."

Razim put out his cigarette. He licked his lips.

"It occurred to me some years ago that everything in this world is measured and that many of these measurements have been named after the great engineers. The most obvious example is the watt, which measures electricity, and which was named after James Watt, the inventor of the modern steam engine. Joule and Newton were both physicists and have been immortalized in the measurement of energy: joules and newtons. Every day we measure the atmospheric heat in either Fahrenheit or Celsius. The first is named after a German physicist, the second a Swedish astronomer.

"We measure distance and height and speed and brightness. If you wish to buy anything from a shoe to a sheet of paper, you ask for it by size. There are measuring units that many people have never heard of. Can you tell me what a pyron is? Or a palmo? Or a petaflop? But here is the strange thing. There has never been a measurement for something we experience almost every day of our lives. There has never been a measurement for pain.

"Can you imagine how useful it would be if you went to the dentist and he was able to reassure you? 'Don't worry, my dear fellow, this is only going to hurt two and a half units.' Or if you went to the doctor with a damaged knee and were able to tell him that it hurt three units down here, but seven and a half units up here, above the knee? Of course, it is very difficult to measure pain. It all depends on how our nerves react and what the stimulus is – knife, electricity, fire, acid – that has caused the pain. But I still believe it is possible to develop a universal scale. And I very much hope that one day the unit of pain will be named after me. The razim. And people will be able to say exactly how many razims will result in certain death."

Fontaine was staring at Razim as if seeing him for the first time. "You're mad," he whispered.

"All great inventors have a certain madness," Razim agreed. "They said the same of Galileo and Einstein. It is what I would expect you to say."

"Please..."

"I would also expect you to beg. But I'm afraid it will do you no good."

Razim leaned over the trolley and considered. It would be interesting to see how long this Frenchman survived. Of course, for the sake of accuracy, he would have to experiment on women. And if one ever came his way, a teenager would be useful too. Everybody reacts to pain in different ways and he needed to examine the full spectrum. He made his decision and chose an instrument.

Moments later the needles on the various monitors leapt forward as the first screams rang out into the night.

# FLY BY NIGHT

The tourist boat was moored at the Quai de Grenelle, on the western edge of the city. But the people who stepped on board on that bright afternoon in June most definitely were not tourists.

It had been Max Grendel, the oldest founding member of Scorpia, who had decided that they should have a floating office in Paris. This had been one of the last decisions he had made, as he had died a few months later, stung to death by scorpions in a gondola in Venice. The *bateau mouche* – literally "fly boat" – looked like any other pleasure craft gliding up and down the river. It was long and narrow with a flat bottom and a low canopy made almost entirely of glass to give its passengers the best possible views. Inside, however, it was very different. Instead of rows of seating for two or three hundred sightseers, there was a single conference table and twelve chairs. A soundproof wall separated this area from the cabin where the captain and the first mate stood at the controls. The rest of the crew, four men in their twenties, stayed outside on the deck. They were not allowed to look into the cabin. They stood as still as the statues that lined the bridges, their eyes fixed on both banks of the river, searching for any movement that might be construed as enemy action.

Grendel's idea wasn't quite as odd as it might seem. Unlike a building, a boat would be impossible to bug, particularly as it was kept under twenty-four-hour guard and thoroughly swept before every meeting. Also, unlike a building, it could move, so anyone trying to eavesdrop on what was being said would have to move too, at equal speed. And as the ship was fitted with a Ruston 12 RK diesel engine stolen from a Royal Navy River Class Offshore Patrol Vessel, that might be very fast indeed. Finally, should a police launch attempt to come close, there was a point-defence weapon system based on the famous Goalkeeper technology developed by the Dutch, with auto-cannon and advanced radar concealed beneath false panels on the foredeck. This was capable of firing seventy rounds per second at a distance of up to fifteen hundred metres. If necessary, Scorpia was both willing and able to start a small war in the heart of Paris.

The boat was called *Le Débiteur,* which might be translated as someone who leaves without paying their debts. Such people used to be called fly-by-nights. As Grendel had argued, there was something very calming about discussing business while cruising past some of the most beautiful buildings in Europe, particularly when the business was as dangerous as theirs.

Sabotage. Corruption. Intelligence. And assassination. These were the four activities that had given Scorpia its name. It was here in Paris that it had been formed, a collection of intelligence agents from around the world who had seen that their services might no longer be needed after the end of the Cold War and who had decided to go into business for themselves. It had been a wise move. Secret agents are generally not highly paid. The head of MI5 in England receives only two hundred thousand pounds a year – a tiny amount compared with any investment banker. Every member of Scorpia had multiplied his annual income by a factor of ten. And none of them paid any tax.

There were once again twelve of them and they were now all men. There had been a woman on the original executive board but she had been killed in London. Altogether, six of the founding members had died – one from natural causes. The current chief executive was Zeljan Kurst, sitting at one end of the table in a charcoal grey suit, white shirt and black tie. As he had explained to Ariston in London, Scorpia had recently taken on six new recruits – although it had been forced to look outside the intelligence community for some of them. There was a ginger-haired Irishman who called himself Seamus and had been a member of the IRA. Twin brothers had been brought in from the Italian Mafia. And finally there was Razim.

Scorpia was on the way up. That was the message it wanted to make clear to the world. It was taking back the control it should never have lost.

The twelve executives arrived individually and at five-minute intervals, some in chauffeured cars, some on foot, one even on a bicycle. Only Giovanni and Eduardo Grimaldi, the twins, arrived together, but then in twenty-five years they had never spent a minute apart. At exactly three o'clock the deckhands lifted the anchor. The captain pushed forward on the throttle and *Le Débiteur* slipped out into the river, beginning its journey east towards the Eiffel Tower and Notre-Dame.

Zeljan Kurst waited until they were on their way before he spoke. He didn't greet anyone by name. Such matters were a waste of words. Nor did he offer anyone a drink, not even a glass of water. None of these people trusted each other so they would only have refused it. If he had any recollection of his narrow escape in London, he didn't show it. His eyes were heavy. He looked almost bored.

"Good day to you, gentlemen," he began. As usual, the English language sounded peculiarly ugly coming from his lips, but it had long since been agreed that English was the only language they would speak. "We have come together today to agree upon our tactics for an operation which we have called Horseman and which will earn us the sum of forty million euros when it is successfully completed. As you all know, I have given the management of this business to Mr Razim..."

Kurst glanced sideways. As he had expected, there was a brief flash of anger in the single eye of the Israeli agent, Levi Kroll. This was the third time he had been passed over for project command. Nobody else had noticed. Their attention was fixed on the man with the silver hair and the round spectacles who had been placed, not by accident, at the head of the table.

"I will add only that the first instalment of the money has been paid into our Cayman Islands account by our client, Ariston Xenopolos," Kurst continued. "We will receive the full amount on the same day that the so-called Elgin Marbles land on Greek soil."

"How is Ariston?" Dr Three asked. He was very small, and as the years went by he seemed to be getting smaller. He had recently completed a two-thousand-page encyclopedia on the subject of torture. The writing had exhausted him, although he had enjoyed the research.

"He is critically ill," Kurst replied. "According to his doctors, he should already be dead."

"And if he dies before our work is complete?"

"The money will still be paid." Kurst blinked heavily, as if to cut off any further discussion. "But it is not just a question of money for us," he went on. "This is a matter of great importance. We have endured two failures in a single year – unheard of in our long history. And I have heard unpleasant whispers, gentlemen. There are some governments and intelligence agencies that no longer trust us with their assignments. The purchase of nuclear material for Iran. A terrorist atrocity in Tel Aviv. The collapse of the banking system in Singapore. Just three recent operations which should have come to us but which instead were given to other organizations. We have to prove to our clients that we are back to our full strength – and this is our opportunity! The work we begin here today will have echoes that will be heard throughout the world."

He nodded in the direction of Razim. "Please. Tell the board what you have planned."

"With great pleasure, Mr Kurst." Razim licked his lips. "Pleasure" was not a word he used often. It was not an emotion that was familiar to him. And yet he had been looking forward to this moment for a long time and he felt something close to a thrill to be the one holding the reins, to be in command of the entire executive board of Scorpia. "The Elgin Marbles," he muttered, his voice barely audible above the drone of the motor. "The British government has refused, time and again, to hand them back. Why? Because they are selfish and arrogant. And the question I have been asking myself for the last few months is what will make them overcome their selfishness and arrogance? What will make them change their mind? And the answer I have come up with is a single word. Fear.

"Somehow we have to arrange matters so that they have no choice. We have to put them in a position where they *must* return the sculptures ... where their survival depends on it. But at the same time, it has to be done very delicately. For example, we could steal a nuclear device and threaten to set it off in the heart of London if they did not comply with our wishes. But this would not be easy and it might not even work. They might not believe us. They might, as it were, call our bluff. And it is not our task to turn the British into victims, no matter how pleasant the thought. It will suit our purposes more if they are hated. They are thieves and aggressors. They deserve the condemnation of every civilized country."

Razim drew a breath. Twenty-one eyes in the room were all turned on him. Outside, the boat was cutting through the bright water, heading towards a bend in the river with the Eiffel Tower and the Field of Mars looming up on the right. They passed underneath a bridge, the Pont d'Iéna, and a bar of shadow swept briefly across the glass ceiling.

"I do not believe violence, or the threat of violence, is the answer," Razim went on. "But suppose we were to arrange a trap for them. Imagine that we were to arrange a scandal so dark and so shocking that it would destroy their reputation for decades to come. No country would do business with them. The Americans would turn their back on them. The European community already hates them, but this would be the final straw. Nobody would trust them. Suddenly Great Britain would be a very small and lonely island indeed. Imagine all that, my friends, and ask yourselves what the British government would do to avoid it. Do you think, perhaps, they would agree to empty one room in a stupid museum in the middle of London? Would they cheerfully send a collection of old statues back to their rightful owners? I think they would. I really think they would."

Razim longed for a cigarette. He could feel the packet pressing inside his jacket pocket – today he was wearing European dress – but he dared not reach for it. It wasn't that smoking was forbidden; it was just that it might be considered a weakness.

"I have already put into operation a plan that will achieve all this," he said. "It is the sort of exercise that carries the unmistakable stamp and authority of Scorpia. And from what I have been told, I think it will give everyone around this table a great deal of personal satisfaction, because, gentlemen, what I have in mind involves a teenage boy..."

He paused for effect.

"The boy's name is Alex Rider."

There was a moment of perfect silence. Even the engine seemed to have stopped. The last two words seemed to have had a paralysing effect on at least half the people in the cabin.

"Alex Rider?" Sitting next to Kroll, the Japanese man called Mikato raised a thumb to his lips and bit at the nail. As he did so, he exposed the diamond set in one of his front teeth. Mikato was a member of the criminal organization known as the yakuza and had tattooed the names of every man he had killed across his body. Unfortunately he had run out of space. "We have encountered this boy twice," he began. "We even tried to kill him with a bullet fired into his heart. The sniper we hired had never failed—"

"Please, hear me out," Razim interrupted. "I have given the matter a great deal of thought." Suddenly he decided – to hell with it. He took out his packet of Black Devils and lit one with a solid gold lighter. Smoke curled in front of his face, reflected in the two circles of his glasses.

"I am perfectly aware that Alex Rider has, incredibly, got the better of this organization on two occasions," he said. "There was a fairly simple affair involving the creation of a tsunami to strike the coast of Australia. And before that, the late Mrs Rothman was responsible for the operation called Invisible Sword. This was a secret weapon using nanoshells with a cyanide core. The plan was to poison thousands of children in Britain."

"We do not need to discuss these matters!" There was a Frenchman at the table, a man with a neat grey beard and the long, slender fingers of a pianist. He was rolling his knuckles across the wooden surface, a sign of his irritation.

"But we do need to discuss them, Monsieur Duval," Razim replied. "How can we understand our one weakness if we don't examine it?" He waved a hand. "There is absolutely nothing special about this child *except that he is a child*. That's the only reason he has been so useful to MI6. Oh yes, he received some training from his uncle, who was a spy himself before he was killed. But do you really think a basic knowledge of karate and the ability to speak a few foreign languages were the reasons he managed to defeat you?

"That's nonsense! Alex Rider won because you underestimated him. Winston Yu should have shot him when he had the chance. And Mrs Rothman too. Maybe they hesitated because he was so young, but that was his strength. He was the world's most unlikely spy. It didn't matter if it was the island of Skeleton Key or Sayle Enterprises in Cornwall, nobody looked at him twice. That was their mistake."

"And our mistake—" Kroll began. He had been listening to all this in growing discomfort. He alone was allowing his emotions to get the better of him. Zeljan Kurst had noticed this. It was what he had expected.

"Let me finish!" Razim cut him off. "I have done a great deal of research into this child. I managed to obtain a copy of a report prepared by a journalist last year and it confirmed what I had already found out for myself. On at least six occasions – it may be more – he was employed by the Special Operations division of MI6. Gentlemen, I ask you to consider the implications.

"Everyone at this table knows only too well that secret agents – spies – aren't really heroes. The work they do is often dirty and unpleasant. They kill people who have to be killed and they do it without a second thought. They have no pity and no sense of shame. They share the sorts of secrets that nobody else wants to know. Do spies have friends? Of course not. Nobody in their right mind would want to get close to them. They cannot be trusted.

"So what would happen if it was discovered that MI6 had recruited a fourteen-year-old schoolboy? Too young to vote. Too young to smoke or get married. But old enough to be sent to foreign countries, to get mixed up in international politics, terrorism and murder! What would that say about that country's government – or its secret service?

"And let us take it one step further. Suppose the boy was sent on a mission that went horribly wrong? But this time it wasn't something brave or clever. He wasn't trying to save the world from some madman like Damian Cray. He wasn't protecting British children from a lethal virus hidden inside a computer. No. This time, he was involved in something that the entire world would condemn."

As Razim spoke, some of the men around the

table were becoming more alert, nodding as they followed the thread of what he was saying.

"And let us also imagine that during the course of this mission the boy was killed."

This brought smiles and a few murmurs of approval.

"Suddenly we have a situation. A fourteen-year-old is shot to death by police in the streets of a major city. There are documents in his pockets. Perhaps he is carrying a gun that can be traced back to London. All the evidence proves, beyond any doubt, that he was working for MI6. Think for a minute what the result of all this would be."

"It would be covered up," Mikato said. "There isn't a newspaper that would dare print such a story."

"Quite possibly. But we would have all the evidence. Scorpia would have collected emails, phone intercepts, photographs, voice recordings. We would have in our hands a bomb that we could detonate at any time. And the result? The reputation of the British government would be destroyed. It would be forced to dismantle its own secret service. The prime minister would resign. And no civilized country would want to do business with Britain for decades to come."

No one spoke. By now *Le Débiteur* had left the Eiffel Tower behind and turned the corner past the Quai d'Orsay. If anyone had looked out of the window, they would have seen the gardens of the Tuileries stretching out on the left bank with the

Louvre museum just beyond. They would have seen couples strolling along the paths between shrubs and fountains that had been arranged so perfectly that it was as if they had been designed by a mathematician rather than a gardener. But nobody was interested in the view. They were all focused on Razim, turning over what he had just said.

"Let me get this straight." The man who had spoken was fair-haired, dressed casually in jeans and an open-necked shirt. His name was Brendan Chase and he had once been the paymaster for ASIS – the Australian Secret Intelligence Service – until one afternoon when, after a drinking session, he had boarded a plane with four hundred thousand dollars of his agency's money stuffed into his backpack. "Somehow you're going to persuade MI6 to send Alex Rider on a mission. You're going to make sure that the mission goes wrong and the boy is killed. Well, I'm with you there. If you want a volunteer, I'll be glad to fire the bullet myself. You're then going to blackmail them. We have all the evidence. We have the photographs and the recordings. We'll make them public unless you persuade your government to send the Elgin Marbles back to Greece. Is that about it?"

"You have expressed it with perfect clarity, Mr Chase."

"OK. But this is what I don't understand. How are you going to do it? These photographs, for example. Are you going to forge them? They'll have

to be pretty good if they're to stand up to exami-
nation..."

"I don't intend to forge anything."

"So how are you going to get the British secret
service to play along?"

Razim tapped ash onto the surface of the table.
His fingernails were stained yellow with nicotine.
"Any forgery is out of the question," he continued.
"We have to be cleverer than that. But I believe it
will be perfectly possible for us to arrange all the
pieces on the board so that we control the entire
game. At the moment, gentlemen, we have the
upper hand. British intelligence have no idea of
our intentions. And the truth is, they are a great
deal less intelligent than they might believe. Alan
Blunt has been in charge for too long; the same is
true of his deputy, Mrs Jones. We have extensive
files on the two of them and I have been examining
them closely. There are certain patterns of behaviour. That is to say, they have become predictable.
I think it will be fairly simple to manipulate them.
We will create a trap. And, with a little nudging
and pushing, they will fall right into it."

"Alex Rider is fifteen years old now," Mikato
said. He had taken out a handkerchief and was
fanning it across his face. He eyed the cigarette
with distaste. "As far as we know, MI6 is no longer
using him. Do you really believe that you can persuade them to involve him again?"

"Certainly." Razim dropped the cigarette and

ground it out on the wooden floor. "All we have to do is create the circumstances that will steer them towards that decision."

"I had heard that he'd refused to work for them again," Dr Three said.

"Alex Rider never had any real choice in the matter. What's so strange is that he never wanted to be a spy in the first place. What this means is that we don't actually have to go anywhere near him. If we provide them with the right sort of bait, MI6 will do our work for us. They're the ones we have to target."

"What bait do you have in mind?" the Frenchman asked.

Razim glanced briefly at Zeljan Kurst as if seeking his consent. The bald head nodded very slightly.

"It has to be done one step at a time," Razim replied. "Our first objective is to get Rider out of England and into a city of our choosing. Although he won't be aware of it, he will be entering a hall of mirrors, as if at a funfair. Every move he makes will be controlled. Certain doors will be closed to him even as others open up. He will be watched from every angle. But, as I say, we have to start with MI6. They are the ones who will draw Alex into our trap.

"So let's begin with the bait. Let's say that a dead body is found floating in the Thames. The body is that of a wanted criminal – a very important criminal. MI6 has been searching for him for some time. And in his pocket is a letter or some other document. Of course, it's in code. MI6 send it to their best scientists and they manage to work out what it means. That is when they discover that an operation is taking place in some distant country which demands their urgent attention. It is something of world-changing importance. An agent must be sent there at once—"

"It could be any agent," Mikato interrupted. "Why should they choose the boy?"

"Because the operation involves a field of activity in which a child might pass unnoticed. This is the key to the whole thing. I've already seen it in the files. The first time MI6 used Rider, it was because he could pass himself off as the winner of a competition in a computer magazine – and this allowed him to infiltrate Herod Sayle's production plant in Cornwall. The next time, it was Point Blanc Academy in France, which he could enter as a student, the teenage son of a multi-millionaire. Then he travelled with two American agents to the island of Skeleton Key. This time he was pretending to be their son, and having him with them turned them into an ordinary, happy family. Do you see? There is a pattern. If a teen-ager is required, they have to choose Alex Rider. There is no one else."

Another pause. The Italian twins turned briefly to each other and knew at once that they had come to the same decision. Mikato's face relaxed and he nodded slowly. The Australian smiled to himself.

*"Lalek et hatahat sheli!"* Any silent agreement in the room was shattered by Levi Kroll spitting out the vile oath in Hebrew. Now he rose to his feet, addressing everyone around the table. "I do not believe what I am hearing!" he roared. His face was livid, the veins on his cheeks standing out. "This is madness. Listen to me. I am not saying that this child is better than us. I do not for a minute believe that he beat us for any other reason than luck. However, let me tell you now, luck has a part to play in our activities. You can plan everything perfectly but still a small, unforeseen detail can destroy you. A chance meeting in the street. A gun jamming. Bad weather! You know that this is true.

"And Alex Rider has the luck of the devil on his side. How else do you explain the death of Julia Rothman – and Nile, her second in command, for that matter? Major Yu was a genius. He ran the most successful snakehead operation in the Far East. But when he came up against Alex Rider he died and his snakehead fell apart. There are a dozen ways we can persuade the British to return these worthless statues! I like the idea of a nuclear bomb. We could kidnap a member of the royal family, maybe one of the princes, and send him back one piece at a time until the government gave in to our demands. But I will not agree to take on this child for a third time. Twice was enough. We cannot risk a third humiliation."

Kroll sat down, breathing heavily.

"Is there anyone else here who shares our colleague's concerns?" Zeljan Kurst asked.

Like poker players about to reveal their hands, the ten other members of Scorpia eyed one another carefully but none of them spoke.

"I take it from your silence, then, that you all agree with Mr Razim's plan?"

"But I disagree," Kroll insisted, not waiting for an answer. "And by our own rules, if we are not unanimous, we do not proceed."

Kurst seemed to consider this. "We could be unanimous," he purred.

"And how might that happen, Zeljan?" Kroll looked at him curiously, daring him to provide an answer.

Nothing had changed. But the atmosphere inside the conference room was suddenly brittle. The sound of the engine shuddered in the air.

Zeljan Kurst shrugged, his huge shoulders rising then falling a few inches. He ignored Kroll, turning instead to Razim. "You suggested that a criminal could be found floating in the Thames," he said. "Might it not be more convincing if it were a member of the executive board of Scorpia?"

"I think that would be excellent," Razim replied.

"Forget it!" Kroll was back on his feet again and as if by magic a gun had appeared in his hand. It was a 9mm SP-21 military pistol, designed by Israel

Military Industries. He couldn't possibly have drawn it from a holster. There must have been a spring mechanism inside his jacket that had delivered it into his hand. He pointed it at Zeljan Kurst, a wild look in his one eye. "I suspected that you'd been thinking of getting rid of me," he murmured. "I'm not surprised. I've given more than twenty years to this organization and I knew the sort of reward I could expect. The same reward as Max Grendel. Nobody retires from Scorpia, do they?" He laughed briefly. "Maybe some of you should consider what future you have here."

The gun didn't move but his eye slid briefly towards the twins and then back again.

"You're not going to kill me, Zeljan. As you can see, I've been prepared for this moment. You think Scorpia is getting stronger? It's not. It's finished. And I'm going to be the first to walk out."

Nobody reacted. It was unheard of for a gun to be produced in the middle of an executive meeting. But they were all confident. Kurst must have known. He must surely have the situation under control.

"You are going to order the captain to steer this boat to the nearest bank and then I am going to leave," Kroll continued. "You don't need to worry about me. I have no interest in you any more. But if any of you ever come after me, I will have stories to tell that will put you all in jail for longer than you can possibly live. Do you understand me?"

Zeljan Kurst's hands were under the table. Kroll

didn't see his right hand stretch out and press a button in the side of his chair.

"I said do you understand me?"

"I understand you completely," Kurst replied.

There was the soft tinkle of glass breaking. A hole had appeared in the window just behind Kroll's head.

Kroll jerked slightly but remained standing. A look of puzzlement spread across his face.

There was a moment's silence. Then Kurst spoke. "You have been shot in the back of the neck, just above the cervical curve," he explained. "I'm afraid your spine has been severed and you are, effectively, already dead."

With an enormous effort, as if knowing this would be the last movement he ever made, Kroll opened his mouth. His hand, with the gun, remained frozen.

"Right now we should be passing the Paris mint." Kurst glanced out of the window. Sure enough, there was a handsome building with arches and columns stretching for some distance along the waterfront. "I knew, of course, that you were carrying a gun and suspected you might be foolish enough to try and use it. So I took the precaution of placing a sniper on the roof. Can you still hear me? I would like to think you have the consolation of knowing that your death will not be wasted."

Kroll's legs gave way and he crashed down into

his chair, his head and shoulders slumping forward onto the table. The hole in his neck was surprisingly small.

"We will have to put Levi in the refrigerator until the time comes to use him," Kurst went on. "We do not want to give away the time of his death. And whatever clue it is that we place in his pocket, it will have to be something very ingenious. We want to make MI6 work. The more clever they think they are, the more easily they will fall into our trap." He glanced again at Razim. "There is something else?"

"Yes." Like everyone else in the room, Razim seemed completely uninterested in the murder that he had just witnessed. It was as if nothing had happened at all. "We can manipulate MI6. And we can ensure that Alex Rider is brought back into service. Once he is in our hands, it will be a simple matter to kill him, although" – he smiled to himself – "I hope you will allow me a little time with him first. There is an experiment that I would like to try."

"Just be careful," Duval said.

"Of course. But there is something else that we need and which I didn't have time to mention before our unfortunate interruption..." He looked briefly at the dead man, sprawled forward over the table. "Although I have said that we cannot forge the evidence, we nonetheless have to be creative. We live in an age of disinformation. That is to say, there isn't a document or a report that anyone trusts. People need to see things with their own eyes. We are going to have to capture Alex Rider on film. I want to be able to show him live on TV, before he is discovered, as it were, dead on TV. I want the whole world to be able to see him in action."

"And how will you manage that?" Dr Three asked.

Razim took out a second cigarette. Nobody was going to ask him to stop smoking. Not now. "Actually it will be very simple," he drawled. "But it will require the assistance of someone very special – someone unique. Fortunately I was able to track this person down and I have already set in motion a plan to communicate with him. He has every reason to wish harm to Alex Rider. In fact, he hates Rider more than any of us here.

"I have not yet been able to speak to him about Horseman but I can assure you that he will be delighted to help us. Although getting him to us will be expensive, I have already put a team in place. It will be money well spent.

"All being well, he should be with us by the end of the week. And then, Operation Horseman can begin."

# PRISONER 7

The boy walking along the garden path and up to the front door of the villa was fifteen years old with fair hair that flopped down over his eyes. He had a thin, rather pale face, well-defined cheekbones and a slender neck. He was wearing jeans, a black sports shirt and trainers. Overall he was slim but he was also athletic and had clearly spent time working out in the gym. His arms and chest were almost too well developed for someone of his age. From the way he moved, it seemed that he had all the time in the world. He was listening to music on an iPod, the white cable snaking down to his back pocket.

It was a warm day, the sun beating down on the well-kept lawn that stretched out on either side of the path. There was a vegetable patch with onions and carrots already poking through and, curving behind it, an old brick wall with pink climbing roses and passion flowers. The villa itself was built in the Spanish style with very pale yellow weatherboarding and blue shutters.

As he approached the door, the boy unplugged his earphones and heard birdsong, along with the *chug-chug-chug* of an automatic sprinkler system. He stood still for a moment. Close his eyes and he might be in some quiet corner of England, perhaps a village in Dorset or Kent. But glancing past the garden, he saw the razor wire fence looming above him. Two guards, both with machine guns, walked past. And once again he was reminded – as if he needed reminding – that he was far from home, in one of the strangest prisons in the world.

Certainly it was a prison like no other. It had no name. It featured on no maps. Very few people even knew it existed. The staff who worked there – from the governor to the guards to the cleaners and the cook – had been told that if they ever breathed a word about their work, they would end up in a cell themselves. The facility had been built at a cost of several million pounds and cost millions more to run, and yet – and this was the most remarkable thing of all – it housed just seven prisoners, each one in his own way so dangerous that there was little chance any of them would ever be released.

This was the problem. There has been no capital punishment in the United Kingdom since 1964, so what was the government to do with its worst enemies, the men and women who had sworn to bring about its destruction by any means? Of course, there were high security prisons such as Belmarsh in the east of London or a psychiatric hospital such as Broadmoor in Berkshire – but even these weren't considered secure enough for the handful of special cases that had to be kept in almost total isolation. These were people who couldn't be allowed to tell their stories. They couldn't be killed. So they had to be put somewhere where they might be forgotten.

And so the compound had been constructed. Not in mainland Britain. That was felt to be too close to home. Northern Ireland had been considered. There were still prisons there from the old days of the Troubles that could have been adapted. But instead the overseas territory of Gibraltar had finally been chosen, jutting out of the southern end of Spain. There were plenty of good reasons. First of all, it was still British soil. Surrounded by sea on three sides and with a well-patrolled border on the fourth, it was virtually a prison in itself. It was very quiet. Apart from the Spanish occasionally demanding that the land be given back, most people would have been hard-pressed to point to it on a map. And best of all, it was a base for both the British Armed Forces and the Royal Navy. There were already military buildings all over the peninsula. Who would notice one more?

The prison was high up on the Rock and overlooked the Bay of Gibraltar and the Mediterranean – or would have done if the walls, six metres high and one metre thick, hadn't got in the way. Electrified razor wire ran inside the walls so that even if a prisoner managed to equip himself with a ladder, perhaps constructed secretly in the prison workshop, he wouldn't be able to place it anywhere close. The position of the fence had been chosen with care. It couldn't be seen from outside and there were no watchtowers, no armed guards visible on patrol. In other words, nothing gave away the true nature of the complex. Nobody lived near by and passing residents and tourists believed that it was a naval communications centre dealing with satellite and Internet traffic.

Most of the security was invisible. There were almost a hundred CCTV cameras and hidden microphones so that prisoners could be observed and listened to from the moment they woke up – and even while they were asleep. Movement sensors and thermal imaging cameras provided data twenty-four hours a day so that the guards could tell instantly where everyone was at any time. The dozen cells (five unoccupied) were built on solid rock, so tunnelling was out of the question, but more sensor wires criss-crossed underneath the floorboards anyway. No visitors were allowed. No letters were ever sent or received. There was just one entrance and exit: a holding area with an electronic gate at each end. Any vehicle entering or leaving the prison was required to drive onto a reinforced glass plate so that it could be examined and searched from all sides before it was allowed to continue.

And yet, surprisingly, the prison was a very comfortable place. It was as if the British government had wanted to convince the inmates that it wasn't completely inhumane. The various buildings scattered inside the walls were low-rise, made of wood and brick. Apart from the bars on the windows in the accommodation block, the complex vaguely resembled a holiday village, an impression heightened by the flower beds, olive and cypress trees, and the sprinkler system dotted around the dusty, winding paths. The governor's villa was almost absurdly pretty. He was a tough ex-navy man and lived there with his Spanish wife. But his home could have come out of Disneyland.

Each prisoner had his own cell with a bed, a work area, a TV and a separate shower and toilet. There was a library, a well-equipped gym, a wood and metal workshop and a dining room. The other buildings included an administration and residential block for the guards, a control room and a punishment block. This was a narrow corridor with three rooms built underground. The rooms were soundproof with no windows, but they had seldom been used. There was no reason to cause any trouble. And as escape was impossible, nobody had ever tried.

Seven prisoners.

Two of them were terrorists, not the people who had carried the bombs but the ones who had decided where they should be placed. They had been captured while planning a nuclear strike on London and had been tried in secret and then brought to Gibraltar. Nobody was ever to know how nearly they had succeeded. Two were secret agents, spies working for foreign powers. They had managed to get deep inside the intelligence services before they were unmasked, and it was what they knew as much as what they were that made them so dangerous. One man – the oldest in the prison – claimed that he had been a weapons inspector in Iraq and was innocent of any crime. Nobody believed him. The sixth man was a freelance assassin. There were very few pages in his file. He had never revealed his name, nationality, age or the number of people he had killed.

But it was the seventh prisoner, the fifteen-year-old boy standing in front of the governor's villa, who was without doubt the most remarkable. In fact, he was almost unique: not born but created, given a face that wasn't his own, taught how to kill – and quite, quite insane.

His name was Julius Grief and he had been one of the sixteen clones created in a French laboratory by his natural father, Dr Hugo Grief. A clone is an exact copy of a human being, manufactured by taking a single cell and cultivating it inside an egg. Julius had not only never met his mother, he didn't really have one. Until he had been born, cloning had been restricted to laboratory animals. The most famous had been Dolly the sheep. But using technology which he had developed first at the University of Johannesburg and later as South Africa's minister of science, Grief had cloned the first human beings: sixteen replicas of himself.

They had all grown up together at Point Blanc Academy, a castle high up in the French Alps, near Grenoble. Dr Grief had been planning to take over the richest and most powerful families on the planet by kidnapping their teenage sons and replacing them with his own brood. One by one the boys had been given painful – and permanent – plastic surgery, making them identical to their targets. None of them had complained. This was the purpose of their entire life. This was what they had been created for. They had never had proper identities of their own. Even their names had been chosen to this end. Each one of them had been named after a great world leader. "Julius" had come from Julius Caesar, the Roman emperor. And there had been other boys named Napoleon, Genghis, Mao Tse and even (the sixteenth) Adolf.

As things had turned out, Julius had been the last of the boys to be given a new identity. He was to be Alex Friend, the son of Sir David Friend, a man who had made a fortune from supermarkets and art galleries. He was going to live in a huge house in Lancashire, in the north of England. He would go riding and shooting with his aristocratic friends. It would be amazing! And one day, after he had murdered Sir David and his family, it would all belong to him.

And so Julius had undergone the surgery. He had begun to learn his new role – how to talk like Alex Friend, how to walk like him, how to *be* him. And then, at the last minute, he had discovered the terrible truth. The boy he was watching day and night, the one he was modelling himself on, was not Alex Friend at all. He was, incredibly, a spy working for British intelligence. Julius Grief had been given the wrong face. The face of Alex Rider.

Worse was to follow. Alex had escaped from Point Blanc, only to return at the head of an armed force. The school had been destroyed; Dr Grief had been killed. Julius had managed to escape and had tracked Alex down to his school near Chelsea; but somehow, even though he'd had surprise on his side and a loaded gun in his hand, Rider had managed to get the better of him. Julius remembered the fight on the roof of the science block. The fire. Plunging down into the inferno. He could still feel the burns that had started at his neck and crisscrossed his body all the way to his thighs. He'd spent two months in hospital and the pain would be with him for the rest of his life. He was reminded of it every time he caught sight of his reflection.

He still had Alex's face.

It drove him mad. When he cleaned his teeth in the morning, there it was, in the mirror, smiling back at him. If he passed a window at night, the ghost of his enemy would glide by beside him. After a heavy rainfall Alex Rider would look up at him from the puddles. There were times when he wanted to tear his face off with his nails – and in his early days at the prison he had tried to do exactly that, leaving deep scratches down his forehead and cheeks. That was when they had decided he needed psychiatric help. He was on his way to his next appointment now.

Julius Grief reached out and rang the bell at the side of the governor's front door. He was expected, of course, but it was against regulations to enter without ringing. The bell sounded both inside the villa and in the control room. A camera had already picked him out and one of the guards was checking that he was meant to be there. Yes. An eleven o'clock appointment. He was exactly on time.

The door opened and a short, grey-haired woman looked out. As always, she was wearing dark colours with a white shirt buttoned to her neck and very little jewellery. She could have been the headmistress of a primary school in some remote English village. She was in her mid forties with a pinched face and a slightly turned-up nose. Her name was Rosemary Flint and she was a child psychiatrist. She had been meeting Julius twice a week for the past six months, talking to him in the living room of the governor's house rather than in the library or his cell because she hoped the homely atmosphere might help.

"Good morning, Julius," she said. She had one of those annoying voices that were always sweet and reasonable. Somehow you knew she would never lose her temper.

"Good morning, Dr Flint," Julius replied.

"How are you today?"

"I'm very well, thank you."

"Come in."

They had spoken almost exactly the same words fifty times and Dr Flint had noted that not once had the boy's expression changed. He was coldly polite. His eyes were empty. She had never told Julius this, but part of her job was to decide if there was any chance he could one day be released and returned to society. After all, it wasn't entirely his fault that he was what he was. That was what he had been made. Someone in British intelligence hoped that he could be turned around and might eventually lead a normal life. But as far as Dr Flint was concerned, that day was still a very long way off.

She led him into the living room and gestured towards a large, comfortable sofa covered with a flower-patterned fabric. There was no need for the gesture. Julius sat in the same place every time. The governor's wife liked flowers. The room had flowery wallpaper too and there was a vase of roses cut from the garden on a low, dark wood table. The curtains were thick and kept out much of the sunlight even when they were open. An antique mirror had once hung on one of the walls but Julius had smashed it in the middle of his third session. The governor hadn't been pleased but Dr Flint had insisted that there should be no punishment. In her view the boy wasn't responsible for his actions. She thought of him, at least in part, as a victim. A painting – a view of Cadiz – now hung in the mirror's place.

"Would you like some orange juice, Julius?" Dr Flint asked.

"No, thank you," Julius replied. He never drank or ate anything during these sessions. Dr Flint had tried biscuits, chocolates, Coke and cream cakes – all without success. She knew exactly what was going on in his mind. To take anything would be giving her power over him. She might set the rules, but he was playing his own game. One day, she hoped, he might accept a Jaffa Cake. Then, at last, she would know that the healing process had begun.

"So how has your week been?"

"I've had a very good week, thank you."

"Are you reading anything from the prison library?"

"I've just started *War Horse*."

"That's excellent, Julius. You should try to read as much as you can." She smiled. "What's it about?"

"Some stupid horses that get killed in the war."

"Aren't you enjoying it?"

"No. Not much."

Dr Flint sighed. The boy was lying. She knew every book he had borrowed and every book he had read. He was the only teenager in the prison and there weren't a great many things he could do with his time. He devoured books. But when he was with her, he pretended otherwise.

"Have you thought more about what we spoke of last time?" she asked.

"We discussed a lot of things, Dr Flint."

"We were talking about anger management."

"I'm not angry."

"I think you are."

Julius didn't answer but he could feel something burning, white hot, inside him. It wasn't anger. How could this stupid woman describe it like that? It was like molten lava, flowing through his intestines. It was like acid. He looked down deliberately, knowing he would be unable to keep the emotion out of his eyes. Dr Flint would spot it and she would write it down in that notebook of hers. She wrote everything down, as if she could even begin to understand him. It was lucky she couldn't see into his imagination. Julius dreamed of killing Alex Rider. Slowly. Painfully. He should have done it on the school roof a year ago. He had come so close.

And he might yet get another chance. Julius thought about the note he had found the night before. It had been waiting for him, hidden in his room ... incredibly, impossibly. He had read it so many times that he knew every word off by heart – but he quickly forced it out of his mind. The woman was still examining him. He didn't dare give anything away.

"I thought we might try some word association today," Dr Flint said.

"Whatever you say, Dr Flint."

It was her favourite game. She said one word; he had to say another, instantly, without any thought. It was supposed to demonstrate what was going on in his mind.

"Right." She looked around her. "I'm going to start with something very ordinary. You know what to do."

There was a pause. Then she began.

"Dog."

"Bone."

"Kitchen."

"Knife."

"Handle."

"Blade."

"Grass."

"Dead body."

Dr Flint stopped. "I don't understand the association," she said. "When you said 'blade', I said 'grass' because I was thinking of a blade of grass."

"And when you said 'grass', I thought about burying someone underneath it."

"Who do you want to bury, Julius?"

Julius didn't answer. They both knew whom he had in mind.

"Let's try again," Dr Flint said. For the first time in her career, she was beginning to wonder if there was any point in continuing. She had been working with this child for months and she had made no progress at all. She touched her lip. "Mouth."

"Throat."

"Drink."

"Poison."

"Bottle."

"Message."

"Letter."

"Bed."

She stopped a second time. "That was a little better," she said. "You were thinking of a message in a bottle, I suppose. But why did you say 'bed'?"

Julius was cursing himself. He couldn't get the message out of his head. He had found it under his pillow when he went to bed. Someone must have placed it there during the day. And now he had almost let it slip, throwing out words without thinking.

"I've got a slight headache. Do you mind if we don't play this any more?" he asked.

"Of course, Julius. Do you want to have a rest?"

"No, Dr Flint."

Only a few minutes of the session had passed. They still had nearly a whole hour together. Julius wondered if he would be able to get through it without screaming at her or even trying to break her neck. He had thrown himself at her once, early on in his therapy, and after he'd been dragged off, they'd put him in the punishment block for a week. He couldn't let that happen now. The message. The secret friends. They wouldn't keep him waiting long. He just had to hold everything together until the right time.

"All right. Why don't we draw some pictures? I'd like you to draw some imaginary place and then you can take me through it and tell me what you can see."

Julius had an imaginary place. It was a forest with Alex Rider hanging from every tree, nailed to every trunk, buried up to his neck in the mud, lying bloody and unconscious in the grass. A whole world of Alex Riders, each one suffering in a different way.

"Can I draw a funfair?" he asked.

"Of course, Julius."

Even as he picked up the child's crayon that had been supplied for him, he thought about the moment he had lifted the pillow and seen the single folded sheet of paper beneath. He had known at once that it was something special. Nobody ever came into his room uninvited. The other prisoners weren't allowed; the guards and cleaners made a point of asking his permission.

He had unfolded it and read:

WE ARE YOUR FRIENDS. WE ARE PREPARING
TO HELP YOU ESCAPE. GO TO THE LIBRARY
TOMORROW AT TWELVE O'CLOCK AND YOU
WILL FIND FURTHER INSTRUCTIONS.

The words had been neatly typed. Instead of a signature there was a little emblem printed in silver at the bottom of the page.

A scorpion.

Julius had read the note a dozen times, then crumpled it into a ball and swallowed it with a cup of water which he had drawn from the tap. After that he had gone to bed – but he hadn't slept.

WE ARE YOUR FRIENDS.

Who? He had no friends. Could it be some of his brothers? Julius had never found out what had happened to them after Point Blanc Academy had been shut down, but he had assumed that they were, like him, prisoners. Perhaps he had been contacted by people who had known his father. They might be from the old South Africa...

TOMORROW AT TWELVE O'CLOCK...

Tomorrow was now today. It was already ten past eleven. Just fifty minutes to go. Julius Grief forced the image of Alex Rider (with a kitchen knife in his chest, his bones exposed, lying in the grass, then under the grass) out of his mind and began to draw a merry-go-round.

Dr Flint watched him and of course she didn't know. Nobody knew.

This was the day he was going to escape.

# *OVER THE EDGE*

The library was the most modern building in the prison, and although it was unusually small and compact, it could have been lifted out of almost any provincial town in England. It was low-rise with red bricks and sliding glass doors and contained about three hundred books – half in English, half in Spanish, for the guards and their families used it too. There was a desk where books had to be signed in and out, a newspaper and magazine section (although all the publications were carefully censored), then the books themselves, divided into the usual classifications. The crime and horror sections were the most popular with the prisoners. New books appeared occasionally, mainly sent by charities. When Julius Grief had arrived, the governor had personally set up a children's section, purchasing the first books – a complete collection of Roald Dahl – with his own money.

Julius headed to the library as soon as his session with Dr Flint was finished, crossing the open space where some of the other prisoners were enjoying the sun, sitting on rickety chairs between the trees. The two terrorists were playing Scrabble. As Julius walked past, one of them noticed him and nodded vaguely in his direction. He had just made the word JIHAD with the J on a triple letter, scoring thirty-six points. The assassin was near by, reading a celebrity magazine and circling some of the heads with a black felt-tip pen. The other prisoners didn't really like having a teenager among them. It offended their sense of dignity.

Julius had to force himself not to hurry. He knew that his every movement was being watched and that any strange behaviour, any indication that he was planning something, would be reported immediately. He even hesitated before he went into the library, as if he wasn't sure whether he needed a book or not. Then, pretending to make up his mind, he passed through the glass doors.

"*Buenos días*, Julius." The librarian was a Spaniard who also worked in the prison accounts office. His name was Carlos and he was plump and good-natured, dressed in the same uniform as the guards: an olive green shirt and dark trousers. "You are coming to the talk tonight?"

"I'm looking forward to it," Julius said.

There were occasional talks in the library, given by the prisoners or by the guards. Two weeks ago one of the secret agents had spoken for an hour on the Cold War. Tonight the chef was demonstrating his mother's paella recipe.

"What is it you want?" Carlos asked.

"I've come to borrow a book."

Carlos glanced at his computer screen. "But you already have three in your cell."

"I know. But I've finished two of them. And I'm not enjoying the third..."

Julius walked towards the bookshelves, feeling the librarian's eyes boring into his back. What exactly was he looking for? The note had told him to come here, where he would find further instructions. But apart from Carlos, there was no one else in the building. Would there be a second letter hidden somewhere – and if so, how was he meant to find it? He decided to head for the children's section. After all, that was where "they" would expect him to go.

He stopped in front of the shelves. The Dahl collection stretched from one side to the other. Julius had never read any, although he had once come across one of the terrorists with *Fantastic Mr Fox*. As far as he could see, nothing had changed since his last visit. He could even make out the gaps where he had pulled out his own choice of books.

And then he saw it. One new book, lying flat on its side. A fat, dusty-looking hardback called *Wildlife in Gibraltar Volume II: Birds and Insects*. It shouldn't even have been here. It should have been on the other side of the room, in natural history. But that wasn't what had caught his eye. It was the cover. There was a picture of a creature that seemed to be gazing at him with its tiny eyes. It couldn't just be a coincidence.

It was a scorpion – the same image that had appeared on the note.

He glanced round. Carlos was sitting tapping at his keyboard. The librarian seemed to have forgotten him. But there were still cameras, mounted in all four corners of the room. They would be watching him from the control room. Julius put on a performance for their benefit. He took out one book, then another – as if considering which to read – then finally picked up the wildlife volume and carried it over to a table.

He had chosen the position carefully. The table was right next to a shelf which screened it from the cameras. Carlos could still see him, but he was fairly certain that the book was out of sight. Very carefully he opened it. And gasped.

How could this have happened? Nobody knew about the prison. Nobody could possibly infiltrate it. And yet, there it was in front of him. The pages of the book had been cut out to provide a hiding place for a gun, a Mauser C96 semi-automatic pistol with the barrel shortened to allow it to fit.

Julius ran a finger over the cold metal. He had been taught to shoot when he was nine years old and had killed for the first time when he was eleven. But it had been more than a year since he had held a gun in his hands, and he had thought he would never have one again. For just one moment he felt an urge to pick it up, to turn round and shoot Carlos in the head. But that was crazy. He had to be sensible, do this one step at a time.

There was a second note, folded into the book. It was much longer and more detailed than the message he had received the night before. Julius read it very carefully. Whoever was helping him, these were serious people. He knew he couldn't make a mistake. Finally, when he was ready, he closed the book and stood up. It was half past twelve, exactly the right time. He knew what he had to do.

*The subject has made no progress at all since his arrival in Gibraltar. It is clear that Julius Grief has a pathological hatred for Alex Rider which is deep-rooted and permanent. And yet, at the same time, surgery has made him identical to the object of his hate. It must surely follow that subconsciously some of that hatred must be directed against himself. In my view, there is a very real danger that this psychological turmoil could drive Grief over the edge and that he could plunge into depression, suicide or total nervous breakdown. Indeed, it is surprising that it hasn't happened yet.*

Dr Flint looked at what she had just written and felt a deep sense of gloom. She had been working with damaged children for her entire professional life but she had never met anyone like Julius

Grief. She wanted to feel sorry for him. He wasn't responsible for what he had become. He had been manipulated from the moment he was born – in fact, even his birth had been manipulated. He was a freak, created for one purpose only: to help his father take over the world. She had read the file on Hugo Grief and it had made her shudder. All sixteen boys had been drip-fed a diet of hatred and insanity and all of them (apart from two who had died) had ended up in institutions like this, locked up for the rest of their lives. It wasn't their fault.

And yet no matter how hard she tried, she couldn't avoid the fact that she felt a deep dislike for Julius. She knew it was unprofessional but at the same time it was almost instinctive. He was a horrible person. And she wasn't fooled by him either. Although he went along with her methods – the discussions, the word association, the different psychological tests – she knew he was toying with her. And he was keeping something back. Even this morning she had been aware of it. He had tried to hide it in his expressionless face and his flat, formal answers. But there had been moments when she sensed it, flickering at the corner of his eye like a moth in candlelight. There was something he wasn't telling her. She wondered if she should mention it to the governor but decided against it. She was the boy's therapist. She had to respect his confidentiality. She went back to her notes.

*I recommend that Julius should be put back on medication with immediate effect. Although I do not like drugging young people, I feel that in his case—*

The doorbell rang. That was surprising. The governor never came back before two o'clock and his wife was out for lunch. Dr Flint went over to the small television screen in the hallway and saw a black and white image of Julius standing outside, holding a bunch of flowers which he must have picked in the prison garden. She was tempted not to open the door. He shouldn't be here. It was against regulations. She remembered how he had tried to attack her in one of their first sessions. And then there had been the time when he had gone berserk and smashed the mirror. She should tell him to go away.

But then she reconsidered. All that had been months ago and maybe he really was trying to make amends for his behaviour that morning. Maybe he had come to tell her what was on his mind. The flowers were a sweet touch. And anyway, there were dozens of cameras that would be trained on him even now. There was no danger.

She opened the door. "What is it, Julius?" she asked.

"It's a bit difficult to explain, Dr Flint."

"Do you want to come back inside?"

"No. As a matter of fact, I'd like you to come with me."

"Where do you want to go?"

"We're leaving here – together."

He dropped the flowers and there it was, in his hand, pointing at her. Dr Flint stared in shock. Julius Grief was holding a gun, his finger curled around the trigger, a glazed look in his eyes. It was like something out of a nightmare. It made no sense at all. How could he possibly have a gun? And yet there was something horribly inevitable about it.

Julius was managing to contain his excitement. He was in total control. Dr Flint knew that if she didn't do exactly what he said, he would shoot her without a second thought.

He stepped forward and suddenly the gun was at her throat and his face was close to hers. She could feel his madness as if she had been slapped with it. He was as tall as her and a great deal stronger. He was armed. For the first time since she had known him his face had cracked into something resembling a smile. Suddenly he was no longer fifteen and the good looks that the plastic surgeon had given him were twisted out of shape. He could have been fifty or even a hundred and fifty. Evil has no age. Dr Flint was terrified. Had she really spent the last six months, twice a week, on her own with this monster?

"I'm going to walk out of here," Julius said and his voice was soft even though it was on the edge of hysteria. "Walk, walk, walk, walk. And you're going to come with me."

"They'll never let you through the gates."

Julius pressed the gun into the side of her neck, the sawn-off muzzle pointing upwards. "Then they'll be scraping your brains off the fence," he told her. "Shall we go, Dr Flint? I think we should."

They walked together like two lovers performing some strange sort of dance. Dr Flint was staring straight ahead, her head tilted. Julius was enjoying himself. The feel of the gun in his hand was giving him strength. He loved the way the hard steel was pressing into the woman's flesh. For months he had endured her stupid questions, her endless mind games. Now, at last, he was the one in command.

Despite all the cameras, Julius Grief and Dr Flint had almost reached the first gate into the holding area before anyone realized that something was wrong. Perhaps they thought it was some sort of exercise, part of the therapy, but finally someone saw the gun and realized what was going on. At once, long-rehearsed emergency procedures sprang into life. A dozen sirens went off, their combined sound echoing all over the peninsula. Guards burst out of doorways, their weapons ready. The other prisoners were rushed at gunpoint back into their cells. An automated phone message was sent instantly to Devil's Tower Camp, home of the Royal Gibraltar Regiment, close to the airport, calling for immediate backup, and before Julius had even had a chance to make his demands, half a dozen Land Rovers were speeding out of the garrison and beginning the long climb uphill.

For a moment, everything froze. It was as if the entire compound had become a photograph of itself. Julius Grief was still holding on to Dr Flint, one hand on her shoulder, the other – with the gun – pressing against her neck. He was surrounded by rifles and automatic machine guns. They were aiming at him from every direction. The sun was still beating down, glinting off the razor wire fence. Somewhere outside the prison, there was a brief chatter of laughter as one of the island's famous apes swung itself off the branch of a tree and disappeared into the undergrowth.

Then the governor appeared. He was a stocky, muscular man with grey hair cut short, dressed in army fatigues. He had been in the control room when the alarm was sounded. He stopped in the holding area, on the other side of the first gate.

"Grief!" he barked. He had been in the Royal Navy for twenty years and had the sort of voice that was used to being obeyed. "What do you think you're doing?"

"Open the gate or I'll put a bullet in her." Julius was loving this. He could feel the world spinning around him. "I'll kill her. I promise."

"Where did you get the gun?"

A stupid question. Julius wasn't going to answer it. "Five seconds..." he called out.

"You're not going anywhere."

"Four..."

The governor had to make a decision. He had no doubt at all that Grief would use the gun. He could see that Rosemary Flint was terrified. The guards were waiting for his command but he couldn't let them fire, not unless they wanted to kill the woman too. How could the boy have possibly got hold of the weapon? Was it even real? He couldn't take the risk of finding out. Dr Flint was a civilian. Her safety came first.

"Three seconds, Governor."

Right now, the boy had the upper hand. But that would change on the other side of the prison gates. Backup would already be on its way and Julius Grief hadn't worked it out properly. He had nowhere to go. He was high above the main city and harbour, with narrow lanes and hairpin bends all the way down. He wouldn't be able to keep Flint close to him all the time and even if he made it to the bottom, there was no way he could leave the peninsula. Nobody was going to let him board a plane or a ship. The Spanish border authorities would already have been alerted. Everything was on the governor's side. Once Grief was out, it would be easy to pick him off.

"Open the gate!" Julius shouted. His face was deathly pale. His arm and the hand with the gun were rigid. Even if someone did shoot him, he would still manage to kill Dr Flint before he died.

"Do what he says!" the governor called out.

For another second, nothing happened, as if the guards couldn't believe what they had just heard. Then there was a click and the heavy gate began to roll aside. Julius grabbed hold of Dr Flint's collar and dragged her forward, the two of them moving side by side. The guns followed them into the holding area.

The inner gate slid shut and now they were trapped inside a pen with fences on three sides, a sentry box on the fourth. The governor had retreated, as if trying to get as far away from the scene as possible. A young guard stared at them from behind a plate-glass window. Nothing like this had ever happened at the prison before.

"Julius," Dr Flint rasped. It was hard for her to talk with the gun pressed against her throat. "Don't do this. It's not going to work."

"I would very much enjoy pulling this trigger," Julius replied. "In fact I'd love it. So if I were you, I'd shut up, Dr Flint. Don't give me the excuse."

The second gate opened and for the first time, Julius was able to see the little olive groves, the scattered boulders and the wild grass on the other side of the gates. In the distance he glimpsed the Mediterranean, a twisting ribbon of blue.

"Off we go!"

He forced Dr Flint forward. This was the critical moment. He knew that as soon as he left the prison, he would have to get rid of her. She would only slow him down. But that would be when he was most exposed. The guards wouldn't hesitate to shoot. Julius was putting all his trust in the people who had sent him his instructions – and he still had no idea who they were. If they had tricked him, if they had failed to deliver, he would be killed. But in a way he didn't care. Better this one minute of freedom than a life behind bars.

Julius and Dr Flint passed through the outer gate and now the prison was behind them. Julius Grief had been brought here in a blacked-out van so he had never seen the view. A narrow track ran downhill past some small, concrete buildings like pillboxes from the Second World War. The ground was dusty and covered in pine needles. He could smell pine and eucalyptus in the air. There was nobody in sight but the letter in the book had warned him that he would only have five minutes before the Royal Gibraltar Regiment Land Rovers reached him. He had to move fast.

He swung his arm, cracking the Mauser across Dr Flint's head. She cried out and fell to her knees, blood pouring down the side of her face. Julius twisted round and fired three shots at the prison gate, the bullets ricocheting off the metal. He hadn't hurt anyone but it would give them something to think about. Certainly nobody would choose to come running out in the next few seconds and he needed all the time he could get.

He began to sprint down the hill. He had kept himself fit while he was in prison, not because he had anywhere to go but because that was how he had been brought up. His father, Hugo Grief, had insisted on six hours' exercise a day, starting with a two-mile run through the snow. They had learned martial arts. They knew how to kill.

And he had taught them how to drive.

The car was waiting exactly where the letter had said it would be, parked just off the track hidden behind a cluster of the date palm trees that were dotted all over Gibraltar. It was a small SUV, a Suzuki Jimny, cheap and box-like and covered in dust. One wing was crumpled. The driver's mirror was cracked. It looked abandoned but the door was unlocked and the keys were in the ignition. Julius scrambled inside. At the same time, he heard a car rush past on the track, heading downhill from the prison. Fortunately the driver hadn't seen him. Somebody shouted. The guards were spreading out on foot as well. It wouldn't take them long to find him. He slammed the door and turned the key.

The 1.3 cylinder engine rattled noisily to life. The guards wouldn't expect him to have a car but they must have heard the sound and would now know – if they hadn't already guessed – that every aspect of this escape had been planned, with help from outside. Julius jammed the car into reverse, then shot out onto the track, the wheels spinning and sending out clouds of dust. The Suzuki handled badly and would struggle to get round the curves. Still, it was better than walking.

A shot rang out, slamming into the bodywork just above one of the rear tyres. One of the guards had seen him. Julius shoved the gearstick into first and accelerated. The Suzuki leapt forward even as the guard fired again, his second shot splintering the branch of a nearby tree. Julius was hunched over the wheel. There was another guard in the track ahead of him. How had he got there so fast? As the guard brought his gun round, Julius floored the accelerator. For a brief second the guard filled the windscreen. Then the car struck him and there was a sickening thud as he was thrown into the air, the gun spinning out of his hands.

Julius was ten metres down the road before the man hit the ground. There were two prison jeeps behind him. He could see them in his rear-view mirror. They were faster than the Jimny, getting closer by the second. If he hadn't been driving downhill, they would already have caught him.

Just ahead the track curved steeply to the right. He spun the wheel and suddenly he was on the very edge of a hundred-metre sheer drop. He saw the huge rocks and the sea far below. He felt the tyres slipping off the track, grit and loose pebbles spraying out. He fought with the steering wheel, forcing the Suzuki back under control. By the time he had rounded the corner, he had put some distance between him and the pursuing vehicles – but he had almost killed himself.

The next corner was easier. It bent to the left so

that this time the car was hugging the cliff face, away from the sea. Even so, Julius miscalculated and there was an explosion of glass and plastic as one of the wing mirrors disintegrated against a rocky outcrop. The jeeps were catching up again too and, looking ahead, he could see the fleet of Land Rovers belonging to the Royal Gibraltar Regiment climbing towards him.

There was no way down. There was no way back. The next hairpin bend and a sheer drop to certain death lay straight ahead.

Julius wrenched the wheel to the right. The driver of the nearest jeep saw the Suzuki leave the road, weaving across a patch of scrubland towards a dilapidated barn. The boy was out of control. He tried to steer the car back onto the track but instead smashed straight into the barn door, disappearing in a blast of shattering wood. For the next few seconds, the car was out of sight, inside the barn, but then it reappeared, breaking through the rear wall, the bonnet crumpled, the windscreen now a spiderweb of cracks. Julius Grief could only be glimpsed, staring out with a rictus smile, his fair hair sweeping down over his eyes, his hands glued to the steering wheel.

There was nowhere to go. The vehicles from the barracks were taking up position lower down the hill, blocking the way ahead. With the rocks on one side and the sheer drop on the other, there was no way past.

Julius didn't even try. Perhaps he couldn't see; perhaps he had been concussed when he hit the barn door. He didn't even attempt to steer, tearing dead straight across the scrubland, rejoining the track, then continuing over it. As the horrified prison guards skidded to a halt, the Suzuki reached the other side of the track, smashed through a barbed wire fence and launched itself into the void. Briefly it seemed to hang in the air. Then it plunged down, following the sheer edge of the Rock in a long, terrible descent towards the sea. About halfway down it hit a boulder. There was a single explosion as it burst into flames, somersaulted, then continued on its way. It was upside down when it hit the water. For a moment it rested there, the flames licking upwards as if trying to set the sea alight. Then it sank. A few pieces of broken metal rolled down the cliff face. Apart from that, there was nothing left.

The nearest Land Rover came to a halt and the driver got out. Gradually more guards appeared, hurrying across the grass to peer over the edge, beside the broken fence. Below them and to one side, the city of Gibraltar lay spread out, the high-rises facing the sea. The Mediterranean itself was a brilliant blue, the sun throwing a million shimmering reflections across the surface.

"Did you see that?" someone asked.

"Poor bastard!"

"You think he did it on purpose? He didn't even try to get back on the road."

"He could still be alive."

"Forget it. Nobody could have survived that. He'll have drowned – if he didn't burn to death first."

"Poor sod. And he was only fifteen..."

There would have to be an inquiry, of course. The most critical question would be how the gun had been smuggled into the prison. One of the guards must have been bribed – but which one? And which organization had been behind the attempted escape? How had they even known about the existence of the prison in the first place? An ambulance was already on its way to take Dr Flint to St Bernard's Hospital in the middle of Gibraltar city. As the last person to see Julius Grief alive, she might be able to fill in a few details. The governor would have to fly to London, to report at the highest level. There would be severe reprimands all round and an inevitable tightening of security.

There were now six prisoners instead of seven. Julius Grief was dead and although frogmen would be sent to the seabed, there was very little chance that much or any of his remains would be discovered in the wreckage of the car. Well, he wouldn't be missed. He was only a kid but he was a mad kid. None of the other prisoners had liked him. Perhaps it was better this way.

And nobody knew the truth.

The trick had been played inside the old barn,

during the few seconds when Julius Grief had been out of sight. As instructed, he had driven into the building, smashing through a door that had been specially weakened for just this purpose. A whole team of Scorpia agents – six of them – had been waiting for him inside the barn, and as he skidded to a halt, a second, identical Suzuki Jimny had burst out of the other side. But this one had no driver. Instead it was radio-controlled with a dummy Julius strapped to the wheel, almost invisible behind all the cracks. It didn't have to travel very far. In fact it had been a simple task to guide it across the open patch of land, through the fence and over the edge.

And while the guards were watching the fall and the explosion, the Scorpia team had got to work. The original Suzuki had been hastily covered with a tarpaulin and then with straw. Julius had been led to a pit with a sliding trapdoor constructed in the floor. There was enough room for him and all the agents to bundle in together, and within seconds they had disappeared. If anyone from the prison had thought to look inside the barn after the crash, they would have found it to be quite abandoned, containing just a few bits of old machinery, a haystack and some mouldy bags of animal feed.

But nobody did. Everything had happened exactly as Scorpia had intended. As far as the world was concerned, Julius Grief was dead. And nobody was watching that night as a fishing boat with a single, smiling passenger slipped out of Gibraltar Harbour beneath a full moon and a starry sky and began its journey south.

# SECRETS AND LIES

The report was marked TOP SECRET with the two words stamped on the cover in red ink, but in fact there was no need for them. Only three copies had been printed: one for Alan Blunt, the head of MI6 Special Operations; one for his deputy, Mrs Jones; and one for the chief science officer; and since almost everything they did was secret in one way or another, they hardly needed to be reminded. Sometimes Blunt wondered how many tens of thousands of documents had passed across the polished surface of his desk, here on the sixteenth floor of the building that called itself the Royal & General Bank in Liverpool Street, London. Each one of them had told its own dirty little story. Some had led nowhere, while others had demanded instant action. An operation might be set up on the other side of the world, an agent sent out to run it. How many people had died on the turn of a page?

But there wouldn't be many more files coming his way. Alan Blunt sat back in his chair and looked around him, his mind still sifting through the details of what he had just read. He had occupied this office for seventeen years and could have described it with his eyes closed – right down to the last paper clip. It was simply furnished with an oak desk and a scattering of chairs on a neutral carpet. A couple of paintings had been hung on the walls recently – landscapes that were barely worth examining. There was a shelf full of reference books that had never been opened. Rooms tell a lot about the people who occupy them. Blunt had made sure that this room said nothing at all.

And soon he would be leaving it. The new prime minister had decided that it was time to make changes, so the entire department was being reorganized. Blunt still didn't know who would be taking his place, but he rather suspected it might be Mrs Jones. She hadn't said anything to him, of course, but nor would he have expected her to. He very much hoped that she would be promoted. She had been recruited straight from Cambridge University, bringing with her a first-class degree in political science. There had been tragedies in her life – the loss of her husband and two children – but she had risen above them. She had a brilliant mind. Blunt wondered if the prime minister would be smart enough to recognize her talents. He had thought of sending a memo to 10 Downing Street but had decided against it. They could make the decision for themselves.

What did the future hold for him? Blunt was in his early fifties, nowhere near retirement age. He would certainly be given a knighthood in the New Year Honours, his name appearing between celebrities and civil servants. "For services to government and inland security." It would be something nice and bland like that. He might be offered the directorship of a bank: a real one this time. He had once considered writing a book but there was no real point. He had signed the Official Secrets Act, and if you took the secrets out of his life, there would be nothing left.

Briefly he found himself examining the empty chairs opposite him. Blunt was not an emotional man but he couldn't stop himself remembering some of the men and women who had sat there. He had given them their orders and they had gone, often not to return. Danvers, Wilson, Rigby and Mortimer, and Singh, who had done so well in Afghanistan until his cover had been blown. And John Rider. Blunt would never have dreamed of saying so but he had always had a special regard for the agent who had finally been assassinated on the orders of Scorpia, just as he was leaving for the South of France with his young wife. John Rider had been a much more effective agent than his younger brother, Ian.

And then, of course, there was Alex Rider, who had in many ways surpassed them both. Blunt half smiled to himself. He had known from the very start that there was something special about the fourteen-year-old, and he had refused to listen to the voices that had insisted it was mad to bring a schoolboy into the world of espionage. Alex had been the perfect weapon because he was so unexpected, and he had achieved something that very few other agents had managed. He had been sent out on eight missions and he had survived.

In a way, though, Alex had been Blunt's undoing. When the prime minister had found out that MI6 was using not just a teenager but one who was under sixteen, he had hit the roof. It went against every rule in the book. The public would have been horrified if the facts had ever leaked out, and of course the prime minister would have shared some of the blame even though it had nothing to do with him. Blunt had no doubt that Alex was the reason he had been asked to step down. He had also been told in no uncertain terms that Alex was not to be used again, nor replaced. So that was that. In a way Blunt was glad. He had seen enough body bags. It would have been difficult to look at one that was child-sized.

The file...

Very unusually, Blunt had let his mind wander. He forced himself to focus again. Forty-eight hours ago a body had been found floating in the Thames, just to the east of Southwark Bridge. The body was that of a middle-aged man wearing a suit and tie, and he had been shot in the back of the neck. Identification had not been difficult, because the man only had one eye and had once served in the Israeli army, which still held his medical records. His name was Levi Kroll and he was known to be an active agent – indeed, one of the founding members – of Scorpia. As soon as that connection had been made, the red lights had begun to flash and the file had been passed to Special Operations.

It seemed almost incredible that such a senior member of Scorpia had been murdered, and even more so that his body should have been allowed to be found. It begged all sorts of questions. What was Kroll doing in London to begin with? Was it in some way connected to the appearance of Zeljan Kurst just a few months before at the British Museum? There were no records of Kroll having entered the country, although that was hardly surprising as he would have had at least a dozen different identities. Who had killed him? According to the report, he had taken a .300 Winchester Short Magnum bullet in the back of the neck, possibly fired by a Belgian FN Special Police Rifle from a distance of around five metres. Could a rival organization have declared war on Scorpia? Blunt considered the possibility. There was no doubt that Scorpia's reputation had declined in the past twelve months. Another group could well have decided to steal its territory.

There were several clues mentioned in the report. Blunt had underlined them in green ink, putting a star beside them in the margin. The MI6 investigators had suggested that Kroll might have been in Egypt before ending up dead in London. The shirt he had been wearing when he died had been purchased at a shop in the Arkadia Mall, overlooking the Nile. It was made by Dalydress, an expensive Egyptian manufacturer, and it was part of their latest spring collection so it must have been bought recently. Of course, the shirt could have been a present, but that was unlikely. They had trawled through hundreds of hours of CCTV footage from all four of London's airports, concentrating on flights that had come in from Egypt, and finally their perseverance had paid off. A man with a beard and an eyepatch had indeed come off a British Midland flight from Cairo, the day before Kroll had been washed up.

He had been carrying two items which gave the MI6 men plenty to play with. The first of these was a crocodile skin wallet in his inner pocket, from Cartier in Paris and fairly new. It contained several credit cards in the name of Goodman, which must have been the identity he had chosen for this visit to England. The cards had been checked for their credit history. Only one purchase had been made. "Goodman" had bought three magazines and a newspaper at Heathrow Airport. The newspaper was the *Times Educational Supplement* – normally read by teachers and academics. Blunt had drawn a line beside this and added a question mark.

The wallet also contained a magnetic key card such as might be used in any hotel in the world, but it was unmarked and, Blunt knew, very hard to trace. Kroll had been carrying three hundred and fifty pounds in different currencies: British pounds, American dollars and Egyptian pounds – another connection with Cairo. Finally, the wallet held a ticket stub from the opera in Milan, dated from one month ago, a receipt for dinner at Harry's Bar in Venice and a photograph of a ten-year-old boy with his arm round a Rottweiler. His son? It wasn't even known if Kroll was married.

But of even greater interest was the iPhone that had been found in the same pocket as the wallet. Of course, the water had almost completely destroyed it, but even so, the MI6 technicians had managed to retrieve a few tiny scraps of information from its memory. These had been printed on a separate sheet for Blunt and he laid it out in front of him.

> ...progress ... the vicar
> Shafik (45) ... payment
> 30 May – 3 Ju
> ...target...

Blunt examined the words, searching for any possible associations. Assuming this referred to a Scorpia operation, Kroll would have been unusually careless to enter anything into his mobile phone. But then, of course, he wouldn't have known he was about to die. The dates, more than three weeks ago, rang a faint bell – although were they referring to June or July? Shafik was an Arabic name. 45 might be his age. Was he the target mentioned in the last line? Or could he be an assassin? That would certainly explain the need for payment. And what of the vicar? The word sat at the top of the page, underlined. That would suggest some sort of operation involving religion, although you wouldn't expect to find a vicar in the Middle East. He would have thought an imam would be more likely.

It was a puzzle but Blunt didn't need to waste any more mental energy trying to decipher it. Half a dozen different departments within Special Operations had been working on the note from the moment it had been found, and he had called a meeting for nine o'clock that morning, expecting to hear results.

As if on cue, there was a knock at the door and Mrs Jones entered, followed by a casually dressed younger woman with fair hair and freckles. This was Samantha Redwing. She was only twenty-seven but she had risen quickly through the ranks of MI6 to become chief science officer. Redwing had a photographic memory and the analytical skills of a world-class chess player. Surprisingly she was also very normal, with a boyfriend who worked in advertising, a flat in Notting Hill Gate and a proper social life. Blunt thought she might well be unique.

The two women sat down. They were each carrying their copy of the Scorpia file. Blunt nodded at them. "Good morning. What progress do we have on this business with Levi Kroll?"

"We've made some headway." Mrs Jones opened her file. She was dressed, as always, in dark colours, which with her jet black hair and black eyes made her look not just businesslike but as if she were on her way to a funeral. The next head of MI6? Blunt noticed a sheaf of pages stapled to the original report. She had, of course, come prepared. "First of all, Kroll had been in the water for approximately ten hours before he was found, suggesting that he was shot around eleven o'clock at night. We've examined the tidal reports for the Thames and if he was going to end up being washed ashore at Southwark then he would have had to enter the water further east, probably somewhere around Woolwich."

That was close to City Airport. A question formed in Blunt's mind but he didn't interrupt as his deputy considered.

"We've been focusing our efforts on the electronic key card and the information we were able to retrieve from his iPhone," Mrs Jones went on. "It's a shame that all his telephone numbers were lost – and the phone itself won't tell us very much. According to the serial number, it was purchased in New York. We're still trying to trace payment details.

"But we think we may have decoded the actual words. They don't mean very much on their own, but you have to put them together with the other items that Kroll was carrying. The key to it all is the *Times Educational Supplement* which he bought at Heathrow. I have the edition here." She produced a copy and laid it on the desk. "What would a man like Kroll want with a paper like this? Was he interested in something that might involve a school? If we assume that 'Ju' means June, not July, then the dates – 30 May to 3 June – just happen to coincide with the last half-term in many schools in the UK and around Europe. We know that Kroll had just come from Cairo. And Shafik – the name on the phone – could well be Egyptian."

"So Scorpia might be interested in a school somewhere in Egypt."

"That's exactly the conclusion we arrived at and that's where we've been directing our attention."

Mrs Jones unwrapped a peppermint and slipped it into her mouth. Blunt waited for her to continue.

"There are twenty-eight men and women with the surname Shafik working in different schools around Egypt," she said. "Eleven are in Cairo. To start with, we assumed that the figure – forty-five – referred to their age. That narrowed the field to three, and only one in Cairo, a Mrs Alifa Shafik, the headmistress at a primary school. But we checked her out and there's nothing that could possibly make her of interest to an organization like Scorpia. The school is in a poor area of the city. We decided that trail went nowhere."

Blunt nodded his agreement. He was quietly impressed. Mrs Jones had moved quickly and there was no doubting the logic of what she had said. "Shafik is a fairly common name," he muttered. "The link with the educational supplement is interesting and it may well be that a school is involved. But it could be in Alexandria or Port Said or even Luxor. Do we have anything more specific?"

"As a matter of fact we do." Mrs Jones flicked through the pages of the paper. "We read the *Times Educational Supplement* from cover to cover, looking for stories that related to Egypt, trying to find a connection. There were none – but in the back there was an advertisement for a new head of security at the Cairo International College of Arts and Education, which is in Sheikh Zayed City on the outskirts of Cairo. That seemed like quite a coincidence so we contacted the school. And we discovered something rather interesting. They needed a new security chief because their last one was run over and killed as he was arriving for work. His name, as it happens, was Mohammed Shafik. The driver didn't stop. The accident – if it was an accident – took place nearly two months ago on 4 May..."

Blunt stared at the page. "The fourth of the fifth," he muttered. "4/5. It's the same numbers."

"Exactly."

"So we can assume that's why Zeljan Kurst was in London," Blunt murmured. "If this school has had to recruit a new security man, Scorpia could have been trying to get someone inside." He quickly read the advertisement in the *Times Educational Supplement*. A recruitment office in London was handling the appointment but it was nowhere near Woolwich, the place where Kroll might have been killed. "Did this agency find anyone to take Mr Shafik's place?" he asked.

"Yes. The new man is called Erik Gunter. Scottish mother, German father. He was brought up in Glasgow and spent time with the 1st Battalion Scots Guards before he was wounded in Afghanistan. He was awarded the Military Cross for courage. I have his file here."

She passed it across. Blunt scanned it briefly. Gunter had come under fire while he was on patrol in Helmand province. According to the report, he had almost certainly saved the lives of his entire platoon but he had taken four bullets himself and had been invalided home.

"What about this business with the vicar?" Blunt asked. "Does the school have a chaplain?"

"No." Mrs Jones glanced at the chief science officer, who had been sitting silently through all this. "The reference to the vicar wasted a great deal of time," she said. "It didn't seem to be at all relevant. At first we assumed it must be a code name. You'll remember that some years ago we dealt with an assassin who was known only as the Priest. But in the end Redwing worked it out."

"It's a mistake," Redwing explained. "If you take the initials of the Cairo International College of Arts and Education – CICAE – and type them into an iPhone, the machine auto-corrects them and you get the word VICAR."

"It's the final confirmation," Mrs Jones added. "Scorpia's operation has to involve this school. But just to make sure, I checked the key card. I sent Crawley out to Cairo and he reported back this morning. The school is guarded, fenced in and monitored twenty-four hours a day. But there's been a security leak. The key opens a door into the kitchen."

Blunt sat in silence. Outside, an ambulance raced along Liverpool Street, the scream of its siren hanging in the air. And what would it find at the end of its journey? Another life or another death? "Tell me about the school," he said.

Mrs Jones was ready for this. She wouldn't have come to Blunt's office without being fully briefed. "The CICAE makes an interesting Scorpia target," she said. *Target*. That was another word that had been retrieved from the phone. "The school maintains a very large security staff – and with good reason. It has about four hundred children from countries all over the world, and if you scroll down the names, it's like a who's who of the rich and famous. They've got parents who are oil millionaires, politicians, diplomats, sheikhs, princes and even pop stars. The Syrian president has a son there. The British ambassador to Egypt has a daughter. The chairman of Texas Oil – one of the biggest petrol companies in America – has no fewer than three children at the CICAE. Can you imagine if one of them was kidnapped – or, worse still, killed? Suppose Scorpia was planning to take over the whole school? They could threaten four hundred of the most powerful parents on the planet. They'd have enough leverage to start a world war."

"We can't be sure that's what they're intending," Blunt said. Suddenly something entirely different flickered across his consciousness. Seventeen years as head of MI6 Special Operations had turned his brain into a computer that never stopped functioning. Always there were connections, connections... What was it? Oh yes. A report that had crossed his desk a week before. The death of that boy in Gibraltar. Julius Grief. All this talk of schoolchildren had reminded him. He considered it for a moment, then moved on. The boy had tried to escape in a car and driven over a cliff. The body still hadn't been recovered but there was no way he could have survived. So that was that. It couldn't be related.

"Why else would they target a school?" Mrs Jones asked.

"Let's examine the possibilities." Blunt thought for a second. The eyes behind the square-framed glasses were bleak. He was weeks away from retirement; he hadn't expected this. "Scorpia is planning an attack of some sort on an international school in Cairo. They send Levi Kroll to London for reasons that are unclear but which seem to be connected to the recruitment of this new head of security. It may well be that Kurst was in London in February for exactly the same purpose...

"It would seem likely that they've put their own man inside the school, although, looking at his file, this man Gunter seems to be beyond reproach. He's a war hero, for heaven's sake! However, I agree with you. It seems a bit of a coincidence that the last head of security should have been taken out by a hit-and-run driver. But we have to assume that Kroll was killed by a rival organization, because if it had been his own people they'd have made sure he had nothing in his pockets when he was found. In fact, the body wouldn't have been found at all. It seems to me there are two questions we have to consider. Is this the most likely explanation of what has occurred? And what should we do?"

"We could warn the school," Mrs Jones suggested.

"I'm not so sure. Warn them about what? We can only guess what Scorpia is planning and we have no idea when it's going to happen. We could talk to the Egyptian government but they're unlikely to listen to us – besides which, we have to look at the bigger picture. What about the Syrians, the Americans and all the other families? If we tell them about this, we'll have half the intelligence agencies in the world at one another's throats. It could all turn into a complete mess."

"But if Scorpia knew we were on to them, they might decide not to proceed."

"Exactly."

Mrs Jones saw the glint in Blunt's eye and suddenly she understood. "You want them to go ahead," she said.

"I want them to try," Blunt agreed. "We could turn this whole thing into a trap. Just for once, we're one step ahead of them and if they decide to make a move, this could be an opportunity to finish them once and for all."

"But you wouldn't seriously risk the lives of the children at this international school?"

"Of course not. We'll put an agent inside to keep an eye on the situation, and the moment Scorpia show themselves, we'll be ready. What we need—" he began.

"No." It was unheard of for Mrs Jones to interrupt her superior. But she did so now. "We can't."

Blunt blinked slowly. "You know what I'm thinking."

Of course she did. Mrs Jones had spent hundreds of hours with Blunt. Soon she might replace him. She knew him inside out. "We can't use Alex," she said.

"I'm sure you're right, Mrs Jones. But you must admit that this would have been exactly the sort of mission for him. Put a fourteen-year-old into a school and nobody would look twice. Just like at Point Blanc."

"Alex is fifteen now," Mrs Jones reminded him. "And that business in Kenya was the end of it, Alan." She didn't often use his Christian name when there were other people in the room, but for now she ignored Redwing, who had lapsed back into silence, waiting her turn. "He was badly hurt ... burnt. He was in hospital again. We both agreed. He's been through enough."

"I'm not sure I agreed."

"We also have orders from Downing Street." Mrs Jones didn't dare disobey an instruction that came direct from the prime minister, not when she might be weeks away from taking over.

Blunt understood that. "I still suggest we put one of our people inside," he said.

Mrs Jones relaxed. "As a teacher?"

"A teacher or a cleaner. Get Crawley on to it. Smithers can provide surveillance and communications equipment. In the meantime, let's keep an eye on all known Scorpia agents, particularly if they show up anywhere near the Egyptian border." He turned to Redwing, as if noticing her for the first time. "Your thoughts, Redwing?"

"I just have a couple of points to add, sir," Redwing said. "I have no argument with anything that Mrs Jones has said, but it does seem a little odd that Kroll should have flown into Heathrow and then travelled all the way across London to Woolwich, if that really was where he was killed. Why didn't he just fly into City Airport? It would have been much closer."

Blunt was pleased. The same thought had already occurred to him. "There are no direct flights from Cairo to City Airport," he said. "Although it makes you wonder why he didn't use a private jet."

"And what really puzzles me is the medical report. First of all, from the contents of the dead man's stomach, we know that the last meal he ate included snails, roast pork, potatoes and some kind of dessert made with Grand Marnier. It's the sort of meal you might eat in Paris or London but it's not exactly what you'd expect from a man who'd just flown in from Cairo."

"What do you mean?"

"Well, even in first class he wouldn't have been served snails on the plane. And pork is an unusual choice in a Muslim country. For that matter we found no Egyptian spices or herbs of any sort. No rice or falafel. Of course, he could have been staying in an international hotel. He may hate Egyptian food. But it still feels strange."

"And there's something else?"

"Yes, sir. When we examined the body, we found a tiny fragment of glass buried in the back of the neck. It had been driven in by the impact of the bullet." Redwing paused. "It's entirely possible that Kroll was shot in London, somewhere close to the Thames. He could have been standing on one of the banks or perhaps on a bridge. He was shot and fell into the water.

"But the fragment of glass tells another story. He was inside, on the other side of a window. In which case the body was then taken and dumped in the river. But if that was what happened, what was the point? Is it possible that the body was meant to be found?"

"And you're suggesting that the note was planted?" Blunt considered. "But why would Scorpia *want* us to know what they were doing?"

"It doesn't make any sense to me, sir," Redwing admitted.

There was a long silence. Blunt made his decision.

"We'll go ahead and put someone in the school," he said. "It may be a complete waste of time but I can't see that it will do any harm. Still, it's a shame to waste the resources of an active agent."

Mrs Jones glanced at him. Once again, she saw what was going through his mind. Alex Rider would already be on the plane to Cairo if Blunt had his way.

But it wasn't going to happen. Alex Rider was history. Mrs Jones had never said as much to him but she had promised it to herself, and no matter what her own future within MI6, it was one promise she was determined not to break.

# PART TWO: ALEX

# ANGLE OF ATTACK

"Alex! You've overslept again. Get yourself out of bed!"

Jack Starbright was standing in the doorway of Alex's bedroom on the second floor of the house they shared together near the King's Road in Chelsea. It was seven forty-five in the morning and he should have been up and getting dressed, but all she could see was the back of his head with a clump of messy fair hair poking out from under the duvet and the curve of his body beneath.

"Alex..." she said again.

A hand appeared, clutched hold of the pillow and dragged it down. "What day is it, Jack?" The voice came from nowhere, muffled beneath the bed-clothes.

"It's Thursday. It's a school day."

"I don't want to go to school."

"Yes, you do."

"What's for breakfast?"

"You'll find out when you've had your shower."

Jack closed the bedroom door and a few seconds later Alex emerged, screwing up his eyes against the morning light. He threw back the duvet and rolled into a sitting position, looking around the wreck that was his room. There were crumpled clothes on the floor, school books and folders everywhere, DVDs and computer games stacked up beside his desk, Chelsea posters peeling off the walls. He and Jack had had one of their very rare arguments a few weeks before. It wasn't that she wanted him to tidy the room. That wasn't the problem. In fact it was the other way round. He had insisted that she stop tidying it for him – as she had done every day for the last eight years. In the end she had understood. This was his space. And this was the way he wanted it.

He stripped off his T-shirt and stumbled into the shower. The blast of hot water woke him up instantly and he stood there, letting it pound onto his shoulders and back. This was his favourite part of the morning, five minutes when he didn't belong to anyone – not to Jack and not to Brookland School – when he could collect his thoughts and prepare himself for whatever the day might throw his way.

He wasn't a spy any more. That was the important thing. That was what he had to keep reminding himself. Nearly five months had passed without so much as a whisper from MI6. He had made it through the second half of the spring term and two thirds of the summer without being recruited, kidnapped or forced into some hare-brained mission on the other side of the world. He was getting used to the fact that it was never going to happen again. He was tall now, five foot ten. His shoulders had broadened and he had virtually lost the little boy looks that had been so useful to Alan Blunt and Mrs Jones. His hair was longer. He was fifteen years old. There had been times when he had thought it was a birthday he would never see.

And what had happened in those five months? School, of course. His second term of GCSEs. Alex had even begun to think about university – it was only three years away. He already knew that science and maths were his strong suits. His physics teacher, Mrs Morant, insisted that he had a natural talent. "I can see you at Oxford or Cambridge, Alex, if you just apply yourself and try to turn up for school a little more often." Then there was sport. Alex had been chosen as captain of the football first team. And drama – he was playing Teen Angel in the summer production of *Grease*, although he still wasn't convinced he could sing.

He seemed to be home less and less, hanging out on the King's Road with Tom Harris and James Hale, who were still his two best mates. He played football at weekends and had joined a rowing club near Hammersmith. He was in the fifteen to twenty-one group and he loved the rhythm of it, slicing through the water early on a Saturday morning, down through Richmond and Twickenham and on to Hampton Court, even if his muscles did ache for the rest of the weekend. The cox, barking out instructions through an old-fashioned megaphone, was a girl of his own age, Rowan Gently, and she was obviously interested in him. He had joked that her name sounded like their progress up the Thames.

But he was still seeing Sabina – even if most of their contact was through Facebook. It wasn't easy being thousands of miles apart with an eight-hour time difference, so that while Alex was getting up and frantically grabbing his clothes, she was still sound asleep. It was almost as if they were on different planets, and part of him knew that if she didn't return to England soon, it would be almost impossible to maintain their relationship.

He had seen her quite recently. Her parents had invited him out to San Francisco for ten days during the Easter holidays and Jack had stumped up the cost of the transatlantic flight. It had given her a chance to have a break too.

It had been a fantastic holiday, something the two of them had promised themselves after their near-death encounter with Desmond McCain in Scotland at the start of the year. They had explored the city – the Golden Gate Bridge, Fisherman's Wharf, Alcatraz prison – and driven down the winding coastal road to Big Sur, where they had spent the weekend hiking and camping in some of the most stunning countryside in California.

As he pulled on his trousers and set about trying to find two matching socks, Alex remembered the last night he had spent with Sabina. The two of them had sat together on the porch of the white-painted wooden house that Edward and Liz Pleasure had rented in Presidio Heights, a quiet, leafy part of the city. It was a brilliant night, the sky deep black and scattered with stars.

"I wish you didn't have to go home."

"Me too."

"It's crazy. You're my closest friend and you're thousands of miles away."

"When do you think you'll come back to England?"

Sabina sighed. "I'm not sure we ever will. Dad's doing really well out here and he's got his green card now, which means he can live here permanently. And Mum likes it." She put her arm round his neck. "Do you think we'll stay together, Alex?"

"I don't know." There didn't seem any point lying. "You'll probably meet some American football player and I'll never hear from you again."

"You know that's not true." Sabina paused. "Maybe you can come back in the summer. You know you're always welcome. We could go to Yellowstone. Or maybe to LA..."

"I'd like that."

Alex remembered how Sabina had looked at him then. But it was the way she had kissed him goodbye that he remembered most.

He grabbed a shirt, but before he put it on he turned round and examined his shoulders in the mirror. It was something he did automatically, every day. The burns had faded but they were still there like a series of exclamation marks, the scars from the burning aviation fuel that had rained down on him in the airfield in Laikipia in Kenya. The doctors had told him they would probably stay with him for life. Well, he could add them to the museum of injuries that his body had become. The bullet wound in his chest, the various scars, the thin white line that had been seared across the back of his hand by, of all things, a poisonous spider's web.

Did he miss it? Did he mind being an ordinary schoolboy again? Alex felt he had passed through a tunnel. There had been a brief time when he had needed the danger, when he was almost glad to be part of the secret world of MI6. After all, that was what he had been trained for virtually all his life. His father had been a spy. His uncle had been a spy. Between them they had made sure he would follow in what had become a family tradition.

But now he was out in the light. Enough time had passed since Kenya to remind him that real life was better. Herod Sayle, Dr Grief, General Sarov, Damian Cray, Mrs Rothman, Winston Yu and, most recently, Desmond McCain. He had come up against them and they were all dead. It was time now to leave them behind.

He glanced at his watch. Despite Jack's wake-up call, he was going to be late for school – and this in the week when the head teacher, Mr Bray, had announced double detention for latecomers, part of Brookland's crackdown on personal discipline. One term it had been crooked ties and untucked shirts. The next it had been chewing gum. Now it was timekeeping. It was good to have such little things to worry about. Alex buttoned up his shirt and looped his tie over his head. Then he hurried down to the kitchen for breakfast.

There were two boiled eggs waiting for him on the table. Alex was amused to see that Jack still insisted on cutting his toast into Marmite soldiers. She was making coffee for herself and tea for him and as he took his place she brought the two cups over.

"Alex, you look a complete mess. Your tie's crooked, you haven't brushed your hair and that shirt's crumpled."

"It's only school, Jack."

"If I ran the school, I wouldn't let you in."

She set the two cups on the table and sat down herself, watching fondly as Alex sliced off the tops of his eggs and dipped the first soldier in. "Have you got any plans this weekend?" she asked. "I thought maybe after you finished rowing we could take off somewhere, get out of London."

"Actually, I'm away this weekend." Alex had forgotten to tell her.

"Where?"

"Tom's invited me over. His brother's coming from Italy and we thought we'd get together."

Tom Harris was as much of a mess as ever,

living with his mother after his father had walked out. Alex had met his brother, Jerry, when he'd first gone chasing after Scorpia, in Venice. Tom and Jerry. As Tom often said, their names told you everything you needed to know about their parents.

"OK. That's fine. I'll put out a toothbrush and a spare set of clothes."

Was there was something in Jack's voice? Alex glanced in her direction but she seemed OK. She looked the way she always did – relaxed and a bit ramshackle, dressed in a T-shirt, jeans and a loose-fitting cardigan. She was sitting with her elbows on the table, cradling her coffee cup and smiling. But just for a moment she hadn't sounded quite herself. It was as if she had something on her mind.

"Is anything wrong?" Alex asked.

"No!" She pulled herself together. "No. I'm sorry. I just stayed up a little too late last night and I'm a bit tired."

That would make sense. Jack had recently started learning Italian. Alex wasn't quite sure why, although one of the reasons might have been the Italian teacher, who was twenty-nine, dark and built like a boxer. She was certainly taking it seriously, with private lessons twice a week and one of those courses that had arrived on so many CDs that it would surely take a year to get through them.

"You're not worrying about me, are you? I haven't heard a thing from MI6."

"I know," Jack said. "It's not that." She shook her head. "It's nothing. I'm fine."

Ten minutes later, Alex was on his way, cycling to school on the new Raleigh Pioneer 160, which he'd bought to replace his old Condor Junior Roadracer. It wouldn't have been his first choice but he'd managed to get a deal from the supplier and it was perfect for getting around London: not too flash, not likely to get stolen. And after he'd changed the saddle for an ergonomically designed RIDO R2, it was comfortable enough too. Glancing back, he saw Jack standing at the door, waving him goodbye. That was strange too. Normally she wouldn't have left the kitchen.

But it was a beautiful summer's day. The sun was shining. Alex forgot about Jack as he accelerated towards the King's Road. A moment later, he had turned the corner and was gone.

Jack closed the front door.

She was annoyed with herself. She still hadn't talked to Alex about the letter she had received a week ago. It was typical of her mother to put it all down on paper rather than phone or send an email. Her parents weren't that old, only in their sixties, but they had always been deliberately old-fashioned – as if they were determined to show that their world was better than the one that was taking shape all around them.

And now her father was ill. He'd had a stroke in

the spring and he needed someone to look after him. Her mother did what she could. Jack had an older sister but she was living in Florida with three young children. Jack had now been in England for coming up to nine years and her mother was suggesting, very gently, that she ought to think about coming home.

And in her heart Jack knew that she was right. Maybe it was time to go.

It wasn't just because of her father. She had her own future to think about. Here she was in London, almost thirty and single. She had first come to England to study law and had taken up the offer of a free room in Chelsea in return for light housekeeping and baby-sitting duties. The baby, of course, was Alex, although in fact he had been seven years old. In the early days she would take Alex to school when Ian Rider was abroad, then slip away to do her studies until it was time to pick him up. But she had soon discovered that law was dry and dusty and simply wasn't for her. At the same time, she loved looking after Alex ... it was almost as if she was his big sister. She felt sorry for him too. She knew that both his parents had died in a plane crash and she could see that Ian Rider was no substitute, not when he travelled so much. Somehow everything happened very naturally. Jack decided to leave university at the same time as Ian offered her a full-time job. Suddenly, without ever really planning it, she had become part of the family.

And then Ian Rider had died and everything had changed.

Had she ever wondered about her employer? He had told her he worked in international banking and she had taken his word for it, but, looking back, she knew she had been foolish. No international banker kept three different passports in his desk drawer. Jack had come across them once, looking for a pair of scissors, and she had asked him about them. It was the only time Ian Rider had ever been angry with her.

*Never ask me about my work, Jack. It's the one thing I'll never talk about. Not with you. Not with Alex...*

She could hear his voice now and wondered how she could have been so stupid. No international banker stayed away for weeks at a time – and certainly none returned with so many inexplicable injuries. Ian had been mugged in Rome, involved in a car crash in Geneva and had broken his arm skiing in Vancouver. He had joked about it, saying he was accident-prone – until, that is, the final accident had revealed the truth.

What Alex didn't know – what Jack had never told him – was that she had decided to leave two weeks before Ian Rider had set off for Cornwall on the mission that had killed him. She had even gone as far as typing her resignation letter. She had felt dreadful, but thinking about it she had been sure she was doing the right thing. She wasn't going to be a nanny and a housekeeper for ever, and the longer she stayed the harder it would finally be to break the bonds with Alex. She would still be his friend, visiting whenever she could. But it was definitely time to move on.

And then had come the news of Ian's death, the funeral, Alex's first meeting with Alan Blunt and the almost incredible truth that Ian had been a spy, working for MI6 all along. That was when Alex had been recruited. And what had persuaded him to risk his life that first time, investigating the Stormbreaker computer? He hadn't done it for his country. He hadn't done it out of respect for his uncle. No – MI6 had threatened to expel Jack from the country and he had agreed to help them in return for a permanent visa so that she could stay.

How could she abandon him after that? As far as Jack knew, Alex had no living relatives. She had tried to find some trace of his grandparents but it seemed that all four had died young. There were no uncles or aunts. The closest relative she'd been able to dig up was a cousin living in Glossop, and she couldn't quite imagine Alex starting a new life there. And so she had stayed. She was almost the only person in the world who knew his secret. So long as he was involved with MI6, nobody could take her place.

All that seemed to be behind them now. The last time she had seen Mrs Jones had been a few days before Alex's fifteenth birthday at St Dominic's

Hospital in north London. Alex had just got back from Kenya – badly hurt – and that was when she had finally put her foot down and insisted that there would be no further missions, that from now on MI6 would leave him alone. Mrs Jones had made no promises but Jack had sensed that maybe she had won the argument. Certainly she had heard nothing since.

In truth Alex was probably too old for them now. He didn't look like a child any more. Jack remembered how he had once crawled up a chimney when he was training with the SAS. He wouldn't be able to manage that again. There were probably SAS men who were smaller than he was now.

But if Jack was relieved that this part of their lives was behind them, there was one side effect which she hadn't foreseen. Alex didn't need her so much now. That was what it all boiled down to. He wasn't going to come home wounded with burns or bullet holes. There was no need to protect him. And the two of them were growing apart. Recently Alex had begun spending more and more time without her, with his friends. Take this coming weekend, for example. He'd casually mentioned that he was taking off with Tom Harris and he hadn't even stopped to consider that he would be leaving her on her own. It was the same at Easter when he'd been away for two weeks with Sabina. Jack didn't mind. It was how it should be. He was a teenager. But she didn't feel wanted. And that told her that – at last – it was time to move on.

All she had to do was tell Alex. She would leave at the end of the summer holidays and together they would find someone to take over. More of a housekeeper. Of course it would be a wrench for Alex too. He'd probably argue with her but in the end he'd see it her way. Jack set about clearing the breakfast things. She had put it off too many times already but her mind was made up. She would talk to him when he got home tonight.

"OK. We're going to start with a warm-up." Grant Donovan, head of maths at Brookland School, pressed a button and six geometric shapes appeared on the whiteboard. Each one had an angle marked X. "In three of these diagrams X equals forty-five degrees," he explained. "You've got five minutes to tell me which, and the first person to finish wins this week's bonus prize."

"I hope it's better than last week's bonus prize," someone called out.

"The last one to finish gets a page of negative multiplications to take home."

There was a general groan and everyone put their heads down.

Alex tried to concentrate on the shapes but they were just floating in front of him, refusing to come into focus. All the triangles looked the same to him, like one of those spot the difference puzzles in a magazine. It had been the same in English lit an hour before, trying to make sense of a passage from Shakespeare's *Twelfth Night*. "If music be the food of love..." Or was it "the love of food", and what did it mean anyway? He was finding it hard to think. He could see the words on the page but they refused to come together to make sentences.

He put his pen down and ignored the triangles. There was something on his mind and he wouldn't be able to do anything until he had worked out what it was. He played back the events of the morning. He had got out of bed as usual, showered and dressed. He'd finished his homework the night before – nothing to worry about there. He knew his lines for the school play. No money worries. He still had plenty left from his weekly allowance.

Then down to breakfast. He replayed the conversation with Jack and in particular the moment he had told her he would be away for the weekend. That was it. She'd been upset. He'd challenged her about it and although she'd denied it, he could tell from her voice...

Now that he thought about it, Alex realized that the two of them had been spending less time together recently. What with homework, the school play, rowing and football and all the rest of it, there were days when they hardly spoke at all. Suddenly he felt ashamed. Jack had always been there for him. She was always looking after him. But he'd given her the impression that she didn't matter to him at all.

He glanced out of the window. There was a building site across the road, a new block of flats going up opposite the school. Everyone was already joking about who exactly would want to live with a view of hundreds of scruffy kids – not to mention the noise at half past eight in the morning and a quarter to four every afternoon. The site was empty today. The builders seemed to come in more or less when they felt like it, but Alex noticed a man making his way across the roof in a crouching run, a bag slung over his shoulder.

What to do about Jack? Alex made a resolution. He would talk to her tonight. He would tell her that he would be lost without her and that he needed her as much now as he had always done. Of course she knew all this but it was still worth saying. And he didn't have to spend the whole weekend with Tom. Maybe he could come back on Sunday afternoon and the two of them could go over to a local street market or something. The thought made Alex feel more comfortable and he turned his attention back to the first of the triangles. ABC was a right angle ... ninety degrees. The other two angles couldn't possibly be the same, so no forty-five degrees here. Cross that one out and move on to the next...

Three desks away, a lean, ginger-haired boy called Spencer was aiming a missile at someone in the front row. He was balancing a rubber on a plastic ruler which he was bending back. He released the ruler, catapulting the rubber across the room. It missed the boy in the front row and bounced off the wall. Someone sniggered.

Mr Donovan had seen him. "If you want to stay in the top group, Spencer, try not to behave like a Year Five. OK?" He sounded more tired than annoyed.

"Yes, sir."

"Two more minutes. You should have cracked nearly all of them by now."

Alex was nowhere near. He was suddenly aware that he wasn't feeling very well. It wasn't particularly hot in the classroom but he was sweating. His forehead and the back of his neck were damp, as if he had a fever. There was a pounding in his head and he was finding it difficult to breathe. What the hell was wrong with him? It was eleven o'clock in the morning. He hadn't had lunch yet, so for once the school canteen couldn't be blamed. He felt a pain in his chest and realized that his old wound was throbbing like some sort of biological alarm clock that had just gone off. As if it were reminding him...

Or warning him.

The man on the roof. All of a sudden Alex was back in Liverpool Street, stepping out of the offices of MI6 seconds before a sniper had opened fire with a bullet that had knocked him to the ground, almost killing him. What had he seen out of the corner of his eye? No. It was impossible. It couldn't be happening again. Not here. Very slowly, forcing himself not to give anything away, Alex turned his head. He was just a bored schoolboy looking out of the window, he told himself. If there really was someone there, if they were focusing on him even now, he mustn't give them an excuse to fire.

Because the man was a sniper. He had no doubt of it. Why else would he be running with his head down and his shoulders hunched unless he was trying not to be noticed? And what sort of builder carries a long, narrow leather bag across his back? There was no sign of him now but Alex visualized the shape and size of the bag and knew with the ice-cold grip of certainty exactly what it contained. Not a spade. Not a drill. Not anything you might use to construct a block of flats. Anyway, nobody was working on the site today. This man was there for something else.

And he was still up there somewhere, hiding. Alex looked again, scanning the seemingly empty roof. Yes. There he was, lying flat on his stomach with his head pointing towards the school. He was partly concealed behind a wall of scaffolding, a plastic sheet hanging in front of him like a flimsy window. Alex couldn't see the gun but he could sense it and knew there could be only one target it was aiming at.

There is a sort of telepathy between the hunter and the hunted, between the sniper and his target. Alex couldn't possibly have known when the man was going to fire, but he jerked back instinctively and it seemed to him that there was a faint tinkle and a thud at exactly that same moment, and right in front of him a gash appeared as if by magic in the surface of his desk, splinters of wood flying upwards. Alex stared at the damage. The enormity of what had just happened flooded over him. Someone had taken a shot at him. Someone had tried to kill him. If he had still been leaning forward over his notepad, the bullet would have driven into the top of his head.

"Alex?" Mr Donovan had seen the movement but he hadn't noticed the tiny round hole in the window. Even if he had, it would have taken him several more seconds to put it all together. Snipers do not fire into school classrooms – certainly not in England. As far as he could see, Alex had just had some sort of fit. Either that or he had been stung by a wasp. One or two of the other pupils were looking round curiously. The diagrams on the whiteboard suddenly seemed a thousand miles away.

"Get down!" There could be no mistaking the urgency in Alex's voice. "Someone's shooting at us."

"What?"

Alex was already on his feet, backing away from his desk, moving out of the gunman's sight line before he could fire a second shot. He knew that while he was in the room, he was putting the entire class in danger. Several of his classmates around him had stood up, making themselves targets. Some had noticed the hole in the window and knew he was telling the truth. Panic was already sweeping through the room.

"Get down!" This time he shouted the words but they still just stood there. Of course, this was Alex Rider. Everyone knew the rumours about him – that he was involved in things it was better not to talk about. But this situation was just too incredible. It couldn't be happening.

And then there was a second shot. Tom Harris yelled and spun round, and to Alex's horror he saw that his best friend had been shot in the arm. His jacket was torn and blood was already seeping through the sleeve.

"Everyone on the floor!" Mr Donovan finally took command and his order was followed by the crash of upturned desks and chairs as twenty-two pupils dived for cover. Tom was the last to react, still in shock, one hand gripping his arm. Alex glanced at the window, knowing that he couldn't offer himself as a target. But if the man tried again, Tom would be directly in his line of fire. Alex ran three paces and threw himself at his friend, rugby tackling him to the floor. Tom howled with pain. His face was completely white.

Bells began to clang all over the school. Alex hadn't seen him do it but he guessed Mr Donovan must have hit the fire alarm before taking cover himself. Everyone was huddling together against the side wall. Alex propped Tom up, quickly examining his wound. There was blood everywhere – it was all over

Alex's hands – but he didn't think his friend had been too badly hurt. A flesh wound only. If Tom had been unlucky, the bullet might have chipped a bone, but Alex was sure it had gone straight in and out.

"Nobody move!" Mr Donovan was shouting. "We're safe here. The police and the fire engines will be on their way."

Brilliant. The rest of the school would be evacuating into the yard, making themselves perfect targets for the man on the roof. Alex thought about warning the maths teacher, trying to explain what had just happened. But then he realized that it didn't matter. This wasn't a case of a psychopath with a grudge against kids. The man had come here for him.

And with that realization came a surge of anger so powerful that Alex felt himself almost overwhelmed. He had given up spying. He hadn't been near MI6 for months. He was just a schoolboy trying to get through the day. But someone thought otherwise. Someone had made the cold-blooded decision to send a man with a gun to kill him and to hurt anyone else who happened to get in the way. Who was it? Was this revenge for something Alex had done in the past? Or was this some new enemy with a new plan of his own?

Alex had to know. If the sniper got away today, he would be free to come back tomorrow or the day after that. In fact, Alex would be in permanent danger. In the space of a second he had been plunged back into his old life and he didn't want to be there. He was furious.

"Alex – what do you think you're doing?"

Alex was already on his feet. Still crouching, Mr Donovan stared at him, afraid to move. "Don't leave, Alex! You've got to stay here!"

But he was too late. Alex had crossed the room and thrown open the door. A second after, he had disappeared, fighting his way past hordes of children as they surged down the corridors following the well-practised fire drills that would take them outside.

As he burst into the yard, he was already fumbling for his keys, heading for the bike shed. The bells were still ringing. All around him two thousand schoolchildren were chattering and laughing, looking out for the smoke while form teachers tried to shout them into straight lines. Alex ignored them. He found his bike, unlocked it and jumped on.

"Alex..." Miss Bedfordshire, the school secretary, had seen him. She tried to wave him down. Alex ignored her. He pushed down on the pedals hard and swerved round her and then he was gone, disappearing through the school gates.

# FLYING LESSON

A sitting target.

That was how Alex felt. He was cycling slowly round the side of the school right next to the building site where the marksman had been concealed and he was very aware that the street was empty with only a few parked cars; there were no witnesses; and if the sniper was still in place, this time he wouldn't miss. He could imagine the cross hairs of the scope sweeping across the street, settling first on his shoulders, then on the back of his neck. Perhaps they were already there and one twitch of a finger would send him catapulting over the handlebars and into oblivion.

He jerked his head up towards the rooftop but saw nothing. Alex was gambling on the fact that the man had already made his getaway. He would have heard the school alarms go off and would have assumed that Alex had been evacuated with the rest of his class and was lost in the crowd, one uniform among hundreds. Surely that was what he would think. And with the police arriving (Alex could hear them now, the whoop of sirens coming from all four points of the compass, closing in on the school), he wouldn't want to hang around.

Where was he? Alex had hoped to spot him as he left. But there was nobody visible on the building site, no sign of any movement on the roof or the ladders leading down. He drew to a halt, resting with one foot against the kerb, listening for the sound of an engine. Somewhere, on the other side of the scaffolding and the half-built walls, there was someone in a hurry to get out of here. Where was he? Every police car in the country would be there in a minute. He wouldn't want to hang around.

Without warning, a car appeared at the top of the road, a silver VW Golf, pulling out of the building site and turning away from where Alex was waiting. He couldn't see the driver but he thought, from the shape, that it was a man and he seemed to be alone. It had to be the sniper. Alex looked and pushed off again. Behind him the alarms were still ringing at Brookland School. He heard the first police cars arrive, the thud of slamming doors and men's voices barking out commands. There was no time to lose. Any minute now, the roads would be cordoned off. If he was really unlucky, the sniper would get away while he was left behind.

The VW was driving quickly but without breaking the speed limit, as if not wanting to draw attention to itself. Alex pedalled harder to catch up, at the same time making sure he didn't get too close. It occurred to him that he had done this before, over a year ago. Then it had been a drug dealer in a Skoda. He had followed the man to a barge on the Thames, near Putney Bridge. He'd never thought he would have to repeat the exercise – and this time it would be more difficult. The dealer had had no idea who he was, but one look in the mirror and the sniper would certainly recognize him. Alex swung his bike off the road and onto the pavement, crouching behind the parked cars to keep out of sight.

London is the slowest-moving city in Europe. Cars drive at an average of twelve miles an hour and it's well known that the fastest way to cross the city is on two wheels. As Alex powered up the pavement, he remembered his uncle complaining as he sat in a jam. *I don't know why I bother with a BMW six-cylinder turbocharged engine. I might as well drive a horse and cart.* Alex knew that his bike would have the edge on the VW. He could weave in and out of the traffic. He could ignore the lights. He could cut corners across the pavement. Provided they didn't reach any of the outer dual carriageways, he'd be able to keep up.

The car reached a T-junction and turned left, heading towards the King's Road. Before it disappeared from sight, Alex memorized its number plate. The letters spelled out a word: BEG. There were plenty of Volkswagens on the London roads and most of them seemed to be silver; it was helpful that this one should have a registration that was so memorable. Still on the pavement, Alex swung round the corner, narrowly missing a woman pushing a pram. The Raleigh Pioneer 160 was perfect for this sort of cycling. It wasn't too heavy and the 700cc alloy wheels were perfectly balanced, making it easy to manipulate, while its twenty-one gears gave him all the speed he could ask for. They were heading west, out of London. The school was already a long way behind.

And then the VW signalled right. Alex looked for the turn-off but there wasn't one. They were passing a parade of shops with an Esso garage at the end. And that was where the car was heading. Alex swore. He must have been chasing the wrong man after all. Snipers pulling away from their latest target didn't usually stop to fill up with petrol or buy a Twix. Alex paused for a second time, catching his breath as the VW rolled across the forecourt. He thought about cycling back to Brookland, then decided against it. There would be too many questions to answer. It would be easier just to go home and find Jack.

But the car wasn't filling up. Without stopping, it had driven straight into the automatic car wash – and that was strange, because there was a large sign reading OUT OF ORDER. From his vantage point on the other side of the road, Alex watched in puzzlement. As far as he could see, the driver hadn't even opened his window to drop a token into a slot, and yet as the VW disappeared behind the plastic screen, the brushes began to rotate and jets of water shot out of the hoses running along the walls. It was as if the car wash had been waiting for it. The sign must have been put there to stop any other drivers getting in ahead.

Alex stayed where he was, waiting for the VW to emerge. He was certain now that something strange was going on and that this was after all connected in some way with the shooting at his school. He could only make out the shape of the car. It was lost in the cloud of white foam that mushroomed against the plastic screen. Water and soapsuds coursed along the concrete floor. The whole process took four minutes. At last the brushes stopped and returned to their starter position, and a few seconds later the VW drove out.

Only it was no longer silver. It was now bright red. Had it been painted inside the car wash? No – exactly the opposite had happened. The silver paint had been stripped off to reveal the red beneath, and the number plate had changed too. Parts of the letters had been washed away so that BEG now read PFC and the number 88 had become 33. This was all part of the plan! The driver had known that the police would be called. After a shooting in a secondary school, every police car in London would be on the lookout for the getaway vehicle. Well, if they were looking for a silver VW with the number plate BEG 88, they would be disappointed. That car had vanished into thin air.

Alex knew now that this wasn't one man operating on his own. It would have taken a serious organization to arrange the trick with the car wash. Scorpia? The triads? They were both enemies of his but he somehow doubted that either of them would come for him now, after five months of inactivity. There would be no point. Even so, he would have to be careful. The car could be leading him into further danger and he was completely on his own. Only Miss Bedfordshire had seen him leave the school and she had no idea which direction he'd taken. Earlier this morning he'd been congratulating himself that all his troubles were over. It didn't look like that now.

He followed the car down the King's Road as far as Eel Brook Common, a small patch of green parkland crowded with Chelsea residents walking their dogs. The car was pulling away, travelling at about thirty miles an hour, but luckily it was forced to stop at a red traffic light and Alex was able to catch up. Whatever happened, he was determined he wasn't going to let it get away. But then the car turned off down Wandsworth Bridge Road, driving straight down to the Thames. Alex gritted his teeth and stamped down hard on the pedals. He knew that the roads widened on the other side of the bridge. A bicycle could keep up with a car in the slow-moving traffic, but once they were over the river he'd have no chance.

The car stopped again and Alex was tempted to move closer, to try to get a look in through the side window. It might help later on if he could give the police a description of the driver. All he could see from here was a hunched-up figure wearing a cap. He wondered what sort of man could bring himself to fire into a crowded school. How much had he been paid? And that made him think again about the car wash. What sort of minds would have dreamed up something like that? What other tricks might they have up their sleeve?

Suddenly he was on Wandsworth Bridge. Only a few weeks ago he had rowed underneath it and he had wondered then how it could possibly have been built. Most of the Thames bridges were very elegant, designed as if to ornament the river. This one was just a slab of reinforced concrete – functional and ugly. It was also very long, with four lanes of traffic, and Alex had to pedal hard to keep up, afraid of being seen but more afraid of losing the VW altogether. He glimpsed the dark grey water beneath him, stretching into the distance with nothing memorable on either side.

The driver came to the roundabout on the other side and accelerated onto it without looking left or right. Alex did the same and was rewarded with the deafening blast of a horn and a fistful of hot, dusty air as a huge truck thundered past, inches away. He wobbled slightly as he fought for balance, aware that his legs were getting tired. It would be just as well if the car did speed off soon. Any further and he might get himself killed.

But it seemed the VW had reached its destination. It turned off into a narrow drive that snaked back towards the river, and as Alex slowed down he saw it draw into a parking space and stop. A sign read WANDSWORTH INDUSTRIAL PARK but it wasn't a park so much as an industrial estate, one of those little pieces of London that had somehow been overlooked. There were a couple of office buildings sitting side by side, facing the river. They were modern and unremarkable, two storeys high with white walls and square windows. One of them advertised a mobile phone company; the other could have been almost anything. A garage and auto repair service stood opposite them near the water's edge, but it seemed to have closed down.

The whole area was covered in rubble and strewn with abandoned tyres, oil drums and empty skips. Alex stopped at the top of the drive, concealing himself behind a broken wire fence. He wondered how a place like this could have just been left to decay. Put a few houses on it, with views over the river, and it would be worth millions. But then again, this wasn't somewhere people would necessarily want to live. The noise of the traffic on Wandsworth Bridge was endless and the air smelled of diesel. Maybe a few run-down businesses was all it was good for.

The man got out of the car, then reached into the back and drew out the bag that he had been carrying up on the roof – the bag that contained his weapon. Peering out over the rubbish, Alex got a better view of him. He was short, in his thirties, dressed in an anorak and jeans, the cap hiding his hair. He was clean-shaven and white. His movements were completely leisurely, as if he were on his way home after a round of golf. He closed the car door, locked it with a remote on his key ring and began to stroll towards the river. Alex chose his moment, then freewheeled down the slope and came to a skidding halt behind one of the skips.

What now? From this new angle he could see a T-shaped concrete jetty sticking out into the fast-flowing water of the Thames, long enough to accommodate a dozen cars. But that wasn't what was parked there. A helicopter was waiting, a two-seater Robinson R22, one of the most popular flying machines in the world. Alex recognized the long tail slanting upwards and the tiny bubble of a cabin resting on its grasshopper legs. It was perched at one end, painted grey like the water behind it. Someone must have landed it here for the man in the VW. But if so, it couldn't be taking him very far. As far as Alex could recall, the Robinson had a range of less than two hundred and fifty miles. Still, that would be enough to get it to France.

There was a narrow three-storey building at the other end of the jetty, right next to the river. It could have been a clubhouse for canoeists or perhaps some sort of outpost for the river police. It was wooden, painted white – but the paint was flaking and some of the windows were cracked. Alex assumed it was empty but then the door opened and a second man came out, walking across the jetty towards the helicopter.

The two men were about to meet. Alex knew he had to get closer to hear what they said. He was still some distance away, crouching behind the skip, but fortunately the men were looking out over the river with their backs to him. Abandoning his bike, he ran down towards them, keeping low behind a slight rise in the ground. He was afraid the sound of his feet on the rubble would give him away but the drone of the traffic was loud enough to cover it. He threw himself face down just as the two men met.

"So how did it go?" the man from the office asked.

"It was fine. Mission accomplished," the sniper replied.

He was lying. Surely he knew that he had missed his target? But maybe it wasn't in his interest to admit that he had failed. Not if he was hoping to be paid.

"Let's go then," the first man said.

They set off together, heading for the helicopter.

So was that it? Was he just going to lie there and let them fly off? Alex memorized the registration number – a5455H – on the helicopter's tail. If he phoned it through to the police, maybe they could intercept the Robinson before it landed. But it wasn't enough. Alex could still feel the anger. These people had broken in on his life. They had tried to kill him and they had hurt his best friend. And calling the police would probably do no good at all. He remembered what had happened to the car. The pilot might press a button and change the registration of the helicopter. Maybe it would turn bright pink in mid-air. Suddenly Alex was determined. He wasn't going to let them get away.

He was up and running before he knew what he was going to do. The men had reached the helicopter and were climbing in, too busy concentrating on their own movements to notice him. Alex sprinted diagonally across the yard and onto the other side of the jetty. Out of the corner of his eye he saw the sniper buckling himself into the back seat, but he had no clear view of the man's face as the pilot was leaning across him. Alex spun to the right, heading away from them, and a moment later he had reached the three-storey building that he had noticed, the one from which the pilot had emerged.

He couldn't take the two men on by himself. He was empty-handed. But there was always a chance he might find something inside – a high-pressure hose maybe, or anything he could use as a weapon. At the very worst, there might be a telephone. He'd left his mobile in his locker at school.

His hopes were dashed even as he burst in through the front door. He was in an office complex that might once have belonged to the river authority. The walls were painted pale green and there were a few old maps of the Thames and tidal charts pinned to a cork noticeboard on a wall. But it was empty, abandoned. The whole place smelled of damp and decay. He tried the door of an office. It wouldn't budge.

Outside, he heard the whine of the four-cylinder air-cooled engine and knew that the Robinson had started up. It would take about a minute for the rotors to achieve maximum speed and then it would be gone, disappearing into the sky and out of his reach for ever. Alex looked around him. There was nothing here, just locked doors and a tatty staircase covered with peeling Formica.

The roof. Alex decided there was only one thing he could do, one way he could get his own back on the sniper. The man in the anorak was pretending that he'd succeeded, that he'd hit his target. Well, Alex would show him otherwise. He would stand on the roof in full view, and then at least the people who'd hired him would know that he'd failed. Perhaps there would be some sort of punishment for lying to them. Certainly he wouldn't get paid.

He took the steps two at a time. On the top floor

he came across a fire extinguisher strapped to the wall and he grabbed it and wrenched it free. He didn't really know what he was doing. In his mind's eye he saw himself spraying the cockpit as the helicopter flew past, blinding the pilot. But that was ridiculous. The wind would whip the foam away before it got anywhere near. Could he hurl the extinguisher at the rotors? It was certainly heavy enough to do serious damage. But it was too heavy to throw – and anyway, the helicopter would be too far away.

But it was all he had and he was still carrying it as he clambered up the last staircase and crashed through a pair of emergency exit doors onto the roof. It took him just a few seconds to scan his surroundings. The river was right in front of him. Wandsworth Bridge stretched out to the left. The Robinson R22 was balancing on its landing skids, already weightless, about to lift off the ground. The pilot, now wearing sunglasses and a headset, was coaxing the joystick. The sniper was in the seat behind him. Alex was above them both but – as he had thought – he was too far away. However, that was about to change. In a few seconds the two men would fly right past him. They couldn't go the other way because of the bridge.

The helicopter lurched off the ground effortlessly. It was moving diagonally, heading towards Alex but at the same time away from him, over the water. By the time it drew level, it would be at least fifteen metres away. He couldn't throw the fire extinguisher that far. If he set off the foam, he would just end up soaking himself.

*If you want to stay in the top group, Spencer, try not to behave like a Year Five.*

Somehow, incredibly, Alex remembered Mike Spencer in the classroom, the moment after he had noticed the sniper. He had been using a bendy ruler to fire a rubber at another pupil. Could it possibly work? Yes! Why not? There was a TV aerial right on the edge of the roof and the fact that it was swaying meant that surely it had to bend. The aerial had four metal antennas that came together in the shape of a V. Alex ran over to it. He hoisted the fire extinguisher up so that it rested inside the V and then, using both hands, pulled it back. The whole thing bent towards him. Alex could feel the metal straining. If he let go now, he would launch the extinguisher halfway across the river. That was one advantage of being fifteen. He hadn't been this strong a year ago.

Suddenly the helicopter was level with him, filling his vision. He could feel the wind from the rotors beating at him, threatening to blow him off the roof, and the engine howled in his ears. His hair whipped around his eyes, half blinding him, but he had a clear view of the sniper through the back window. The man turned and saw him. His eyes widened in shock. He shouted something. The pilot seemed to have frozen too; the helicopter wasn't moving. It was just dangling there, a perfect target, right in front of him.

Alex let go of the fire extinguisher. The TV aerial whipped forward, propelling it like a medieval catapult. The red metal cylinder hit the cockpit, an oversized bullet that smashed into the glass, sending cracks in every direction. It wasn't enough to bring the helicopter down, but the pilot jerked back instinctively, losing control.

Alex threw himself to the ground as the tail of the helicopter swung round, scything through the air inches above where his head had just been. He felt another blast of air tearing at his shirt and jacket, trying to drag them off his shoulders. For a brief second he glimpsed the terrified face of the sniper, upside down – or at least that was how it seemed to him. The pilot was fighting for control and might have regained it, but then the tail rotor clipped the edge of the building and there was a dreadful grinding and a snapping sound as part of the blade broke off. Lying flat on the roof, Alex covered his head with his hands, afraid that he was about to be torn to pieces. A slice of broken metal shot past him and shuddered into the brickwork.

And then the helicopter was gone, yanked into the air as if it were a fish on the end of an invisible line. It was completely directionless, spinning round and round. Alex dragged himself to his knees, gazing at his handiwork with a sense of disbelief. The helicopter was like a mad thing. He wondered what sort of nightmare the pilot and his passenger were experiencing inside. It was still moving fast.

Already it was a quarter of a mile away, mercifully flying upriver, away from Wandsworth Bridge. Alex stood up. The helicopter tried to right itself but it wasn't going anywhere. It hovered briefly, then crashed down into the river. There was a great explosion of white water and then nothing. Alex couldn't see any more.

Were the two men dead? Alex didn't know and, in truth, he didn't really care. He'd given them a lesson they'd richly deserved. After all, one of them had just tried to kill him. He had opened fire on a classroom full of kids and hadn't cared what might result. Alex wondered if Tom Harris was all right. He was sure the injury hadn't been too serious but he knew all too well the shock of being wounded by gunfire. He thought about phoning him, then remembered again that he had left his mobile at school.

He limped back in through the emergency exit, climbed down the stairs and went in search of his bike.

# SAFETY MEASURES

Sitting in the back seat of his chauffeur-driven Jaguar XJ6, Alan Blunt was in a bad mood. He hadn't spoken a word in the thirty minutes it had taken them to drive from Liverpool Street, gazing out of the window with narrow, expressionless eyes as if the entire city had somehow offended him. Mrs Jones was next to him and she knew exactly what he was thinking. The two of them were breaking every rule in the book. They were on their way to see Alex Rider when really he should have been summoned to see them.

They already knew what had happened at Brookland – but then, of course, the whole country did. A gun attack on a school in west London was the sort of story that would travel instantly all over the world – and the intelligence services had been forced to act quickly to rein it in. This was Alex Rider's school. They had made the connection immediately and had done everything they could to turn media attention away. There was no sniper, they said, and certainly no sniper rifle. It was just some local vandal with an air gun who had managed to break into a building site and had fired a couple of shots at the school windows. One boy had been slightly injured but nobody had been killed.

Even so, the shooting had been the main story on all the six o'clock bulletins and would be on the front pages the next day. Tom Harris had been filmed in his hospital bed with one arm in a sling, surrounded by cards and chocolates and looking quite happy to be the centre of so much attention. The police had mounted roadblocks all over Fulham and Chelsea. The home secretary had promised that she would be making a statement to the House. All the children at Brookland were being offered counselling and the school would be closed for the rest of the week.

As a result of the media frenzy, two other stories were given less attention than they might otherwise have received. In a completely unrelated incident, a helicopter had crashed into the River Thames near Wandsworth Bridge. The police were still looking for the pilot and any passengers. No names had been released. And in Greece one of the world's richest men, Yannis Ariston Xenopolos, had died after a long fight against cancer. He had left behind a fortune of more than twenty billion pounds.

Alan Blunt had been in one of his regular meetings with the Chiefs of Staff when the news came in. He had left at once, joining Mrs Jones for an emergency briefing. It was obvious to both of them that Alex had been the target. The sniper had missed – that much was known. But Alex seemed to have disappeared. He had last been seen cycling away from the school. When Blunt had heard about the helicopter crash just one hour later, he had assumed at once that there must be a connection. That would have been typical of Alex. He was a boy of extraordinary resource.

Alex finally arrived home in the middle of the afternoon. Jack was shocked by what had happened, and when Mrs Jones called her a short while later, she was in no mood for an argument.

"We need to talk to Alex," Mrs Jones said. "We'll send a car round to bring him to Liverpool Street."

"I'm sorry, Mrs Jones." There was ice in Jack's voice. "Alex isn't going anywhere. I can under- stand that you want to debrief him. But if you want to see him, you'll have to come here."

"That's out of the question."

"Fine. Then you can forget about talking to him." Before Mrs Jones could interrupt, Jack continued. "Every time Alex has been into that building of yours, he's had nothing but trouble. The last time was January. He came to see you because he had a journalist chasing after him – and what happened? You sent him to spy on Desmond McCain and he ended up in Kenya being almost fed to the croco- diles. Well, that's all over now. He doesn't work for you any more. If you want to talk to him about what happened this morning, you can come over here, but don't leave it too late. He's had a tough day and I want him in bed before ten."

It was unheard of for the head of MI6 Special Operations and his deputy to be summoned in this way. Secret conversations need to take place in a secure environment and Blunt's office was exactly that. Nobody could enter without being scanned for weapons or recording devices. Any form of eavesdropping was out of the question. The windows had even been treated to deflect radio and microwave beams. It was impossible to find out who had been there and for what reason. Visiting Alex at his home in Chelsea would change all that. It was a completely unacceptable risk.

And yet, early that evening, the car drew up outside the elegant, white-fronted house that had once belonged to Ian Rider, and Alan Blunt and Mrs Jones stepped out. Jack had refused to budge from her position and in the end they'd had to accept that this was the only way. But then, of course, Alex was no ordinary agent. Recruiting him in the first place had broken all the rules. So perhaps they should have been prepared to make an exception.

Alex was waiting for them in the living room. Blunt could see at once that he was very different from the fourteen-year-old he had so often employed. It wasn't just that he was bigger, that he had filled out more. He was more confident too. Looking at him, Blunt was suddenly reminded of Alex's father. The resemblance was really quite remarkable.

Jack offered coffee, which was politely declined. She had already given Mrs Jones a full description of what had happened after Alex left the school and the deputy head of Special Operations didn't waste any time.

"We've had divers and police down at the river," she began. "It seems likely that both the pilot and his passenger managed to escape from the helicopter. Certainly no bodies have been washed up."

"You'd have thought someone would have seen two dripping wet men climbing out of the Thames," Jack growled.

"We're making inquiries. We're still looking." Mrs Jones glanced at Alan Blunt sitting opposite her. "It does seem strange that they managed to vanish into thin air. This was broad daylight, in the middle of London. They must have been injured. And yet as far as we can tell, no one's had any sight of them."

"Did you see the sniper, Alex?" Blunt asked.

"Not clearly." Alex had changed into jeans and a T-shirt. He was barefoot, as if to stress that this was his home and he would dress how he liked. It felt strange having Blunt in the room, as if two worlds which should have been kept apart had somehow collided. "He was too far away and he had his back to me. But I got the numbers of the car and the helicopter."

"They were both fake," Mrs Jones said. "We've found the car – we picked it up from Wandsworth Park – and we're running tests for fingerprints and DNA. We've also salvaged the wreckage of the helicopter. But I have my doubts that either of them will lead us anywhere."

"These were professional people," Blunt agreed. "That trick with the car wash, for example. That showed a certain style..."

"Whose style?" Jack asked.

"We don't know. We've spoken to the owner of the garage. He says he was paid to close the car wash for a couple of days and he doesn't know anything else. We think he's telling the truth. But the main questions we have to ask ourselves are who would want to kill Alex and why now? And, more to the point, how do we stop them trying again?"

Alex examined the head of MI6 Special Operations, who was sitting on the edge of the sofa with a very straight back, as if he was determined not to make himself comfortable. As usual Blunt was completely businesslike, dressed in a slate grey suit, with steel-rimmed spectacles and highly polished black leather shoes. Despite what he had said, he had somehow made it clear that it didn't really matter to him if Alex lived or died. This whole thing was just a nuisance, something else to be dealt with in a busy day.

"They think I'm dead," Alex said. "The sniper

told the pilot. He said *mission accomplished*. I heard him."

"That may not necessarily be the case," Mrs Jones said – and once again she half glanced at Blunt, as if she wasn't sure she should continue. "First of all, we have to assume that the sniper was aiming at you. This will have been a very risky and expensive operation, so whoever was behind it must have a very serious reason to wish you harm. It's clear from what you say that the sniper lied to his employers, but even so they've probably guessed you're alive. And when his helicopter crashed ten minutes later, they'd have known for sure. Whichever way you look at it, Alex, you're probably still in danger, and I'm afraid your going back to school is out of the question until we've sorted this out."

"How long will that be?" Alex asked with a sense of despair. Some people might have thought him mad, wanting to go back to school. But he'd been enjoying the term. Everything had been going well for him. He wanted to be with his friends.

"It's impossible to say. We have no idea who the enemy is or even why they've chosen now to attack you. At the moment, we have no clues. We're as much in the dark as you."

"So how are you going to keep Alex safe?" Jack demanded. "How are you going to stop them trying again?"

Blunt and Mrs Jones exchanged a look, and suddenly Alex realized they had already worked this out, that they had known what they were going to say before they had walked through the front door. The same thing had happened after he had been attacked in Cornwall while surfing with Sabina. They had used the situation then; they would do the same now.

"I think Alex has to leave the country," Blunt began.

"No way!" Jack exclaimed.

"Please, Miss Starbright. Allow me to finish. He can't go back to Brookland and he can't stay here. As Mrs Jones just said, it's too dangerous."

"You could give him twenty-four-hour protection."

"We'll have people watching the house tonight – but in the long term, twenty-four-hour protection doesn't exist. If an enemy is determined enough, he'll break through the tightest barrier no matter how carefully it's been constructed. No. While we investigate this business, Alex would be much safer with a new identity somewhere far away."

"Do you have somewhere in mind?"

"As a matter of fact, I do." Blunt coughed delicately, his hand forming a comma in front of his mouth. "I want him to go to Egypt," he said.

"Egypt?"

"To Cairo, to be precise. It just so happens that I needed to send one of my people out there anyway—"

"Alex isn't one of your people!" Jack cut in.

Blunt ignored her. He turned directly to Alex.

"I wasn't going to involve you, Alex. You've made your feelings very clear, and of course I've tried to respect that. But circumstances have changed. You need our help; we need yours. I have a job which is ideally suited to you. At the same time, it'll take you far away and keep you safe."

"What job?" Alex asked. The two words fell heavily from his lips.

"It's just a question of being in the right place and keeping your eyes open. All we want you to do is report back and we'll do the rest." Blunt paused, waiting for any argument, and when none came he went on. "The place is a school – a very good school, as it happens – so you won't even need to miss any of your studies. It's called the Cairo International College of Arts and Education, although the students just refer to it as CC, or Cairo College. It's for boys and girls aged thirteen to eighteen, and there's a junior school too. Many of their parents are working in the Middle East. Some of them are high profile; some of them are very rich.

"We have received information that suggests some sort of hostile activity could take place there sometime soon. Unfortunately we don't know when and we have no idea what exactly it might entail. A kidnapping might be a possibility. Some of these parents could afford millions of pounds as a ransom, if it were demanded."

"Have you warned the school?" Jack asked.

"We're not sure a warning would do any good,"

Blunt replied. "Not until we know more. However, we do have one line of investigation. Last week the school appointed a new head of security, a man by the name of Erik Gunter. It seems very unlikely that he would be involved in anything illegal. As a matter of fact, he's a war hero. He was decorated by the queen. But we don't believe his arrival is just a coincidence."

"What happened to the last head of security?" Alex asked.

Blunt swallowed. "He had an accident. All we're asking you to do, Alex, is to keep an eye on this man and report anything suspicious back to us. There's no need for you to get involved. At the first sign of any trouble, we'll step in."

"Wait a minute!" Jack exclaimed. "I can't believe you people! We asked you to come here because someone just took a shot at Alex. His best friend was almost killed! But all you want is to use him again."

"We want to protect him," Mrs Jones insisted. "Honestly, Jack. It does seem to be the best solution. Nobody would think of looking for him in Cairo. We'll give him a false name. And the best thing about an international school is that the students come and go. The parents are always on the move. Nobody will ask any questions when a new face shows up. Meanwhile, we'll investigate the car, the helicopter, everything. We'll let you know as soon as it's safe for Alex to come home. It shouldn't be more than a few weeks."

She fell silent. Blunt was looking straight at Alex, waiting for him to reply. Jack shook her head, clearly unhappy. Alex realized it was all up to him. At the same time, he wondered if he really had any choice. Only that morning, he had been celebrating the fact that his life had returned to normal. Out of the tunnel – that was what he had thought. How could he have been so naive? The tunnel had reached out to draw him back in and once again he was lost in its darkness.

"I don't mind going," he said. "Mr Blunt is right. If there's someone after me, I can't stay here. I can't risk anyone else getting hurt because of me."

"I could take you to America. We could go anywhere in the world!"

"I need to be at school somewhere, Jack. I've started my GCSEs. I don't want to get any further behind."

"Then we're agreed—" Blunt said.

"Actually, I have a few questions," Jack cut in. "Where is Alex going to live in Cairo? Who's going to look after him? Is this international college a boarding school?"

"No." Mrs Jones shook her head. "We'll have to find him a flat."

"Then make sure it has two bedrooms because I'm going too!"

Alex turned to Jack in surprise. He could tell from the tone of her voice that there would be no argument.

"I'm fed up with sitting at home while you put Alex in harm's way," Jack went on. "I know you've said he won't be in any danger – but that's what you said last time, and the time before. Well, if Alex agrees to go, that's his decision. But I'm not letting him go alone. That's mine. Both of us or not at all. Your call, Mrs Jones."

Mrs Jones thought for a moment, then nodded. "I think it's a good idea," she said. "Alex?"

Alex was still gazing at Jack. "Are you really sure?" he asked.

"I've never been more certain about anything."

"That's great." Alex smiled. "We can see the Pyramids together. And the Nile. It'll be fun to have you with me."

"You can leave all the arrangements to us," Blunt said. "I'll alert our Cairo office that you're on your way. They'll give you everything you need."

"Then it seems we're all agreed," Jack said.

She got up and led Alan Blunt and Mrs Jones to the door. Their car was waiting for them, parked outside. Meanwhile, Alex stayed sitting on his own, his head in a whirl. Part of him was excited. He couldn't help himself. Cairo! It was an amazing city. Somewhere he had never been before. And yet at the same time, he felt a great weight on his shoulders. It was all happening again.

Jack came back in. "They've gone," she said.

"Thanks, Jack." Alex stood up. "Thanks for saying you'd come with me."

"I wasn't going to let it happen any other way." Just for a moment, Jack remembered that she had been planning to tell Alex her plans this very evening. Had she really been thinking of abandoning him, of moving on? Well, Washington and her parents would have to wait. "I guess they'll have to give me a new ID too," she said. "I wonder what I'll look like with a fake moustache?" She sighed. "Are you going to do your homework?"

"I don't think there's any point."

"Then why don't I make us some supper? And you see what's on TV..."

Alan Blunt was in a better mood as they headed back towards Liverpool Street. Mrs Jones had noticed the difference. "So you got what you wanted," she said.

"Yes." Blunt avoided her eye. "It's funny how things work out sometimes."

"I think you forgot to mention that Scorpia might be involved."

"I didn't forget. I preferred not to alarm him."

"He might have decided not to go."

"I would have said, all in all, that it's better for him to keep an open mind."

They drove on in silence.

"I want him to have backup in Cairo," Mrs Jones announced suddenly.

"Who do you have in mind?" Blunt knew there was a time when his deputy would never have spoken to him so directly. But he would soon be gone. Power was already transferring to her. "We could send Crawley back out, perhaps. Or Gerrard..."

"I was thinking of Smithers."

"An interesting choice."

"Alex trusts him. And he may come in useful, particularly if Scorpia do show up. Do you have any objection?"

"Of course not, Mrs Jones. Whatever you think best."

The strange thing was that Blunt had been right all along. He never should have left Liverpool Street and he certainly shouldn't have visited Alex at home.

He and Mrs Jones had been filmed getting out of the car from the window of the house opposite. The owners were on holiday in Thailand and should have returned by now, but they had fallen ill with food poisoning and were being treated in a hospital in Bangkok. Scorpia had arranged this, just as they had arranged for one of their teams to break into the house and set up their cameras on the second floor.

Alex's home had also been bugged. Two men dressed as telephone engineers had slipped in while Jack was out at the shops and had placed recording devices in the kitchen, living room, both bedrooms and even dotted around the garden. The entire conversation with Alan Blunt and Mrs Jones had been recorded.

*I want him to go to Egypt... I have a job which is ideally suited to you... I'll alert our Cairo office that you're on your way. They'll give you everything you need.*

*We'll give him a false name...*

It had all been recorded, time-coded and filed, proof that MI6 had once again employed Alex Rider and sent him to the Middle East. It would be added to the Horseman file and over the next few days, that file would start to grow. Ariston might be dead, but his work would continue. Scorpia's operation had begun.

# WELCOME TO CAIRO

The man from the embassy had introduced himself as Blakeway but Alex wondered if that was his real name. It somehow suited him too well. He was thin, elderly, hollowed out by the sun and very English – wearing a crumpled linen jacket, a striped tie and a panama hat. He had been waiting for Alex and Jack at Cairo International Airport, standing at the end of the metal tunnel that led from the plane.

"Miss Starbright? Alex? Very good to meet you. I've got a car waiting for you. Do come this way..."

They set off at a leisurely pace. Blakeway didn't look like the sort of man who ever hurried. But it was good having him with them. They were waved through passport control. They didn't have to join the long queues or buy twenty-dollar entry visas from the banking kiosks. Blakeway stood with them until their luggage arrived on the carousel, then carried Jack's cases for her, leading them through the crowds of taxi drivers and tour operators clamouring on the other side of the arrivals gate.

The heat hit Alex full in the face. As they passed through the sliding doors, leaving the terminal behind them, it was almost like stepping into a furnace. Within seconds his clothes were sticking to him and he felt his case dragging him down.

Meanwhile, Blakeway was looking around the concourse. "Where's Ahmed? I told him I'd only be a few minutes. Ah! There he is!"

He waved at an official-looking black saloon car, which drew up in front of him, and a small, round-faced man in a white shirt and dark trousers leapt out and began to busy himself with the luggage.

"That's better. You two can hop in the back. The car's got air conditioning, thank goodness. It shouldn't take us too long to get across Cairo – apart from the blasted traffic."

A minute later they were on their way. The car was cool inside and the seats were soft and comfortable, but Alex couldn't relax. He was worn out from the long journey, and although he desperately wanted to fall asleep he knew it wasn't going to happen. London didn't just seem a five-hour flight away; it was another world. He wondered when he would see it again. What a fool he had been to think that MI6 would ever leave him alone. Perhaps it had been the same for his uncle, Ian Rider – and his parents. They had all discovered the same thing. In the end, there was no way out.

Sitting next to him, her head resting against the window, Jack Starbright seemed to know exactly what he was thinking. She was wearing large sunglasses that covered most of her face, along with a floppy white hat, but he could tell she was concerned about him. She suddenly reached across and put a hand on his arm.

"We don't have to stay," she said, quietly, so that Blakeway wouldn't hear.

"I know."

"I noticed a flight to New York leaving in three hours. We could be on it."

"We're here now, Jack. We might as well see what it's like."

Was that even possible? Could they still leave? Alex wondered what would happen if he asked the car to turn round, if he tried to get back on a plane. Would MI6 let him leave Cairo? Alan Blunt wanted him here and that was where he was. There would be no departure until the job had been done.

"All right in the back?" Blakeway asked. He might have overheard them talking after all. "We've got some water here if you need it. Just shout."

He had said the traffic would be bad and he hadn't been exaggerating. It was horrendous. They had joined a six-lane motorway but there still wasn't enough room for the thousands of cars jammed together, the drivers hooting at one another furiously as if it would make any difference at all. Alex stared out of the window. It seemed to him that

they had driven into a nightmare of steel and concrete, of sand and dust. Old-fashioned office blocks
stood next to crumbling houses. Here and there,
slender towers rose over the domes of mosques, but
they were hemmed in by radio masts, electricity
pylons and cranes, tons and tons of ironwork fighting for control of the sky. Alex's first impression was
that Cairo was a very ugly city. It certainly wasn't
somewhere he would have chosen to live.

Somehow they fought their way through to the
other side. The traffic thinned out a little and they
found themselves in a suburb, quieter and less
densely populated but still less than welcoming.
Everything seemed half finished. They were driving down a street with palm trees and expensive
Arabic-style villas on one side, but piles of rubble
and broken-down fences on the other. For the first
time, Alex saw the desert. It was there, in the middle distance, an endless wave of drab yellow sand.
It was as if Cairo didn't dare go any further. It just
stopped. And next to it there was nothing.

"Not much further," Blakeway said. He sounded
remarkably cheerful. Alex wondered how long he
had been here. He turned to the driver and said
something in Arabic. The two of them laughed.

And then they drove into a bright, modern complex, automatic gates opening and closing behind
them. It was called Golden Palm Heights and was
a private community of about fifty bleached-out
houses and flats surrounding well-kept lawns with

sprinklers twisting in the sunshine and a good-sized swimming pool. It reminded Alex of a holiday village, the sort of place you might rent for a week in the sun. The car drew up beside a neat block of flats with terraces overlooking the pool.

"This is it! Let's go in. Ahmed can bring up the luggage."

They followed Blakeway up a staircase to a two-bedroom flat on the first floor. The door was open and he showed them into a light, modern space with marble floors, air conditioning and an open-plan living room with sliding windows leading onto the balcony. There was a large fridge-freezer, an electric oven and microwave opposite a breakfast bar with stools. A slightly old-fashioned TV stood in a corner with a cactus sitting on the top. Everything was very clean. It looked comfortable. After the long journey, Alex had to admit that he was pleasantly surprised.

"I'll leave you now," Blakeway announced. "You'll want to unpack and go for a swim. If you need anything, this is my number here." He took out a business card and snapped it down. "You're only five minutes from Cairo College and I'm sure someone will turn up to show you round. Quite a lot of the students and some of the teachers live here at Golden Palm Heights. They'll be back around four o'clock, after school, and there's usually a rush for the pool. I expect it'll be quite strange for you, Alex, being the new boy and all that."

He went over to the window and glanced out, as if to make sure they were alone. When he turned round, his voice was lower and he sounded almost nervous. "I'm told that one of your people will be coming here on Sunday evening," he went on. "He'll pass on further instructions and see that you're properly equipped. But that gives you the weekend to acclimatize yourselves, see a bit of Cairo. It's not such a bad place once you get to know it. Well, I'll wish you good luck, Alex. For what it's worth, I've heard about you. A few whispers, anyway. It's very good to have met you."

He called for Ahmed and the two of them left. Jack watched the car disappear through the gates. They were finally alone.

"A swim, something to eat or a sleep?" she asked.

"All three," Alex replied. "But let's start with the swim."

Jack was keen to unpack so Alex dragged a pair of trunks out of his case, changed and went down alone. He dived straight in and did six lengths, pounding through the cold water, leaving the heat and the grime behind him. He was still there, splashing around and enjoying himself, when the first students from Cairo College arrived back at Golden Palm Heights, threw off their backpacks and clothes and dived in with him. Almost at once he found himself surrounded by two boys and a girl who were all about the same age as him and who seemed delighted to have a new face in the complex.

The two boys were Australian: Craig Stevens and Simon Shaw. Craig was tall for his age – in fact he was huge – and needed to shave but didn't. Simon looked like a surfer, from his tanned skin and long fair hair right down to the bead necklace and brightly coloured swimming trunks. The girl was called Jodie, and although she had been born in England, she had lived most of her life abroad. Her parents were both teachers, fortunately not at the CICAE. She had freckles and straw-coloured hair cut short and Alex liked her at once.

"Cairo College isn't too bad," she told him in answer to his questions. "It's pretty relaxed and the teachers are OK. I spent two years in Singapore and that was miserable."

"How come you're out here?" Craig asked Alex. Like Simon, his father worked in the oil industry. Quite a few of the families at the school were supported by Shell or BP.

It was the moment Alex had been dreading. It was hard enough making new friends; doing so on the basis of a lie made it ten times worse. But he had no choice. MI6 had given him a false name – Alex Brenner – and he had already rehearsed his backstory with Jack. She would support him if anyone asked her.

"I don't have parents," he explained. "My uncle works for an international bank and the company's recently started working in the Middle East. He's not here right now. I have a sort of guardian who looks after me. Everyone just decided it would be easier for us to be here."

Like all good lies, the story contained a lot of truth. Ian Rider had pretended to be a banker before he'd died. MI6 were certainly active in the Middle East. And Jack was his legal guardian. In any event, it seemed to make sense to Alex's three new friends.

"It's OK," Craig said, "once you get used to the heat and the noise."

"And the hawkers," Simon added.

"And Miss Watson." The three of them groaned.

"Welcome to Cairo, Alex. You're going to love it here."

And over the next few days, almost despite himself, Alex began to relax. He would start at the school on Monday. Until then, he and Jack were tourists, on holiday together, and they could put everything else out of their minds. The first thing they did was to visit the famous Pyramids at Giza, slipping in as the sun was rising, and wandering almost alone around the extraordinary monuments built to house the bodies of dead kings almost five thousand years before. They took a felucca, a traditional wooden sailing boat, along the Nile. They explored Cairo together, strolling through the crowded streets of the souk – the local market – and haggling for things they didn't even want. They popped into mosques and museums, staying just long enough to say they had been. They visited the place where Moses had supposedly been found in the bulrushes and Jack got a picture taken of the two of them, arm in arm, grinning like idiots.

Craig and Simon had both been right. The heat in the city was almost unbearable, at least forty degrees without any desert breeze, and the hawkers never left them alone, trying to sell them everything from spices to pornographic postcards. Cairo had no centre and seemed to have no way out. It was as though half of humanity had just piled in and decided to stay.

But they didn't care. They were enjoying themselves, closer than they'd been for a long time. Alex felt as if he had gone back five years, as if Ian Rider were still alive and Jack was looking after him and every day in its own way was fun. He was almost glad that he'd been shot at. This wouldn't be happening otherwise.

They didn't hear from Blakeway again, but returning home on Sunday evening they noticed a new car parked outside the flats and realized that the MI6 agent he had mentioned must have turned up. Sure enough, someone called to them from the main door, and to his surprise Alex saw a familiar, plump figure waddling slowly towards them.

He had last seen Smithers in his office on the eleventh floor of the Royal & General Bank in London, just before he had broken into the Greenfields Bio Centre on Salisbury Plain. Alex had always had a soft spot for the man who had provided him with so many bizarre and useful gadgets during his time with MI6. Seeing him now, he wondered how Smithers could possibly manage in this heat. It wasn't just the huge stomach, it was the three chins, the round cheeks, the neck that seemed to be melting slowly into the shoulders. Smithers was bald with a small black moustache, reminding Alex of a comedian in one of those old silent black and white films. He was wearing a linen suit that billowed around him like a parachute. He was mopping his head with an oversized silk handkerchief but as he drew up in front of them he stuffed it back into his pocket.

"*As-Salaam Alaikum*, Alex," Smithers chortled. "That's Arabic for good evening. And you must be Jack Starbright. How very nice to meet you."

"What are you doing out here, Mr Smithers?" Alex asked.

"Believe it or not, Mrs Jones sent me to look after you." Smithers beamed. "Let's go and talk inside, shall we? I'm told you have a first-floor flat. I hope there's not too many steps!"

They made their way up and soon the three of them were sitting round the living room table. Alex had a glass of iced grenadine – still his favourite drink. Smithers had a beer.

"So you begin at Cairo College tomorrow, Alex,"

he said. "My job is to help you and also, as it were, to be the interface between you and London."

"What's going on in London?" Jack asked.

"They still haven't found the helicopter pilot or the sniper," Smithers said. "And no bodies have turned up, so we're assuming they got away."

"They tried to kill Alex. You must know who they were."

"I'm afraid not, Miss Starbright." Smithers lifted his beer. "Can I call you Jack? I feel I know you rather well even though we've only just met. And I have to agree with you. It's all rather mysterious. I'm not sure how the helicopter managed to land in the middle of London in the first place. It would have needed a flight plan and for that it would have had to have a proper licence. But so far all the trails have led nowhere."

"Was it Scorpia?" Alex asked. He didn't know why he said that. The name had just popped into his head.

"I don't know, Alex, old chap. They haven't told me. The good thing is that nobody knows you're here in Cairo. At least you're safe."

"You mean he's safe until someone tries to blow up the school," Jack growled. "Then he'll be right in the middle of it."

"What exactly am I meant to do?" Alex asked. His face brightened. "And what gadgets have you got for me, Mr Smithers? I'm sure you've got an exploding camel or something."

Smithers shook his head. For once, he was completely serious. "This is a very rum situation," he said. "And we have to be careful. All we know is that the school is a target and a lot of young lives may be at stake. Imagine if the whole place was taken over by armed criminals. Such a thing has happened before, you know. Or suppose some of these teenagers were taken prisoner..." He pulled out a list of names and laid it flat on the table. "For what it's worth, these are the ten wealthiest students at Cairo College."

Alex glanced at the names. The third one down was Simon Shaw, the blond-haired boy he'd met on his first day. "I know him," he said. "He was in the swimming pool."

"His father is William Shaw. He owns about half the petrol stations in Australia." Smithers took the list and folded it away. "Don't be fooled by the fact that his son is living in a flat just like yours," he said. "A lot of them don't want people to know how rich their families are."

That was an interesting thought. Perhaps Alex wouldn't be the only person at Cairo College with secrets to hide.

"We have to examine all the security systems in the school," Smithers continued. "Put simply, Alex, we need to be sure that it's safe. What about members of the staff? Are there any teachers with drinking or gambling problems? Now I come to think of it, my old history teacher suffered from both. But we want to know about anything that could open them up to blackmail.

"And then there's this chap, Erik Gunter. Now, I've seen his file and I find it hard to believe he's turned bad. He took four bullets for his regiment while he was in Afghanistan and spent nine weeks in hospital recovering. He has no criminal record of any sort. But at the same time, he is their new head of security and it can't just be a coincidence that he's popped up now. That's where you should concentrate your efforts. We want to know everything he's up to. Who he meets, how much he spends – even what he has for lunch."

Smithers had brought a small attaché case with him and he opened it. The first things he took out were a pair of rather chunky sunglasses and a bright red plastic water bottle, the sort of thing sportsmen might use.

"These work together," he explained. "Everyone at Cairo College carries water – and you can pour about a quarter of a litre in the top part of this bottle. The equipment is concealed in the bottom part; it's new technology, Alex, and highly classified. It uses people's mobile phones against them. Point the bottle in their direction when they're making a call and you'll hear everything they're hearing. The speakers are inside the handles of the dark glasses and go behind your ears. But it's better than that. You can activate mobile phones at a distance of up to fifty metres and turn them into bugs. Two teachers having a conversation in the schoolyard? You'll hear every word they say."

He took out what looked like an ordinary plastic light switch. "This is the same design as all the light switches at Cairo College," he explained. "You can stick it on any wall – there's a resin on the back – and nobody will notice it's there: one more switch among so many. It doesn't actually turn anything on or off, of course, but it's got a highly sensitive listening device inside and you can use it to hear through walls. Again, it's connected to the glasses.

"Now, if you want to communicate with me, you'll need this." He produced an old-fashioned notepad and a ballpoint pen and handed them to Alex. Both objects felt slightly too heavy. "Anything you write or draw on this notepad will appear instantly on my computer screen," Smithers said. "Scribble down SOS and I'll be on my way. I've taken a house in the middle of the city, just off al-Azhar Street, round the corner from the souk. I'll give you directions or you can use this."

He brought out a baseball cap with a fancy logo on the side. "There's a miniaturized satnav system inside the fabric," he explained. "The whole thing is self-powered. The logo is a solar panel and there's an audio feed that connects to the sunglasses. I've got rather a good name for it."

"Hat-Nav?" Alex suggested.

"You're one step ahead of me!" Smithers chortled, then took out his handkerchief and patted at his face. "Trouble with this country is it's damnably hot," he said.

"I'm going for a swim," Alex said. "You can come with me if you like."

"No, thank you, old chap. I never swim. I once invented a miniature submarine but it was pretty hopeless. For a start, I couldn't fit into it. And floating doesn't come naturally to me. But you enjoy yourself!" He got up and went over to the door. "Delighted to meet you, Jack. And take care, Alex. I'll show myself out!"

Alex and Jack waited until he had gone. Then Jack picked up the sunglasses and examined them. "So that was the famous Mr Smithers," she said. "He was completely unbelievable."

"You mean his gadgets?"

"I mean the size of him! But I guess it's good he's on your side." Jack handed Alex the sunglasses and went into the kitchen. "I'll make us some supper while you have a quick swim," she said. "And then you'd better have an early night. You've got to be ready for your first day at school."

# THE NEW BOY

The Cairo International College of Arts and Education was only a five-minute walk from the flat, just as Blakeway had said. When Monday morning finally arrived, Alex set off with the two Australian boys, Craig and Simon, who had offered to deliver him to the main reception. Jack would have liked to go too but understood that Alex would feel more comfortable with kids of his own age. But she still grabbed hold of him before he went and gave him a quick kiss goodbye.

"It reminds me of the first time you went to Brookland," she said.

And the strange thing was, Alex was aware of the same nervousness that he'd felt when he'd left for secondary school. His new uniform – dark blue trousers and light blue polo shirt – felt ridiculous and he had to remind himself that everyone would be wearing the same thing. He guessed it didn't matter how old you were. These feelings never went away.

Cairo College even looked a bit like Brookland. It was halfway down a wide, tree-lined avenue, a modern complex with a main gate and coaches turning in, cars already pulling up outside, children of every age and size tumbling out, dragging backpacks and lunch boxes and peculiar class projects made out of wobbling cardboard and paper. It occurred to Alex that schools all over the world are more or less alike. After all, a classroom is a classroom, a football pitch a football pitch – and Cairo College had plenty of both. Even the noise was the same: the medley of shouting voices, the first bell, the stampede of feet on concrete. Is there any other type of building that identifies itself so quickly by the sound it makes?

What made Cairo College different was the burning sunlight, the brightly painted yellow walls (surely no school in England was ever painted yellow), the exotic plants and palm trees and the thin scattering of sand in the main yard. The buildings had been designed so that the passageways were light and airy, opening onto different courtyards with benches and tables grouped together under wooden canopies so that everyone could have their lunch outside. There was also a junior school, with about a hundred children aged eight to thirteen. But they were all contained in a single block, next to an Olympic-sized swimming pool. The three hundred boys and girls in the senior school had the rest of the place to themselves.

Craig and Simon escorted Alex through the main gate. They weren't allowed to continue without presenting their passes, which were electronically scanned by an Egyptian guard. Alex noticed that the same was being done for all the other students as they arrived. He was held up while his own pass was issued with a photograph that made him look as if he had just been mugged. Finally the two boys left him at an office on the other side, where he was greeted by the school secretary: a smiling, motherly woman with a thick Yorkshire accent who made him fill out a lot of forms, gave him a copy of the school regulations and then took him into the room next door. Here he was surprised to find himself shaking hands with the head teacher of Cairo College, a man in his fifties who introduced himself as Matthew Jordan – "But everyone calls me Monty." He was a New Zealander, a shaggy, easy-going man who obviously liked his job.

"Alex, welcome to Cairo College. I hope you'll enjoy yourself. I guess it'll all be a bit strange at first but we try to take things easy here. We don't like bullies and we don't like show-offs, but you don't look like either so I'm sure you'll fit in fine. If you have any problems, my office is always open. Every new kid who comes here gets a mentor. Yours is waiting outside. Her name is Gabriela and I'm sure the two of you will get along. Good luck. I'll see you around."

Gabriela was sixteen and, it turned out, the daughter of the Italian ambassador in Cairo. She had been at the school for three years and – she wasted no time telling Alex – was looking forward to leaving. She already seemed to be bursting out of her uniform. Her nails were painted bright red. From the way she walked, it was as if the whole place belonged to her. She took Alex to morning assembly, class registration, and then to his first lesson. After that, he didn't see her again.

Monday at Cairo College...

It began with four one-hour lessons followed by lunch. The college taught exactly the same subjects as an English school, with the single exception that there was no religious studies – perhaps it was too sensitive an area in an Islamic country. The lessons were also more relaxed, and the class sizes, with only fifteen or sixteen students, were small. Like the students, the teachers came from all over the world, and maybe because they were so far from home, they all felt a need to mix in. Alex's maths teacher was from America, his history teacher was South African and his English teacher was actually Japanese. He wasn't quite on first-name terms with them, but Alex thought that if he stayed at the school long enough, he could easily become so.

Lunch was served in the courtyard, a choice of salads, sandwiches, wraps and pizzas. Again, because this was Egypt, there was no ham or pork.

Alex wondered where he should sit but he needn't have worried. Craig, Simon and Jodie were waiting for him, and called him over to their table. They seemed keen to introduce him to their Year Ten friends, and from the way they described him they might have met him months ago rather than a few days before.

"Brenner? That's a Scottish name." The speaker was a stocky, ginger-haired boy called Andrew Macdonald, who was of course Scottish himself. There were quite a few boys from Scotland at Cairo College, connected by the oil industry. Alex had already noticed that they were the one national group that preferred to stick together.

"I'm not Scottish," Alex said.

"That's your bad luck. So why are you here?"

Once again Alex went through his story. The fake name, the fake history. He still hated having to do it. He could feel it separating him from the rest of them.

"So where are your parents?" someone asked.

"They died a long time ago."

"That's tough..."

"I've got used to it."

"How long do you reckon you'll be here?" Andrew asked.

"I don't know. They haven't really said..."

There were two more lessons in the afternoon, then sport, then ECAs, which stood for extra-curricular activities and included everything from drama to swimming to trekking in the desert for an International Award. The school secretary had told Alex to put his name down for at least two activities and he had chosen drama and football – although he couldn't imagine kicking a ball around in the intense heat. The last lesson was French, which was hardly needed as most of the students at Cairo College spoke two or three languages anyway. It was taken by Joanna Watson, the teacher whose name had been mentioned in the pool at Golden Palm Heights. Alex supposed that every school had to have a Miss Watson: permanently scowling and short-tempered, unloved and proud of it. She was short and bullish and had threatened him with his first detention before she'd even introduced herself.

It was at the very end of the day that Alex had his first encounter with Erik Gunter.

The head of security came out of his office on the ground floor as Alex was leaving. The two of them were suddenly face to face, and they eyed each other warily.

"Good afternoon. You're the new boy, Alex Brenner. Isn't that right?"

"Yes, sir."

"I'm Erik Gunter." Alex recognized the Glasgow accent. "I'm also new here. I just started a few weeks ago."

Gunter was younger than Alex had expected, not quite thirty. It was obvious that he had been in the army. He was incredibly fit with the sort of overdeveloped muscles that might have been made for tattoos – not that Alex could actually see them beneath the black suit he was wearing. His dark hair was shaved close to the scalp, leaving only a shadow on his skin. He had a high forehead and glinting, sunken eyes. He wasn't tall – in fact, he and Alex were about the same height – but Alex had no doubt that if it ever came to a fight, Gunter would be faster, stronger and dirtier than him. He decided at once that it would never happen. If Gunter really was involved in some sort of conspiracy, MI6 could deal with him. This was one man he would leave well alone.

"Are you a teacher here?" Alex asked. He felt a need to say something.

"No. I look after security. Do you feel secure, Brenner?"

"Yes, sir."

"Good. Well, keep out of trouble and you'll stay that way. I'll see you around."

Gunter walked down to the main entrance. Alex saw that he moved with difficulty, and even had trouble opening the door. He wasn't slow but his whole body was somehow lopsided, as if the different parts weren't receiving the right signals from his brain. Nothing about him quite worked and Alex remembered that he had been shot several times in Afghanistan. Was he really the enemy? The man was a war hero – and in his own way he had been friendly enough. Alex already felt bad about spying on him.

As far as Alex was concerned, that should have been the end of his first day at Cairo College. He was looking forward to getting back to the flat and telling Jack everything that had happened. But there was still one last encounter waiting for him and it was a very strange one.

He had managed to drift behind the other students and was virtually alone as he walked towards the main gate. The guards were checking everyone's IDs and the last coach was just pulling out. The sun hadn't started to sink but there was a pink hue in the sky and a sense of calm in the air. Alex dug out his card so that it could be scanned. And it was then that he got the impression he was being watched. Actually, it was stronger than that. He was quite certain of it. It was like an electric shock, a shudder of something running through him as he became aware of somebody's eyes boring into him.

Slowly he turned his head, and for just a moment he spotted a figure in a downstairs window, looking at him from behind the glass. It was Gunter's office. Alex was sure of it. But it couldn't be Gunter as Alex had just seen him leave. It looked like a boy; Alex could see he was wearing school uniform. He glimpsed fair hair. The boy's face was just a blur. Alex tried to make it out, but almost at once the boy moved away and instantly disappeared, like a mirage in the desert. Perhaps he had never been there at all.

But in that brief second, the heat of the afternoon was replaced by a shiver of something that Alex didn't quite recognize, as if something unpleasant from the past had chosen to reappear. He stopped and took a deep breath, forcing himself to forget what had just happened. He was allowing things to get on top of him. He had to focus his mind on what lay ahead.

The window was empty.

Alex hurried through the main gate. He didn't look back.

Jack was waiting for him when he got home. She'd spent the morning at the famous Egyptian Museum looking at the treasures of the boy king, Tutankhamen. In the afternoon she'd gone shopping and she'd even met some of the parents living at Golden Palm Heights. They'd all been very welcoming. Like their children, they were displaced and needed to make friends.

Alex quickly told her about his first day at the college. "You know, I think I'm actually going to quite like it there. Everyone's really friendly. The school's OK. And at least it's not raining..."

"That's good, Alex. Maybe this is going to work out, after all."

And yet, much later that night, after he'd had dinner, done his first batch of homework and watched half a bad film on TV, Alex wondered. He had taken the smaller of the two bedrooms and was sitting at a desk with views over the back of the complex. There were no curtains and the night was very black, dotted with stars. The air conditioning was on full and he could feel it blasting over his shoulders. He'd opened his laptop and logged into Facebook. The photograph on his profile page had been taken on a mountaineering holiday with his uncle, Ian Rider. The two of them were sitting next to each other on a ridge, both with ropes coiled over their shoulders. He wondered why he had chosen it.

He had eighteen messages, nearly all from his friends at Brookland. The first one was from Tom Harris:

Hey, Alex. Where are you, man? I'm out of hodpital and now I know whatit feels like to be shot. Hurt like hell. ThANKs for dragging me down, as I'd have just stod there and let that nutter hit me a secod time. I guess he ws aiming at you. Yes? Hope this doesn't mean you're in troubble again. Let me know, if you can. EVEryone talking about it. Brookland on News at 10, Daily Mail, Sun ETC. Now we're not allowed to talk to anyone. Typimg this with one hand. Two weeks off school plus counselling. Ha ha ha. TOM

He quickly looked through the others but didn't

reply. How could he explain what had happened in the last few days? Finally he opened a message from Sabina:

Alex, we saw Brookland on the TV and heard what happened. I can't believe someone tried to shoot you. Where are you now? Mum and Dad really worried about you and guess this has got something to do with you-know-who. You said you weren't getting into all that again. James told me you've disappeared so hope you're somewhere safe. Let me know!!! Sab xxx

Sitting on his own, framed against the darkness, Alex suddenly felt isolated, as if he were trapped in some sort of cyberspace, between two worlds. Here in Egypt he was Alex Brenner, in a new school, making new friends. But none of it was true, and as soon as the job was done, MI6 would pull him out and he would disappear so totally and so immediately that it would be as if someone had just pressed the delete key. And yet, what of his old friends, his real life in London? After what had happened, would he ever be able to return to it? Or had the sniper snatched it away for good?

He was about to turn the computer off and go to bed, when he noticed he'd been sent a new email. He drew his finger across the touch pad and double-clicked.

Hi Alex,
Julius G added you as a friend on Facebook.

For a long minute he gazed at the screen, at the brief message and the green panel: ADD FRIEND. He didn't know anyone called Julius but that wasn't so unusual. He'd connected with lots of people he'd never met. So why did the name make him feel so uneasy? He thought again of the boy he had glimpsed in the window at Cairo College. It had been a boy, he was sure of it.

Right now, Alex felt he needed all the friends he could get. But not this one. He didn't know why but some instinct told him to stay away.

Alex clicked IGNORE on his Facebook page.

He turned off the computer and went to bed.

Over the next fortnight, Alex fell into the natural rhythm of Cairo College. Mondays were the quietest day of the week; Wednesdays were the worst, with the biggest pile of homework. School food was OK so long as you avoided the pasta. He worked out which teachers he liked best and which he preferred to avoid, and he made plenty of friends. He was still the new boy, but in an international school like this, with students coming and going all the time, people were more quickly accepted. Early in the second week he was called into Monty Jordan's office and given his first report.

"You're doing very well, Alex," the head teacher told him. "Your teachers all say you're making good progress, although Miss Watson thinks you could focus a little more in French. How are you finding it?"

"I'm OK, thank you, sir."

"Good. I'm glad to hear it. By the way, I see you've applied to join my politics set."

This was one of the extra-curricular activities. Alex knew that Craig and the Scottish boy, Andrew, were both in this group, which met once a week to discuss stories that had appeared in the newspapers. They also took part in a miniature version of the United Nations, with everyone pretending to be a different country. According to Craig, the last session had ended with Belgium invading Holland and China declaring war on everyone else.

But Alex wasn't interested in politics. He looked puzzled. "Actually, sir, I didn't apply."

Mr Jordan frowned. "Didn't you? That's strange. Your name's down on the list." He took out a sheet of paper and examined it. "That's right. You're definitely here. Why don't you join us anyway? We've got a couple of interesting events coming up and you might find it's fun."

Alex shrugged. It didn't make any difference to him – and it made sense not to offend the head. "All right," he said.

"Great. I'll see you later in the week."

And so he talked politics, played football (five-a-side in the air-conditioned gymnasium) and even got a small part in the Cairo College production of *Blood Brothers*. That made him think of Brookland. Right now he should have been rehearsing for their production of *Grease*. It struck him as odd that no matter where in the world he went, there were people trying to make him sing.

And yet Alex couldn't settle in completely. Although part of him felt ashamed of himself, he had a job to do. He wasn't here as a schoolboy; he was here as a spy. And that set him apart. There wasn't a moment when he was able to forget it.

The transmitting device that Smithers had given him, concealed in the bottom of his water bottle, worked brilliantly. It turned every mobile phone into a bug and, wearing the sunglasses, Alex was able to pick up conversations across the school-yard. At the same time, though, he learned a lot of things he didn't want to know. Miss Kennedy, who taught chemistry and physics, was having an affair with Mr Jackson, the head of sports. Miss Watson had a mother in hospital in England and was desperately worried about her. Monty Jordan had just applied for another job in a school in New Zealand. These people weren't criminals or terrorists and Alex hated prying on them. It made him feel shabby.

There was also a limit as to how much he could pick up. The guards spoke Arabic so there was no point eavesdropping on them. And although he saw Erik Gunter a few times, the head of security seemed determined never to speak to anyone. Alex had positioned one of the fake light switches outside Gunter's office and had spent as much time lingering in the corridor as he dared, listening to what was said inside the room. Gunter had made just a couple of phone calls – one to a company that maintained the school alarm systems and one to a doctor to order more painkillers. Either he was very careful or completely innocent. Alex still wasn't sure which.

At the same time, he did his best to assess security at Cairo College – the other half of the job that MI6 had given him. It was strange to sit in the courtyard and try to imagine himself as a terrorist. But if he were going to target the school, where would he begin? Who would be his first target?

And the truth was fairly bleak. The school had guards, identity cards, security cameras, wire fences and alarms. But none of the guards were armed and any well-organized group would be able to break in and take over the place in minutes. And if they were thinking about kidnap – perhaps one of the names on the list that Smithers had shown him – they wouldn't even need to come close. Simon Shaw, the son of the Australian petrol king, walked home every day. Anyone in a car could just pull up and drag him inside. All the rich kids at Cairo College were determined to live an ordinary life. And that meant no bodyguards, no armour-plated saloons, hardly any security at all.

The one weak link, the only lead they had, was Erik Gunter. He was the new security head; he must have been recruited for a purpose. If Alex could just break into his office, perhaps he might be able to pick up a clue and bring this whole business to an end.

On Friday afternoon at the end of his second week, Alex stopped in front of the room on the ground floor. The window was locked and barred, but he had often seen Gunter going in and out through the door. He didn't use a key. He pressed his thumb against an electronic scanner and the door clicked open. Alex quickly checked out the technology. Behind the glass panel was a light sensor system, the same sort of thing that could be found in any digital camera. This took a picture of Gunter's thumb, which was then turned into a series of dots by an analogue to digital converter. Somewhere in the system, there was a second picture. If the two matched, the door would open.

Alex needed Gunter's thumb ... and it needed to be connected to his hand. Cairo College had installed a sophisticated system which also incorporated a pulse and a heat sensor. Only the real, living thing would do.

But surely that was possible.

Alex took out the notepad and pen that Smithers had given him. Working quickly, he sketched an illustration of the door and the keypad. He wrote down the brand name – Securi-Scan – and the serial number. Then, underneath, he scribbled a message: *Can you get me in?*

He underlined it, then closed the pad and put it away. The image and the question should have instantly appeared on Smithers' computer screen. Hopefully he would come up with a solution over the weekend.

Alex picked up his backpack, threw it over his shoulder and set off home.

# *IN THE PICTURE*

Erik Gunter was away for the whole of Monday at some sort of conference in Alexandria, handing over security to his assistant, an Egyptian called Naquib, who spent the entire day either smoking or dozing in the sun. It was infuriating to know that Gunter's office was empty – but Alex couldn't break in without him. He realized he had to wait for his return, and it wasn't until the end of Tuesday that he finally got his chance.

It had been another ordinary school day but Alex had been unable to concentrate, knowing that he was about to make his move. He had noticed Gunter at lunchtime sitting with some of the teachers and drinking a glass of milk. He had never actually seen the head of security eat anything solid. Somehow Alex had managed to get through French, history, maths and all the rest of it. He'd gone swimming, and rehearsed the school play. And finally he was on his own, hanging back after the last lesson had ended. He was fairly sure that he was the only student left in the school. It was just after three thirty. The gate would be locked at four o'clock – allowing him a window of just thirty minutes. It might not be enough.

By now, Alex knew the movements of Gunter, Naquib and everyone else whose job it was to patrol the school and keep it safe. Gunter returned to his office at a quarter past three every day. He worked there for about twenty minutes, then went over to the main gate to watch the students leave. It was surprising that this was one part of his army training that he seemed to have forgotten. He repeated himself – and repetition is a gift to the enemy. It makes you predictable. It makes you an easy target.

Alex waited in the corridor close to the office until there was a click and the door opened. He moved forward, timing it so that he arrived outside just as Gunter emerged. He glanced briefly inside before Gunter closed the door. The lock engaged automatically.

"Brenner!" The security man was surprised to see him. "What are you doing here?"

"I came to see you," Alex said.

"Why?"

Alex put his hand in his pocket. "I found this." He took out an iPhone and handed it to Gunter.

"What about it?"

"Well, someone left it in class. I tried to start it up but it's locked. I thought you could find out who it belongs to and hand it back."

Gunter scowled. With his shaven head and hostile eyes, he had the sort of face that showed anger very easily. "Lost property is no business of mine. You've got to hand it in at the gate. They'll put up a notice and whoever's left this can claim it when they get in tomorrow." He gave it back and began to move away, again with that strange, fumbling progress that suggested his muscles and skeleton weren't quite working together.

He had only taken two steps when he turned round. "How are you getting on here?" he asked.

"I'm fine," Alex said.

"But you must be missing your friends in London."

"Yes. But I've got a lot of friends here too."

"Good. I'm glad to hear it."

Gunter clomped his way down the corridor, leaving Alex wondering how he could possibly have known that he came from London. Of course, Gunter could have looked at his file. But that was in the main office – and why would he have bothered to search it out? It was an interesting slip. Alex made a mental note of it.

The corridor was now empty. It was three thirty-six. Alex was still holding the iPhone, cradling it in the palm of his hand, careful not to place his own fingers on the screen. He hadn't actually found it. In fact it had arrived at the weekend, sent by Smithers and delivered in a padded envelope with a single sheet of instructions. Alex tilted the iPhone, checking the screen. Yes. Gunter had left a perfect thumbprint. He searched for the little button on the side and pressed it. There was a slight buzzing sound and the whole thing began to vibrate in his hand as the image was reversed and then reproduced. It took about twenty seconds and then a thin sheet of pink latex slid out of a slot where the power cable would normally be attached. Alex pressed his own thumb onto it, then wrapped the sides round. If the machine had worked, he would now be "wearing" Gunter's thumbprint – but then, when had Smithers ever let him down?

He touched his thumb with the latex covering to the screen. The machine read the thumbprint, at the same time registering the blood temperature behind it, and the door clicked open immediately. Somewhere nearby someone called out. Alex didn't move. It was one of the guards. If he came along the corridor now and saw the open door, that would be the end of it. But then he heard footsteps going up the stairs to the first floor. He looked left and right. He knew there were no cameras here but one of the guards could appear at any moment. Gunter would be back in less than twenty minutes. He had to move fast.

He went in and closed the door behind him.

The office was exactly as he had imagined it: clean, very tidy, half empty. There was a desk, a couple of chairs, a steel filing cabinet, bookshelves and very little else. A large window, barred on the outside, looked towards the main gate. This was surely where the boy had been standing, spying on Alex as he left. Fortunately Gunter had lowered the blinds before he left so Alex could move freely without fear of being seen.

He began with the desktop. There was a diary with a few notes scribbled in English, but they all seemed to relate to meetings within the school and there were no addresses or telephone numbers of any interest. Gunter had received about a dozen letters. Alex flicked through them. There were several job applications. A salesman from an alarm company was trying to make an appointment. The wife of the Italian ambassador had written to complain about locals at the school gate wolf-whistling Gabriela. There was nothing to suggest any conspiracy, but then of course Gunter was a careful man. Even though his office was locked, he wouldn't have left any evidence in view.

Alex examined the bookshelves. Gunter seemed to like murder mysteries and thrillers. There were books by Agatha Christie and Andy McNab. A guide to Egypt stood next to a thick volume called *Teach Yourself Arabic*. Neither of them seemed to have been opened. Otherwise the shelves were empty. Nor were there any pictures on the walls. The room gave the impression of someone who had just arrived or who was about to leave. Maybe Gunter didn't expect to be at Cairo College very long.

Next, Alex turned to the filing cabinet. It was locked and he was annoyed that he hadn't asked Smithers for something to help him break in. He remembered the zit cream he had been given on his first assignment. A few drops of that would have quickly burnt through the metal. Well, he could always come back to the office another time, provided he hung on to the latex thumb.

He returned to the desk and tried the drawers. The first contained pens, envelopes, a torch and a pile of report sheets which Gunter was expected to fill in every day. The second drawer looked like a medicine chest. It was crammed with different pills and a bottle of some sort of white liquid which smelled of peppermint. It reminded Alex that Gunter was a sick man, a wounded soldier – and for a brief moment, he was tempted to leave. He had no right being here, trawling through someone's private life. But it was too late to worry now. He had a job to do. He might as well get it over with.

Somebody knocked on the door.

Alex froze as a voice on the other side called out in Arabic. It might have been the guard he had heard earlier. Was he looking for Gunter? Or had he somehow worked out that there was an intruder inside? There was nothing Alex could do. If the door opened, there was nowhere to hide.

Ten seconds passed. Alex listened to the sound of his own heart. Nobody came in. Whoever had been there must have gone.

Moving more quickly now, afraid that he might be discovered at any minute, Alex tried the third drawer. It was empty apart from a couple of brochures advertising the college. He swung it shut again, then opened it a second time. Was it his imagination, or had something metallic moved, somewhere inside the drawer? He had heard it, a distinct rolling sound followed by a clunk as it hit the wooden edge. He took the brochures out. There was nothing beneath them. Unless...

Alex placed his hand flat on the bottom of the drawer and pushed. It tilted and he saw that he had discovered a false bottom: there was a secret compartment underneath. He wouldn't have ever noticed it but for an accident. A biro had somehow dropped into the hidden space and had rolled from one end to the other with the movement of the drawer.

What else was in there? Alex put his hand in and pulled out a gun, made in Russia with a star engraved in the handle. Was that something Gunter kept for his job at the school? And if so, why was it concealed here? It had been resting on top of a map ... the edge of the Sahara and an oasis town called Siwa. It seemed an unlikely holiday destination, although Cairo College did sometimes organize trips into the desert. Next out was a newspaper, a copy of the *Washington Post*, about a week old. The front page was given over to a big article about the president's plummeting approval ratings and, underneath it, a smaller one about pollution in the Gulf of Mexico. There might be something relevant inside but Alex didn't have time to read it. MI6 could buy the same edition and do that themselves. Alex memorized the date and set the paper aside.

There was nothing else in the drawer except for a bundle of photographs. Alex spread them out over the surface of the desk and examined them. Most showed a large domed building which reminded him of the Royal Albert Hall in London but which, from the palm trees that surrounded it, was more likely to be somewhere in Cairo. The pictures had been taken from every angle. There were cars parked outside and people – many of them young and carrying books – crossing the lawns that surrounded it. A school or university? This was a modern, liberated place. Some of the women were in jeans and hardly any were wearing head-scarves or veils.

And then there was a picture of a room, per-haps inside the domed building. It wasn't so much a room as a wide storage cupboard or cellar. Alex saw red tiles, old paint cans and a mop in a bucket, leaning against a wall. What on earth could Gunter want with a photograph of this? The next picture was even stranger. It was a close-up shot of a coat hook, presumably in the same room. The hook was in the middle of a brick wall, shaped like a swan's neck. The edge of the metal had caught the flash, which was blurring much of the image. It certainly wasn't going to win any prizes in a "Views of Cairo" competition.

There was one picture left. Alex turned it over and frowned. He was looking at a photograph of himself at the school gate. It showed him in full school uniform, glancing back as he left at the end of the day. The photographer must have been inside Gunter's office. Alex was in the far distance, barely more than a centimetre high. But it was certainly him. The definition was good enough for him to see his own face. Even so, there was something about it that puzzled him. He examined it carefully. There was definitely something wrong.

Alex dug out his own iPhone – a real one with an eight megapixel camera – and took snaps of all the photographs he had looked at. Then he carefully returned them with the map and newspaper to the secret drawer, making sure they were in the same order he had found them, and laid the gun on top. He wondered if MI6 would be able to make anything out of them. Well, it was up to them now. He had finally achieved something. Maybe he had even bought his ticket back home.

Finally he reached into his pocket and took out a dead cockroach with its legs bent in the air. It was, of course, a bug – one of Smithers' jokes. He placed it on the carpet, right in the corner. With a bit of luck the cleaners wouldn't hoover it up and from now on Smithers would be able to listen in on anything that was said in the room. Alex made sure he had left nothing behind, then tiptoed over to the door and listened. There was nobody outside. He slipped out into the corridor and quickly walked away.

It was almost four o'clock. He was very late leaving. If anybody asked him what he was doing, he would say he had forgotten his homework and had gone back for it. He passed the school secretary's office – it was empty – and went through the main doors, back into the searing heat of the yard. The gate was ahead of him. A couple of guards were standing there, smoking cigarettes, thinking their work was done.

And then he saw Gunter on the far side of the yard. He was talking on his mobile with his back slightly towards the school as if afraid of being seen. It was too good an opportunity to miss. Alex was already wearing his sunglasses. He stepped back into the shadows and took out his water bottle. He pointed it in the right direction and, a second later, he heard Gunter's voice so clearly, he could have been standing next to him.

"The House of Gold. Yes, of course I know it." There was a pause. "Five o'clock tomorrow. I'll come alone – do you think I'm an idiot? And if I'm satisfied, I'll authorize the final payment."

Gunter rang off, then walked away, disappearing round the side of the building. Alex waited a minute, then darted towards the main gate. Suddenly things seemed to be happening very quickly. The head of security had to be on his way to some sort of secret meeting. A payment was involved. It had to be part of the conspiracy that MI6 was looking for.

Alex passed through the gate, and suddenly he realized he was standing in exactly the same spot where his picture had been taken. And it was then he knew what was wrong.

In the photo that he had seen he had been stand-ing on his own, as he was now. But he had never once left the school on his own. He was sure of it. Simon or Craig walked home with him every day and if it wasn't them, it was Andrew or one of the other Scottish boys. There were always other kids around. Alex left at the same time as everyone else.

So where had they gone? Had they all been air-brushed out? Or was he simply wrong? Had there been a moment when his image could have been captured with nobody else about?

It didn't matter. The House of Gold at five o'clock the next day. Wherever it was, Alex planned to be there.

In his hurry to get back to the flat, he didn't look round and see Gunter emerge from the side of the school and watch him, his lips stretched in a thin smile. Nor did he hear him make a second call.

"He listened in on the conversation. He's taken the bait. He's clearly not quite as clever as he's cracked up to be. He'll be there tomorrow. I know what to do."

# THE HOUSE OF GOLD

Alex found it easily enough on the Internet. The House of Gold turned out to be some sort of shopping centre specializing in jewellery. FINE GEMS AND ALL YOUR GOLD & SILVER DREAMS. That was how it advertised itself on the website. COME AND SEEK US FOR THE BEST PRICES IN CAIRO. The name should have given it away but it still seemed an unlikely destination for a man like Erik Gunter.

"Perhaps he's just going to buy a ring for his girlfriend or wife, if he has one," Jack suggested.

"He said he was going to authorize the final payment," Alex said. "You don't do that with a wedding ring."

"It doesn't have to be a jeweller. He could be meeting anyone."

"It's a strange place to want to meet."

The two of them were sitting in the living room of their flat. Jack had been waiting for Alex with two glasses of ice-cold lemonade and a plate of sandwiches; he was normally hungry when he got

225

back from school. Outside, the pool was crowded; there was a rough version of water polo going on and Craig and Jodie had called out to Alex to join them as he passed. But he had gone straight to the computer: **houseofgold.com**. Then he had told Jack what had happened, and what he had found inside Gunter's office. It wasn't a lot to go on, he realized. Not after almost three weeks in Egypt.

"He wasn't buying jewellery," Alex insisted. "He sounded ... I don't know ... mysterious. As if he didn't want to be overheard."

"You're sure he wasn't leading you on? Maybe he wants you to follow him."

Alex shook his head. "He couldn't have known I was listening to him. I was miles away, on the other side of the yard."

"What about the pictures you found in his desk?" Jack had Alex's iPhone. She flicked through the images on the screen.

"I don't know. We'd better pass them on to Smithers. He can send them to MI6. Why would anyone take a photo of a hook on a wall? And what's this building? Do you think it's somewhere in Cairo?"

Jack held up the iPhone. "Nice shot of you," she said.

"Yes. But if Gunter took it, then it means he knows who I am."

"Not necessarily."

"Why else would he have it? You think he takes photos of all the new students?"

They fell silent. Jack had been out in the sun and she was looking tanned. They both were. It reminded Alex how long they'd been away.

"What are you going to do about Gunter?"

"I suppose I'd better follow him." Alex went on before she could argue. "I'll make sure he doesn't see me, Jack. But I know that the House of Gold has got something to do with whatever's going on. Five o'clock. I can go there after school."

"You mean *we* can go there after school. That's why I'm here, Alex. I'm keeping an eye on you."

"Thanks, Jack." Alex gulped down his lemonade. It was deliciously cold. "I'm really glad you came."

"Are you?"

"I don't know what I'd do without you. You're always there for me. And you make the best sandwiches."

Jack smiled. "You'd better get on with your homework," she said. "You don't want Miss Watson breathing down your neck."

An hour and a half of French grammar. Alex wondered if there were any other secret agents in Cairo being sent upstairs to do their homework. But he didn't complain. And an hour later, immersed in the future perfect of *avoir* and *être*, he was almost grateful that he could put everything else out of his mind.

\* \* \*

The next day was a Wednesday. It was also the day when Alex realized that his time at Cairo College was drawing to a close.

He was having lunch with Andrew and some of the Scottish boys, when one of the sixth-formers came over to their table. It was unusual for the older students to mix with the Year Tens but he realized that this one was examining him. He looked up into a face that he vaguely recognized: dark spiky hair, blue eyes, pockmarked cheeks.

"Alex?" the boy said. "You don't remember me?"

Alex did remember him. But he pretended not to.

"I'm Graham Barnes. I was at Brookland until last year when my dad got sent out here. You're Alex Rider, aren't you?"

It was the worst coincidence in the world. In their first term at Brookland new pupils were paired up with sixth-formers, more or less the same system that they had here. Alex had been looked after – quite well – by Graham. There was no point denying who he was.

"Yes," he said. "That's me."

"Rider?" Andrew made a face. "I thought your name was Brenner."

"My mother remarried." It was the first thing Alex could think of to say. "Before she died," he added weakly.

"Yeah. Well, it's good to see you." Graham nodded at the other kids. "I'll see you around."

The rest of them went on talking as they had before, but Alex noticed Andrew glancing at him once or twice and knew that he had been caught out. Andrew might not know the reason but he knew that Alex had lied. It was like the seed of a poisonous plan – and very quickly it would start to grow.

The day seemed to last for ever as far as Alex was concerned, but at last three thirty came and with it the end of school. The usual fleet of buses arrived, clumsily manoeuvring around each other in the space outside the main gate. Most of the school left on foot and Alex was among them. He noticed that Andrew avoided him. And maybe he had spoken to Craig and Simon, because even they left him alone.

He was glad to see Jack, who was waiting for him beside a black and white cab. "Are you sure about this?" she asked.

Alex nodded. He was more sure of it than ever. "Let's go," he said.

The two of them got in and Jack leaned forward and gave the driver his instructions. She had printed out the home page for the House of Gold and the address was there in Arabic as well as English. She also made sure that the meter was actually running. It was a common trick for Cairo drivers to leave it off and then charge double when they arrived.

The traffic in Cairo was as bad as ever, the air full of exhaust fumes and bad-tempered hooting. By the time the driver dropped them outside a smart hotel next to the river, Alex and Jack were grateful to get out. Jack had brought Alex a change of clothes and he had wriggled into them on the back seat. Now he was wearing a khaki T-shirt, knee-length shorts and sandals. Jack took care of his uniform. Dressed in two shades of blue, he would have stood out at twenty paces.

It was only now that they saw the House of Gold wasn't a house at all. It was an old paddle steamer, like something out of another age, permanently moored on the sluggish brown water of the Nile. The boat was three levels high, painted white, with two huge paddles at the back and a single funnel close to the bow. At some point it had been converted into a gaggle of jewellery shops, each one built into the old cabins and staterooms. A gangplank led up from the quay. The boat's name was written in gold over the entrance on the main deck.

"What now?" Jack asked.

"We wait," Alex said.

They found a little park with trees shading them from the sun and sat down on a wooden bench, tucked out of sight. From here they could see everyone entering or leaving the boat. Alex looked at his watch. It was five to five.

"I should come with you," Jack said.

"No. It's better if you stay here. If anything happens, you can call for help."

*If anything happens.* Three small words. But Alex knew how easily they could tear his life apart.

And then another taxi drew up and Erik Gunter got out. He had on the same black suit that he wore at school and a small backpack on his shoulder. He paid the driver, then made his way up the gangplank and onto the boat. Alex didn't hesitate. He was already on his feet following, leaving Jack behind. And with all his attention focused on the head of security, he didn't notice the grey Chevrolet parked in the street, on the other side of the park. Nor did he see the two men sitting inside it, watching the paddle steamer just like him. But they saw him.

"Hey – that kid. Quickly. Get his picture." The man spoke with an American accent.

"Why? What do you—?"

"Just do it."

The second man raised a Nikon D3 digital SLR camera and pressed the button, capturing Alex as he reached the gangplank, as he stepped on it, as he began to climb. "What are you interested in a kid for?" he demanded sourly.

"I know who that kid is," the first man replied. "And you'd better get ready. It looks like we've got trouble."

Erik Gunter made his way through the *House of Gold*, squeezing between the tourists and local visitors who crowded out the narrow passages.

There were shops and stalls on both sides with jewellers standing outside, some of them wearing the dark red Egyptian fez, like magicians about to do card tricks. There was jewellery everywhere: the same necklaces and brooches that hung in every souk in Cairo. Little pyramids on chains, Egyptian hieroglyphs, lucky cats, scarabs, portraits of Queen Nefertiti and Tutankhamen ... thousands and thousands of different pieces on sale, all of them overpriced, half of them fake.

Gunter stopped next to one of the stalls. Immediately the owner, a fat little man, was beside him. "What you want? I show you the best. I make you the best price."

Gunter ignored him. There was a mirror on the counter and he reached out and tilted it, as if examining himself. But in fact he was looking back the way he'd come, over his shoulder. And there he was, skulking in the doorway of an antique shop about fifteen metres behind him. Alex Rider. Gunter almost smiled to himself. It was just as he had said. This fifteen-year-old whizz kid from British intelligence wasn't quite so smart after all.

The trap was set. Everything was in its right place. Now all he had to do was finish it.

He continued forward until he arrived at a doorway with a closed sign – the one place on the paddle steamer that wasn't ready for business. He rang a bell and waited. There was a buzz and the door clicked open. He paused for a moment, then went in.

The shop sold antique weapons. There were hundreds of them spread out on shelves and in glass cases, and hanging from the walls on hooks. Gunter ran his eye over swords and sabres, flintlock pistols, old army rifles and muskets, and daggers with huge jewels set in the hilts. It was an interesting collision, he thought. Beauty and death. All these weapons had once been used by armies or nomadic tribes. The blades had severed flesh and bone. The guns had cut down men, women and children, sending them crashing into the sand. And now they were being sold as ornaments to hang in people's houses. Gunter wouldn't have been able to live with them. He knew too well the truth about the pain that these things brought.

An old man, an Egyptian, had appeared behind the counter: round glasses, thin face, an old-fashioned wing collar and tie. He hadn't shaved, and grey hair had spread over his chin and cheeks as if they were diseased. He had narrow lips and bad teeth. His fingers were long and very precise – like those of a pianist. This was a man who had spent his whole life working with his hands.

"Mr Habib?" Gunter asked.

"That is my name." He spoke perfect English.

"I'm Erik Gunter. I think you were expecting me."

The old man didn't move. Gunter reached into his pocket and placed a small metal object on the counter. It was a silver scorpion.

The old man nodded slowly. "I was indeed expecting you," he said.

"Do you have it?"

"Of course."

Habib reached below the counter and produced another gun. But there was nothing antique about this one. It was an L96A1 Arctic Warfare sniper rifle, gleaming and deadly, a perfectly machined and balanced piece of equipment. He laid it out for Gunter to examine. "I have made all the adjustments as requested," he said. "Particularly to the trigger and the static iron sights."

"What about the ammo?"

"I will supply you with fifty 8.59mm bullets. The gun has a ten-round box magazine."

"Can it be traced?"

Habib looked pained. "I do not ask you foolish questions, Mr Gunter. I do not ask why you require a piece of killing machinery as finely crafted as this. I would suggest you do the same."

"I apologize, Mr Habib," Gunter said and, reaching behind him, drew a pistol out from the waistband of his trousers and shot the Egyptian once, in the middle of his forehead. There had been almost no sound. The pistol was silenced. The Egyptian stared, as if he couldn't quite believe what had happened, then slumped forward. Gunter snatched the rifle up. He didn't want it to be contaminated by the rapidly spreading pool of blood.

Moving quickly, he went behind the counter

and found what he was looking for: a golf bag, big enough to hold the rifle. He took a cloth out of his backpack and wiped the barrel clean. This was the only part of the gun he had touched and he wasn't going to leave fingerprints. Using the cloth, he lowered the L96A1 into the bag and zipped it shut. Finally he reached into the backpack and found a cumbersome package with several wires and a switch. He flicked the switch, closed the backpack and stuffed it behind the counter. He took one last look around. Then he left, satisfied with what he had done.

In his haste he didn't quite close the door.

Alex Rider saw him go past. He noticed that Gunter had swapped the backpack for what looked like a golf bag. For a moment, the two of them were almost next to each other. Alex was inside one of the stalls, pretending to examine a mother-of-pearl jewellery box. He glanced back as Gunter disappeared, then stepped out into the corridor. The obvious thing would be to follow the head of security. That was what Gunter seemed to be inviting. But then he noticed that the door of the shop wasn't quite closed.

He took out his iPhone and texted Jack. **Gunter leaving. Follow him. Will meet later.** That was him taken care of. Now to see whom he had met and, perhaps, what he had been given.

Alex made his way down the corridor, pushing

through the crowds. The *House of Gold* had an air conditioning system but even so it felt hot and sticky. A couple of salesmen waved gold necklaces at him but he ignored them. He reached the door and gently pushed it open. It took his eyes a few moments to get used to the gloom. His gaze swept over all the weapons. The place was like a medieval arsenal. Then he saw the man lying with the top part of his body on the counter and his arms spread out protectively around him. He could have been asleep but Alex knew instantly that he wasn't. And it wasn't a red cushion beneath his head. He could smell the blood in the sluggish air.

He backed out fast. He knew that he had finally arrived at the heart of the conspiracy. Gunter had just killed this man and it was easy enough to guess what he had been carrying in the golf bag. But still it made no sense. Was he acting alone or was he part of a larger organization? And what was the connection with Cairo College? Despite everything, this trail had led him nowhere. He still had no idea what was going on.

Alex was feeling sick. He just wanted to get back into the open air and he wished now that he hadn't sent the instruction to Jack. Gunter was a killer. If Jack got too close, she could be in danger. He would call her again, the moment he was out. But for now he was fighting his way back down the corridor. The gold and silver jewellery seemed to hammer at him from every direction. He was almost suffocating.

And then there was an explosion. Alex was blown off his feet and he felt the entire paddle steamer tilt violently to one side. All around him people began to scream, thrown off balance. Gold chains, ornaments and brass plates came raining down. At the same time, a plume of black smoke came surging through the corridor, instantly wiping out his vision. He could hardly breathe. All the electric lights had gone off.

Somebody fell on top of him. He pushed them off and crawled onto his hands and knees. The steamer rocked back again; it was like being on some hideous fairground ride. The crowds were still screaming. And then there was a gushing sound and Alex felt water – warm and evil-smelling – surge around his hands and knees. God! Erik Gunter – or someone working with him – had blown a hole in the side of the paddle steamer and it was sinking. If he didn't get out, he would go down with it.

Everyone else had had the same idea. The jewellers were stuffing necklaces and chains into their pockets, saving what they could. They had forgotten that once they were in the water it would only drag them down. The floor moved again, slanting backwards, and Alex found himself clawing his way uphill. There were people everywhere, all around him. He drew next to a sobbing Egyptian girl who couldn't have been more than six years old. She was on her own. He reached out and put an arm round her, pulling her with him. Behind him he heard the sound of shattering glass. One of the counters had come loose and rolled down the deck into the wall. Gold coins and medals exploded out of it.

The girl was snatched away. Her father or uncle had found her and took her without a word of thanks. Alex could see the exit in front of him, a rectangle of light that slanted heavily to one side. He climbed towards it, dragging himself up with his hands. A minute later, he was out on the open deck, sucking in the air, still tasting the smoke. The gangplank had fallen away. The paddle steamer was jammed into the side of the quay as if it had just crashed into it. Alex saw that the thick mooring ropes were preventing it from sinking altogether, although they were already straining and would surely snap at any moment. People were hurling themselves over the side. Some of them preferred the river to the hard fall and solid concrete below. Alex decided to join them. He was already soaking wet. There was no point in risking a broken leg.

He slid down the deck and dived into the murky water of the Nile. He vaguely wondered what germs he was exposing himself to. He broke the surface and swam towards the quay, making his way through the pieces of debris that floated all over the surface. At the same time, he noticed half-naked Egyptian boys diving off the edge into the water. They weren't trying to help anyone. They were scavengers, looking for anything of value that might float.

Jack, of course, was gone. How would he contact her now? His iPhone would be ruined. Alex reached the side of the quay and pulled himself out. He examined himself. At least he wasn't hurt. But he was filthy and battered by the force of the blast. He could taste the Nile water on his lips and wondered how many millions of germs he had managed to swallow. The bomb hadn't killed him; the river quite possibly might.

He crossed the quay, making for the park where he and Jack had waited. He guessed that as soon as she heard what had happened, she would make her way back to the same spot. He found the bench and sat down heavily. All around him people were milling past, many of them dripping wet. There were white-suited police officers everywhere, already taking command, blowing whistles and shouting out orders. Of course, the police were all over Cairo. This was a country that was always on high alert against terrorism. They would have spent months training for an event just like this. Alex shook his head. How could this have happened? It was the last thing he had expected.

And then there was a man standing in front of him. Alex looked up.

"Come with me," the man said.

"What?"

The man opened his jacket, revealing a gun in

a holster under his arm. "You heard what I said."

A second man had crept up behind him and dragged him to his feet. Both of them were in their thirties, clean-shaven, with sunglasses. The man with the gun had spoken with an American accent.

"We have a car. We're going to walk you there. If you try anything, we'll shoot."

Alex didn't doubt them. There was a seriousness about them, a sense that they knew exactly what they were doing. This was something they had done before. One man stood in front of him; the other was right behind. Alex was pulled up and frogmarched out of the park and into the road. There was a grey Chevrolet parked right in front of him. For a brief moment he considered a countermove. Right now, before it was too late, jabbing with an elbow then swinging round to kick out.

But the first man had been expecting it. Suddenly Alex's arm was seized and twisted behind his back. "Don't even think about it," the man warned.

Alex was bundled in. He was face down on the back seat of the Chevrolet. The door slammed. Both men got into the front.

The road was clogged up with traffic but the car swerved round, performing a U-turn. And then they were clear, picking up speed, leaving the dead man and the wreckage of the *House of Gold* far behind.

# THE BELL ROOM

They drove for forty minutes, heading for one of the many suburbs that were hardly separate from the city itself. That was the thing about Cairo. It was almost impossible to say where one area ended and the next began. If ever a city could be described as sprawling, this was it.

Alex tried to work out where they were going but soon gave up. He was lying on the back seat with his head facing the floor. This was what the two men had instructed. For the first part of the journey, he did what he was told, feeling as the car lurched left and right like a rat caught in a maze. But the further they went from the *House of Gold*, the more the two men relaxed, and he was able to twist round so that at least he had a partial view out of the window. Most of what he saw was sky but a few landmarks flashed by – the hideous modern construction that was the Cairo Tower, the American University, the minaret of one of the main mosques. Alex made a mental note of each one. Later on, it might help to work out where he had been taken.

He had been dripping wet when the journey began but gradually – a combination of the heat and the air conditioning – he dried out a little as they continued. Eventually the driver signalled and the car began to slow down. Alex guessed they had arrived and he suddenly sat up, determined to see where they were.

He was pushed down immediately, but in that one brief second, he was just able to see an old-fashioned, possibly abandoned office block and a sign that read CAIRO ISLAMIC AUTHORITY before they turned off the road and drove down a ramp leading under the building.

The Cairo Islamic Authority? Alex wondered what he had got himself into. Why should a religious group have any interest in him?

The car stopped. There was a third man waiting for them. The back door was thrown open and Alex was dragged out. He found himself standing in a drab underground car park illuminated by strip lights that threw a hard white gloss over the concrete walls and floors. One of the lights was malfunctioning, buzzing and flickering. It made the place seem more nightmarish. There were about a dozen cars already parked but no other drivers. Alex was alone with three dangerous men. Their hostility bristled in the air.

For the moment, none of them spoke and Alex

was able to examine them for the first time. They were all of a type, about the same age, all in dark suits and white ties. They reminded Alex of the sort of people who went round towns, knocking on doors, trying to convert you to some religion. The man who had first approached him – and who seemed to be in charge – was built like an American football player, with huge shoulders and a thick neck. He had a small, upturned nose, fair hair cut like a nail brush and watery, blue eyes. His partner was similarly built, fit, possibly ex-army. His hair was dark and he was obviously mixed race – Native American, maybe. The third man, the one who had been waiting, was black, angry-looking, smaller and lighter on his feet than the others. He was staring at Alex in disbelief.

"Is this him?" he demanded.

"Yeah." The fair-haired one nodded.

"What about Habib?"

"Habib is probably dead. The boat blew up."

"What?"

"You heard what I said, Franklin. Right now, the *House of Gold* is on the bottom of the Nile. And this kid was there—"

"I had nothing to do with it," Alex said.

"Shut up!" Fair Hair snapped out the two words.

"What are we going to do with him, Lewinsky?" Franklin, the black man, asked.

"We're going to take him to the bell room."

"Whoa!" The second man was unhappy. "We can't do that!"

"We don't have time to talk about this," Lewinsky snarled. "And we're not going to discuss it in front of him. We need answers to questions and we need them now. So let's take him down and get on with it."

Down? They were already in the basement. Alex didn't like the sound of this or the way things were going.

"You're making a mistake—" he began.

"Save your breath," Lewinsky said. "You're going to need it."

Alex felt a hand shove him in the back and he was propelled towards a lift. The second man pressed the button and the doors slid open at once. The lift was a steel box. It was like walking into a refrigerator. The four of them bundled in and they were carried down. Alex was trying to quell a rising sense of panic. Too much had happened in the past hour – the discovery of the dead man, the explosion, the way he had been kidnapped in broad daylight. He had no idea who these people were or what they wanted. And what was the bell room?

But more than anything, he was desperately worried about Jack. He had sent her chasing after Erik Gunter. Right now, he needed to warn her about what he had seen on the boat. She needed to know the danger she was in. And it might well be that she had heard about the explosion. If so, she would be sick with worry herself. The least he could do was tell her he was still alive.

"I want to talk to Jack," Alex said.

"Who's Jack?" Lewinsky asked.

"She's a friend. She looks after me."

"What? You mean she's your nanny?"

Alex ignored the taunt. "I have her mobile number." There was no response. "I just want to let her know that I'm OK," he said.

Lewinsky smiled unpleasantly. "What makes you think you're OK?"

They had travelled some distance underground. Alex could feel it in his stomach and in the sense of weight pressing on his shoulders. The lift doors slid open to reveal a short, windowless corridor leading to a single wooden door at the end. Somehow Alex knew he didn't want to find out what was on the other side. But he had no choice. Franklin and the unnamed man had already left the lift. Lewinsky laid a heavy hand on his shoulder and pushed him forward.

He walked down the corridor with a sense of dread, a long shadow stretching ahead of him. Franklin opened the door. It led into a large room that was indeed shaped like the inside of a bell, round with bare brick walls that narrowed as they rose at least two storeys above his head. Alex didn't like anything he saw. The room had no windows and was lit by a single bulb dangling on a wire. The door was soundproofed. The floor was covered with a thick rubber mat. In the middle was a wooden chair, and to one side a narrow table constructed so that one end sloped downwards. The table had three leather belts and Alex could see at once that they were meant for him: one for his ankles, one for his stomach, one for his shoulders and arms. There were a bucket and a tap. The room had been designed for one purpose. There was no escaping it. It screamed at him everywhere he looked.

Lewinsky gestured at the chair. "Take a seat."

"I'm OK standing."

"You want to quit wisecracking and do as you're told? I can make this much, much worse for you."

"Why don't you tell me who you are?"

Franklin and the other man exchanged a look but Lewinsky didn't blink. "You're the one who's going to answer the questions," he said. "Now sit down!"

Alex went over to the chair. He sat down and watched with a mixture of curiosity and disgust as Lewinsky leaned down and pulled off his damp sandals. Meanwhile, Franklin closed the door. Lewinsky straightened up and stood in front of him. Alex's clothes were sticking to him. His bare feet dangled above the floor.

"Let's start at the beginning," Lewinsky said. "What were you doing on the paddle steamer?"

"What do you think I was doing?" Alex replied. "I was buying a present for my teacher. I'm a schoolboy. I go to the Cairo International College of Arts and Education. You can ring them if you don't believe me."

"Right – let's cut this out and get one thing straight," Lewinsky spat. "I know exactly who you are. You're not a schoolboy – or at least, you may be. But you're also a spy working for the British secret service. Your name is Alex Rider. So let me ask you again. What are you doing here in Cairo? Why were you on that boat?"

Alex's head spun. He wasn't quite sure how to respond. These people knew who he was. But how? Cairo Islamic Authority. Who were they?

"Look, I don't know who you people are or what you want," Alex said. "But I've got nothing to tell you." He sighed. There didn't seem any point holding information back. They would beat it out of him anyway. And why should he suffer in silence to protect MI6? It wasn't as if he had chosen to work for them. "I was following someone," he said. "A man called Erik Gunter. He's the head of security at Cairo College."

"Why were you following him?"

"To see where he went!" Alex couldn't resist the answer but immediately regretted it, seeing Lewinsky's face darken. "There's a possible threat against the school," he went on. "I thought Gunter might be part of it. I heard him talking on the phone and he led me to the *House of Gold*."

"And then?"

"He went into a shop. It was full of old weapons. I went in afterwards and saw a dead man there. I think Gunter must have shot him."

"Describe this dead man."

Alex did the best he could. "He was old. He had grey hair. To be honest with you, I didn't look at him that closely. There was a lot of blood."

"Habib..." Franklin muttered. "Habib's dead?"

"That's right. I saw the body and I left the shop and about ten seconds later the whole ship blew up. That's all I know – and if you want to interrogate anyone, you should be looking for Gunter. I can get you his address if you like. It might stop you wasting your time with me."

Lewinsky considered for a moment. Alex could almost see the thought processes whirring behind his eyes. At last he came to a conclusion and Alex knew at once that it was the wrong one. "You're working for MI6," he said.

"Yes."

"Why are you in Cairo?"

"I've already told you."

"I don't believe you."

Suddenly Alex had had enough. "Then why don't you go and —— yourself." He spat out the swear word. "What's the point of asking me questions if you don't believe the answers?"

"You can make us believe you."

"And how do I do that?"

Lewinsky must have given a signal, because the other two men grabbed hold of Alex and pulled him to his feet. There was nothing he could do; they were much stronger than he was. They hauled him over to the table and forced him down on his back. Then, while Franklin held him, the man with no name tied his ankles, arms and chest, pulling the belts tight. When they stepped back, Alex couldn't move. He was lying at a slant with his bare feet slightly above his head. Meanwhile, Lewinsky had filled the bucket with water from the tap. It was the last thing Alex saw. A moment later, a black hood was drawn over his head, blocking his sight and much of his air.

And with a surge of panic that he couldn't control, Alex knew what they were going to do. He knew what this was called. Waterboarding. It was a method of torture that American soldiers had supposedly used in Guantánamo Bay, one that they favoured because it left no bruises or signs of injury. And yet it was horribly effective. Alex had read somewhere that a grown man was unlikely to last more than fourteen seconds before he begged to tell his inquisitors everything.

In short, they were going to drown him.

"I want to know why you're here and what really happened on that boat." Lewinsky's voice was muffled. It came out of nowhere.

"I've told you!" Alex shouted through the hood.

"You haven't told me anything. But you will..."

Alex felt the extra weight as a towel was laid across his face. Desperately he shook his head from side to side, trying to throw it off, but then two hands clamped down on him, holding him still.

Alex's hands curled. All the muscles in his legs and abdomen loosened as sheer terror took control. And then the first drops of water were poured onto the towel. He felt the dampness against his face and immediately afterwards the first symptoms of suffocation. He couldn't breathe. Worse than that. His lungs were tearing themselves apart, his whole body trying to swallow itself. He was going mad.

"What the hell is going on in here? What do you think you're doing?"

It was a new voice, coming from somewhere miles away. Alex tried to scream. No sound came out. He thought he was about to die.

"Get that thing off him!"

There was a hand scrabbling at his face. The towel had gone. The hood was torn off and light and air hit him at the same time. Alex was gasping. His mouth was wide open. He knew he wouldn't have been able to survive a second longer.

A man loomed over him and at that moment, Alex knew exactly where he was and who these people were. He would almost have laughed if he hadn't still been in shock. He should have recognized the sign. In Miami they had been Centurion International Advertising. In New York it was Creative Ideas Animation. And here – Cairo Islamic Authority. Always the same initials. CIA.

The man's name was Joe Byrne. He was black, in his sixties, with white hair, a moustache and the earnest, caring face of a family doctor about to deliver bad news. Alex had met him twice before and, despite everything, knew him to be a decent man, one who was usually on his side.

"Alex, I don't know what to say..." Byrne exclaimed. The belts had been untied and Alex had been helped to sit upright. "I only just heard what was going on."

"Sir—" Lewinsky began.

"Save it for the court martial, Lewinsky," Byrne snapped. "God in heaven! What did you three think you were doing? This is a kid!"

"He's a British spy!" Lewinsky insisted.

"He's on our side. He's helped us on two separate occasions. If it wasn't for Alex Rider, Washington DC would no longer exist. Get out of here! I don't want to see any of you right now. I'll talk to you later!" The three men left. Byrne turned back to Alex. "Are you feeling strong enough to get out of here?" he asked. "Or do you need more time?"

"I'm fine." Alex was still in shock but he slid himself off the table and picked up his sandals.

Byrne waited until he'd put them on. "Let's get some coffee in my office," he suggested.

He led Alex out of the bell room and back to the lift. They took it up to the ground floor, neither of them speaking. Alex guessed that Byrne was giving him a few moments to recover – or maybe he was still fuming with anger himself. This time the doors opened onto a more comfortable area with a reception desk, potted plants, mirrors and chandeliers. "We rent this place from the Egyptian government," Byrne explained. "Half of it is pretty run-down but the rest of it is fine for our needs. This way..."

Byrne's office was on the same level, with smoked glass blocking out the view. Alex remembered his room in Miami. This one was almost exactly the same, with fairly standard furniture, a thick-pile carpet and a picture of the American president on the wall. The CIA had offices all over the world and they were probably all identical. Byrne waved Alex to a seat, then picked up the phone and ordered two coffees. He sat down himself.

"First of all, I'm sorry about Blake Lewinsky," Byrne began. "He's not actually a bad agent but this new breed ... they're young and have no sense of proportion. Ever since 9/11 you only have to whisper the word 'terrorism' and everyone starts behaving like Nazis or fascists. But this time he went too far. I swear to you, Alex, I'll have him sent back to Langley and he'll end up working in the canteen!"

"Forget it," Alex said. "He didn't hurt me."

"He would have if I hadn't arrived in time." Byrne sighed. "I'm afraid there are some questions I have to ask you..."

"There's not much I can tell you," Alex said. "But first I'd like to call Jack Starbright, if you don't mind."

"Sure. Be my guest."

Byrne handed Alex the phone and he dialled Jack's mobile. It rang several times, then went to voicemail. That worried Alex. There were plenty of areas in Cairo where it was impossible to get a signal, but he still wouldn't be able to relax until he had spoken to her. "Jack," he said. "It's me. I'm OK. I'll meet you back at the flat." He didn't want to add any more with Byrne listening. He hung up.

The door opened and a young woman came in with two cups of coffee and a plate of biscuits. She set them down and left again.

"You know, Alex, I can't believe you're out here," Byrne said. "Don't tell me Alan Blunt persuaded you to work for him again!"

Alex didn't answer. He trusted Byrne but he also felt uneasy being trapped between the two intelligence services. He would have to be careful what he said.

"So why are you here, Alex?"

"Why don't you start by telling me what you're up to?" Alex replied. "Why were your men watching the *House of Gold*? And who is Habib?"

"Did you meet with him?"

"No. Your men asked me about him. But by the time I saw him, he was already dead."

"You didn't shoot him then?" It was impossible to say if Byrne was joking or not.

"Of course I didn't."

Byrne nodded. "I believe you. This whole thing is a mess. It's just a miracle that no one from that paddle steamer was killed. Apart from Habib, that is." He paused. "All right, Alex. I'll tell you what's going on. I guess I owe you that much. But if you're involved – you and MI6 – I want to know. Is that a deal?"

"Sure." Alex helped himself to a coffee.

"OK. We're out here because the secretary of state is arriving this weekend. I don't know how acquainted you are with American politics, but our secretary of state is like your foreign secretary. You could say she's number two after the president – in fact, there are a lot of people who say she could be the next president. She's outspoken and she's a hardliner but she's also very popular. And she's about to give a speech in Cairo."

Byrne took his own coffee. He looked uncomfortable about what he was about to say, unsure whether he should give away his secrets, but then he made up his mind and went on. "This is being hushed up at the moment, but the speech is all about power. Who are the big hitters in the world right now? When it comes to talking about the important issues – nuclear weapons, war, terrorism – who should be sitting at the top table? Up to now it's always been the Americans, you British, the Europeans and so on. But there are new powers in the world. The Chinese. India. She thinks it's time to make a few changes. And – you're not going to like this, Alex – she doesn't think the Brits have a place any more."

"It doesn't matter to me one way or the other," Alex said.

"No, of course not. Why should it? But it's going to make a lot of your politicians very angry. If you ask me, the secretary of state is playing politics. It's coming up to election time and there's a lot of anti-British feeling in the States right now. You remember that big oil spill in the Gulf of Mexico? And then there was that secret deal with Libya. A speech like this will make all the right head-lines – for her. She's way out of line. Even the president has tried to rein her in. But she's going ahead anyway."

"How does Habib fit into this?"

"I'm coming to him. Our job is to protect the sec-retary of state while she's in Cairo. It doesn't matter what she's doing or saying; that has nothing to do with us. We're just here – we've been here for two weeks now – to look after her. And a few days ago we got a tip-off that somebody might take a shot at her to prevent her making the speech."

"Habib..."

"That was just one of the names he used. Mostly he was known as the Engineer. He sold weapons, Alex. Very precise, high-calibre weapons such as sniper rifles. Actually, he'd provide you with any-thing from a samurai sword to a hand grenade. But he was a craftsman. Everything he supplied was deadly accurate. Now do you begin to get the picture? We receive a tip-off. We know that the Engineer is in town, so we start to watch him. And then, three days before our secretary of state is about to make a big, anti-British speech, a British secret agent turns up and – boom – there's an explosion and Habib is shot."

Byrne slumped in his chair. Maybe it was the heat. Maybe he was feeling his age.

"I'm not saying that Blake Lewinsky was right, but perhaps it explains what he did to you. Habib was dead and he needed to know why."

Alex's mind was in a whirl. There was so much he had to take on board. The main question was – how much should he tell Joe Byrne?

First, Erik Gunter. When he left the boat, he'd been carrying a golf bag and Alex had no doubt now that it must have had some sort of weapon inside. Was he here to assassinate the American secretary of state? And if so, who was paying him? Then there were the pictures he had seen in Gunter's desk. He couldn't show them to Byrne as his iPhone had been destroyed by the Nile water. But the building, the room, the *Washington Post* ... they all had to be connected. And what about Cairo College? That was the reason he had been sent here. It was the school, not some American politician, that was meant to be the target.

He needed to see Smithers. That was the impor-tant thing. Smithers could talk to Blunt and Blunt could talk to Byrne. Suddenly Alex felt an overwhelming desire to get out of Cairo. He didn't understand why, but he didn't like the way this was going. Not for the first time, he had a sense of invisible forces...

*The boy at the window.*

*Julius G added you as a friend on Facebook.*

...wheels within wheels. There was something happening here in Egypt that none of them understood.

"There's not much I can tell you, Mr Byrne." Alex found himself talking before he even knew quite what he was going to say. "The reason I'm in Cairo has nothing to do with your secretary of state. I was simply sent here to keep an eye on the Cairo International College of Arts and Education in Sheikh Zayed City. There's a possibility that some of the students may be targeted; I don't know much more than that. I was following their head of security, a man called Erik Gunter, and he led me to the *House of Gold*. I told Lewinsky this but he didn't believe me. Gunter was the last person to see Habib alive. I think he was the one who killed him, and if I were you I'd strap *him* to your table and see where you get with the water torture, and leave me alone."

Alex stood up. "And now I'd like to go home. I'm worried about Jack."

Byrne nodded. "And I'd better put a call in to your Mr Blunt," he said. "By the way, I hear he's on the way out."

Alex was surprised to hear it. "He's retiring?"

"Not by choice." Byrne reached for the telephone. "I'll get a car to take you home. Once again, I'm sorry about what happened."

A few moments later, the woman who had brought the coffee came back in and led Alex out to the street. Joe Byrne stayed where he was, deep in thought. Despite all the evidence, he had never believed that there was a British plot to kill the secretary of state. Now, after what Alex had told him, he wondered if he should change his mind. For a start, there needed to be round-the-clock surveillance on this man Gunter. He would raise the security level to red and order another search of the Grand Hall, where the speech was to take place. It had been searched twice already and on Friday night, twenty-four hours before the secretary of state arrived, it would be sealed.

The Grand Hall. A huge domed building surrounded by palm trees in the middle of the University of Cairo. How could he ever hope to make such a place completely secure?

And what of Alex Rider? With a bit of luck he'd be on the next plane back to England. Safely out of the picture. In fact, if the boy had had any sense, he would never have come at all.

# PLAN A ... PLAN B

Jack was waiting for Alex when he got back to Golden Palm Heights. In fact she was out and running towards him before the CIA driver had even come to a halt. She half dragged him out of the car and into her embrace. "Alex? What happened to you? I've been so worried." She pulled away from him. "Your clothes are wet!"

"Yes. I took a dip in the Nile."

"You were on the boat when...?" She didn't want to put it into words. "I couldn't believe it when I saw what had happened. For a minute, I thought ... well, I didn't know what to think. But then I got your message."

The CIA car drove off.

Jack noticed it as if for the first time. "Who was that?" she asked.

"It's a long story, Jack. If you don't mind, I'm going to have a shower and get changed first. I stink. And I don't suppose you've got anything for supper? I'm starving."

A short while later, Alex and Jack sat down to eat together on the balcony, allowing the warmth of the evening to wash over them. The sun was dipping behind the buildings, throwing soft shadows across the complex. The pool was empty. Alex knew that Craig and Simon and all the others would be inside by now, slumped over their homework. He wished he had so little to worry about.

Alex had changed into a baggy T-shirt and shorts. His hair was still wet from the shower and there was a plaster on his knee. He wasn't even sure when he'd scratched himself but Jack had noticed it at once and had insisted on rubbing in half a tube of antiseptic cream. He had, after all, taken a dip in the Nile. It reminded Alex of all the times she had looked after him in the past. Some things never changed.

She had prepared an assortment of Egyptian dishes: hummus, olives, stuffed vine leaves, fried meatballs and smoked aubergine – all served with warm *aash baladi* or Egyptian flatbread. She was drinking chilled pink wine. Alex stuck to water.

"I was sitting outside the *House of Gold*, wondering what was going on, when I got your text," she said. "I didn't like the idea of leaving you but I waited for Gunter to come out and I followed him like you told me to. He looked like he was going to play golf or something. He had a golf bag..."

"I know."

"Well, he flagged down a taxi and I managed

to get one just behind him. It was like being in a film. I followed him all the way across Cairo and I thought he might be going somewhere exciting, but in the end he went into a flat just round the corner from here. I made a note of the address; I think it's where he lives. Anyway, after that I wasn't sure what to do, but I was worried about you so I went all the way back to the *House of Gold* – except it wasn't there any more. There were police everywhere and they were talking about a terrorist attack or something. My first thought was to call Mr Smithers but when I took out my mobile I saw that you'd rung. I got your message and rushed back here."

She poured herself another glass of wine. "Now it's your turn. What happened on the boat? How did you escape? And who was the man in the car?"

Quickly Alex told her about his ordeal, starting with the dead man in the antique shop, the explosion, his capture by the CIA and the bell room. He left out the waterboarding. He didn't really want to relive the experience and he knew Jack would have been sickened. "That was a CIA car that brought me here," he concluded. "At least they were decent enough to give me a lift."

Jack shook her head. "This is absolutely typical of Mr Blunt," she said. "He promised us there wouldn't be any danger, but we've already got dead bodies on boats, bombs and threats of political assassination. So what are we going to do?"

The question had been hanging in the air since

he got back and Alex had already been considering the answer. "I think it's time to do what Mr Byrne suggested," he said. "We ought to leave."

"Back to England?"

"I suppose so." Alex had eaten enough. He put down his knife and fork and leaned back contentedly. In the distance he could hear insects of some sort – cicadas – that had started up in the undergrowth. "And my cover's been blown. There's a boy here from Brookland who recognized me, and it won't be long before people start asking questions. It's all getting out of hand and I don't want to be part of it."

"Do you think the school's under threat?"

"If I thought that, I'd stay. Cairo College is OK ... even Miss Watson. But I've been there for almost three weeks and it all seems completely ordinary. The only reason we think it might be a target is because Mr Blunt told us – and you're right: we can't believe a word he says. Anyway, after what happened today, it seems almost certain that he's wrong."

Alex went over it all in his head once again. But he couldn't see any other possibility.

"Erik Gunter must be involved with this visit," he said. "The American secretary of state. He'd been to see this big weapons dealer and that bag he was carrying..."

"It wasn't golf clubs."

"Exactly. Maybe he's a hired assassin. Maybe he's

using his position at the school as some sort of cover. But the CIA will be watching him from now on. It has nothing to do with the school and it has nothing to do with me. So I might as well leave."

Jack nodded. "Are you going to tell Mr Smithers?"

"Yes. I'll go and see him tomorrow while you're packing. You'd better also call the school and tell them I'm not well or something." Alex felt a little sad about that. He'd have liked to say goodbye to some of the friends he'd made. But he knew it was better not to. There would have been too much to explain. "We can get a flight tomorrow afternoon."

"I agree with you," Jack said. She lifted her glass and swirled the wine round. "But there's just one problem. I'm not sure England's going to be safe for you, Alex. Remember how this all started. Someone tried to kill you."

Alex knew she was right. "Where, then?" he asked.

"Well, I've been thinking. It's probably a crazy idea and you don't have to make a decision. But I was wondering if you wouldn't be happier in America."

"America?"

Jack nodded. "It's just a thought, Alex. You might be safer there – in every sense. Away from Alan Blunt and Mrs Jones. You could start a new life, maybe in Washington. You know my parents are there." She paused. "The funny thing is, I was going to talk to you about it before all this began."

"You want to go home?"

"I wouldn't go without you."

"I don't know, Jack. I really don't." Alex tried to imagine leaving Brookland School behind him, all his friends, the house in Chelsea. And would MI6 leave him alone, even if he was on the other side of the world? "London's got to be safer than it is here. Let's go home and see how things work out."

"Sure." Jack smiled. "Two business-class tickets to Heathrow. We might as well travel in style – we can always get MI6 to pay. The important thing is that we're leaving Cairo. Are you certain you don't want me to come with you to see Mr Smithers?"

"No. I'll be all right."

"You won't let him change your mind?"

"I don't think he'll even try. I've always had the feeling that he's on my side."

"Well, that sounds like a plan." Jack lifted her glass. "So the toast is – home!"

Alex raised his own. "Home!"

The two of them clinked glasses in the gathering dark.

Night comes slowly in the Sahara Desert.

By eight o'clock the sands were burning a deep yellow and the shadows from the olive trees were stretching out as if trying to escape from the trunks that bound them. But the sun was still there, sitting on the horizon, and the heat of the day was only just beginning to retreat. The salt lakes were like sheets of steel, utterly still. There didn't seem to be a breath of wind.

The crack of the bullet tore through the great silence, splitting the very air. Seventy metres away from the tip of the rifle a black and white photograph of Alex Rider shuddered briefly, pinned to a wooden stake driven into the sand. It was a perfect shot. A round hole appeared where his right eye had once been, the last in a row of five that snaked across his forehead. Lying on his stomach, Julius Grief lowered the sniper rifle – the L96A1 Arctic Warfare that had been brought to him from Cairo. It was a beautiful weapon, he thought. He couldn't wait to use it for real.

In the distance he heard soft applause. Razim was standing on the parapet of the old French fort, wearing a freshly laundered, very white dishdasha.

"Come inside, Julius," he called out. "We're about to turn on the night defences and I wouldn't want to see you blown apart."

Julius stood up, brushing sand off his chest and thighs. He was wearing loose-fitting shorts and a striped shirt with the sleeves rolled up. His hair had been cut a little shorter since his escape from the Gibraltar prison. He was also thickly smeared with sun cream; he burned easily and it was important that his appearance remained the same.

He had been brought by ship from Gibraltar all

the way round the northern tip of Africa to the resort town of Marsa Matruh and then driven south to Siwa. He had been at the fort for more than two weeks, almost exactly the same length of time that Alex had spent at the Cairo International College of Arts and Education. Razim had been keeping him well out of sight. The entire world thought he was dead and it was vital that it stayed that way. Of course, Julius had complained. It was as if he had been transferred from one prison to another, and Razim had allowed him to visit Cairo with the promise that he would wear a baseball cap and dark glasses to conceal his identity and would stay well clear of Alex Rider. Razim had been furious to learn that Julius had disobeyed his instructions. So far, however, he hadn't mentioned it.

Julius passed through the main entrance and heard the whirr of machinery as the solid wooden and steel gates swung shut behind him. He knew that miniature landmines buried in the sand would have been activated all round the fort. A few nights ago a stray desert fox had tried to approach the compound, scavenging for food. They had all been woken up as the unfortunate animal had been blown apart.

Drinks had been served on the terrace outside the house where Razim lived. This was a neat, very square building with two floors; in fact it could have been drawn by a child. It had a front door and five shuttered windows, one on each side of the door on the ground floor and three above, positioned with perfect symmetry. Wooden rods carved from palm trunks jutted out of the side of the house, just below the tiled roof, part of the Berber tradition. Local tribesmen would have hung bones – animal and human – from the rods to keep away devils. But looking at the two people who had come together to watch the sun set, they might have decided that they were already too late.

Razim had a tall glass of gin and tonic with ice and lemon in front of him and, as usual, he was smoking one of his Black Devil cigarettes. Julius Grief sat down opposite him, resting the gun against the table. He raised a hand and one of Razim's men hurried over with a beer.

"That was excellent shooting," Razim said.

"My father trained me," Julius replied. "He trained all of us. And every time we missed, we got three strokes of the cane. By the end of it we were all pretty good shots."

"He was a remarkable man."

"He was brilliant." Julius drank some of his beer and wiped the foam off his top lip. "You know, they say it's impossible to clone a human being. Well, he managed it. In fact he did it sixteen times."

"And the plastic surgery?"

"That was done by some doctor he found. A man called Baxter."

"It must have been very disappointing to find you had been given the wrong face."

"You have no idea." Julius's hand tightened around his glass. "It wasn't just that. I'd spent ages learning about David and Caroline Friend. They were stinking rich; they owned supermarkets and art galleries and stuff. And I was going to move in as their son and take it all from them. It would all have been mine. But then Dad had to come and tell me that Alex Friend didn't actually exist. His real name was Alex Rider. And everything I'd done, everything I'd been through, was for nothing!"

Razim had already noticed that when Julius became angry, he spoke with a South African accent. He was angry now.

"He was a bloody spy! I couldn't believe it! And after that, everything went pear-shaped. He managed to escape, and then he killed Dad and that was the end of it."

"I can understand how much you must hate him. But even so, you were wrong to disobey me." Razim spoke softly but there was an edge to his voice. "Going to the school was foolish. If you had been seen, it could have ruined everything."

"I *was* seen!" Julius laughed. "I put on that uniform you gave me and I just walked in through the school gate. So much for all their precious security! They took one look at me and they thought I was him. I went into Gunter's office and I waited and I saw Alex Rider leave. He actually turned round."

"He saw you?"

"No. Don't worry. But I think he sensed me. It was quite interesting, really. It was like a sort of telepathy."

"And how did you feel?"

"Now you're sounding like my bloody psychiatrist, if you don't mind my saying so, Razim. How do you think I felt? If I'd had a gun, I'd have used it then and there. I had to stop myself running out and strangling him with my bare hands. I'd have loved to do it. I really would."

In the courtyard two of the guards had appeared with spades and a wheelbarrow, walking towards a great pile of salt directly underneath the rope bridge on the other side of the well. The salt had been pounded until it was fine and it seemed to Julius that it had a life of its own, shifting and swirling in the breeze. A third guard stood above, watching them.

"What are they doing?" Julius asked. The men had begun to scoop out the salt, loading it into the wheelbarrow.

"The salt has come out of the lakes. We mix it with sand to make bricks." Razim gestured at one of the half-finished buildings. "One day this will be a library. I also plan to construct a small concert hall."

Julius sniffed. "You'd have thought it would all dissolve in the rain."

"It has not rained here for a hundred and ten years."

"That's a lot of salt. Maybe we could strip off

all Alex's skin and roll him in it. That would really hurt." Julius giggled. "You are going to let me torture him, aren't you, Razim?"

Julius had already attended several of Razim's experiments. Only that morning, they had been working on a street merchant they had picked up in Alexandria. Julius had watched with fascination as Razim jotted down his findings. Unfortunately the man hadn't lived very long.

"You enjoy my experiments?" Razim asked.

"Yes. Very much. Don't you?"

"I do not derive pleasure from them. I have never really understood pleasure. For me they are a scientific necessity – nothing more, nothing less."

"Well, I like them a lot."

"And in answer to your question, I will allow you to spend a little time with Alex Rider. And I can promise you that you will cause him more pain than he has ever known. You will have your revenge, my friend. But only if you do as you are told. I will not have you putting this operation at risk again. Do you understand?"

Julius scowled. "Yes."

"Good. Scorpia have made too many mistakes in the past. I do not intend to make any myself. Alex Rider will be with us very soon, and from the moment he arrives, we will have to take extreme care."

Julius finished his beer. Almost immediately, and without being signalled, a servant ran forward with another.

"The gun will have to be decontaminated tonight," Razim continued. "And make sure you don't handle it again until it's in place. Meanwhile, it would seem that we do have one small problem which we will have to deal with."

"Oh? What's that?"

"This morning I received a coded transmission from Zeljan Kurst in Paris. MI6 have taken one precaution that we could not have foreseen. They have sent an agent out here to keep a watch over Alex Rider while he is in Cairo. He is a very fat man by the name of Smithers."

"Is that bad?"

"No. On the contrary. He visited Alex at his flat a few days after he arrived and we have photographic evidence which we can add to the Horseman file. It's further proof that MI6 have been running a covert operation in Egypt. However, as we move towards the critical stage, I do not think we can afford to have him on the scene. It's too dangerous."

"So?"

"So this is my plan." Razim took a last drag on his cigarette and for a moment the tip glowed, the same colour as the sun. "Mr Smithers must die. I will have it done tomorrow. From what I have heard, and despite his appearance, he is an extremely effective secret agent. So I think I will send perhaps a dozen men."

"That seems a bit OTT."

"Learn from me, Julius. Maybe one day, when

this present operation is concluded, you will join the ranks of Scorpia."

"Really? Do you think they'd have me? I'd love that!"

Razim smiled. He had already decided that he would kill Julius as soon as he had no further use for him. That idea he had just suggested ... flaying him alive and then rolling him in salt. That might be interesting.

"We take no risks; we make no mistakes. Tomorrow morning we kill Smithers and tomorrow evening..."

"Alex Rider!"

"That's when it begins."

# INSIDE EVERY FAT MAN...

The street was less than five minutes from the souk but it was surprisingly quiet and empty, with just a few children kicking a football around in the dust and not a tourist in sight. The taxi dropped Alex off a few minutes before eleven o'clock. He had already contacted Smithers using the notepad with its hidden circuitry. Smithers had rung back immediately to confirm.

The house wasn't difficult to find.

When Alex had been walking around the city with Jack, he had noticed a few old European buildings here and there, elegant and somehow out of place, as if the Egyptians hadn't noticed they were there and so had forgotten to knock them down. They dated back to the nineteenth century – the Suez Canal had been built at the same time – and might once have housed French noblemen or engineers. Smithers had chosen one of these and added a few touches of his own.

It was a tall, narrow, three-storey building,

constructed out of grey stone with dark brown shutters and a little balcony protruding over the front door. What made it unusual in this crowded city was that it stood alone, set back from the street. A gate opened onto a path which swept up the middle of a lawn that was more dust and sand than grass. There were two stone lions facing each other about halfway up and, to one side, a tall fountain with water tinkling down in graceful loops. It was obvious that the house belonged to an Englishman. There was a large mat in front of the door with the single word: WELCOME. A small Union Jack fluttered on the roof.

Alex was already dressed for the flight home in jeans and a dark red Hollister polo shirt. It was too warm for Cairo but Jack was packing the rest of his clothes and she had told him it was raining in London. He walked up the path, his feet crunching on the gravel, and rang the doorbell. There was a mirror set in the wall on either side of the door and he examined the two reflections of himself as he waited. A moment later, the door opened and Smithers appeared.

"Do come in, Alex. Very good to see you. I was just boiling the kettle. I hope you'll have a cup of tea and perhaps a slice of home-made cake?"

Smithers was more informally dressed than he had been at the flat, wearing pale trousers and a brilliantly coloured short-sleeve shirt. He could have walked straight off a cruise ship – all that was missing was the straw hat and camera. He stepped aside to allow Alex into a hexagonal-shaped hall with a marble floor; a chandelier; and, rather strangely, golden-framed pictures of the royal family on each of the walls, the queen and the duke of Edinburgh glancing at one another, side by side, opposite the door. There was an ornate table with what looked like a TV remote control sitting on the top. But there was no sign of a TV.

"This way!" Smithers bustled ahead into the kitchen, which was dominated by a stainless steel fridge. He threw it open to reveal shelves stacked with food, much of it flown in from England. There was a large cake on the middle shelf. "A Victoria sponge," he said. "Can I interest you?"

"No, thanks, Mr Smithers. I'll just have a Coke."

"Will you stay for lunch?"

"I haven't got time."

"A short visit, then! Very well. Let me see..."

Smithers put the cake back, then carried two Cokes and a bowl of crisps into the living room, an airy, old-fashioned space with plump sofas, bookshelves, a mahogany coffee table and a splendid rug that must surely have come from the souk. And yet, as Alex sat down, it occurred to him that the house told him very little about the man himself. It could have belonged to anyone. What did he actually know about Smithers, now that he thought about it? Was he married? Was he gay? Where did he live when he was in England? What did he do in his spare time – apart from baking Victoria sponges? But of course, that was the world of MI6 and all its agents. They didn't just live with secrets. Secrecy surrounded their entire lives.

Smithers helped himself to a handful of crisps. "So you've decided to leave," he said.

"Yes." Alex hadn't told Smithers anything. "How did you know?"

"I'm afraid I was tipped off the moment your Miss Starbright booked the flights over the Internet," Smithers explained. "We keep a very careful watch on the movements of our agents, Alex. Half past three this afternoon. You're right. That doesn't leave us time for lunch."

"I came to say goodbye."

"That's very decent of you."

For some reason, Alex felt a sudden twinge of guilt. "I hope you don't think I'm walking out on you, Mr Smithers," he said.

"Not at all, my dear boy. Although I do wonder if this has something to do with the explosion in Cairo yesterday afternoon. The *House of Gold*. There's been a great deal of excitement about that – and not just in London. I don't suppose you were in any way involved?"

Quickly Alex brought Smithers up to date, starting with the office break-in and the contents of Gunter's desk, then the phone call and the events on the paddle steamer. This time he didn't leave anything out, and after he'd finished describing the waterboarding, Smithers pounded the table with his fist, making the rest of the crisps jump.

"I like the Americans," he exclaimed, "but sometimes they're completely intolerable. I shall make an official complaint, Alex. They had no right to do that to you."

"It's OK, Mr Smithers. I'm fine now." Alex shrugged. "Anyway, maybe Gunter really is going to take a shot at the secretary of state when she comes to Cairo. But as far as I can see, there's nothing going on at Cairo College. I don't have any need to be there. So I'm going home."

He took out his iPhone and laid it on the table.

"I'm afraid this was completely ruined when it went into the Nile. But you might be able to get something off it. I took pictures of all the stuff in Gunter's desk. I still don't know why he had a picture of a coat hook. And there was also a brochure about a place called Siwa." Alex stopped – then remembered. There was one other thing. "I managed to leave the bug behind."

"I know, Alex. I've been listening in to Mr Gunter's office all morning but so far he hasn't said a single thing of any interest. In fact he barely says anything at all."

"I'm sorry," Alex said. "I haven't really been very helpful to you this time."

"You shouldn't apologize." Smithers' voice had changed. He was suddenly very serious, talking in a way that Alex had never heard before. And he got the strange feeling that this new voice didn't belong to the man he had known for more than a year. It was as if he was seeing the real Smithers for the first time. "And what you said just now – about walking out on us. Complete stuff and nonsense. I'm glad you're going. If you want the truth, I was always opposed to your getting involved in our business in the first place."

He paused, then continued more slowly.

"I never spoke my mind, because it's not my job. I do what I'm told, like everyone else. But it was wrong, quite wrong, getting you involved. People think that being a spy is fun and exciting. Your uncle was a bit like that. It was all a big adventure as far as he was concerned – and look what happened to him. The truth is that spying is dirty, dangerous work, quite unfit for a child who's still at school. I won't deny that you've been useful to us, Alex. But at what cost? You were very nearly killed at Liverpool Street – that was unforgivable – and you've spent more than a whole year surrounded by death and deception. Nobody should have asked you to do that.

"So you're absolutely right to be getting out now. I don't know what's happening here in Cairo but I'll tell you this: it's got a very nasty smell. Leave it. Go home. And the next time Mr Blunt or Mrs Jones calls you, don't pick up the phone. You should forget about us all."

Smithers stood up. Alex knew that in his own

way he had just said goodbye. Permanently. Alex stood up too and the two of them shook hands.

And then the doorbell rang.

"That's very strange," Smithers said. "I'm not expecting any visitors."

Alex followed him back out into the hall. Smithers snatched up the remote control that Alex had noticed earlier and pressed a button. At once the royal family disappeared. Each gold frame now contained a television screen with several views of the house, taken from different angles. The garden was empty but there was a man outside wearing a FedEx uniform and carrying a small parcel.

Smithers moved over to the wall and spoke into a microphone close to the door. "What do you want?" he asked.

"I've got a parcel for a Mr Derek Smithers," the man said.

"I'm afraid I'm rather busy at the moment. Can you leave it outside?"

"I'm sorry, sir. You have to sign for it."

"Just give me a minute..." He clicked the microphone off and turned to Alex. "I think we may be in trouble," he said. "This is an MI6 safe house. I designed it myself. But nobody knows I'm here – and certainly not any parcel delivery companies."

"Who do you think...?" Alex looked at the screen, at the man waiting outside.

"Let's take a closer look."

The buttons on the remote control were almost

too small for his pudgy fingers but he chose another one and pointed the device at the TV screen. The image flickered and changed. Now the man in the FedEx uniform had become a grey and white ghost of himself. Alex remembered the mirrored panels he had seen. That had to be where the X-ray cameras were hidden. And they revealed two things. The box that the man was delivering was empty. And he was carrying a gun. The shape of the weapon, tucked into the back of his trousers, was unmistakable.

"Now that's interesting," Smithers muttered. "Do you think this chap followed you here? Or has he come for me?"

"Either way, I hope you're not going to let him in," Alex said.

Smithers smiled. "I don't think so." He pointed the remote at the door. "I put the welcome mat in myself. Occasionally, though, it becomes an unwelcome mat, as he's about to find out."

His thumb stabbed down. The doormat collapsed. It was hinged, like a trapdoor, and the fake FedEx man had been standing right in the middle of it. With a yell he disappeared from sight.

"What's underneath?" Alex asked.

"It heads directly to the Cairo sewers about ten metres down," Smithers replied. "He'll have a soft landing but I'm afraid it won't be a pleasant one."

"Mr Smithers..."

Alex pointed at another of the screens, which

only moments before had been a portrait of the prince of Wales. Now it showed the front gate. Two cars had pulled up and even as he watched, half a dozen Egyptians poured out, dressed in dark clothes. Perhaps they were all in radio contact, because somehow they seemed to know what had just happened. Warily they made their way up the garden path. Two of them had machine guns slung across their chests; the others were carrying automatic pistols.

"How many gadgets do you have in this house?" Alex asked.

"Not enough." Smithers nodded at a third screen. Four more men had joined the others, coming round the side of the building, bringing the total to ten. They were spreading out, surrounding the house like an invading army.

"What time did we say your plane was?" Smithers asked.

"Three thirty."

The men were getting closer.

"Then we'd better get a move on. We don't want you to be late."

Smithers was still holding the remote control device and Alex wondered what else it could do. The collapsing doormat had been simple but effective and at least it had reduced the odds by one. But there were a lot of determined-looking men crossing the garden, approaching the front door – and as far as Alex could see, that was the only way out. The attackers were all armed and they were taking no chances, moving carefully one step at a time as if they were in a minefield. Smithers looked from one TV screen to the next. Alex had never seen him like this before. Like so many fat men, he had always seemed carefree and jolly. But right now, as he timed his next move, he was deadly.

One of the screens showed the pair of stone lions. Two men were passing between them, each one clutching a nasty-looking snub-nosed miniature machine gun, and Alex wondered if they would really dare use them here, in the middle of a city that was always on the alert against terrorism. But there could be no doubting the determination in their eyes and in their body language. They had come here for the kill. By the time the police arrived, they would be far away.

Smithers waited for the exact moment, then hit the next button. The two men partially disappeared in a cloud of white dust that sprayed out of the lions' mouths. They were still there when it cleared, gazing at each other, wondering what had just happened. Alex had no idea either. He glanced at Smithers, who said nothing. Then one of the men threw away his gun and began to roll about on the grass. A second later, the other did exactly the same. They were like small children, writhing on their backs, kicking their legs and screaming. They had completely forgotten where they were or why they had come here.

"Itching powder," Smithers muttered. "Super-strength. It was actually developed in the last war but I've made a few improvements. To be honest with you, I've been itching to try it!"

The others had seen what had happened and looked at the two men, still rolling helplessly, in disbelief. Somebody shouted a command and they advanced on the house, colder and more angry than ever. Alex could see all eight of them spread over the TV screens. He glanced at the door. Would it be strong enough to hold them back?

As if to answer the question, that was when they opened fire. Their weapons had been silenced but even so the sound of the bullets slamming into the walls, the windows and the front door was deafening. It was like being inside a tin box in a hailstorm and Alex flinched despite himself. But the door didn't so much as splinter. The window-panes didn't crack.

"The door's armour-plated!" Smithers shouted out. "And the windows are bulletproof glass. They're not going to shoot their way in."

"Can they cut their way in?" Alex asked.

"Yes. But they'd need..."

Smithers stopped. Alex had already seen it on the screens. Two of the men had run forward, both wearing body armour, their heads protected by welding masks. They carried with them an oxyacetylene torch with a cutting head capable of reaching temperatures up to three and a half thousand degrees Celsius. While the others fell back, these two knelt in front of the door and a moment later, there was a whoosh of harsh blue flame as they fired up the torch. Almost at once, Alex smelled burning. The inside of the door began to change colour as it was attacked by the fierce heat and a tiny tongue of flame burst through and began to move, curving around the handle and the lock.

"Well, they're certainly well prepared," Smithers muttered. He sounded more irritated than afraid.

"Can you hold them off?" Alex asked.

"Unfortunately not. This is only a grade three safe house. Now, if we were in Jerusalem or Baghdad, that would be a different matter..."

Alex caught sight of a man swinging his arm. He was halfway down the garden, captured on one of the screens. For a crazy moment, Alex thought he was playing catch ... then he understood. It wasn't a ball; it was a grenade. It hit the roof and exploded. The whole house shook, sending the chandelier into a furious, jingling dance. Dust and broken plaster rained down and smoke billowed down the main staircase. Meanwhile, the oxyacetylene torch was making steady progress. The hissing flame had already moved from twelve o'clock to half past four.

"I think we're going to have to make a run for it," Smithers said.

"Run?" It wasn't a word that Alex would ever have associated with Smithers. A fast waddle would surely be the best he could manage. And anyway, how were they going to get out?

"There's a back way." Smithers must have known what he was thinking. "Don't you worry about me," he added. "The main thing is that you don't get hurt." He searched out another button on the remote control. Outside, the fountain stopped, and even as the last drops of water splashed down it released a cloud of yellow smoke instead. The gunmen began to stagger across the lawn, covering their eyes and coughing. "Tear gas!" Smithers explained. "Shame this isn't England or I could have had them with my exploding gnomes..."

Despite the defences, the men had almost cut through the front door. The circle had reached ten o'clock. Smithers hurried back through the hall and into the kitchen and to Alex's astonishment headed straight for the fridge. Surely this wasn't the time for a snack! But when Smithers threw open the door, the food and the shelves had disappeared. Instead there was a stainless steel tunnel leading straight to the street. Behind them Alex heard the front door crash open.

"After you!" Smithers cried.

Alex went first. It was a tight squeeze for Smithers but he followed right behind and a few seconds later they were out in the street. Smithers still had the remote control. He pressed one last button and began to move away as fast as his legs would take him.

There was an explosion inside the house. Then another. Alex heard screams and wondered what exactly had blown up. The sofas? The toilet? With Smithers it could be anything.

It seemed to Alex that their best plan would be to disappear as quickly as possible into the crowd before reinforcements arrived – but that wasn't going to be easy. For a start the streets were too quiet. And they had already been spotted. Alex heard a van screech to a halt. The back doors were thrown open and five more men came bundling out. Alex didn't have time to see if they were armed too – but he didn't have to look. There was a gunshot and a bullet spat into the brickwork close to his head. A few children had been playing football but they scattered instantly. An old man with a donkey and cart stood trembling with wide eyes, unsure what to do. Alex could hear the sirens of approaching police cars. They must have been alerted by the first grenade. But it was impossible to tell how near they were or, given the Cairo traffic, how quickly they might arrive.

Alex and Smithers ran round a corner, past the entrance to a mosque, and down an alleyway with fresh laundry hanging on lines above their heads. It was close to midday. The sun was directly overhead and the heat was fearsome. Alex wondered how far Smithers would be able to run before his heart gave out. But he had already decided. No matter what happened, he wasn't going to leave the gadget master behind.

Smithers reached the end of the alley and came to a breathless halt, glancing left and right as he weighed up their options. "The souk!" he gasped. "We can lose them in the souk."

"Who are they?" Alex demanded.

"Scorpia," Smithers replied, and the single word told Alex everything he needed to know. Nobody else would have dared mount an armed assault in the middle of a highly populated Middle Eastern city. Nobody else was more determined to see him dead. From the very start, even when he had been attacked at Brookland, he had been aware of something unseen, some old enemy stealing out of his past. Well, now he knew. Part of him was grateful to Smithers for telling him the truth. But he was also angry. Blunt must have known that Scorpia were active in Egypt. Yet even so, he had sent Alex here like some sort of sacrificial lamb, forcing them to make their move.

For just a brief pause, Alex and Smithers were alone. Alex guessed that the Scorpia agents had decided to regroup. They would be waiting to see if any survivors came out of the house.

"Did you tell anyone you were coming to see me?" Smithers asked.

"No. Only Jack."

"Were you followed?"

"No. I don't think so."

"Then they didn't know you were coming. It's

just bad luck you were with me. I'm the one they're after."

A figure appeared at the top of the alleyway. Alex and Smithers set off again, crossing a court-yard of debris, past a couple of shops with interiors so dark it was impossible to see what they actually sold. The main road was in front of them, divided in half by ugly concrete pillars supporting a second road overhead. The traffic had become a solid, unmoving wall – in fact the explosions and the approaching police must have brought the entire city to a halt. There were people streaming past in every direction. The pavements simply weren't wide enough to contain them and much of the available space was taken up by stallholders selling sandals, cigarette lighters, scarves, souvenirs, each one blocking the way ahead.

Smithers pointed. A metal footbridge led above the chaos, up and over to the other side. Alex could feel the sweat pouring off him. The clothes he was wearing were for England. He certainly hadn't expected to run in them in Egypt. He didn't look back. Somehow he had the idea that if he managed to reach the other side he would be safe.

It wasn't the case. Halfway across the bridge, Smithers stopped to catch his breath. Alex turned and saw the five men from the van appear at the side of the road. There were two or three more behind them, the survivors from Smithers' safe house. He and Smithers were in plain sight – but surely even Scorpia wouldn't try to take them out in front of so many witnesses? He shouldn't even have framed the question. A hail of bullets hit the side of the metal bridge and as Alex dived for cover, they ricocheted all around. Remarkably, in all the noise and the confusion, nobody seemed to hear the shots. The two of them could have been killed without anyone even noticing.

Alex caught Smithers' eye. The big man was crouching uncomfortably beside him. "Can you call for help?" he asked.

"I'm afraid not, old bean."

"You must have more gadgets!"

"Just one!" Smithers checked the way was clear, then stood up again and ran forward. Alex had no choice but to follow – across the bridge and down the other side.

Behind them the five Scorpia agents were already clambering up the first steps, determined to follow them into the souk.

For that was where they were now. Alex had plunged into a series of courtyards and alleyways so densely packed together that it was hard to say if he was inside or out. The Khan al-Khalili souk was the biggest in Cairo, a twisting labyrinth of tiny shops connected by steps, arches and passages with all manner of goods piled high on shelves, dangling from walls and spilling out onto the street. Alex and Jack had already been there and had found the experience almost too much.

"You want gold? I make you good price."

"Please – come in, my friend. No need to buy!"

"You English? Jolly good chap!"

Every shop had its own hawker trying to draw them in. And every hawker seemed to be selling the same things: the same earrings, rugs, spices, decorated boxes and incense sticks that Alex had already seen in the *House of Gold* and which were sold by everyone else. Everything here was somehow desirable. There was nothing that anyone really needed.

And now Alex was back in the middle of it with at least eight armed men thirty seconds behind him.

"This way!" Smithers commanded.

He had already lurched down a corridor that specialized in *sheeshas*, the slender glass pipes that many Egyptians used to smoke fruit-flavoured tobacco over bubbling water. As he went, his arm or leg must have knocked into one. The result was a domino effect. Pipe after pipe toppled into the next with a terrible smashing of glass. Alex felt someone reach out and try to grab them. He wrenched himself free and kept going, leaving the outraged howls of the hawkers behind them.

They passed through a soaring archway, part of a stone tower that could have housed a princess out of an ancient fable. There were thick pillars and narrow, barred windows. The archway led into a square filled with stalls and shops on all sides. The tourists were already evacuating the area. It was obvious that something was going on. They were surrounded by police cars, there were sirens howling in the air and people were running! Nobody ever ran in the souk. The whole point of life there was to take it slowly. By the time Alex and Smithers stumbled to a halt to consider their options, they were almost alone. Only the astonished shopkeepers gazed at them from behind half-open doors, wondering what was going to happen next.

There were three ways out of the square but Alex saw at once that they were blocked. Yet more Scorpia men had been brought in and these ones had somehow second-guessed them. They were closing in from every direction. At least these new arrivals didn't seem to have guns. But they were carrying knives with long, vicious blades and they were ready to use them. Alex and Smithers were unarmed apart from the one gadget he had mentioned, and that might be anything. What next?

"Mr Smithers!" Alex called out the warning as one of the men raised his knife and moved in for the kill. At the same time, Alex ducked sideways and grabbed a brass pyramid, one of thousands on sale in the souk. It made an ugly souvenir – but it was heavy, with a lethal point, and that made it a useful weapon. Alex hurled it with all his strength, watching with satisfaction as it sailed over Smithers' shoulder and hit the knifeman in the centre of his forehead. The man went down like a stone, dropping his knife. Smithers snatched it up, spun it in his hand and threw it across the square. Alex looked round. A man had appeared just behind him, carrying a machine gun. The knife turned in the air, then buried itself in his chest. As the man fell back, his trigger finger tightened and suddenly he was spraying the air with bullets. About a dozen glass lamps exploded. Brass plates were blown off their hooks, falling with a great clatter. The windows of a silversmith's shattered. Then it was over – but the silence after the last bullet was immediately broken by more sirens, frantic shouting, the panic of people trying to get away.

There were still two more knifemen. Before he could react, Alex was seized from behind. He felt himself being dragged away and tried to struggle, but his attacker was too strong for him. He writhed helplessly, expecting to feel the point of the knife slide into his back at any moment. He wondered why it hadn't happened already. Out of the corner of his eye he saw the other knifeman close in on Smithers, who was standing in front of him, his great chest rising and falling as he caught his breath.

Alex had to break free. As he was pulled back, he passed a spice shop with sacks of powder and leaves piled up outside. He knew at once what he had to do. His hand shot out and scooped up as much red powder as it could hold. Then he twisted round and flung it into the man's face. It was chilli powder. The man screamed as it invaded his eyes and nostrils. He couldn't breathe. He was blind. Alex felt the man release him. He pulled free, then turned round and lashed out with a side kick – the *yoko-geri* he had been taught in karate – his foot powering into the man's solar plexus. The man was thrown back into a counter filled with silver jewellery. He smashed through the glass, his head and shoulders disappearing. His legs twitched for a moment, then became still.

Alex wanted to rest, but he could see the last knifeman moving towards Smithers on the other side of the square. The man was smiling, perfectly balanced on the balls of his feet, about to strike. Alex looked around for another weapon. There were none – but then he noticed a brass plate that had been shot off its hook. He picked it up and threw it in a single movement. Unconsciously he was back on the beach – with Tom Harris, with Sabina – playing Frisbee. The plate was heavier but it was exactly the same shape and its aerodynamics were more or less the same. It was a perfect throw. The plate sailed across the square, curving slightly, then crashed into the side of the knifeman's neck. Alex saw his eyes go white and his legs crumple. He collapsed, leaving Alex and Smithers facing each other, alone.

Smithers seemed amused by the whole affair. "Well done, Alex," he crowed. "I always wanted to see you in action, and you really are as good as they say!"

"I think we have to get out of here, Mr Smithers," Alex panted. They had taken out four more of the men but he knew there were plenty left.

"Quite right. It's time I disappeared."

"What?"

"No time to argue. It's me they're after. That much is obvious. Heaven knows why. Mr Blunt will find out. The important thing is for you to get on that plane and go home."

"But what about you?" Alex couldn't keep a note of dismay out of his voice. Smithers would be easy to spot wherever he went. It wasn't just his clothes. It was his bald head, his size.

"They won't be able to find me if they don't know what they're looking for," Smithers replied. He reached down between his legs. "This may come as a bit of a shock, Alex, old chap."

For a moment, Alex thought that Smithers was about to unzip his trousers. He was certainly unzipping something. As he straightened up, there was a tearing sound and the waistband of his trousers divided into two. His shirt did the same, and to Alex's horror he saw that Smithers' bulging stomach was also splitting in half. It was like a snake shedding its skin. The brightly coloured shirt and the plump, oversized arms fell aside as a second pair of arms, lean and suntanned, appeared from inside, pushing their way out. The shoulders rolled away, and finally the bald head with its round cheeks and several chins crumpled and fell back as a younger head emerged and Alex saw what should have been obvious from the start.

A fat suit! That was Smithers' last and most brilliant gadget – and he had been wearing it from the day the two of them had met. The real Smithers was thin and wiry and about ten years younger – in his late thirties, with short brown hair and blue eyes. He was looking at Alex with a mischievous smile and when he spoke again even his public school accent had gone. It seemed that he was actually Irish.

"I never meant to deceive you, Alex," he explained. "I developed the Smithers disguise for work in the field but somehow I got used to it. It was like my office suit, you know?" Quickly he tucked the rubber and latex body behind one of the stalls. He was now wearing scruffy jeans and a T-shirt. For his part, Alex was too astonished to speak. "I don't feel comfortable taking it off now, if you want the truth. I feel as if I'm exposing myself. But needs must if I'm going to get out of this place alive. No time to worry about it now. We'd better go in different directions. Get home to Jack. Give her my best wishes. Try not to mention this if you can help it."

And then Smithers was walking briskly away. Alex watched him climb down a flight of stairs and turn a corner and then he was gone. He was reminded of an advertisement he had once seen in a newspaper for diet pills. What had it said? *Inside*

*every fat man there's a thin man trying to get out.*
Well, he'd just witnessed a vivid demonstration of
that – although if he hadn't seen it with his own
eyes, he wouldn't have believed it.

He retraced his steps, putting as much distance between himself and the square as possible.
Smithers might be wrong. The Scorpia people
could still be looking for him. As he hurried away,
a group of white-suited tourist police ran past. The
*House of Gold* yesterday and now this! Cairo had to
be wondering what had hit it. All the shops had
locked their doors. Alex joined a crowd of fright-
ened tourists and followed them as they made
their way out of the souk.

Somehow he managed to find a route back to
the footbridge that he and Smithers had crossed.
He tried to hail a cab but realized at once that he
didn't have a hope. They had all been taken by
people wanting to get back to the safety of their
hotels; and anyway, the police must have set up
roadblocks everywhere. Nothing was moving.

He looked at his watch. Just after one. He still
had time to make the plane. Jack had given him
her own mobile phone and he used it to call her at
the flat.

There was no answer. That was odd. Maybe he
had misdialled. Jack had definitely told him she
would wait for his call. He tried again and allowed
the phone to ring ten times but there was still no
answer. Where was she?

Suddenly Alex had a bad feeling. Jack wouldn't have left the flat. She might have heard that there'd been a further disturbance in Cairo but she wouldn't have come out looking for him. So if she wasn't answering the phone, where was she?

Alex was on his own. Smithers had gone and he had no one else to call. Pushing through the crowds, he hurried away from the souk, following the main road back into the centre of the city, searching for a taxi or a bus or anything that would give him a lift, knowing with a sense of dread that he had to get home.

# CITY OF THE DEAD

Alex finally managed to flag down a taxi in Opera Square, an open space full of modern shops and ugly offices, and cut in half by a flyover. It still took him nearly an hour to get back to Golden Palm Heights and half that time he found himself motionless, sweating on the back seat, surrounded by traffic. He rang the flat three more times. There was still no answer and he had to clamp down on his imagination, trying not to think the worst. But the fact was that if Jack had had to go out, if there had been some problem with the school or with the air tickets, she would have called him first. There was something terrible about the silence and Alex clutched the mobile until his hand was aching, hoping against hope that it would ring.

He was also worried about Smithers. It still made his head spin to think of the young Irishman who had stepped out of the fat suit. His work clothes ... that was what he had said, but it must have taken a bizarre frame of mind to get rigged up like that every day. It just went to show that you couldn't trust anyone or anything that belonged to the world of espionage.

As he sat in the back of the cab, waiting for a traffic light that seemed to be stuck deliberately on red, Alex cursed Alan Blunt and Mrs Jones – and himself for listening to them. They had set him up against Scorpia without even telling him. And Alex was absolutely certain now that whatever was going on in Egypt had nothing to do with the Cairo International College of Arts and Education. It was as if he had been lured there on purpose, part of the evil jigsaw puzzle that Scorpia were putting together. Well, to hell with all of them. Alex just wanted to find Jack. It was time to get out.

After what seemed like an eternity, the taxi turned into the complex – empty now as there was still more than an hour to go before the end of school. Alex gave the driver a handful of banknotes without even bothering to count them, got out of the car and ran up to the flat. The front door was open. Was that a good sign or a bad one?

"Jack!" He called out her name, standing in the middle of the living room. Despite everything, he had still hoped she would be here and he was shocked by the silence, by the knowledge that he was alone. He could see that she had been packing. There were two suitcases open on the floor, both of them full. The few books and bits and pieces that they had brought from England were neatly stacked beside them, along with some cash and their passports. There was a half-finished glass of Coke on the kitchen table. Alex examined it. The ice had melted and the liquid was lukewarm. She had been here. She had been getting ready to leave. Something or someone had disturbed her.

Then Alex saw the letter pinned to his bedroom door. A white envelope with his name written on it. It wasn't Jack's handwriting. There was already a hollow pit in his stomach as he took it down and opened it. What he read made it worse.

WE HAVE JACK STARBRIGHT. IF YOU WANT TO SEE HER AGAIN, COME TO THE CITY OF THE DEAD AT 3.00PM THIS AFTERNOON. THE TOMB OF THE BROKEN MOON. DO NOT BE LATE. DO NOT SPEAK TO ANYONE. IF YOU CALL MI6, SHE WILL DIE. IF YOU CONTACT THE SCHOOL, SHE WILL DIE. IF YOU ARE NOT ALONE, SHE WILL DIE. WE ARE WATCHING YOU NOW. WE ARE LISTENING. OBEY THESE INSTRUCTIONS OR YOU WILL NEVER SEE YOUR FRIEND AGAIN.

Alex felt physically sick. The marble floor seemed to be shifting beneath his feet. Three o'clock! He looked at his watch. It was already well after two. They had left him hardly any time – presumably on purpose. Despite that, he forced himself to slow down, to think this through. The wrong decision now could kill them both.

He knew about the City of the Dead. They had been talking about it at school only a couple of days ago. It was a vast cemetery in the north of the city, not far from the Citadel. The Tomb of the Broken Moon? He could find that when he got there. But should he go at all? If he allowed himself to be captured, he would be no use to Jack. They might simply kill him then and there. After all, this was Scorpia he was talking about and he had given them more than enough reason.

But that didn't make sense. If they wanted him dead, that would have been easy enough to arrange. They could have had someone waiting with a gun in the flat. They needed him for some reason – perhaps the same reason that had drawn him to Egypt in the first place. This wasn't about Cairo College; it was about him. If he walked into their trap, who could say what the consequences might be? But if he didn't, Jack would die.

He could get a message to Smithers. He still had the electronic notepad. But it wasn't worth the risk. Anyway, Smithers had been forced to abandon his safe house and might not even have access to his computer. Alex could ring England. He could leave some sort of written message here. But he had no doubt that the flat would be thoroughly searched. It was probably already bugged. Scorpia might be watching him even now, and the note had made it perfectly clear what would happen if he tried to disobey the instructions.

It took him about fifteen seconds to run through all the options and to come to the only possible conclusion. He had to do what he was told. He had to deliver himself into Scorpia's hands and hope that some sort of opportunity would arise further down the line. The one thing he wouldn't do was put Jack's life at risk. He remembered how she had insisted on coming with him on this trip. He wished now that he had persuaded her to stay behind.

He was already out the door and back down the stairs – and at least there was one piece of luck. The taxi that had brought him was still parked outside, the driver talking on his mobile. Alex had snatched up another handful of cash before he left and he banged a fist on the window, showing it to the driver.

"The City of the Dead," he instructed. "Can you take me there?"

The driver nodded.

"Do you know a place called the Tomb of the Broken Moon?"

The driver's eyes were still fixed on the money. "I know it."

"You can have all this if you get me there in half an hour."

The driver must have had enough English to understand, because Alex had no sooner got in than they were away, the back tyres spinning and spitting up dust. He gazed out of the window, trying to assemble his thoughts. Why did they want him to come to a cemetery? Was there something ominous about the choice? Perhaps he should try calling someone now after all, using Jack's mobile. But that was too dangerous. It was always possible that Scorpia agents were following in another car. And the iPhone itself could be bugged.

The City of the Dead, also known as the Northern Cemetery, lay sprawled out next to the Salah Salem Highway. Lanes of traffic roared past continuously, filling the air with fumes of burnt rubber and petrol. It really was a city in itself, dusty and crumbling, hammered by the sun. For centuries the Egyptians had brought their dead here, building not just tombs but miniature complexes with mosques, mausoleums and even living rooms for visiting relatives. The wealthier the family, the more elaborate the construction, with high brick walls and arched doorways leading into courtyards that really could be someone's home. Indeed, a lot of the poorer people of Cairo had seen an opportunity and had moved in, so that many of the buildings were now occupied. TV screens flickered behind windows, television aerials were mounted on the roofs and laundry hung on lines that stretched over the graves. There were even a few bars and supermarkets with cans and bottles spread out on wooden shelves that might once have held dead bodies.

The taxi slowed down once they entered the

cemetery. It was impossible to speed through the narrow twisting streets. The driver seemed to be looking for something and suddenly drew in, stopping beside a wooden door. Alex saw a name – Torun – written in Arabic and English characters on a plaque. Was this the place? The driver pointed and he looked up. There were a dome and a minaret surmounted with a crescent moon that someone had shot at. The bullet had snapped off one end. The moon was a Turkish symbol. Torun could well be a Turkish name too. Had a Turkish family moved to Cairo, died in Cairo and decided to be buried in Cairo? At least Alex could be fairly sure that he was in the right place.

He gave the driver all his money. With his nerves tingling, he got out of the car and went through the door. He heard the taxi pull away behind him, leaving him on his own. He looked at his watch. It was five to three. He had completed his part of the bargain. He wondered what would happen next.

Alex was surrounded by three walls. The fourth had crumbled away, revealing more tombs scattered haphazardly and a few shrubs and trees. No squatters seemed to have moved into this part of the cemetery and Alex was quite alone. He felt trapped, hemmed in. As far as he could tell, the City of the Dead stretched out for at least a mile and at this time of the afternoon, in the full heat of the sun, there would be few tourists or visitors.

He heard footsteps. Somebody was approaching. Alex drew himself up, his whole body tensed, not sure what to expect.

A figure appeared.

Alex stood where he was, completely shocked, as he watched himself walk between the graves.

It was him. The boy had his face, his hair – cut in exactly the same style. He was even dressed similarly, as if he had deliberately checked out what Alex was wearing. The only thing that was different was the cruelty in his eyes. Alex had never smiled like that, with such a degree of malevolence. And suddenly he knew who it was – who it had to be.

Julius Grief stopped. "Surprised?" he asked.

Alex didn't speak. He was angry with himself. He remembered the face he had glimpsed at the window as he left Cairo College. He should have recognized him then. And the photograph he had seen in Gunter's desk. At the time it had puzzled him – when had it been taken? But the answer was simple. It hadn't been a photograph of him.

"My name is Julius Grief," the other boy said. "You knew my father."

"Where's Jack?" Alex demanded.

"You don't ask questions," Grief replied. He was obviously relishing this. He couldn't contain his glee. "From now on you do exactly as you're told or she gets killed. Do you understand? We're going on a little journey together, you and me. And if you cause me any trouble, she's the one who'll pay."

"I'm not going anywhere until I've spoken to her," Alex said.

Grief's face darkened. "I don't think you understand how this works. You're nothing now, Alex Rider. You're not special. You're not a superspy. You have no idea what's coming your way. I'm in charge; I'm the one who says what you do." Suddenly, as if changing his mind, he took out a mobile, pressed the redial button and spoke a few words. "All right," he went on. "You can talk to Jack. But only if you ask me nicely. You have to say please."

"Please may I speak to Jack?" Alex measured out the words.

"Get on your knees."

Grief was taunting him with the phone. He was behaving like any schoolyard bully. But Alex had to know if Jack was alive. He knelt down in the dust. Grief nodded, pleased with himself. He stepped forward, towering over Alex, and handed him the phone.

"Jack?" Alex muttered the single word.

"Alex – don't do anything they say. Get help—" It was definitely Jack's voice. But then the phone was snatched away at her end and the line went dead.

"Satisfied?" Grief held out his hand for the phone. Alex handed it back. He was already wondering how the boy had escaped from wherever MI6 had sent him. What was his part in all this? And did anyone know he was free? One thing was already certain: he was quite mad, worse even than he had been the last time they'd met, on the roof at Brookland. "From now on, you call me sir," Grief continued. "And you only speak to me when you're spoken to. Do you understand?"

"Yes."

The phone slammed into the side of Alex's head, almost knocking him off his knees. He swayed and reached out to steady himself against a tomb.

"Do you understand?"

"Yes, sir."

Grief held all the cards. There was no point fighting him yet.

"That's good. Now get up and start moving. There's a car waiting for us near by."

Grief gestured and Alex stood up. The side of his head was pounding. He wondered briefly what would happen if he took Grief out here and now. It would be easy enough. Twist round, a side kick to the stomach. But they still had Jack. Until she was safe, there was nothing he could do.

They made their way back through the cemetery. Alex knew this was bad – worse than anything that had ever happened to him. Scorpia had their own agenda, still unknown to him; but Grief clearly had just one thing on his mind. He wanted revenge and he was going to make him suffer. Alex walked slowly, trying to ignore the pain in his head. He wouldn't give up. His chance would come. He just had to make sure he didn't miss it.

A black limousine was parked, not far from where the taxi had dropped him off, and standing beside it was a man that Alex knew. Erik Gunter was waiting, the sun reflecting off his forehead, his eyes dark and watchful. He was dressed in the same suit and tie that he wore every day at Cairo College ... presumably he had left school early today to be here. The only difference was that there was a gun in his hand, but Julius nodded at him and he tucked it away, seeing that the situation was under control.

"Hello, Brenner," he said jovially. "Or maybe I should call you by your real name now. Rider! It looks like you've reached the end of the line."

"So have you," Alex replied. "MI6 have a file on you. You may have been a war hero in Afghanistan, but they know you've switched sides and that you're working for Scorpia. When this is over, they'll come looking for you. And they'll find you. There's nowhere in the world you'll be able to hide."

Gunter smiled but his eyes were troubled. "Maybe I'll have to change my face," he said. "Like Julius." He glanced at the mark on the side of Alex's head, then at the other boy. He scowled. "You weren't supposed to mark him," he said.

"He was rude to me."

"Razim won't be pleased."

Alex filed the information away. It might be useful later. Who was Razim? Presumably the man in charge. For some reason he needed Alex not just alive but unhurt.

Gunter went over to the car and opened the boot. He leaned in, and when he straightened up Alex saw that he was holding a sophisticated weapon, a sniper rifle, complete with scope. Alex remembered the golf bag that he had seen at the *House of Gold*. He had no doubt that this weapon must have been inside. Gunter had also slipped a glove onto his right hand. He was holding the rifle by the barrel, taking care not to leave fingerprints.

"Before we go, I want you to hold this," he said. "And don't get any funny ideas. It's not loaded."

"What do you want me to do with it?"

He had no sooner spoken the words than he felt a sharp jab in the ribs. He had been hit, hard, from behind. "You don't ask questions. You just do as you're told," Julius said.

Alex took the gun. It was heavier than he had expected. He held it awkwardly, unsure what they wanted him to do.

"Aim it at me," Gunter said. "Go on. I'm sure you'd love to kill me. Aim it at my head."

Alex did as he was told.

"Now pull the trigger."

Alex hesitated.

"Go on. Do it."

Alex put his finger on the trigger and squeezed. There was a click but no explosion. As Gunter had said, the gun wasn't loaded.

"I bet that felt good," Gunter mocked him. "Now – hold it there." He took out a digital camera and fired off a few shots: Alex and the gun, a brick wall behind him, nobody else in the picture. "That's great," he said. "That'll make a nice addition to the Horseman file." He held out the gloved hand. "Now, let's have the gun back, please."

Alex handed it over. He had a good idea what was going on. He also knew that there was nothing he could do. Gunter put the rifle back in the boot, then opened the car door. "Get in," he instructed.

"Where are we going?"

"I'd just do what I tell you – unless you want Julius to hit you again."

Alex climbed in. Gunter closed the door and wandered round to the driver's seat. Julius Grief sat next to him, a bundle of scowling, angry energy. Alex guessed that he was still angry at being told off.

They drove back onto the highway and turned off about a mile out of Cairo, following a rough track to a patch of wasteland – yet another unfinished building site. There a large, old-fashioned heli-copter was waiting, the pilot already checking the controls. The helicopter was a Sikorsky H-34, once popular with the US military but no longer in pro-duction, with the engine mounted in the nose and a cabin big enough for at least a dozen men. It was much bigger than the machine that Alex had brought down over the Thames.

"This is as far as I come," Gunter said. "I have to take the gun back where it belongs. But I'll be seeing you again the day after tomorrow, Alex. Enjoy the flight! In fact, if you want some advice, you'll enjoy everything while you can. You don't have a lot of time left."

Alex got out of the car. Julius Grief pushed him forward, his hand slamming into Alex's back. Alex climbed into the Sikorsky. The cabin had been constructed to house an entire squadron and it was so spacious that he could almost have parked a car inside. There were straps and rigging hanging off the walls and the door slid back far enough to allow parachutists to exit cleanly. Two benches faced each other across the void. Alex wondered if Jack had sat on one of them before him.

Julius had followed him in. "Sit there." He pointed at one of the benches.

Alex did as he was told. The blades began to rotate and he heard the whine of the engine increase until it overwhelmed him. At last it was ready. The pilot pulled at the controls and the helicopter lurched off the ground. It hovered for a moment, then turned and rose up, carrying Alex away.

# HELL IS WAITING

The scorpion was about two and a half centimetres long, perched on the windowsill as if trying to catch the first rays of the morning sun. It was an unpleasant colour, a strange sickly yellow that was almost transparent against the light. It had barely moved for the last ten minutes, its tail curving above its head. This one had to be a baby. The *Androctonus australis* – or yellow fat-tailed scorpion – can be more than ten centimetres in length and a full-grown adult is one of the deadliest insects in the world, with a sting that is often fatal.

Alex lay on his bunk, watching it. This was the second scorpion he had seen since he had woken up, climbing over the brickwork on the other side of the bars, and he guessed that there was a nest somewhere below. Fortunately neither of them had come any further into the cell.

He had only a vague idea where he was – some sort of ancient fort in the Sahara Desert. The sun had been setting when they arrived, the helicopter touching down on an area of sand that must have been treated in some way so that it wasn't sent spinning into the rotors. As he had climbed out, the first thing he had seen was a miniature fort about two hundred metres away that looked like something out of an old film or perhaps a Tintin book. There was no other sign of life. About a mile on, the sand turned silvery grey and he realized that he was staring at the edge of a huge lake. There was something odd about the water. It looked utterly dead.

The heat was intense, buffeting his face. He could smell aviation fuel from the helicopter. He already knew that even if he managed to escape, there would be no way out. There was simply nowhere to go. Where was Siwa? That was the name on the brochure he had found. But if the oasis town was anywhere around, it was out of sight.

"Get in the jeep, Rider." Julius Grief had climbed out of the helicopter and stood beside him. "There's someone waiting to meet you."

Alex said nothing but did as he was told. The jeep had been waiting beside the landing area, the driver in Bedouin dress and another man with him, carrying a rifle. Alex got in the back; Julius sat in the front. They started up and drove the short distance to an arched entrance with two massive gates. As they passed into the fort, the gates swung slowly shut behind them, eventually meeting with a solid and conclusive thud.

And now there was activity all around him. As the jeep slowed down, Alex took it all in: Arab guards with machine guns, a radio tower, satellite dishes, more jeeps, watchtowers and spotlights. There was a man drawing water from the well, another digging at some sort of salt pile. Overhead, a rope bridge stretched from one side to the other. He counted about a dozen buildings of different sizes, including one that looked like a chapel, and one that was more like a doll's house.

There was no sign of Jack.

"This way," Julius said.

Alex followed his doppelgänger into a long, narrow building set right next to one of the walls. He found himself in a cool, empty space with a wooden floor and a fan turning in the ceiling. There was a chair with a Cairo College uniform neatly folded and hanging on the back. Two guards, silent and emotionless, stood waiting for him.

There was a movement at the door and someone else came in. Before they had even spoken, Alex felt the atmosphere in the room change. He turned and found himself facing a short, very slender man with close-cropped silver hair and round glasses. The man looked too small and girlish to be dangerous but Alex knew he must be in charge.

He stopped in front of Alex and examined him. "What happened to his face?" he demanded.

"I hit him," Grief replied.

"That's very displeasing, Julius. I specifically asked you not to do that."

"He annoyed me."

The man turned to Alex. "Welcome to Siwa," he said. "My name is Abdul-Aziz al-Razim and I've been looking forward very much to meeting you. I have to say, you do bear a remarkable similarity to Julius here, a credit to the artistry of modern plastic surgery. I hope you didn't find the journey too stressful."

"Where's Jack?" Alex demanded.

"She's here. She's unhurt – for the time being."

"I want to see her."

"I'm sure you do, but that won't be possible. As a matter of fact, I'm afraid you have a rather distasteful experience ahead of you. Believe me when I say that I take no pleasure in it, but I'm aware that in the past you have been equipped with certain ingenious gadgets, and I also know that your Mr Smithers has been in Cairo. So I'm afraid you'll have to be stripped and searched from head to foot. I won't actually witness this myself; I'll spare your blushes. But I would advise you to cooperate with my guards or they will hurt you quite considerably.

"After that you will take a shower and all your clothes will be replaced. We have a school uniform for you, there, on the chair. We don't want any exploding buttons or anything like that. As you can see, Alex, I am not a man who makes mistakes.

You are now in my power and will remain so until the end of your life."

"Which isn't a very long time," Julius muttered.

"That is indeed the case." Razim sounded almost sad. "But we can discuss that in the morning. After the guards have finished with you, they'll take you to a cell. You might be interested to know that we are in an eighteenth-century French fort and this used to be the prison block. You will be given dinner and then left to sleep. I advise you to take advantage of it. You'll need all the rest you can get."

Julius smirked. Razim nodded at the guards, who moved forward.

"Goodnight, Alex. We will meet again tomorrow."

"Sleep well!" Julius crowed.

The two of them left together, and the guards began their work.

Two hours later, Alex found himself back in school uniform, alone in a cell that measured about ten metres square with a bunk, a table and a bucket for him to use in the night. There was a single, barred window that overlooked the outer wall, a long shadow stretching out in the corridor in between.

After about twenty minutes the door opened and a guard came in with a tray holding bread, soup and a bottle of water. This was all he was going to get for the night. But there was no point starving himself. Alex ate the food and drank half the water. He curled up on the bunk and a short while later, despite everything, he was asleep.

And now it was morning and the scorpion, alarmed by something, suddenly scuttled forward and disappeared over the windowsill. Alex looked up at the sun and guessed it must be about eight. A moment later, the guard who had brought Alex's dinner returned, dressed in baggy trousers with a scarf around his head. There was a machine gun slung across his back. He signalled with one hand. The message was clear. *Come with me.*

Alex was led back out of the cell and down the passageway to the area where he had been received the night before. As he went, he heard a familiar voice.

"Take your hands off me, you creep. Who do you think you are, anyway? Just because you've got a gun."

It was Jack. Alex hurried forward and there she was, poking her finger into the chest of a man who was twice her size. She was dressed in the clothes she must have been planning to wear for the flight: pale jeans and a shirt with the ends knotted around her waist. Her hair was a bit bedraggled and there was a tiredness in her eyes, but otherwise she looked fine.

"Jack!" Ignoring the guard who was right behind him, Alex ran over to her.

"Alex!"

The two of them embraced. They were surrounded by armed men but for the moment all of them were forgotten.

"Are you OK?" Alex asked.

"I'm fine. But I told you. You shouldn't have come."

"I didn't have any choice, Jack. I couldn't just leave you."

"I know." She held him close. "Don't worry," she whispered. "I think I've found a way out of here." Then, louder: "Who are these people, Alex? What is this place?"

"I don't know," he replied. "But I think we're about to find out."

"Come. Now." One of the guards had managed two words of English. He pointed at the door.

It was early morning but the sun was already hot. Alex and Jack were led past the main gates and across to the house where Razim lived. Alex looked around him. He had already counted a dozen guards and there were probably more. This was the home of someone who liked to feel extremely secure. Razim was waiting for them on a small terrace that he had constructed in front of his home. There was a stone table surrounded by dwarf palms sprouting out of terracotta pots. A stone lion dribbled water into a basin, the tinkling sound giving an illusion of cool in the desert heat. Razim was wearing a white dishdasha that looked brand new. He was eating breakfast: fresh figs, yoghurt, pastries and tea. There was also a packet of cigarettes – Black Devils – beside him. Alex was glad to see that the table was set for three. It seemed that Julius Grief wouldn't be joining them.

Seeing them, Razim got to his feet. "Please join me. I hope you don't mind my starting without you. I never sleep after five o'clock and I'm always rather hungry by the time it comes to breakfast. However, there's plenty left. Do sit down."

Jack glanced at Alex as if for advice. Alex nodded and they took their places.

Razim seemed pleased. He fussed over them, moving dishes and pouring the tea as if they were guests who had chanced to pop in rather than his prisoners. Meanwhile, Alex continued to look around him. It was already obvious that it would be almost impossible to escape from the fort, and yet, he remembered what Jack had just said. *I think I've found a way out...* She'd been here a little longer than him. Could she have possibly seen something that he'd missed?

"Will you have some tea, Alex?" Razim held out the pot.

"Thank you." Alex hated the fake politeness, the pretence that all this was civilized. He'd been here before. Tea in the garden with Damian Cray. Dinner with Julia Rothman. All these people had to act like they were human. To disguise the fact that they were anything but.

But Jack wasn't having any of it. "What do you

want with us?" she demanded. "Alex ought to be at school. You've got no right to bring him here."

Razim set down the teapot and helped himself to a spoonful of yoghurt. "Let's not keep up the pretence that Alex is an ordinary schoolboy, Miss Starbright," he said. "We all know who he is and what he is. And, for that matter, you really shouldn't speak to me as if I were an ordinary man. Of course I have no right to keep you prisoners here. But I am a criminal. Why not be honest about it? The law means nothing to me. I do exactly what I want."

"What *do* you want?"

"You're very direct! Please have some breakfast. You both need to eat and – particularly in this heat – to drink."

Alex took some fruit. Jack hesitated, then did the same. A man walked past them pushing a wheelbarrow piled high with salt crystals.

Razim licked his spoon clean. "That's better," he said. "I'm sure the two of you have a lot of questions, so let me put your minds at rest by answering at least a few of them."

"You don't need to tell us anything," Alex interrupted. "I already know that you're part of Scorpia and that you're planning to assassinate the American secretary of state when she gives her speech in Cairo this weekend. I also know where we are. We're close to the town of Siwa."

At least some of this was guesswork but Alex was pleased to see a flicker of surprise behind the two circles of glass. Razim had been thrown and couldn't conceal it.

"I know this," he went on. "And MI6 know it too. By now they'll have realized that Jack and I are missing and they'll come looking for us. If you let us go now, you might have time to save yourself. But otherwise I'd say you're pretty much finished."

There was a long silence. Then Razim broke into a forced, unnatural laugh. "Well spoken, Alex," he said. "My friends at Scorpia told me you were someone to be reckoned with and they were certainly right. I am willing to accept that you have managed to work out at least part of what we are planning. You have seen the rifle. It is common knowledge that the secretary of state will be here tomorrow. But it is too late to stop us, and I can assure you that you have no idea at all of our true aims.

"As to the arrival of MI6, which I am inclined to doubt, they may find it more difficult than you think to reach us. This fort was built more than two hundred years ago, but I have made certain modifications. We are in the middle of a minefield. There is what you might call a necklace of road-side devices similar to those used in Afghanistan around the compound. We can activate them the moment we come under attack – there's a series of switches in the control room." He gestured at the old bakehouse with its brick chimney. "You might also like to know that the watchtowers are equipped with radar warning and electronic warfare antennas. We have enough firepower here to blast an entire fleet of aircraft out of the sky. The Iranians kindly provided us with several of their SA-2 medium-range, high-altitude surface-to-air missiles. At a price, of course. But I am a man who likes to feel safe and were any enemy forces to show themselves – in the air or on land – I can assure you that it would be a simple matter to blow them to smithereens."

He smiled and laid down his spoon, lining it up exactly with his plate.

"But even if by some miracle MI6 did manage to find us and break in, they would still be too late," he continued. "I am leaving Egypt tomorrow night. I have a new identity and a new life waiting for me in another part of the world. And as for you, Alex ... well, that was what I wanted to talk to you about. That's why I invited you to join me."

He paused. Alex glanced at Jack, willing her to stay quiet, not to endanger herself. He knew she wasn't going to like what they were about to hear.

"I will make no secret of the fact that you have been a considerable nuisance to my colleagues in Scorpia," he began. "Indeed, one of the things that attracted them to this operation was that you were going to be at the centre of it. Speaking personally, I have no interest in revenge. And I want you to understand that I have no particular feelings about you. You seem a pleasant enough boy. But unfortunately for you, you are now completely in my power and, as it happens, I am a scientist. Recently I have been doing a great deal of research into the subject of pain. This evening, when the sun sets, I intend to perform an experiment on you. In effect, my aim is to cause you more pain than you have ever known; more pain than you can begin to imagine."

"You're mad..." Jack whispered.

Razim ignored her. "It's strange, but imagining pain actually makes it worse when it finally arrives. This is something I have discovered through my research. I notice that you are clutching a fruit knife, Miss Starbright, and perhaps plan to attack me with it. I can assure you that my guards will shoot you before you can even rise out of your chair."

Jack's hand had indeed closed around one of the knives. She was hardly breathing and her eyes were pinpricks of fury. Alex reached out and touched her arm. She put the knife down.

"Thank you. Now, where was I? Yes. It's a bit like entering a swimming pool. The child who imagines the cold water, who enters it one inch at a time, has a much worse experience than the child who simply runs off the diving board and jumps in. The dread that one feels before visiting the dentist is often as unpleasant as the visit itself. That is why I'm telling you this now, Alex. I want you to start thinking about what lies in store for you tonight.

You see that building over there?" He pointed to what looked like a chapel on the far side of the fort. "That is where you will be taken. That is where, for you, hell is waiting."

"You can't do this," Jack said. "You're a monster! Alex is a fifteen-year-old boy!"

"It is because he is fifteen that he is so useful to me. And please don't bore me with this stupid name-calling. I have already made it quite clear to you that Alex Rider is nothing to me. I am not like Julius, for example, who hates him very much; who is, indeed, consumed by hatred. I have no such emotions. For me, hate is as much a waste of time as love. Alex has been a useful device in a plan that I have created for Scorpia. Tonight he will be useful to me. That is all. I simply want the two of you to prepare."

Razim pulled the cigarette packet towards him and opened it. There was one cigarette left. He took it out and lit it. "You have the rest of the day to yourselves," he said. "You are free to walk in the desert; the salt lakes have a certain beauty and you may like a swim. I can lend you both costumes. Do not take this as a sign of weakness on my part. You have no water and it would be quite impossible for you to walk the ten miles to the town of Siwa in the full heat of the day. And anyway, you will be watched at all times. As you may have appreciated when you were brought here, Alex, I have reasons for not wanting to damage you. But if you stray too far from the fort, if you attempt to do anything that gives me reason to believe that you are trying to escape, I will not hesitate to put a bullet in your friend. Do you understand me?"

"I understand you completely," Alex said. There was contempt in his voice.

"Good." Razim stood up. "I have a few last-minute preparations to take care of, but please feel free to have as much breakfast as you want. Lunch will be served here as well. The guards will take you back to your cells at four o'clock – you'll need to get as much rest as you can before your experience tonight. I hope you both enjoy what time is left to you."

Jack waited until Razim had disappeared into the house before she began to speak. "Oh, Alex..." The words came out almost as a sob.

"Let's not talk here," Alex said. "We might be overheard." He looked briefly at the archway and the open gates that led out of the fort. It was still hard to believe that Razim was just letting them walk out. But then again, they were in the middle of the desert – a perfect prison even if it didn't have any walls. "He said we could go for a swim, so let's do that. No one will be able to hear us in the middle of a lake."

In the end they didn't swim. Two of the guards had followed them and stood watching, twenty paces away. Instead they walked along the shore-line of one of the extraordinary lakes that had somehow sprung up in the middle of the desert with so much salt in the water that strange crystal formations were spreading out across the sand. The fort was about a quarter of a mile away and reminded Alex of something he might have built when he was six or seven years old.

They had both heard what Razim had said. Neither of them knew quite what to say. Alex realized that Razim had done this on purpose. He might pretend to be a scientist. He might claim to have no feelings. But deep down he was getting some foul pleasure from their pain.

It was Jack who broke the silence. "What a bastard! What a little jerk! I won't let him hurt you, Alex. I swear to God..." Suddenly there were tears in her eyes and she didn't try to wipe them away. "I never had any idea," she went on. "When you went away on all those missions, I knew it was bad, but I never thought it was like this. How could we have let this happen to you all this time? And your uncle actually wanted you to be a spy! They're all as bad as each other – Alan Blunt, Mrs Jones ... even Mr Smithers. They should never have allowed it."

Alex put an arm round her. "Don't worry, Jack," he said. "I'll get away." He forced a smile. "I always do."

Jack nodded and used the backs of her hands to wipe her eyes. "If we could steal one of the cars..."

"We don't have the keys."

"Didn't MI6 teach you how to hot-wire an engine?" Jack said, shaking her head. "Typical! There is one other thing, Alex." She looked round, checking that the guards were far enough away. "Before you arrived, I was alone in my cell for a time and there was something I noticed. The walls are brick but the cement is some sort of mixture of salt and mud. And one of the bars of my window is a little loose."

"Can you get it out?"

"I might be able to. Look!" Carefully she lifted her shirt to show Alex a knife tucked into her waistband. "I stole it at the end of breakfast, after that creep had left. I can use it to dig into the cement. It's very soft. And if I can get the bar out, I can squeeze through."

Alex felt the first stirrings of hope. "And then?"

"Somehow I get you out of your cell and off we go. When they flew me here, we passed over Siwa. I saw it, and it can't be more than about fifteen minutes away by car. If we can get there and raise the alarm ... we just have to make one phone call. And that'll be the end of Abdul-Aziz al-Ratface, or whatever he calls himself. He won't have time to come after us. He'll have to get out fast."

"What about the keys?" Alex asked.

"I noticed that too. They leave them in the cars." Jack smiled. "You see – they're not as smart as they think they are."

Alex thought about what Jack had just said. Everything made sense, and yet at the same time, something worried him. Three basic errors. The loose bar, the car keys, the knife that had gone missing without anyone noticing. It seemed almost too good to be true. On the other hand, Jack could be right. Razim thought he had all the odds on his side. That could be making him careless.

"All right," Alex said. "But listen to me, Jack. If you get a chance to escape without me, that's what you have to do."

"I'd never leave you behind," Jack said.

"You might have to. If it's a choice between one of us or neither of us, you have to go." He reached out and held her hand. "And please, watch out for yourself, Jack. I've met people like this before and I'm telling you, they know what they're doing. This is Scorpia we're talking about."

"You've beaten them twice," Jack reminded him.

Alex nodded. "Let's hope it's third time lucky."

They spent the rest of the day together, sitting in the shade, talking about anything that would take their minds off the clock ticking away, the evening drawing in. Alex tried to forget what Razim had said.

*...more pain than you have ever known...*

They talked about Brookland, Sabina, the house in Chelsea ... anything that would fill the silence. There was no sign of Julius Grief, and Razim seemed to have disappeared too. Maybe they were both inside. The sun was blazing down and there was barely any breeze. The two of them could have swum in the salt lake but neither of them felt like it. Eventually a guard appeared and in broken English told them that it was time to go back to their cells. Neither of them wanted to show any emotion in front of these people so they embraced briefly.

"Good luck," Alex whispered.

"I'll come for you. I promise..."

Alex was taken to his cell. Jack's was further down the corridor, on the opposite side. Before the doors were locked, Alex was able to look around him and he saw, with a heavy heart, that Razim was being true to his word. He was taking no chances. A wooden chair had been placed in the middle of the corridor and there was already another guard sitting there. If he heard the slightest sound he would raise the alarm.

The two doors slammed shut. The keys were turned.

Time slowed down. Alex felt every minute as it lumbered past. He knew that all this was part of Razim's plan. He wanted Alex to think about what lay ahead, and he tried as best he could to put it out of his mind.

...*more pain than you can begin to imagine*...

But of course he couldn't. What were they going to do to him? Alex remembered the scorpions he had seen that morning. Maybe that was their plan.

No. Stop. Don't even think about it. Don't let your imagination do their work for them.

All too quickly the sun began to set. Why couldn't it hover in the sky a little longer? Why was it suddenly so eager for the end of the day?

Darkness fell. The door swung open and Julius Grief was there. He had also changed into Cairo College uniform, as if determined to mimic Alex to the bitter end.

"It's time!" he crowed. "I can't tell you how much I'm looking forward to this!"

There were two guards with him, both of them armed. Alex stood up. He had no choice. He stepped out into the corridor. There was no sign of Jack.

With Julius Grief striding ahead, the three of them led him out.

# *HELL IS HERE*

Alex couldn't move.

He was sitting under bright spotlights in a high-backed leather chair, strapped in place by soft cords around his wrists, ankles and neck. No matter how much he struggled, they would make no mark. A series of wires ran down his naked chest; each one had been carefully positioned and stuck in place by an unsmiling female technician in a white coat, the only woman Alex had seen since he had arrived at the fort. There were more wires attached to two of his fingers, his pulse, his forehead and the side of his neck.

The air conditioning had been turned up high and Alex could feel his own sweat chilling against his skin. With its thick, white-painted walls curving around him, the room reminded him of an oversized igloo. He was connected to a variety of machines that were already measuring everything that was happening inside him. Out of the corner of his eye he could see a green dot pulsing across a screen, and knew it was recording his heartbeat. The dot was moving very fast. He tried willing it to slow down but he was no longer in control. Alex hated the way that he had been reduced to nothing more than a laboratory specimen, but there was nothing he could do.

They had finished by wheeling a large TV screen in front of him and he had wondered what it was for. Was Razim going to show him some sort of horror film? Nothing could be worse than the horror that was all around him. For the moment, the television was turned off. The technician and the guards had withdrawn, leaving him alone.

Alex waited to see what would happen next. He thought about Jack. Even now, there was a part of him that was more scared for her than for himself. He had been in situations like this before. A lot of unpleasant people had threatened him with a lot of unpleasant things, yet somehow he had always come through. But this was all new to her. While he sat here, she would be putting her plan into operation, trying to escape. He just hoped she would take care. She had no idea what she was up against.

Footsteps on the concrete floor. Julius Grief had returned, this time in the company of Abdul-Aziz al-Razim. The boy's face was flushed with excitement and anticipation, and it made Alex's stomach churn to see this grotesque version of himself capering towards him. Razim had changed into a pale grey collarless jacket and trousers that made him look like an upmarket dentist. He was wearing an earpiece with a wire snaking down behind his shoulder. As he stopped in front of the chair, the spotlights reflected in his spectacles and his eyes briefly disappeared behind two blazing circles of white.

"Are you afraid, Alex?" he asked.

Alex didn't answer. He didn't trust himself to speak.

"Would you like a glass of water before we begin?"

Still Alex said nothing.

"A great many people have sat where you are sitting now," Razim went on. "I have conducted many experiments in this room, and one day the world will be grateful for the information I have gathered. It is very unusual for me to have a teenager, and in normal circumstances it would suggest to me many possibilities."

He reached out. He was standing next to a trolley draped with a sheet and he uncovered it to reveal a long line of knives and scalpels, neatly laid out. Alex knew that he was doing it on purpose for effect. It was the act of a bad stage magician in a cheap theatre. He tried not to look at the gleaming instruments. He already knew that he couldn't break free. All he could do was sit and wait.

"As you can see, there are all sorts of ways that I could cause you pain, Alex," Razim murmured. "My young friend Julius has ideas of his own. Left to himself he would, I am sure, do unspeakable things to you, starting perhaps with your toes and working up. He would enjoy that very much. Unfortunately I cannot allow him to go ahead. We are both somewhat limited as, for reasons I won't go into at the moment, you cannot be marked in any way. No cuts or bruises! No bits missing! And so, with regret, we must say farewell to the knives and the syringes. There will be no blood-shed tonight."

He re-covered the trolley and pushed it away.

"However, do not believe for a minute that this offers you some sort of easy way out. I have made it my life's work to study pain in all its different forms, and the pain I intend to inflict on you will be perhaps even worse. There are two instruments that I am going to use. Earlier today I promised you hell. And now, my dear child, it is here."

He reached down and took hold of two plastic boxes. Alex recognized one immediately. It was a remote control, presumably for the television screen in front of him. The other was similar, about the size of a mobile phone, with a single red button in the centre. Razim handed this to Julius, who took it gratefully, licking his lips and rolling it in his palm.

Razim tapped his earpiece as if awaiting instructions. "Are you ready, Alex?" he asked. "There's something I want you to see."

He turned on the TV.

* * *

Jack had begun working on the bar the moment she had heard Alex being taken from his cell. As the footsteps faded into the distance, she felt a black steel mesh of shock and disbelief slamming down in her mind. Jack had always thought the best of people. She had refused to believe that anyone could be completely heartless and evil. Her breakfast with Razim had proved her wrong.

She had seen the guard sitting outside in the corridor and had no idea if he was still there. Hopefully Razim wouldn't have considered her important enough to watch over while he dealt with Alex. Even so, she would have to work quietly. And quickly. What were they going to do to him? How soon would they start? Jack felt the tears rising and angrily wiped them away. Crying wasn't going to help Alex. She had to get out of here.

The window looked out onto a strip of sand and rubble with another building, possibly a store-house, directly opposite. There were just two vertical bars, solid steel, set side by side as if in a cartoon. She only had to remove one and she would have enough space to squeeze out. And one of them, as she had discovered, was loose.

The fruit knife that she had stolen from the breakfast table was small, with a blunt edge. Even if she had been able to use it to attack Razim, it was unlikely that she would have done him much harm. But it was surprisingly effective against the crumbling cement that surrounded the bar. She was using it like a chisel, chipping away, making sure that the rubble fell into the cell where nobody could see it. The cement was very soft, almost like putty. And maybe it had rained – did it ever rain in the desert? – because it was damp to the touch. The bar was already wobbling. Soon she would be able to pull it free.

But how soon? Alex had been gone for about ten minutes and she dreaded to think what they might be doing to him. It was worse than that. She had to use all her mental strength not to think about Alex, to put him out of her mind. Otherwise she would be too sick to continue. She was his only hope. She was going to break out and bring help. She had come all the way to Egypt to look after him and she wasn't going to let him down.

She had scooped out a lot of the cement, forming a cavity around the bar. She tugged and it came free. It happened so suddenly that she actually dropped it, trying to grab it with fumbling fingers and only half catching it as, with a dull clang, it hit the floor. She froze, terrified that the sound of metal on concrete would alert the guard if he was still sitting outside. She waited a minute, her heart pounding. Nobody came. The door didn't open.

She pulled herself up and stuck her head out of the gap she had made.

The prison block was in one corner of the fort, on the opposite side to Razim's house. Leaning out, Jack could just glimpse the main courtyard with the salt pile that the guards had collected. The sun had set long ago and the sky was that strange, intense black that seems unique to the desert. Even the stars seemed very distant, barely glimmering, and there was a sense of stillness, of the world holding its breath until the coming of the next dawn.

Jack was about to heave herself up, then had second thoughts and grabbed the metal bar and looped it through her belt. It was the only weapon she had and she might need it. Getting out of the cell wasn't going to be easy. The bunk was in the wrong place and screwed down to the floor. There was no chair. She had to hoist herself up, straining the muscles in her arms, and then pull her head and shoulders through the narrow space between the remaining bar and the edge of the window.

Somehow she managed to manoeuvre herself so that she was dangling half outside, and she twisted round, wincing as the loose metal bar dug into her stomach. For a moment, she thought she was stuck. Her hips were the widest part of her body and they refused to pass through. She was almost prepared for the humiliation of being discovered and dragged back inside. If anyone walked round the back of the storehouse, they would be certain to see her. The thought gave her extra strength. One final squeeze and she had made it, falling in a tangle of arms and legs to the ground below.

She landed heavily, winding herself. There were bruises all the way down the side of her body where she had positioned the bar. For about five seconds she didn't move. Surely someone must have heard her. She had made so much noise! But perhaps the guards were at dinner. Perhaps they were helping to deal with Alex.

Alex, what are they doing to you? I can't wait. I have to get help.

Nobody came. Jack picked up the bar and got to her feet. Now all she had to do was steal a car and drive away.

The main courtyard was about fifteen paces away on her right, and this was where she headed, following the wall of the storehouse. It seemed to her that the shadows were darker on the other side, away from the prison block. The courtyard was where the cars were parked; she had seen them earlier. About halfway along she came to an open doorway with a pile of crates and boxes stacked up around it. There were lights on inside and she peered in nervously. It was a kitchen. She saw a fridge, a microwave, some cupboards, a table and chairs. Maybe this was where the guards came to eat and relax when they were off duty. But nobody was there now.

She continued to the end, crouching low in case one of the guards was on the rope bridge that stretched high up from wall to wall. But the whole fort seemed abandoned. Her pulse raced. There was a car, a very old and beaten-up Land Rover, parked right in front of her. Incredibly she could even see the keys in the ignition. Surely it couldn't be as easy as this!

It wasn't. A young, bearded guard was standing right next to it, leaning on the bonnet smoking a cigarette. There was a rifle slung over his shoulder. To reach the car she would have to get past him. Or she could knock him out with the bar. But she would never be able to sneak up on him without being heard. Sound carries too easily in the desert evening, particularly when surrounded by the great silence of the sands. Somehow she had to distract him. She had to make him come to her.

And quickly. They're hurting Alex. They've already started.

She remembered the kitchen. It was just a few steps back and she darted in. She threw open the fridge and, with a surge of relief, found what she was looking for: a carton of eggs. Why should she have remembered this now? It was the sight of the microwave that had done it. A failed experiment by a ten-year-old Alex Rider. How she had yelled at him at the time! But now she could use it.

She put one of the eggs in the microwave, swivelled the knob to five minutes and turned it on. Then she hurried back outside and hid behind the boxes. She wondered if it would have been sensible to have armed herself with a kitchen knife, but the idea revolted her; and anyway, she hadn't seen

339

one around. She waited, counting the seconds. She could imagine the egg turning slowly behind the glass door on its rotating plate. As Alex had discovered, you can't cook an egg that way. There was a bang as the egg exploded, showering itself all over the inside of the microwave.

As she had hoped, the guard had heard the noise and came running almost immediately. He stopped at the entrance to the kitchen and looked inside, wondering what had happened. That was when Jack tiptoed forward and hit him on the back of the head with the iron bar, using all her strength. He grunted and fell sideways. Jack made sure he was really unconscious, then turned and ran for the car.

All sorts of thoughts were flying through her mind. Should she have taken the guard's rifle? Could she make her way through the fort, find Alex and take him with her? No – that would be too dangerous. Right now, she had the element of surprise, but the moment she tried to start a fight, Razim would have her outnumbered by about twenty to one. She hated leaving Alex behind but she remembered what he had said beside the lake. Better one of them out than neither of them. Siwa wasn't too far away. She would drive there and come back with reinforcements: the local police, the army, whatever. And the moment Razim heard the car leaving, as soon as he found out what had happened, he would stop whatever he was doing and come after her. Alex would be all right.

She got into the car, closing the door softly behind her so that it made no sound. There was nobody guarding the gates. They were open, with the desert and a single track stretching out beyond. This was somehow all too good to be true. Would the car start? She turned the key and the engine purred into life. Nobody shouted at her. Nobody came running.

What about the mines? Razim had said there was a defensive circle all the way round the fort. But she remembered his words. They were only turned on if he believed he was under attack. She would just have to hope for the best. There might be other tyre tracks she could follow through the sand.

Hang on, Alex. Help is on its way.

She pushed the car into first gear and moved off.

It took the television screen several seconds to warm up. Alex found himself looking at a black and white image that was so fuzzy, at first he didn't understand what he was seeing. Julius Grief was leering at him, waiting for him to work it out. Razim was standing to one side, resting the TV remote control in his palm. Alex thought of closing his eyes, of looking away. Whatever these two freaks were trying to show him, it couldn't be good. But then he realized what was happening and knew that he was trapped, that it was already too late.

There must have been a camera hidden somewhere high up in Jack's cell. Jack had her back to him but he could see her attacking the bar of the window with the knife she had taken, cutting into the cement. Alex still didn't know why they were doing this, what they wanted. But as he watched her, Razim began a soft, mocking commentary.

"So it would seem that your friend Miss Starbright stole a knife from the breakfast table this morning. That was very bad of her. But shall I tell you a little secret, Alex? I had an idea that she might. In fact, I rather wanted her to. And she didn't disappoint me."

On the screen Alex saw the bar fall out of the window. Jack only half caught it before it hit the concrete floor.

"And there you are," Razim continued. "Who would have thought that someone as careful as me would put your friend in a cell with a metal bar just waiting to come loose? And how foolish of me to dismiss the guards who usually patrol the prison block, leaving her free to wriggle out. What could I have been thinking of?"

Alex was beginning to see where this was going. All around him the machines pulsed and flickered and the needles began to twitch. Julius Grief was grinning, still clutching the black plastic box that Razim had given him.

"Now look at that! She's out! She's free. And despite all the noise she's made, nobody has heard. I wonder if anyone has left a car for her to help her get away?"

There were other cameras outside. Alex saw Jack look into the kitchen, then continue down the passageway, where a third camera picked up the main courtyard with the waiting Land Rover.

"Just one guard," Razim crooned. "We didn't want to make this too easy, did we!"

"You wanted this to happen." Alex wasn't sure how he found the words. There was a terrible crushing feeling in his chest, as if he were being scooped hollow.

"Of course. We were using a long-range listening device when you were at the lake this morning. Why else do you think I let the two of you walk alone? It might amuse you to know that the technology was almost exactly the same as that water bottle gadget you were given by Mr Smithers. Yes. I know about that too."

Razim moved closer, so close that when he spoke again, Alex could feel his breath on his cheek. "Have you not yet learned? I am a master of manipulation. I manipulated MI6 into sending you here. I manipulated your arrival at the Cairo International College of Arts and Education. And very soon I will manipulate the British government into doing exactly what I demand. From the start I have been pushing the buttons and pulling the strings. All along you have been dancing to my tune..."

Razim nodded at the screen. Alex watched Jack come out of her hiding place and knock out the guard.

Julius giggled. "She thinks she's being so clever!" he exclaimed.

"I must say, I hadn't expected her to injure my guard," Razim said. "But as to the rest of it ... shall we tell Alex?"

"Yes!" Grief's eyes were blazing. "Tell him!"

"There are two types of pain, Alex. Physical and emotional. Up until now, my experiments have all been physical. But as I have already told you, I need you intact. So it is emotional pain that I am measuring right now, and so far, the results are already impressive."

The needles were jumping and swaying like grass in the wind. Pulses of light were shooting across the screens. Alex's entire body was tense, his hands straining at the bonds, his eyes staring. He knew what was coming. He had worked it out.

"Please," he pleaded. "She has nothing to do with this. You don't have to hurt her."

Jack had got into the car.

"Miss Starbright is now sitting on thirty pounds of high explosive," Razim said. "Consider the situation, Alex. She has been with you all your life. She is, I am sure you would agree, your best friend."

"Leave her!" The machines had gone mad. Alex was writhing, trying to break free.

"She is your best friend. And the remote control, the device that will detonate the explosive, is in the hands of someone who hates you, who has been dreaming for more than a year of destroying you.

344

Why don't you speak to him, Alex? Why don't you ask him to take pity on you?"

On the screen Jack had driven out of the fort. The Land Rover was already on the track and picking up speed.

"Please!" Alex felt hot liquid pouring from his eyes. He couldn't help it. "Don't..."

"I'm sorry?" Julius pushed his face into Alex's. "I don't think I heard you."

"Please, Julius. I'll do anything you want..."

"You're doing *exactly* what I want," Julius said. He was holding the remote control right in Alex's face.

Alex saw his thumb press down.

The car blew up.

The images weren't black and white after all. The fireball was bright red and orange at the centre. The explosion seemed to swallow up the entire desert and sky. For a moment, there was no image at all. Then the cameras picked up the flaming skeleton of the car, fire roaring through the shattered windows, and Alex knew that Jack Starbright was dead.

Jack Starbright, who had looked after him since he was seven. Who had been by his side at the funeral of his uncle and who had tried to protect him once Ian Rider's secrets had taken over his life. Jack Starbright, who had packed his books for school and taken care of his injuries, always cheerful, always on his side. Jack Starbright, the one person he could confide in, who understood him better than anyone and who should never have set foot in the terrible, shadowy world that he had inherited.

Alex Rider's grief burst out of him. There was no stopping it. The tears coursed down his cheeks. He was howling, his whole body contorted, his eyes tight shut. At the same time, Julius Grief was capering about him, laughing while Razim examined his apparatus, tapping at a keyboard, comparing different readings.

"It's extraordinary," he muttered. "We've never had readings like this. Never. It seems that I have completely underestimated the power of emotional pain. I may even have to create a second scale of measurement. This is really quite remarkable."

Alex slumped forward, his head lolling against his chest. He had blacked out. But still the machines sucked out and translated his emotions: the computers, the monitors, the printers, the gauges.

"Wasn't that great!" Julius exclaimed. "Wasn't that cool!"

"Go to bed, Julius," Razim replied. He picked up a printout and held it up to examine the figures. "I have work to do."

Two guards had arrived. They untied Alex and dragged him away. Julius followed them out of the room. Razim stayed where he was, deep in thought.

Out in the desert the flames flickered in the darkness, throwing jagged red shadows across the sand.

# HALF AN INCH

The convoy was moving swiftly through the streets of Cairo. There were nine vehicles in all, starting with two police cars and four outriders on motorbikes. The three cars at the centre of the procession were identical: oversized black limousines with tinted windows and a miniature Stars and Stripes fluttering at the corner. The limos had begun their journey a mile away, at the American embassy in Garden City, and from the moment they had swung out of the gates and onto the main road, a whole army of Egyptian police had been deployed to keep them moving, with officers holding back the traffic at every corner and every light. From the air the convoy might have looked like a living animal, a snake perhaps, burrowing its way through a hundred thousand ants.

The secretary of state was in the first limousine. It might have been safer for her to ride in the middle one with CIA agents in front and behind, but that was also the more obvious target. Even though the cars were armour-plated, an armour-piercing missile launched from a rooftop was always a possibility. All the roofs had been checked. Armed police had taken up strategic positions all the way along the route and would remain there until the night was over. Habib, the man known as the Engineer, had been seen in Cairo. He might have been killed, but not before he had given someone a weapon. Nothing could be left to chance.

Sitting in the back seat, next to the window, the secretary of state watched the drab buildings and the stationary traffic as they flashed by. She was a small woman with steely eyes and tied-back silver hair, wearing an off-white silk jacket and skirt, a white shirt and a jade necklace that had been given to her by the Chinese premier on a recent visit. There was a short, bald man in a dark suit next to her. He looked nervous but she knew it had nothing to do with the security arrangements. He was her foreign policy adviser and he was already thinking about what she was going to say. It was always a dangerous business making new enemies, and her speech tonight would do just that. Her driver and bodyguard – both CIA – were in the front. They knew nothing. To them it was just another trip.

It seemed to have got dark very early. It was only half past six but the sky was already black. It was going to rain. The temperature had risen too high even for this sweltering city and it was obvious that something was going to break soon. The clouds were so heavy that they looked as if they were about to fall out of the sky, and the air seemed to be sticking to everything it touched. Even the air conditioning inside the car seemed to be fighting a losing battle.

"It's a pretty nasty night, Jeff," she said.

Jeff Townsend was the name of her foreign policy adviser. "There could be a downpour," he agreed.

"I thought it didn't rain in Cairo."

"It doesn't rain often, ma'am. But when it rains, it rains."

The secretary of state had a headache. It had been nagging at her ever since she had touched down in the presidential plane. She leaned forward. "Do you have an aspirin, Harry?"

"Sure thing, ma'am." Her bodyguard was also a trained medic. He handed her two pills, which she swallowed with a sip of mineral water from a bottle.

The convoy crossed the Nile on University Bridge and swept round al-Gamaa Square – actually a circular area and one that would normally have been jammed with traffic. It continued up a wide avenue with palm trees on each side and lawns and fountains in the centre. The university lay straight ahead. Even on a normal day security at the campus was high, with students passing through a single gateway and showing ID before they were allowed to continue. But this week security levels had soared, with triple checks, full body searches, metal detectors, the works. The Grand Hall had been in lockdown for the past twenty-four hours. Egyptian police with sniffer dogs had finished searching the place for the fifth time just a few hours ago.

The limousine drove through the gate. White-suited police stood to attention and saluted as it passed. And then the convoy was in the campus itself, with searchlights sweeping across the ground, people everywhere, helicopters hovering overhead. Even the secretary of state began to feel a little anxious. She noticed that inside, the police were wearing black and carried machine guns. Of course, she was used to this. She couldn't even cross Washington DC without the same sort of security. But she was in a strange place, far from home. And this thick, unnatural darkness felt like the end of the world.

The driver stopped exactly where he had been told. Even with the unpredictable Cairo traffic, everything had been planned with such precision that the secretary of state was only fifty seconds late. Someone ran forward and opened the door. She got out.

She was standing in front of a massive building that resembled a museum or an opera house, or perhaps a library with a million books. It stretched all the way across the main campus, its huge dome supported by five columns, and with steps that could have been purposely designed for the arrival of a president or a head of state. A red carpet led the way, with crash barriers on both sides holding back the crowds of journalists and photographers. There was the usual line of VIPs waiting to meet her, and the secretary of state found herself shaking hands with politicians, academics and businessmen – people she had never met before and would never see again. A hundred cameras flashed in the heavy heat. She felt a drop of rain on her shoulder and looked up. There were huge clouds rolling in.

Around the corner from the main entrance, in a separate space where they could be kept out of sight, a whole fleet of brightly coloured vans stood silently, feeding on the images of the arrival. These were OBUs – outside broadcast units – and they had been sent to record the speech for worldwide transmission. The BBC was there, along with Sky, CNN, Fox, al-Jazeera and news teams from all over the Middle East, jammed together in a tangle of thick black cables and satellite dishes. As the secretary of state continued along the line, shaking hands and nodding at smiling faces, her image was captured on a hundred television screens.

The OBUs were small and packed with equipment: monitor stacks, sound desks, vision racks, electric generators. Some of them had two or three producers already playing with the images, dissolving from one to another then cutting to some presenter in a studio miles away. A little girl handed the secretary of state some flowers, and the producers grabbed the moment, zooming in for the close-up, the reaction shot, the applause from the crowd. This was the big speech. It had to have a big build-up too.

The OBUs had arrived earlier in the day, filing in one at a time through the main gate. Each one carried a special permit on the window and every driver had shown his ID. But the vans themselves had not been searched. They were, after all, going to remain outside the building, and even if a journalist or sound engineer wanted to break into the Grand Hall, it would be impossible. Security was too tight. The outside broadcast units were part of the event. Nobody had considered that they might represent a threat.

But they were wrong.

One of the vans belonged to a television company called al-Minya and had arrived with the name in bright red letters and a pyramid logo painted on the side. It carried the right permit and the driver, dressed in white overalls with the same red pyramid on his top pocket, had shown what seemed to be an authentic ID. But if security had decided to telephone al-Minya – which was a real cable company – they would have been told that they weren't covering the speech. They hadn't sent an OBU, although, as it happened, one of their vehicles had recently had to go in for repairs.

If security had checked the number plate, they would have discovered that this was the missing vehicle. They might then have discovered that the driver – shaven-headed and built like a bulldog – had never worked in television and that his real name was Erik Gunter.

And finally they might have searched the van and found an English schoolboy, sitting with his arms tied and a gag in his mouth, a prisoner inside.

They had brought Alex Rider back from Siwa Oasis that afternoon, landing the Sikorsky H-34 at the same building site that he had been taken from after leaving the Northern Cemetery. He was wearing his Cairo College uniform and was securely belted in place. Without the belt he would have slumped forward. He seemed to be half asleep.

Gunter was waiting with the al-Minya van when the helicopter landed, and even he was a little surprised by the change in the boy who had been captured forty-eight hours ago. Despite his time in the sun Alex was an ashen white, and there was a lost, empty look in his eyes. When he was ordered to step down from the cabin, he did just that, and he didn't move as his hands were tied in front of him. Gunter led him into the van. Alex stumbled briefly at the doorway, steadying himself against one of the worktops. But he said nothing and he didn't try to resist. There hardly seemed any point gagging him. He looked completely defeated.

"What have you done to him?" Gunter asked.

Julius Grief had sprung down from the helicopter and followed them across the rubble-strewn ground. Like Alex he was in school uniform. "We played a little joke on him," he explained. "But I don't think he enjoyed it."

Four hours later, the al-Minya van was in its place at the very end of the line, furthest away from the entrance where the secretary of state had arrived. Along with all the other OBUs, it was plugged into the main feed being delivered by the television network inside the Grand Hall and received the same images as all the news channels. Julius Grief hadn't come with them. Gunter and Alex were alone.

Gunter was beginning to feel unnerved by the long silence and by the semi-conscious boy sitting bound by his arms and feet to a metal chair between two banks of machinery. He took out his gun – it was a black Russian-made Tokarev TT-33, the same gun that Alex had found in his office – and laid it on the desk, within easy reach. He had checked that the door of the OBU was locked but if anyone tried to come in, he wouldn't hesitate to kill them. Then he clicked open a can of Coke and turned one of the dials on the control panel in front of him.

"...the secretary of state has just arrived, and we can see her entering the building. The man beside her is Jeff Townsend, who has been her foreign policy adviser for the past two years..."

The voice was that of a CNN newsreader. Gunter could see the secretary of state on one of the monitors. She was walking down a wide corridor with officials applauding on both sides. Then the image cut to the audience waiting inside the Grand Hall. Two thousand people were sitting on three levels. Everyone was dressed smartly, packed together in rows that curved round in front of a stage decorated with a single lectern and two American flags.

From where he was sitting, Alex had a good view of the screen. But he didn't seem to be interested. Gunter wondered if he even knew where he was. Well, it didn't matter. He glanced at his watch. The speech was due to start in twelve minutes. And five minutes after that, Alex would be dead.

He stretched a hand out and turned off the sound. "I expect you want to know what this is all about," he said. He didn't really care if Alex wanted to know or not. He just felt a need to break the silence.

With the gag in his mouth, Alex couldn't talk. He didn't look as if he wanted to.

Gunter thought for a moment, then took out a knife, which flicked open in his hand. "I'm going to untie you," he said. "Because you'll be leaving here shortly. But if you even try to stand up or get out of that chair before I give you permission, I will shoot you in the stomach. Do you understand?"

Alex nodded very slightly.

"Good..."

Gunter would have had to untie Alex later anyway. It was part of the plan. He couldn't see any harm in doing it now. He stood up and leaned over him, cutting the ropes and releasing his arms. He stepped back quickly in case Alex tried to lash out, but the boy didn't even seem to be aware that he was free. Gunter cut the rest of the cords, took off the gag and sat down again. There was very little space between them. The gun was right next to him and his eyes had never left Alex's. The different screens inside the OBU showed pictures of the audience, the Grand Hall from outside, the empty stage.

"That's better," Gunter said. "We still have a bit of time together and I'd quite like to explain what's going on. The fact of the matter is that Scorpia have put together a rather brilliant plan and this is where it ends – just you and me, in this van. You get a bullet, I'm afraid. And do you know what I get? A million quid – just for moving one finger half an inch.

"I've never killed a kid before and for what it's worth, I don't feel too good about it. But it's not my fault. You don't know anything about me, so let me tell you. When I came out of Afghanistan ... do you know how many bullets I have in me? They dug two of them out but there are still two lodged inside – they couldn't reach them – and they're killing me. I can feel them. I took those bullets for my men and I was glad to do it. But when I got home, well, suddenly I discovered I wasn't quite the hero that I thought. They stuck me in a hospital in Birmingham – it was even a mixed ward. Can you believe that? I was in pain all the time; you have no idea how much pain. But when I rang the bell, nobody came. Sometimes I was just left there to soil the bed. It was disgusting.

"And in the end, when I was able to limp out of there, oh yes, they gave me the medal. But they didn't give me a decent pension. The army didn't want to know. I couldn't even get a job. Nobody gives a damn about the war in Afghanistan. Nobody cares. So when Scorpia came along, when they offered me this opportunity, do you think I was going to say no? A million quid, Alex. And too bad that I have to kill a kid. But right now I have to look out for number one."

Alex didn't speak. Gunter leaned over and suddenly slapped him. Alex's head rocked backwards.

"Talk to me, dammit," he said. "I want to know what you think."

"I don't think anything," Alex said.

Gunter nodded, as if this was enough. "I wonder if you've heard of the Elgin Marbles," he went on. "Did you ever study them in class? Or perhaps you went to see them at the British Museum. Well, believe it or not – and this must sound very strange to you, sitting here in the middle of Cairo – that's what this is all about. There was this rich Greek guy called Ariston and he wanted them sent back to Athens. Can you believe that? He was the one who hired Scorpia – and they've been playing you like a puppet on a string, you and MI6. You've been complete idiots from the very start.

"This is how it works." Gunter tilted his watch again. "In ten minutes' time the American secretary of state is going to begin a speech. She'll make some general remarks about the Middle East; we've already seen a draft of what she's going to say. And then she'll start talking about the balance of power in the world and how totally and utterly useless and untrustworthy we Brits have become. And at that moment, there'll be a shot in the auditorium – a hidden assassin – and I'm afraid the poor woman will be killed. There will, of course, be an immediate panic. There are two thousand people in the audience and they'll all come stampeding out. It's dark and it looks like it's about to rain, which will help. Nobody will have any idea what's going on – which is exactly what we want. Because in all the confusion, I'm going to kill you too."

Gunter was about to continue, but just then an image came up on one of the screens and he reached out and jabbed a button on the console, freezing it. Still keeping half an eye on Alex, he turned a dial. The image zoomed in and Alex saw exactly what he was meant to see. A row of boys and girls in dark blue and light blue uniform – the politics set from the Cairo International College of Arts and Education. The head teacher, Monty

Jordan, was at one end of the line; Miss Watson was at the other. Julius Grief was in the middle, chatting to Gabriela, the daughter of the Italian ambassador. Of course, she would think he was Alex. He looked like Alex and he sounded like Alex and she hadn't known him long enough to tell the difference.

"Ah – there you are!" Gunter exclaimed. "Did you ever wonder how your name got on the politics set list? I put it there, of course. They do lots of visits like this and there was no way they were going to miss the American secretary of state. Mr Jordan got tickets for the whole group and there you are, right in the middle.

"Any minute now, you'll stand up and leave the auditorium. You'll tell the head teacher that you're not feeling well and need some fresh air. You'll slip round the back, passing quite close to this van, as it happens. Then you'll go back inside through a service door and that's when the shot will be fired. And the next time anyone sees you, you'll be lying dead on the tarmac with a bullet in your head."

"You want people to think I killed her." It was the first time that Alex had volunteered anything and he sounded almost matter-of-fact, as if he didn't care what happened.

"Exactly. You've finally worked it out. You see, Scorpia have been recording and filming you for quite a few weeks now. They've created a whole file about you – the Horseman file, they call it.

What's in it? Well, there's a lot of information about your other missions, proving that you've worked for MI6 in the past. And there's also a film of the evening Alan Blunt and Mrs Jones drove to see you in Chelsea, including a recording of the entire conversation. With a little editing, it will prove conclusively that they sent you to Cairo, although it won't say why. We even intercepted the email booking which shows that MI6 paid for your flight tickets.

"And then there's the matter of the weapon used to kill the secretary of state. You'll remember that I took several pictures of you holding it, and at the same time you'll have left your DNA and fingerprints all over it. We've also got plenty of evidence tying you to the death of Habib. I was actually quite surprised that you fell for that old trick, listening in on my telephone call in the schoolyard. I knew you'd followed me to the *House of Gold*. And what does everyone think? You see Habib, you get the gun, and the next minute he's dead and the boat's blown up. Who did it? Well, you did, of course."

Gunter drank some Coke, then put the can down.

"So what happens now?" he went on. "The secretary of state has been assassinated just as she was about to launch into an anti-British speech. The whole of Cairo is in an uproar. And a British schoolboy is found dead at the scene. His classmates can testify that he was behaving very strangely and left the Grand Hall minutes before the shot was fired. Rumours begin to swirl around. As always, there are conspiracy theories. People say that British intelligence were involved in the shooting and that the dead teenager was working for them. Of course, they deny it. And after a few days or maybe weeks, the press move on and everything becomes quiet again. It looks as if they've got away with it.

"And then Scorpia turns up with the Horseman file. They have all the proof they need to show that in this case the conspiracy theories are true. Alex Rider *was* an MI6 agent. He *was* the killer. They have photographic evidence, forensic evidence, films, recordings, intercepts ... and they'll pass the whole lot over to the Americans unless the British government do exactly what they say. They will have no choice! The Horseman file would quite simply blow Britain apart. It would make them the enemy of the entire world. Can you imagine how nervous they will be, Alex? They will be at the complete mercy of Scorpia. What is it that they want? A billion pounds? A trillion? But no! All Scorpia ask for is an announcement that the Elgin Marbles will be returned – immediately – to their correct home. Maybe it'll upset a few art historians and some pompous professors, but it's really a tiny price to pay.

"And here's a funny thing. As it happens, the secretary of state has Greek parentage. Her mother was born in Athens. So the British government can announce that they're sending back the Marbles in her honour! Everyone will be happy. The prime minister will even be congratulated on his consideration. He will see at once that he has no choice but to agree.

"Everyone wins. I get paid; Scorpia gets paid. The Greeks get their Marbles; MI6 gets the file. The only losers, I suppose, are the secretary of state and you. She'll be killed in" – another turn of the watch – "seven minutes' time. And you will die the moment Julius Grief returns to this van. He's asked to watch when I pull the trigger, by the way. I don't think he likes you very much."

Gunter finished speaking and looked back at the screens. All the cameras were now fixed on the stage inside the Grand Hall and even as he watched, a tall, dark-haired Egyptian man appeared and began to address the crowd in Arabic. The secretary of state was about to walk on. Her speech was about to begin. He turned up the volume but kept it low.

"Julius should have left by now," Gunter said. "You have very little time left, Alex. In a way I feel sorry for you. But if there's a moral in all this, it's that kids shouldn't get mixed up in adult affairs. You should have known that. Now it's too late."

"I want something," Alex said. His voice was neutral.

"Oh yes?" Gunter was surprised that Alex had asked for anything at all.

"I want a cigarette."

"A cigarette?"

"Yes."

"When did you start smoking?"

"A year ago."

Gunter shook his head. "It's a bad habit. You're too young to smoke."

"It's not going to kill me now. What difference does it make?"

"You have a point." Gunter shrugged. "But I'm afraid I don't smoke. I don't have any cigarettes."

"There's a packet over there." Alex nodded at the work surface near the door, just behind Gunter. Sure enough, there was a packet of Black Devils – the cigarettes smoked by Razim – lying on the top.

Gunter glanced over his shoulder. The cigarette packet was within easy reach. "I hope you're not trying to trick me," he said. "You think you can distract my attention? Let me assure you that I could shoot you dead before you'd even realized I'd picked up the gun."

"I don't care what you do to me," Alex said. "I just want a cigarette."

"All right. If you want the truth, Alex, I think you're a little pathetic. But if that really is your last wish..."

Without taking his eyes off Alex, Gunter reached back for the cigarette packet, opened it and slid his hand inside to take out a cigarette.

And screamed.

In half a second all his poise and self-control

had vanished. The gun was forgotten. Even Alex didn't matter any more. All he was aware of was the pain blasting its way through his hand and up his arm – all the way to his shoulder. The pain was crippling. It was tearing at his heart.

And from out of the cigarette packet crawled a mature, angry fat-tailed scorpion. The sting of such a creature is not always lethal but this one had been a prisoner inside the packet for almost twelve hours, and in that time it had been filling its glandular sacs with poison, waiting for the moment when it could attack. As soon as Gunter had opened the packet it had struck, its barb – or *hypodermic aculeus* – injecting a dose of fast-acting neurotoxins into his palm.

At the same instant, Alex had come back to life, springing out of the chair and snatching up the gun in one movement. He didn't have time to aim it. Instead he swung it with all his strength into Gunter's face. He heard the man's nose break. With blood spurting, still clutching his injured hand, Gunter reeled back, lost his balance and fell. His head hit the edge of the worktop with a sickening thud and his neck snapped forward. He lay still.

Alex stood where he was, breathing heavily.

He had noticed the nest of scorpions outside his cell his first morning at Siwa Oasis. With no gadgets and no weapons, he had begun to formulate a plan long before Jack Starbright had tried to escape.

He had stolen the cigarette packet at breakfast and had concealed it in his cell. And he had been awake all night – the longest night of his life – hoping that a scorpion would reappear. The adult had climbed in through the window a few hours after sunrise. Alex had managed to trap it in the cigarette packet and had been keeping it in his pocket ever since. He had slipped the cigarette packet into position as he entered the OBU, pretending to stumble.

Alex's face had barely changed. His eyes were still far away. But now there was a pinprick of something deep inside them. Had Gunter been conscious or even alive, he might have described it as a spark of fury. Alex examined the gun. It was quite heavy in his hand but he could see that it would be fairly simple to use, with an external hammer, no safety catch and a detachable box magazine in the handle holding eight bullets. It was fully loaded. Alex slipped it into the waistband of his trousers. He was going to need it.

There was a round of applause and Alex glanced at the screens. The American secretary of state was walking onto the stage. The audience had risen to their feet. Alex took one last look at Gunter. The Scorpia man didn't seem to be breathing. His hand looked like a washing-up glove that someone had pumped full of air, and it reminded Alex that there was an angry scorpion somewhere inside the OBU. It was time to go.

He found the lock and slid the door open to find himself facing the Grand Hall just a few metres in front of him. It was very dark but the rain hadn't started yet. A blast of warm, heavy air rubbed against his face, taking over from the air conditioning. He could see the other OBUs. Some had kept their doors open, allowing the grey and white flicker of their television monitors to escape into the night. There were no police or guards in sight and he guessed that they were either around the main entrance or inside the Grand Hall, concentrating on the audience and the stage.

Just then a single figure flitted past him, keeping close to the main wall, hurrying round the back of the building. He was dressed in dark blue trousers and a light blue polo shirt and he was breathing heavily. He must have been delayed. Perhaps one of the CIA men had tried to stop him leaving the building. He wasn't carrying any weapon, of course. He would have been searched on the way in and possibly on the way out too.

It was Julius Grief.

Alex slid the door of the OBU shut behind him and set off in pursuit.

# CAIRO STORM

"Good evening, ladies and gentlemen. It's a real pleasure to find myself back in Egypt, a country that has always been a good friend to democracy. It's certainly warm this evening, but it's nothing compared with the warmth of your welcome."

An image of the American secretary of state was being projected onto a vast television monitor at the back of the stage, her head and shoulders looming over the actual woman herself. She was standing between the two flags with the lectern in front of her. Her opening words had scrolled down onto a glass screen that stood just on the edge of her vision and they could only be read from her side. Two thousand people greeted her introduction with a ripple of applause that seemed to spread out and grow, rising all the way to the dome.

The front rows and special galleries to the left and right were taken up by Egyptian politicians, sheikhs, diplomats and business people, dressed in smart suits, bright white dishdashas, sparkling evening dresses and jewellery. In the far distance, three tiers up, the spectators at the very back were little more than grey smudges in the shadows. Security men stood at every door and at intervals along the aisles, watching not the secretary of state but the people watching her. All the exits had been closed moments before she had begun to speak. Nobody would be allowed in until she had finished.

The lights had been dimmed but there were spotlights focused on the stage, trapping the speaker in a perfect white circle. The light and sound levels were being controlled by two technicians in a soundproof cabin with a plate-glass window constructed underneath the first tier. But most of the machinery, including the projection equipment for the TV monitor, was actually concealed much higher up. A winding staircase led all the way up from the ground floor, following the curve of the dome. At the top, there was a low, arched doorway leading into an area packed with fuses, circuit boards and temperature gauges. This second control room had been built into the ceiling at the very centre of the dome and resembled the cockpit of a spaceship: completely circular with narrow slits that would have given someone a bird's-eye view of the stage – if they had been allowed inside.

The room had been quickly identified as a grade one security risk, an ideal position for a would-be assassin. It had been thoroughly searched – not once but several times. The door was locked from outside and a CIA man had been in place, sitting there on his own, since nine o'clock that morning. He was there now, trying to listen to the speech, which sounded muffled and distant. He was bored. When Joe Byrne had named the protection details and started handing out jobs, he had certainly drawn the short straw.

The CIA agent couldn't have known that the weapon which was going to be used to kill the secretary of state, the L96A1 Arctic Warfare sniper rifle, was already in place and that Julius Grief, who had been trained as a sharpshooter since the age of nine, was already on his way to collect it. In a few minutes he would take his place inside the room and the moment the secretary of state uttered the word "Britain" for the first time, he would fire, sending a .300 Winchester Magnum bullet travelling at eight hundred and fifty metres per second into her head.

Far below, she was already developing her theme.

"The point of my talk this evening is friendship. Who are the long-term partners? Who can we still trust in a rapidly changing world?"

Her voice rang out, echoing around the great Grand Hall. The words scrolled, line by line, up the Plexiglas autocue. Another page of general introduction. Then she would read the word that would spell her death.

* * *

Alex Rider watched as Julius Grief crept round the side of the building, doing his best to keep out of sight behind the parked cars and OBUs. The other boy was close enough for Alex to make out the fair hair, the lightly tanned skin and even his intense, cold-blooded gaze. But Julius hadn't noticed him. He was in too much of a hurry, making up for lost time, and his attention was fixed on the way ahead as he stepped over the cables that were strewn along the tarmac. Alex followed. He could feel the heat of the night bearing down on him. It was as if he were carrying the whole weight of the world on his shoulders; as if the coming storm were trying to pound him down.

On the other side of the wall a major international speech was being delivered by the second most powerful politician in the United States. Her words were about to cause a political firestorm. And here, out in the darkness, identical twins were stalking each other, one of them with murder on his mind. What would a security guard have made of it? But there were no CCTV cameras back here and there didn't seem to be anyone around apart from the television crews, locked up in their steel boxes. Why should there be? There was surely only one way into the Grand Hall and that was round the front.

And yet...

Alex saw the open door even as Julius began to make his way towards it. That was insanity. The whole place was crawling with police and security men. After all the preparation and with the speech meaning so much, were the authorities just going to let anyone stroll in?

Julius disappeared through the doorway. Alex allowed a few seconds to pass, but before he could sprint across the open space and go in himself, two armed soldiers suddenly appeared round the corner, talking together. Alex ducked behind one of the parked cars, waiting for them to move on. But they didn't seem to be in any hurry. They were standing right outside the door – it didn't seem to bother them that it was open – and had chosen this moment to have a cigarette. Alex saw one of them produce a packet and offer it to the other. Then both of them lit up. Alex was so close that he even caught a whiff of the burning tobacco cutting through the heavy air.

What should he do? Julius Grief would be well on his way to his position, wherever that might be. Seven minutes – that was what Gunter had said – and at least six of them must have already passed. Alex was tempted to make himself known, to raise the alarm. But he knew it would do no good. The soldiers probably spoke little or no English – and even if they did, it was unlikely they would believe a fifteen-year-old boy. He would be arrested and dragged out of the area, and by the time he had spoken to someone in authority, the American secretary of state would be dead.

Of course, Scorpia's plan would still have failed. Alex would be able to prove that he hadn't been involved and the so-called Horseman file would be useless. But that wasn't enough. In the confusion, after the shot had been fired, Julius Grief might escape; Razim had said that he was planning to slip away to another country. Alex had already decided. That wasn't going to happen.

He looked around him, searching for a stone, a brick, anything heavy. It was hard to see in the darkness but he noticed a shard of light glinting off a steel nut that must have come unscrewed from a piece of equipment. Alex reached out and picked it up, balancing it in the palm of his hand. Yes. It would do. He twisted round and threw it with all his strength. The nut arced through the darkness and hit the side of a car, denting the metalwork. The noise was loud enough to make the two soldiers jump. At once they dropped their cigarettes and hurried forward to see what had happened. Alex watched them go past, then darted over to the door. He didn't need to be careful any more. Julius Grief would be well ahead of him by now. The real worry was that he might already be too late.

And now he understood why no one had shown any interest in the open door. It led into a narrow service room, hardly more than a corridor, illuminated by two bare light bulbs dangling on wires. There were a couple of metal buckets and a mop, some empty crates and, about five metres away, a brick wall with a row of hooks and a pair of dirty overalls hanging above the floor. Some old furniture – folding chairs and filing cabinets – had been stored on one side. A bank of very old dusty fuse boxes lined the other. It was nothing more than a dead end. The corridor went nowhere.

Alex would have moved on. He would have thought he'd made a mistake. But he recognized the room. He had seen it in one of the photographs in Gunter's desk. He stepped inside. Julius Grief had definitely come in here – but how could he possibly have disappeared? Alex had watched him enter; he had been watching the entrance ever since. There were no other doors, no other way out. If Julius had slipped back out again, Alex would have seen him.

The hooks.

It seemed like years ago that Alex had been in Gunter's office at Cairo College. Razim had boasted that he had manipulated Alex from the start – but breaking in had been the one thing that he couldn't have foreseen. Razim had arranged for Alex to come to the school. The fake telephone call had led him to the *House of Gold*. But nobody could have guessed that Alex would use one of Smithers' gadgets to break into the head of security's office. And so it surely followed that whatever he had found in the secret drawer had to mean something. It hadn't been left there for him to find.

The newspaper – the *Washington Post* – must have

been reporting the visit of the secretary of state. The pictures of the Grand Hall – that was where her speech was taking place. This room. And the photograph of a hook, shaped like a swan's neck. It was identical to the ones he was looking at now.

Alex had moved even before he had arrived at the end of his thought process. He reached out and grabbed one of the hooks, then another. He was expecting them to twist and turn, but in fact the third one pulled down like an oversized switch. He heard a click and a section of the wall swung open, revealing a metal staircase constructed between two solid concrete walls so narrow that he would have to turn sideways to climb it.

At once he understood the cleverness of Scorpia's plan. How do you put an assassin inside a building that will be surrounded, searched from top to bottom, kept under constant surveillance and locked up for twenty-four hours? Answer: you build a secret passage weeks or months before your target arrives. Alex had no doubt at all that the sniper rifle had been concealed here, ready for Julius Grief to find and carry up with him. No wonder he had been empty-handed when he had gone in. All he had to do was pick it up, climb to a good vantage point and fire. He wouldn't even have to leave if he didn't want to. He could stay hidden for days.

Alex was already climbing the staircase, which had been built between the inner and outer shell of the Grand Hall in a space that might have been used for pipework or perhaps to help with the circulation of cool air. There were no lights and after about ten steps, away from the secret opening, he was plunged into blackness. Presumably Julius had brought a torch. But Alex didn't need to see. The staircase was made out of metal slabs, each one placed at a regular interval, so provided he kept to the same rhythm, moving his feet the same distance, he wouldn't stumble or fall. The walls on either side helped too, keeping him wedged in place. He was blind but it didn't matter. He knew where he was going and what he had to do.

He continued up, knowing from the ache in his legs that the staircase was taking him all the way to the top of the Grand Hall. He felt himself curving round and guessed that he was inside the dome. He hadn't been counting but he knew he must have climbed at least two hundred steps. How much time had it taken? That didn't matter, as long as he wasn't already too late.

He saw light at the same time as he heard a voice – a woman speaking in an American accent – a long way away, as if on the other side of a curtain.

"...the United States has always valued its special relationships with countries all over the world. However, I believe that with the shift in global power, we have to look at those relationships again..."

Alex reached into his waistband and drew out the Tokarev TT-33 that he had taken from Gunter. Clutching it in his hand, he edged forward. Part of him was screaming at himself to hurry. But at the same time, he knew he could make no noise. He was moving towards an entrance, not a door but a jagged opening cut into the brickwork, barely big enough to crawl through. The light was flickering, as if projected from a television screen.

"One country in particular has, in my view, failed to move forward with the times..."

Alex looked through the opening and saw Julius Grief lying on his stomach with the sniper rifle that he himself had once handled pressed against his shoulder, the tip of the barrel resting on the sill of a narrow, slit-like window at floor level. Julius was wearing latex gloves so he wouldn't leave his own fingerprints on the stock or the trigger.

"That country is our friend and will remain our friend. But I think it is time to recognize that it no longer has very much influence in international affairs..."

The circular control room was like an upturned bowl, and looked as if it hadn't been used for years. It had a shabby grey carpet, and was full of banks of old machinery, pulleys and wheels, electric generators, and tin boxes that might have contained air conditioning units. All of these were connected by a tangle of pipes and cables.

Julius was lying with his feet towards Alex.

Looking over his shoulder out of the window, Alex saw what he was aiming at: a huge head, a smart-looking woman with silver hair. No. That was the television screen. The actual target was much smaller, leaning on a lectern in front of it. The secretary of state. He could imagine the cross hairs in the scope centring on her head.

"We all know which country I'm referring to..."

Alex saw Julius tighten his grip on the rifle and knew that the moment had come and that he had to act.

"Julius!" he shouted.

On the stage the woman heard the shout. It had broken through the silence of the auditorium. She paused and looked up.

Julius Grief reacted with incredible speed. He had been about to fire at his target but instead he whipped round like an injured snake, turning the gun on Alex. Alex ducked back into the darkness as Julius fired, the sound of the bullet explosive in the small space. The gunshot was incredibly loud – purposely so. It had always been part of Scorpia's plan to cause panic, to help Julius and Gunter make their escape.

The secretary of state never uttered the word "Britain". Her security men were already on the stage, rushing towards her, forming a protective human shield, covering every angle. In an instant she had disappeared from sight. It took the audience a few more seconds to realize what had happened. The people in the front rows were the first to spring to their feet, pushing sideways, fighting with one another in their hurry to get out. Panic spread like some incredible virus, rippling in every direction, transforming the crowd which seconds before had been seated and silent into a seething, surging mass.

Grief's first bullet had missed Alex, smashing into the brickwork above his head even as he had jerked back. Alex had misjudged his own movement. Either a piece of broken pipe or a part of the wall – it was impossible to tell in the darkness – had jabbed into his right arm, sending a bolt of pain all the way up to his shoulder, numbing him. He was forced to waste precious seconds recovering, then lunged back into the control room, knowing that the narrow entrance would slow him down and that Julius would have the advantage over him.

Sure enough, as Alex re-entered the circular chamber he saw that Julius had already reloaded and the gun was now aimed directly at him, no more than a few metres away. At this range it would be impossible to miss. He saw death in the other boy's eyes.

And then the door – the real door to the room – flew open and the CIA man who had been standing guard burst in. He was young, in his twenties, with the same clean-cut, boyish looks that all the agents seemed to share. There was a gun clasped in his hands. He had taken up a stance with his legs apart, ready to fire.

For two or maybe three seconds, nobody did anything. Julius and Alex had been aiming at each other. The agent was right between them. He had a gun in his hand but didn't know which way to turn it. It was obvious to him that there had been a major security breach, but what he was seeing didn't make any sense. He was looking at two boys, both dressed the same in some sort of school uniform, identical to each other in every way. All his training and experience in the field hadn't prepared him for anything like this.

It was the weapon that decided him. Someone had just taken a shot at the secretary of state and although one of these kids had a pistol, the other was holding a rifle. He had to be the enemy. The agent brought his gun round. Julius did the same and he was the first to fire. The bullet smashed into the man's chest, throwing him back towards Alex. The two of them fell backwards. For a moment, the dead man was on top of him, pinning him down, and he couldn't raise the Tokarev to fire at Julius. But nor could Julius take another shot at him; he didn't have time to reload. He threw the rifle down and ran out of the door that the agent had opened. Alex clambered to his feet and went after him.

This was the real service staircase. It was made up of wide concrete slabs with white-painted walls and was lit by a series of neon strips. Alex took the steps three at a time. He was fairly certain that Julius was unarmed. If he'd had another gun on him, he'd have surely tried to use it. The real danger was that once the other boy reached the bottom, he would all too easily lose himself in the crowd. Alex knew that there were two thousand people down below, surging out into the night. If Julius got too far ahead of him he would disappear in seconds, and Alex was grimly determined that he was going to end this tonight.

The staircase emerged on the far side of the building, away from the OBUs, with the main gate visible ahead. Alex burst out into a scene of pure chaos. There were people everywhere, scattering across the ornamental lawns. Tourist police were shouting at them, blowing whistles, waving frantically with gloved hands, but everyone was ignoring them. More police cars were arriving with lights stabbing at the darkness, sirens adding to the confusion. Here and there, Alex caught sight of security men, Americans, shouting into their throat mikes, barely able to hear a word. The night was thicker than ever and the Grand Hall loomed over them, massive and swollen, like a bomb about to go off. Alex sucked in the warm air. He was already sweating. It was like being inside a gigantic oven.

Where was Grief? Alex searched for him, trying to pick out the blue uniform from the swirl of suits and cocktail dresses. There was no sign of the other students from Cairo College but they could have been anywhere. A voice erupted in Arabic, speaking through a loudhailer. It was accompanied by an electric whine of static. Where was he? Alex was afraid that he was too late, that Grief had already got away.

And then he saw a movement out of the corner of his eye that somehow didn't fit into the pattern of fear and people taking flight. A flash of blue colliding with white. There he was! Julius had attacked one of the tourist police. Why would he want to do that? Alex watched the man go down with a knee in his solar plexus and saw Julius sweep something up from the edge of the lawn. Now he understood. Julius had decided to arm himself and he had taken the lightweight Vzor 27 pistol that was standard issue for the Egyptian police. Well, that made two of them. Alex was still holding the Tokarev and he gripped it more tightly. The chase had become more dangerous, but somehow it felt right. After all, the two of them were meant to be identical. Well, now they were.

He set off in pursuit. Julius must have sensed he was coming, because he suddenly twisted round, and although they were a good twenty metres apart, separated by hundreds of people racing in every direction across the campus, their eyes locked. Alex wondered if Julius was going to shoot it out right here, but the other boy was in no mood for a fight. He had a policeman lying unconscious at his feet and it wouldn't be long before others noticed. With something like a snarl, he turned and began to run.

Alex went after him. He wasn't even trying to hide his own gun. The police and security men might be looking for a would-be assassin, but they would barely glance twice at a teenager in school uniform. Julius was getting close to the gate, burrowing through the crowd, using his elbow and fist to strike out at anyone who got in his way. Alex seemed to be moving more slowly, taking his time. But the distance between them remained the same, and he knew with a cold certainty that he wasn't going to let the other boy slip out of his sight.

Julius was through. On the other side of the gate was a wide, circular parking area with dozens of hawkers and taxi drivers, and more policemen and soldiers, some of whom still seemed unsure what exactly had taken place. A long avenue with fountains and statues led down to the main road but the traffic had tied itself into an impossible knot as everyone tried to get away. As Alex reached the gate, he felt something hard hit him on the shoulder and wondered if someone had struck him from behind. He turned briefly but there was no one there. Behind him the Grand Hall was lit by huge spotlights, bathed in a brilliant white glow. There were still people pouring out between the great pillars, streaming towards him.

He was hit again, this time on the head, and felt water trickling down the side of his face. Now he understood. The storm was finally breaking. The first raindrops – as big as tennis balls – were already falling. He looked up in time to see a flash of lightning with all the power of the universe come scorching across the Cairo skyline. At the same moment, there was a roll of thunder so loud it was as if the whole world had split in two. Then the rain came down in earnest.

It was incredible – a vertical flood. Within five seconds Alex was completely drenched. The rain washed through his hair, swept over his shoulders and down into his shirt. He felt it coursing over his lips and into his mouth. It half blinded him. But he ignored it. Julius might think that the rain was on his side, that it would help to conceal him. Alex would prove him wrong.

The traffic, which had been barely moving, shuffling forward in fits and starts, had come to a complete halt. The cars were deluged. Windscreen wipers that hadn't been used in months were being pushed into life, sluggishly sweeping curtains of water off the glass. Windows were being wound up, sunroofs desperately fastened. And still the drivers were hooting, as if they could somehow persuade the bad weather to go away. Alex pressed forward, feeling the water surging over his ankles. The roads in Cairo had no drains. Already the cars seemed to be sitting in the middle of a river. There was a second, blinding burst of lightning. The rain hammered down.

Julius was weaving between the stationary cars. Where was he going? Gunter had said that he was returning to the OBU. He had wanted to be there when Alex died. That plan was no longer open to him, but maybe there was a second getaway vehicle out there, a driver waiting to take him to the helicopter. Alex quickened his pace. He had reached the queue of traffic himself now. He moved past the cars, glimpsing the figures inside, almost invisible on the other side of the rain-soaked glass.

A gunshot. Alex wasn't even aware that Julius had fired but he heard the bullet twang into the side of a grey Peugeot and saw the dent appear in the bodywork. Inside, the driver and two passengers screamed and threw themselves down. He couldn't imagine what it must have sounded like for them, with the rain already pounding down on the roof. Perhaps they thought they'd just been struck by lightning. There was another shot and the wing mirror of the car next to Alex exploded.

Alex didn't even try to dodge the bullets. He lifted his own weapon, water dripping off the muzzle and the back of his hand. It occurred to him that from the day he had first joined MI6, he had wanted his own gun but had never been given one. Well, he had one now. Blunt and Mrs Jones were nowhere near. This was between him and Julius Grief.

Julius had ducked out of sight but suddenly he reappeared, darting from one side of the road to the other, firing twice more. The windscreen of a white van shattered and the driver must have panicked with his foot on the accelerator because the vehicle shot forward, smashing into the car in front. A man got out of the second car, rising into the rain in front of Alex, already shouting in Arabic. Julius fired again and the man spun sideways, a flower of blood sprouting out of his shoulder. Alex saw him slump down beside his car, his face white. The driver of the van was staring out, terrified. The hooting was louder than ever. Alex held his pistol out in front of him. Julius had fired five times. He couldn't have many bullets left.

There were only half a dozen cars between them now. The two of them were like duellists, trapped in a long line of traffic that stretched as far as the eye could see, in front of them, behind them, all around them. Water was streaming off Alex's hair, pouring down his face. He could feel it dripping off his chin. His shoes were full of water; his clothes had turned into sodden rags. He wiped his eyes with the back of his arm, then took aim and fired for the first time.

The trigger moved easily – the half an inch that Gunter had described – but he was shocked by the noise as the bullet detonated, and by the way the Tokarev recoiled, almost dislocating his wrist. His bullet slanted uselessly into the air. A woman in a burka stared at him from behind the window of a four-by-four. Her eyes – all he could see of her – were full of outrage. He had been standing close to her when he fired. This was the middle of a city. You couldn't start a gunfight here!

But even if Alex had missed, the shot had an effect. Julius took fright, ducking behind the traffic, trying to find a way of escape. Alex saw him run back across the road in front of one car, behind another, disappearing behind an open-back truck. There was a park over to one side and next to it a sign advertising Cairo Zoo. He leapt over the barrier in the middle of the road, past one line of traffic. Perhaps he thought that the trees and bushes would give him shelter.

He was in the outer lane, almost at the grass verge, when the taxi hit him. This was the only lane where the traffic was moving – heading towards the university. The taxi hadn't been doing more than ten miles an hour but it was enough. It struck Julius on his left thigh and shoulder, sending him spinning into the darkness. Alex saw him fall, then get up again, then fall a second time like a wounded animal. The driver didn't stop. He might not have realized what he'd done, or he could have seen the gun that Julius was holding. He didn't want to get involved.

Alex stepped over the barrier and made it across to the other side. Now he was on grass. Was it his imagination or was the rain already easing?

It had been falling so heavily that there simply couldn't be much more left in the sky. He crossed the pavement and walked onto the lawn. Julius had vanished from sight but Alex knew he couldn't have gone far. He wasn't walking any more; he was crawling.

Alex found him stretched out on the grass next to a flower bed. He was cradling his injured shoulder, the gun lying beside him. He had cut himself badly in the collision with the taxi and there was blood oozing through his shirt. His hair was plastered across his forehead; his eyes were wide and staring. Alex came closer and stood over him. The traffic was behind them. The university campus and the Grand Hall were suddenly a long way away. They were on their own.

"Are you going to kill me?" Julius screamed. He didn't sound afraid. His voice was on the edge of hysteria. "Are you going to shoot me?"

Alex said nothing. The Tokarev was at his side, pointing down.

Julius drew a breath. It seemed to Alex that he couldn't have stood up even if he'd wanted to. "What happened to Gunter?" he asked. "Don't tell me he let you go!"

"Gunter is dead," Alex said.

"And you think you've won? You've saved the boring secretary of state and everyone is going to be all over you? 'Good old Alex has done it again!' But it's not like that, is it?" Julius writhed on the grass. His shoulder might have been dislocated. There was a lot of blood, mixing with the rain. "You won't shoot me," he sniggered. "You can't shoot me. You don't have it in you. You're just a goody-goody. Alex Rider, the reluctant spy. And I'll tell you what's going to happen. Very soon the police will come and they'll send me back to prison but – you know? – prison isn't that bad. It's just like being at school. And they can't keep me there for ever. They'll wait five years or ten years and then they'll set me free.

"But you'll never be free, will you, Alex? Not after what we've done to you. We've taken away the one thing that mattered to you. We've killed your best friend. Do you think she knew what had happened when the bomb went off? Do you think she died instantly? You'll be asking yourself that for the rest of your life, and from now on you'll always be on your own. No parents. No friends. No Jack. Nothing.

"And look at you now! I can see how much you hate me..."

"You're wrong," Alex said. "You're nothing to me."

The rain was a mask, hiding his face. His eyes were dark and empty. In his sodden clothes he was almost a skeleton of himself. He turned and began to walk away.

That was when Julius went for the gun, his hand scrabbling through the wet grass. He lifted it and aimed.

Alex heard him. Some tiny movement. Some instinct. He spun round.

Julius fired a single shot.

But Alex fired first.

# SELKET

The grey Chevrolet swept into the university campus and pulled up in front of the Grand Hall. Joe Byrne stepped out into a scene of chaos.

He had been less than half a mile away at the Four Seasons Hotel, watching the speech on television, when the shot was fired and his evening suddenly became very unpleasant indeed. It was extremely unlikely that an assassin could have slipped into the Grand Hall with the crowd. It was almost impossible that anyone could have smuggled a gun inside. Not if Byrne had done his job properly. His BlackBerry had already been buzzing as he stormed out to the waiting car. Of course, the journey had been endless. It would have been faster to walk.

And now here he was in the damp and the darkness, trying to get answers to questions he should never have had to ask. It had stopped raining as suddenly as it had started but there were still huge puddles everywhere. At least it was a little less hot.

His second in command, a man called Tanner, had seen him arrive and came over to him. The man was experienced, a former Marine, and he didn't waste any time.

"We have two fatalities, sir. I'm afraid Edwards was shot dead in the room where the sniper was concealed. It was some sort of control centre high up in the roof. And they've found a TV technician in one of the OBUs. Cause of death is still unclear."

"What about the secretary of state?"

"She's fine, sir. We put the usual protocol into place and got her out of the building unharmed. She's already back at the embassy, a little shaken up but otherwise OK."

"The weapon?"

"Arctic Warfare, sniper rifle. The Egyptians are hanging on to it, sir. Their man's already here."

The Egyptians! Joe Byrne was looking old and tired, as if all the cares of the world had been dumped on his shoulders, which in a way they had. If he wasn't careful, this whole situation would disintegrate into a who-did-what spat with each country blaming the other. An armed assassin had walked past fifteen CIA agents and ten times as many Egyptian security guards and police. That meant an awful lot of egg on an awful lot of faces.

As if on cue, a short, dark man with heavy eyes and a moustache drooping all the way down the sides of his chin came striding towards them. Byrne recognized him at once. His name was Ali Manzour and he was the head of Jihaz Amn al Daoula, the Egyptian State Security Service. He was wearing a white striped suit and there were several heavy gold rings on his fingers. Byrne noticed that the Egyptian's clothes were drenched and he wondered if it was the rain. It was just as likely to be sweat. Manzour was seriously overweight.

Even so, it was good news that he was here. Byrne knew Manzour fairly well. He was smart and efficient. Over a glass of raki he could also be warm and good-humoured. But right now, his stress levels were out of control. Even as he approached, he took out a bottle of white tablets and dry-swallowed a handful.

"This is a disgrace!" he exploded. "This is an outrage!"

"You told me the building was secure." Byrne had decided to play it tough. The buck stops here ... and not with me.

"The building *was* secure!"

"There was some sort of secret staircase constructed in the walls," Tanner said. "It led all the way up."

"I know nothing about this secret staircase!" Manzour exclaimed. "But I am telling you now that this is a British plot. In my opinion it has the fingerprints of the British secret service all over it. The gun that the sniper used is of British design. The British did not wish the secretary of state to make this speech. And it is a British citizen who was found in the television van."

"How do you know that?"

"We have his ID. His name is Erik Gunter. And he does not work for al-Minya. The van has been stolen from them. They know nothing about him."

Erik Gunter. Byrne's heart sank. It was the name that Alex had told him. He had given instructions for the man to be kept under surveillance but somehow he must have slipped through the net. "How did he die?" he asked.

Manzour's eyes bulged almost comically, as if he couldn't believe what he was about to say. "My people tell me that he was stung by a scorpion. But this is madness. You don't see scorpions in Cairo. There are no scorpions in television broadcasting vans." He signalled frantically and a junior officer came running over with a folding chair. He plumped himself down and fished out a handkerchief to wipe his brow. It took him a few moments to regain his composure but when he spoke again it was in a softer voice. "I do not understand any of this. I get the sense of a great conspiracy. Let us give thanks that it does not seem to have worked and that the secretary of state is unharmed."

A soldier appeared, walking hastily towards them. He stopped in front of Manzour, saluted, then bent forward and whispered a few words. Manzour looked up, his face filled with new alarm. "The business becomes even more strange," he said. "I have just been told that a boy has been arrested at the main gate."

"A boy?"

"He was carrying a gun. Russian manufacture. It appears to have been fired. He simply walked up to my men and allowed himself to be taken. He didn't try to resist. And now he is asking for you."

"Where is he?" Suddenly Byrne knew. It couldn't be anyone else. "Can you ask your man to describe him?"

Manzour turned to the soldier and there was a brief exchange of words. "He is a British schoolboy. Aged fifteen. Light-coloured hair. He was wearing the uniform of one of our international colleges."

"The Cairo International College of Arts and Education?"

"Yes." Manzour's eyes narrowed. "You know him?"

"Yes, I do. And it's absolutely vital that we speak to him immediately – somewhere private."

Manzour nodded. He stood up, then noticed the soldier, still waiting for instructions. "You heard what he said!" he bellowed. "Fetch the boy. Bring him to me in the director's office. Nobody is to speak to him. Not even his name! I'll see him at once…"

It was Alex Rider, of course. It couldn't have been anyone else. But Joe Byrne was shocked by what he saw. Only a few days had passed since the two of them had last met, but in that time the boy seemed to have aged ten years. Alex didn't appear to be physically hurt. He walked into the room, an office inside the Grand Hall, and sat down without limping or showing any obvious sign of injury. He seemed pleased to see Byrne. But he looked haggard and exhausted. His clothes, soaking wet, hung off a body that was almost broken. The light had gone out in his eyes. It was obvious to Byrne that something terrible had happened. And for the first time in his long career with the CIA, he was almost afraid to ask.

Alex told his story briefly, as if he wanted to get it over with as quickly as possible. He explained that he had been kidnapped by a man called Abdul-Aziz al-Razim and taken into the desert. There was a conspiracy, put together by Scorpia, to blackmail the British government. An exact lookalike of Alex had entered the Grand Hall with the party from Cairo College and would have shot the secretary of state if Alex hadn't stopped him.

"A lookalike?" Manzour repeated the words. From the expression on his face, he hadn't believed anything Alex had said.

"Yes. His name is Julius Grief. His father was Dr Hugo Grief. He had plastic surgery that made him look like me."

"And where is he now?"

"You'll find him on the side of the road leading down from the university."

"Alive?"

"No. I killed him."

Manzour turned to one of his officers and snapped out a command in Arabic. The officer hurried out of the room.

Byrne waited until he had gone. "I don't think you should doubt anything Alex says, Ali," he muttered. "I know him. I've worked with him twice in the past. You can trust him."

The use of his first name signalled something to the Egyptian head of security. He nodded slowly then turned back to Alex, examining him more carefully. "We found a dead man in an outside broadcast unit," he said.

Alex nodded. "That was Erik Gunter. He was part of it. He was the head of security at Cairo College. But he was also working for Scorpia."

"He was stung by a scorpion."

"That's right." Alex didn't offer any explanation.

Byrne leaned forward. "Tell me," he said. "Where can we find this man, al-Razim?"

"I'll tell you," Alex said. "But there's a condition. I want to come with you when you take him out."

Manzour frowned. "Out of the question. I have men who are experienced in this sort of thing. Unit Triple Seven. They do not need your help."

Unit 777 was the Egyptian counter-terrorism and special operations unit. It had got its name from the year it was founded – 1977. It was based in southern Cairo.

"I think you've done enough, Alex," Byrne agreed. "You can leave this to us."

Alex shook his head. "Razim is in a fort near the town of Siwa," he said. "And he has enough firepower to hold back an army. He's put mines in the sand all around him, so even if your men are experienced, they'll be blown to pieces before they get anywhere near. Razim boasted to me about radar warning systems and surface-to-air missiles. Do you really want to get into a fight with him? If you let me help you, you won't have to."

Neither man spoke, so Alex went on.

"There's a helicopter waiting to take Julius Grief back to the fort. I can show you where it is and you'll be able to hide a dozen of your men inside. If we move fast enough, we might be able to catch Razim before he hears what happened here tonight. I can walk right in. He'll think I'm Julius."

"And then?" Manzour was suddenly interested.

"Your men wait in the helicopter. There's a central control room. If I can get in there, I can disable all the machinery in the fort. No power. No missiles. No mines. Then you attack. He still has at least a dozen guards but you'll take them by surprise."

"Everything depends upon your being able to reach this control room," Manzour said.

"It's in an old bakehouse. I noticed it when I was there. That's the weak spot."

There was a brief silence, then Byrne nodded. "He's right," he said. "The question is – is it too late for a news blackout?"

"The television stations have already broadcast

that an attempt was made on the life of your secretary of state," Manzour replied. "But they have not reported if it was successful. I can make sure that they say nothing more tonight. That would give you the time you need."

"So it's agreed?"

There was a movement at the door and the officer that Manzour had sent out returned, chattering excitedly in Arabic. He was staring at Alex as if he had just seen a ghost. Manzour nodded and dismissed him. "It's true about the other boy," he said. "He's an exact duplicate – apart from the bullet hole in his head."

Alex shrugged.

Manzour glanced at Byrne. "What do you think?"

"A joint American–Egyptian operation. It's your country but it was our politician. Six of your men; six of mine. Plus Alex, of course."

"I agree. But we must move quickly."

Byrne reached out and put a hand on Alex's shoulder. He had to know. "What did Razim do to you, Alex?" he asked.

He felt Alex flinch, as if the contact was painful to him. He didn't answer Byrne's question. "Razim has an interest in pain," he said. "I think it's time he experienced some." He stood up. "We shouldn't be sitting here talking. We should be on our way. And there is one other thing.

"This time I want a gun."

\*   \*   \*

The Sikorsky H-34 was waiting exactly where Alex had said it would be, sitting in the darkness beside a half-built office block. The pilot didn't even see them coming. One moment he was sitting in the cockpit, waiting for Erik Gunter and Julius Grief, the next he had been dragged out and found himself spreadeagled on the rubble with a gun pressed into the back of his neck.

A signal was given and four jeeps pulled up. Alex was in the first, sitting next to Joe Byrne. There were a dozen men behind them, all dressed in desert khakis and combat boots and carrying a selection of Heckler & Koch MP5 sub-machine guns, grenade launchers, automatic pistols and enough weaponry to launch a small war. This was the American–Egyptian assault team put together by the two intelligence chiefs. Alex was still in his Cairo College uniform. He had assumed it was what Julius would have been wearing on the return flight.

Jihaz Amn al Daoula, the Egyptian security service, had so far managed to control the night's news. All the radio and television stations had reported that an attempt had been made on the life of the secretary of state but it was still unconfirmed whether she had been hurt or not. Of course, there were thousands of witnesses who had actually been there but most of them were unsure exactly what they had seen, and the CIA had quickly put out their own version of events, which had the secretary of state in hospital in Cairo and the assassin still at large. Razim might wonder why Erik Gunter hadn't reported back. But there was every chance that, in the middle of the desert, he was still in the dark – in every sense.

As Alex climbed out of the jeep, the man in charge of the CIA team came over to him. Alex recognized him. Fair-haired, square-shouldered, blue eyes: it was Lewinsky, the agent who had interrogated him in the bell room.

"I guess I owe you an apology," he said, holding out a hand. "I never told you my name. It's Blake Lewinsky. I know now I was way out of line."

"That's all right." Alex shook his hand briefly.

"I hope you don't think I make a habit out of this, but we need to get some information out of the pilot."

"What information?"

"He probably has a password, an identification signal he has to give, before he can land at the fort. If we don't know it, we could get blown out of the sky."

"Are you going to waterboard him?" Alex asked.

Lewinsky nodded, acknowledging the jibe. "I think Manzour has other ideas," he said. "But I just thought I'd come over and warn you. It's not going to be pleasant. You may not want to watch."

Ali Manzour had got out of one of the jeeps and had picked his way across the rubble to where the helicopter pilot was waiting. He crouched down and Alex heard a few soft words in Arabic. There was silence, followed by a sudden scream. Standing next to Alex, Joe Byrne grimaced and looked away. A moment later, Manzour walked over to them, wiping blood off his hands with his handkerchief. At the same time, two of his men dragged the unfortunate pilot away.

"It's just as well we asked," Manzour said. "The password is Selket. It is certainly appropriate. Selket is an ancient Egyptian goddess of death. She is also known as the scorpion goddess."

"You're sure he wasn't lying to you?" Byrne asked.

"He did lie to me." Manzour folded the handkerchief and put it away. "But then I asked him a second time and he told me the truth." He turned to Alex. "Everything now depends on you, my friend. But I ask you again, as the father of two sons, are you quite certain you are prepared for this?"

Alex nodded.

"Then I wish you success."

The twelve men climbed into the helicopter, arranging themselves with the Americans on one side and the Egyptians on the other, like opposing baseball teams. Unit 777 had also provided a pilot to fly them into the desert.

Joe Byrne shook hands with Alex. "Take care, Alex," he said. "You look after yourself."

"Don't worry about me," Alex said.

He climbed into the helicopter. The blades began to turn, picking up speed until finally they became a blur and the helicopter rose into the air. Byrne was left standing next to Manzour.

"So that is the famous Alex Rider," Manzour muttered.

"That's right," Byrne said.

"It is not my place to say it, but I think something very bad has happened to that child. Did you see it in his eyes?"

Byrne nodded. He had already put in a call to Alan Blunt in London and the two of them would speak as soon as Alex returned ... assuming, of course, that he did. Alex had told him not to worry. But he was very worried indeed.

He watched the helicopter until it had disappeared into the night. Then Ali Manzour clapped a hand on his shoulder and the two men returned to the waiting cars.

# *A PINCH OF SALT*

The helicopter shuddered through the night sky, carrying its load of twelve silent men and one boy. As it reached the edge of Cairo, the street lights fell away and suddenly it was alone with the stars. Alex was sitting at the very front, closest to the pilot, and looking out through the cockpit window he was aware of the desert, vast and empty, an infinite blackness below. He slumped back and perhaps he dozed off – there was little difference between being asleep and being awake – with the rotors beating out their progress, hammering in his ears.

And then someone was tapping his arm and he knew that they were there. How much time had passed? It couldn't have been more than an hour or so. Lewinsky stood in front of him and Alex could see the tension in his eyes. This was the moment of truth. The fort with all its defence systems was ahead. If the original pilot had lied to them, they were all dead.

The radio crackled into life. A voice rapped out

a single sentence, speaking in Arabic. The pilot replied with one word.

"Selket."

A long pause. They seemed to be hovering in mid-air, as if they had come to a standstill. Then more instructions and the pilot visibly relaxed. They had been given clearance to land.

Looking out, Alex could see the fort, illuminated by hundreds of lights. The whole place was a hive of activity as Razim prepared to make his getaway. There were men criss-crossing the courtyard, carrying files and boxes out of the various storerooms and loading up the Land Rovers and open-top trucks that were parked in a long line. Nobody would be allowed any sleep tonight. Guards were patrolling the parapets and the rope bridge. All four towers were manned. The huge gates were closed and there were more armed guards watching the helicopter as it swept down out of the blackness.

And abruptly night became day as two spotlights crashed on, slanting up into the sky from opposite corners of the fort, capturing the helicopter between them. Brilliant light blazed into the cockpit. Lewinsky winced, covering his eyes. But the light gave Alex an idea. The helicopter was expected. It was being watched. He knew that Razim would be nervous, wondering about the long silence. Well, he would give him a signal, set his mind at rest.

Alex unbuckled himself and stood up. The door

of the helicopter was operated by a heavy lever and he pulled it down, then slid the door open, allowing the blast of the engine and the desert heat to come rushing in. One of the CIA men called out to him, but Alex ignored him. He knew what he was doing and he was certain that Razim would be watching. Holding on to a strap that dangled from the ceiling, he leaned out of the helicopter into the light and waved at the fort, grinning as if he had just done something very clever. This was how Julius Grief would have behaved. He wouldn't have waited for the helicopter to land.

Lewinsky understood what he was doing and nodded his approval. Alex gesticulated at the pilot, directing him towards the area of sand that had been hardened to create a safe landing pad. He saw the main gates swing slowly open and a jeep burst out towards them. So far so good. The password had been accepted and perhaps Alex had been seen. Razim was turning off his defences, inviting them in.

There was a slight jolt as the helicopter touched down. The pilot killed the engine. Lewinsky got up and came over to him, taking care to keep out of sight.

"We'll give you ten minutes." He still had to shout over the whine of the engine. "Then we're coming in."

Alex nodded.

The Sikorsky had landed about two hundred

metres from the gates. Alex jumped down onto the sand and waited for the jeep to arrive. It was being driven by a bearded man in long robes and a headdress. Alex recognized him as the guard who had brought him food the night he had been captured. He pulled up and Alex got in.

"Where are the others?" the driver asked. He must have been referring to Gunter and the pilot. He couldn't possibly know that there were twelve armed men waiting in the Sikorsky.

"Take me to Razim," Alex commanded. The driver hesitated. "Now!"

The driver was used to obeying orders. He shoved the gearstick forward and they set off, bouncing back across the track. The gates were still open. No one had any idea that anything was wrong. They entered the fort, steering away from the prison block where Alex and Jack had been held, heading towards Razim's house. Alex noticed the old bakehouse which was also the control centre. He had hoped that the door to the control room would be open but it was closed – presumably locked – and there were no windows. He could see light showing through the cracks in the wood. There was someone inside. Even now they might be turning on the mines that surrounded the fort, and if anyone inside the helicopter so much as sneezed, motion and sound detectors would instantly pick them up.

The jeep pulled up. Alex threw open the door and leapt out.

"Julius!"

Razim had come out of his house, a cigarette in one hand, the smoke captured in the glow of the electric lights as it curled upwards. He was wearing Western dress: jeans, a loose shirt and sandals. Perhaps this was part of a new identity, but the round glasses and close-cropped silver hair were unmistakable. The two of them met on the terrace with the stone lion and the terracotta pots. This was where they had had breakfast. Razim examined Alex with a mixture of curiosity and annoyance.

"What happened?" he snapped. "I was expecting to hear from you an hour ago."

So Julius had been given instructions to radio in before he left Cairo. Alex couldn't have known that.

"She's dead," Alex said. He didn't want to talk too much to begin with. He was afraid of giving himself away.

"The secretary of state is in hospital. I heard it on the radio. But they didn't say she was dead."

"Then they're lying." Alex tapped the middle of his forehead with a finger. "I hit her here."

"And Rider?"

Still acting as Julius, Alex smirked. "He begged for mercy. He was crying at the end. But Gunter let me watch when he killed him and that's what I did."

"Where is Gunter?"

"In the helicopter."

"Why didn't he come with you?"

"I don't know, Razim. What's the matter? I thought you'd be pleased."

Out of the corner of his eye Alex saw the main gates begin to swing shut, the two halves folding towards each other. They were moving slowly and he knew it would take them a full minute to close. That gave him a minute to act. He turned his back on Razim and began to saunter away his hands in his pockets.

"Where are you going?" Razim was uneasy. He might not have guessed whom he was really talking to. But some inner sense, some instinct, was shouting a warning. "What are you doing?" he demanded.

"I'm going to bed."

"We're not going to bed. We're leaving."

"Then I'll get my things."

"But that's not the way to your room!"

And that was what gave him away. Julius had been staying in Razim's house. But Alex was walking in the opposite direction, heading towards the well.

"Julius!" Razim called one last time.

Alex didn't know what to do. Should he just ignore him or turn round and continue to bluff it out? Julius Grief would have been angry. He would have expected rewards and congratulations, not an interrogation. The bakehouse was straight ahead. The chimney stood out in all the electric light. There were guards all around but so far none had shown any interest in him.

"Stop him!"

The two words came cutting across the court-yard. Almost immediately Razim repeated them in Arabic. He had guessed what had happened. He knew that he had been tricked. Right in front of Alex, standing between him and the control room, two guards twisted round, untangling their weapons. The gap between the gates was narrow-ing one centimetre at a time. In half a minute they would meet, cutting Alex off.

He had no choice. He broke into a run, veering round the well and away from the control room. The outer wall was ahead of him, with a flight of stone stairs leading up. He took them two at a time. At the same time, one hand came out of his pocket. He was holding the grenade that had been there from the moment he had left the helicopter. He had already worked the ring loose with his index finger. He heard two shots and almost felt the bul-lets as they thudded into the steps just below him. Who was shooting? It didn't matter. Nothing mat-tered any more except finishing this business once and for all.

There were guards running towards him from every direction. Everyone was shouting. An alarm had gone off, jangling in the night air. Alex was utterly focused on what he had to do. Two more steps and he reached the top, standing on the parapet with the fort on one side of him, the desert on the other. A third shot whipped past his shoulder. He was horribly exposed. Everything depended on what happened next.

The bakehouse was below him but he was on the same level as the chimney, about five metres away. He could see the square opening and could imagine the brickwork running all the way down to the oven. He knew he only had this one shot. There was a second grenade in his other pocket but he would never get the chance to throw both. How much time did he have left? How long had it been since he had pulled out the pin? He shut all the noise out of his head. The shouting, the clang of the alarm, the gunshots. He was back at school. Tossing a Coke can into a bin. Easy. Nothing to it.

He threw the grenade, saw it arc through the air, knew that it was going to find its target, that it couldn't miss.

The grenade disappeared into the chimney without even touching the brickwork.

It took so long for the explosion to happen that Alex was afraid that something had gone wrong, that the grenade was faulty. He was just scrabbling for the second one when the blast came. The door of the control room was blown off from inside and a great roar of fire and smoke rushed out into the courtyard. All the lights went out and the darkness of the Sahara threw itself onto the fort like a magician's cloak. Alex hurled himself to the ground as a machine gun opened fire, splattering the brickwork behind him. But even as he rolled he saw that the main gates hadn't quite met, that they were frozen with a gap in between. He knew Lewinsky and the others would have heard the grenade go off and they would be out of the helicopter by now, crossing the desert. If he could survive for a minute more, he would no longer be on his own.

His eyes had already got used to the darkness. The fort was illuminated by the moon and the stars – and also by the flames coming from the bakehouse. Alex twisted round and saw Razim moving towards him, now halfway up the staircase. He was holding a gun. His whole body was bathed in a red glow. He had once promised to send Alex to hell and now he looked like the devil himself. There was a crackle of machine-gun fire from the main gates. Somebody screamed. The Egyptians and the American agents were nearly there.

But it wasn't over yet. Razim was climbing, closing in on him. Suddenly the night shimmered and white light washed over the parapet as a back-up generator kicked in. Alex was in full view. He reached behind him and brought out the Tokarev that he had taken from Gunter. It had already served him well and he had demanded it back from Ali Manzour. Somehow it seemed right. It was the only gun Alex had ever called his own. He had wanted it with him at the end.

There were eight rounds in the magazine. Alex fired three of them at Razim, then ran round the side of the parapet, trying to find shadows, somewhere he would be less of a target. He could see one of the towers ahead of him and suddenly there was a guard blocking his path, taking aim with his rifle. Alex took out the second grenade and threw it, diving to the floor at the same time. He felt the blast, covering his head with both arms, and when he looked up, the way ahead was clear. He glanced down. The Americans and the Unit 777 men had reached the fort. Alex saw them pouring through the gates, spreading out and taking up positions across the courtyard. Razim's guards had almost forgotten him. They knew that a far more dangerous enemy had arrived.

Alex got to his feet. He didn't know where to go but he certainly didn't want to stay where he was. He was trapped on the narrow ledge with the edge of the wall on one side and the courtyard on the other. There was gunfire all around him. He glimpsed an object flying through the air. It soared through the open door of Razim's house. There was an explosion and the building was torn apart. Two guards had been standing in front of it. There was a burst of automatic fire and they twisted round, dropping their weapons before collapsing to the ground.

He came to the rope bridge and ran onto it almost without thinking. The other side of the fort looked darker and quieter, and right now all he wanted was to get out of sight and leave all this to the special forces. He saw three of Razim's men rush past underneath him. They seemed to have given up the fight and were running away. One of the Americans appeared behind them, wearing night vision goggles. He stopped, took aim, and picked them off one at a time. Alex realized that the fight was rapidly becoming a massacre. The invaders were better trained and better equipped. They'd had the advantage of surprise. And with all the defences down, the fort was nothing more than a killing ground. He felt sickened. He wanted this to be over.

And then a voice surprisingly close to him spoke two words.

"Don't move."

Alex turned round. It was Razim. Somehow he had caught up with Alex. He was standing with one hand on the side of the bridge, holding on to keep his balance. The other hand held a gun. Alex raised his own gun. His legs were slightly apart. He could feel himself swaying in the air.

"It's you. I knew it was you. I knew it the moment I saw you." For the first time in his life, Razim felt the full force of his emotions as they rushed in, overwhelming him. Fury. Despair. He was out of control, unable to believe what had just occurred, that everything he had planned – so carefully, so brilliantly – had been suddenly taken away from him. "What happened? How did you do it?"

Alex didn't answer. The fight was raging on in the courtyard below them. Some of Razim's men were still firing but even they must have seen that it was all over for them. Razim no longer cared. All the blood seemed to have drained out of him. He was staring at Alex with tears in his eyes.

"I beat you!" Razim whimpered. "I crushed you. I killed your friend. And you still came back. Well, this is where it ends, Alex Rider. I will finish you now. Not a slow death. Alas, we have no time. But every death is the same for the one who dies."

He raised his gun.

"Alex!"

The shout came from below. Blake Lewinsky had seen what was about to happen and reacted immediately, swinging his machine gun round and firing upwards. A volley of bullets cut into the bridge between Alex and Razim. Alex lost his balance as the ground gave way beneath his feet. He flailed out, catching his hand on the side, and cursed as he dropped the gun. He saw Lewinsky taking aim a second time. But then someone opened fire from one of the towers and the American spun round, a bloody stitchwork erupting across his chest. Alex knew he had been killed instantly. But he had done enough.

Razim had fallen back, dazed. His gun had dropped onto the bridge; it was right beside him. Alex sprang forward, using all the coiled-up power in his legs. He caught hold of Razim, his hands closing around his throat. The bridge had almost been torn in half but somehow it was managing to support the two of them and for a moment they stood there, swaying in mid-air. There was more gunfire and Alex saw a guard topple from one of the towers. Razim reached out, trying to retrieve his gun. Alex fell on him, grabbing his arm, pulling it away.

And then the bridge snapped. Alex felt the gap open up. He could keep hold of Razim and drop with him or he could let go and save himself. At the last microsecond, self-preservation took over. He fell backwards, wrapping himself in the severed ropes, twisting them around his arm to tie himself in place. Suddenly his feet were dangling in the air. He felt the strain on his shoulders and wrists. Only part of the bridge had collapsed. There was enough of it left to prevent him hitting the ground.

Razim hadn't been so fortunate. He had been trying to reach his gun and had left it too late to get a handhold. With a last, desperate effort he snatched at the ropes but they had been whipped away and there was nothing to prevent him falling into the courtyard. If he had hit the ground he would have broken both his legs, but instead he plunged into the mound of salt that his men had collected from the desert. He went in feet first, burying himself up to the waist. His glasses were gone. His gun had landed near by. He was stuck fast.

All around him the fighting had stopped. His men were surrendering. The American and Egyptian special forces were taking control.

Razim wriggled. His eyes widened in fear as he felt himself being sucked into the salt. Alex was still dangling above him on his half of the broken bridge. He was out of reach.

"Help me," Razim said.

Alex didn't move. If he shifted his weight, the rest of the bridge might collapse.

Razim sank into the salt. It was already up to his armpits. And it was as if he knew what was going to happen, that the game was finally over. Somehow, in the last seconds of his life, he managed to force a smile. To Alex it looked like a hideous grimace. "Please..." he whimpered. "Help me. Throw me a rope."

The salt climbed higher.

Razim could feel the pressure crushing his stomach and chest. The salt pile was like some hideous creature drawing him in, inch by inch, swallowing him alive. "You cheated me," he screeched. "I was better than you. I should have won."

Alex did nothing. There was nothing he could do.

With the last of his strength Razim lunged for the gun, stretching his arm across the surface of the salt pile. His fingertips brushed against it, but he wasn't close enough to grasp it. He gave up the struggle. His arm was dragged beneath the surface. The salt rose over his shoulders. Now only his head and neck were visible, as if he had been decapitated in the fight.

"Don't move, Alex!" One of the CIA men had

reached the bridge and was crawling towards Alex. "We're coming to get you."

Alex watched.

Something horrible was happening to Razim. The salt had penetrated his skin, working its way through the pores. It was as if he were being cooked alive inside the huge pile. White foam began to bubble out of his mouth. It trailed out his eyes. Alex was reminded of a garden slug. He had heard it said that slugs died horribly if they were rolled in salt.

"Alex..."

It was Razim's last word. His eyes were completely white. He managed to swallow one last breath, as if it would do him any good, and then he was pulled beneath the surface. For a brief moment, there was a dent in the surface where he had been, then the salt poured in, filling it.

"We've got you!"

Alex felt hands grab hold of him and then he was being led back along the bridge. There were other men waiting for him. Perhaps they had seen what had happened to Razim; perhaps they had been watching and had simply allowed events to take their course. Alex didn't care. He was exhausted.

The fighting was over. As Alex was helped back down the stone staircase, he saw guards lined up against the wall with their hands over their heads. There were bodies everywhere. Two Americans and a Unit 777 man had been killed, along with Blake

Lewinsky. But most of the casualties were Razim's people, lying stretched out on the bloodstained sand.

Someone gave Alex a bottle of water. "Are you OK?"

Alex nodded.

"Stay here. We've radioed Cairo. It's over now. There are more people on the way."

But ten minutes later, Alex had disappeared, and at first there was panic among the special forces fighters as they searched for him, wondering what had happened. It was only much later that they found him, on his own outside the fort, kneeling beside a burnt-out car.

# DEPARTURES

It was time to go.

Alan Blunt had reached his last day as head of MI6 Special Operations. He had just finished packing his personal possessions. It hadn't taken him very long. In fact they all fitted inside a small shoebox which now sat in the middle of his otherwise empty desk. Of course, what he would really be taking from here would be his memories, and he certainly had enough of those. It had briefly occurred to him that he might write a memoir – it was very much the trend with politicians and departing civil servants. But that was out of the question. It was part of the job description that he should take his secrets to the grave. And if he tried to sell them, he might arrive there sooner than he had expected.

He took one last look outside. It was a hot summer. Liverpool Street was unusually bright, the sun flaring off the plate-glass windows. There was a pigeon half asleep on the ledge outside. Did birds sleep? Blunt tapped on the glass and it flew away. He had once discussed with Smithers the possibility of using homing pigeons to listen in on foreign ambassadors. Homing pigeons with homing devices around one leg. The Covert Weapons division had conducted a feasibility study but nothing had come of it. Blunt had seen Smithers a few weeks ago, after his return from Cairo. There had been a formal debriefing. The two of them had not said goodbye.

Blunt went back to his desk and rested a hand on the shoebox. He was tempted to throw it in the dustbin. There was nothing inside that he really wanted. Suddenly he just needed to be out of there. In two days he was leaving for Venice, the first stop on a six-week tour of Europe. His wife was going with him. It would be the longest time the two of them had spent together since the day they were married.

The door opened and Mrs Jones came in. The new head of Special Operations, just as he had expected. She seemed surprised to see him, but that couldn't be the case because she had requested a final meeting before he left. For a moment, the two of them looked at each other uneasily across the desk. It occurred to Blunt that they should switch round. Her place was behind it now.

He moved back to the window and sat down in an armchair that looked antique but which was actually modern. Like so many things in this building, it wasn't what it seemed. Mrs Jones perched on the edge of the desk. She was wearing black: a smart suit with a silver chain around her neck. She was sucking one of her peppermints. That was bad news. Blunt knew her habits. She sucked mints when she had something unpleasant to say.

"Congratulations," he said. He had only been officially told about her new appointment that morning. "I wish you every success."

"Thank you." Mrs Jones nodded briefly. "Have you made plans?"

"Travel. A little golf perhaps. The BBC's asked me to join the board."

"I know. I recommended you." She paused, her hands resting behind her on the desk. "Before you leave, we have to talk about Alex."

"Yes. I thought he might be on your mind. How is he?"

"I'm afraid he's not at all well. What did you expect?"

"It was very unfortunate, the loss of that house-keeper of his."

"Jack Starbright was more than a housekeeper. She was his closest friend. She was the only adult friend he had. Certainly the only adult he could ever trust."

"Nobody could have foreseen what would happen."

"Is that really true?" Mrs Jones walked behind the desk and sat down: she had taken Blunt's chair and the message was clear: she was taking his authority too. "Scorpia set a trap for us and we walked straight into it. Levi Kroll turning up in the Thames with an iPhone conveniently lodged in his top pocket. A handful of clues leading us to the Cairo International College of Arts and Education. They played us for fools and that's how we behaved. If it hadn't been for Alex, the secretary of state would be dead and we'd be at war with the Americans. And all this for the Elgin Marbles! It almost beggars belief."

Blunt spread his hands. "I take full responsibility. You don't need to worry. You can start your new job with a clear conscience."

"I wish that were the case. But I agreed to use Alex Rider from the very start – and I'm talking now about the Stormbreaker affair over a year ago. I may have had my doubts about bringing a fourteen-year-old boy into our world, but I ignored them. He was too useful to us. And in that respect I'm as guilty as you."

Blunt was impressed. There was a quality to his former deputy, a steel in her voice, that he had never noticed before. "How bad is he?" he asked.

"As I'm sure you know, he killed Julius Grief," Mrs Jones said. "That was something else, by the way. We should never have accepted Grief's supposed death in Gibraltar, and I've already given instructions for the whole facility to be shut down. Anyway, Alex has had guns before but this was the first time he actually used one to kill. He was forced to shoot Julius in cold blood. I don't think he can be blamed. Unfortunately the effect on him has been traumatic."

She fell silent for a moment. Blunt waited.

"I've talked to the psychologists and they say that for Alex it was almost as if he were killing himself. After all, the two of them were identical. What it boils down to is that part of Alex Rider died with Julius Grief. He shot himself – or perhaps a part of himself that should never have been born."

"Maybe that was the part we created," Blunt suggested.

"Maybe it was. But as far as I'm concerned, the file on Alex Rider is now closed. It was an experiment that we should never have attempted. There's no point raking over it all now, but we were wrong – both of us. It will never happen again."

"Is that why you wanted to see me?"

"No. There's one other thing you have to answer for before you leave. The attack on Alex Rider at Brookland School." Mrs Jones waited for Blunt to respond, but he said nothing. He showed nothing more than polite interest. She wasn't surprised. "A gunman was sent to shoot Alex," she went on. "But curiously Erik Gunter never mentioned it. Nor did Razim. One might almost think they knew nothing about it. And there are two other questions that have puzzled me. The first is very simple. Why did the sniper miss? It's true that Alex noticed him and reacted quickly, but even so the bullet hit his desk, not his chair. It's as if the sniper wasn't aiming at him at all.

"And then there's the business at the Wandsworth industrial estate. Alex overheard the gunman talking to the helicopter pilot. *It was fine. Mission accomplished.* That was what he said. Was he lying? Or was he actually telling the truth? Had he achieved what he set out to do?"

"Where are you going with this?" Blunt asked.

"I think you know exactly where I'm going. You thought Cairo College was in danger and you were determined to send Alex there. So you recruited the sniper and the helicopter pilot. You set up the whole thing. If Alex believed he was in danger – worse than that, that his friends might also be in danger – he would have no choice but to leave. I've traced the ownership of the Robinson R22, by the way, so there's no point denying it."

"I wouldn't insult your intelligence by denying it, Mrs Jones," Blunt replied.

"What happened to the pilot and the sniper?"

"They survived. They broke a few bones. Nothing serious. They're both recuperating on the Isle of Man."

"Do you have any idea how serious this is? You arranged a shooting in a British school! You brought half of London to a standstill and you've wasted thousands of hours of police time – and all so you could get your way. And you were wrong all along. Scorpia tricked you."

Alan Blunt took off his glasses, wiped them with a handkerchief, then put them on again. His eyes were suddenly tired. "Who knows about this?" he asked.

"Only me."

"And what do you intend to do?"

There was a brief silence.

"Nothing." Mrs Jones might have made the decision before she came into the room. Or she might have made it just then. It made no difference. "I can't separate myself from the responsibility in all this," she went on. "I can understand why you did what you did. And I won't stand in the way of your knighthood. So go to Venice. Enjoy your holiday. We've been together for a very long time. We won't see each other again."

Blunt stood up. He went over to the desk and laid his hands on the shoebox. But he didn't pick it up. He looked at Mrs Jones. "I'll say two things if I may," he said.

"Go ahead."

"Try not to forget that some good came out of all this. I understand that Scorpia has disbanded."

"Scorpia is a laughing stock," Mrs Jones agreed. "They'll never work again. Several of their agents – including Zeljan Kurst – have been arrested and the international police forces are cooperating to track down the rest of them. They took on Alex three times and three times they failed. That was the end of them."

"Well, one might argue that that made it all worthwhile."

"One might. What else?"

"Only this. Let me give you some parting advice, Mrs Jones." Blunt lifted the shoebox. Now the desk was entirely hers. "The Brookland business was a mistake, as it turned out. But I had no hesitation in arranging it. And if you are going to succeed in this job, Mrs Jones – my job – then there will come a time when you will have to do the same. Of course, you know that. You know the sort of decisions I've had to make. But I wonder if you know what it's like to live with them? A German philosopher once wrote that he who fights monsters must take care that he doesn't become one himself. Our work is often monstrous. I'm afraid there's no escaping it."

Mrs Jones considered this and nodded. There was nothing more to say.

"Goodbye, Alan."

"Goodbye, Mrs Jones."

Carrying the shoebox, Blunt left the room, closing the door behind him.

"Virgin Atlantic Flight 20 to San Francisco has begun boarding. Will all passengers please proceed directly to Gate 3."

Sitting in the Virgin business-class lounge at Heathrow, Edward Pleasure closed the book he had been reading and put it away.

"Time to go," he said.

"OK."

Alex Rider was sitting next to him, dressed in jeans and a dark jersey. He had a carry-on bag for the flight, packed with books and computer games for his Nintendo DS. He had checked in two other cases and they contained just about everything he now owned. The house in Chelsea had been cleared and was on the market. Alex had taken his clothes, a few photographs, his tennis racquet and a football signed by members of the Chelsea squad that he had once won in a raffle. He could have kept more. Edward had offered to arrange for a whole crate to be shipped out. But Alex had preferred to leave it all behind.

He was going to live in San Francisco with Edward and Liz Pleasure – and, of course, Sabina. The two of them had spoken on the phone and she was thrilled he was coming. "It'll be great," she had said. "We'll be together all the time. And you'll love it here, Alex. I know you will. I've already got your room ready. And Mum can't wait to see you."

Edward and Liz were now legally responsible for Alex. It was almost as if he had been adopted.

Curiously it had been Mrs Jones who had suggested it; perhaps it had been her way of making up for everything that had happened. She had called Edward Pleasure even before Alex had arrived back in England. She had sorted out the legal paperwork and had managed to get Alex a permanent visa to stay in America. MI6 had a manor house – part hospital, part rest home – in fifty acres of parkland down in the New Forest, and Alex had stayed there while the arrangements were being made. Edward had finally arrived two days ago. And now they were on their way.

Edward Pleasure was a journalist and, following the success of his book about Damian Cray, he was also a wealthy man. He was in big demand in America, writing for several of the major newspapers and magazines. He owed a lot of his success to Alex. After all, it had been Alex who had discovered the truth about Cray in the first place. And Alex had ties with the family that went far beyond his friendship with Sabina. He had stayed with them in Cornwall, Scotland and the South of France – where Edward had nearly died when a bomb exploded in their house. He walked with a limp and still needed painkillers but he hadn't let what had happened to him destroy his life. He had a beautiful home in Presidio Heights with views of the ocean. Sabina went to the local high school. Liz was writing a book about fashion, which had once been her career. At the same time she cooked and looked after the garden and walked the dog (they had recently taken on a chocolate Labrador). It had taken them time to get used to life on the other side of the world but they were comfortable and happy.

And Alex was going to join them and be part of their family. Edward examined him as they left the lounge and began to walk to the departure gate. He knew very little about what had happened out in Egypt. It wasn't just that Mrs Jones had been unwilling to tell him. He didn't want to ask. Jack Starbright was dead. He knew that much and understood what it meant to Alex. He also knew that Alex's spying days really were behind him, that MI6 would never contact him again.

Alex had barely spoken during the two days they had been together. There was something terrible about the silence that had taken hold of him like some sort of illness. He showed no interest in food and barely ate. If he was asked something, he would respond politely. But he never volunteered anything and there were long minutes when he didn't seem to be in the room, when his eyes were somewhere else. At their first meeting, it seemed to Edward that something inside Alex had broken and would never be repaired. He even wondered if he was doing the right thing, taking responsibility for him, bringing him into his home.

But even in the past forty-eight hours he had noticed small differences. Alex was more alert. And now his pace was quickening as he headed down the long tunnel towards the plane, as if he was in a hurry to be on his way. He had overheard Alex talking to Sabina on the phone and knew that he was looking forward to seeing her.

Was it too much to hope that Alex was already starting to heal? Suddenly Edward was determined.

It would all work out. Alex would be part of a family, something he had never experienced in his
life. He would be thousands of miles away from the
forces that had done so much to damage him. It
was a fresh start. He would finally be what he had
always wanted to be. An ordinary boy.

Twenty minutes later, they were sitting beside
each other with their seat belts fastened. Alex was
next to the window, looking out. The plane had
reached the start of the runway and was waiting
there while the pilots made the final checks.

"Are you feeling all right, Alex?" Edward asked.

Alex nodded. "Yes. I'm fine."

The engines roared. The plane rolled forward,
picking up speed, then rose into the sky.

# Read the next mission in the Alex Rider series: Russian Roulette

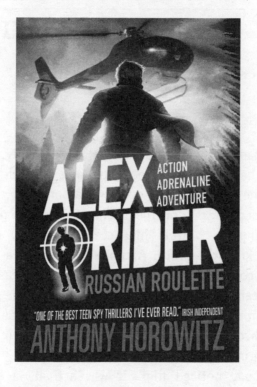

What does it take to make a killer?

*Turn over for a short taster...*

# BEFORE THE KILL

He had chosen the hotel room very carefully.

As he crossed the reception area towards the lifts, he was aware of everyone around him. Two receptionists, one on the phone. A Japanese guest checking in ... from his accent, obviously from Miyazaki in the south. A concierge printing a map for a couple of tourists. A security man, Eastern European, bored, standing by the door. He saw everything. If the lights had suddenly gone out, or if he had closed his eyes, he would have been able to continue forward at exactly the same pace.

Nobody noticed him. It was actually a skill, something he had learned, the art of not being seen. Even the clothes he wore – expensive jeans, a grey cashmere jersey and a loose coat – had been chosen because it made no statement at all. They were well-known brands but he had cut out the labels. In the unlikely event that he was stopped by the police, it would be very difficult for them to know where the outfit had been bought.

He was in his thirties but looked younger. He had fair hair, cut short, and ice-cold eyes with just the faintest trace of blue. He was not large or well built but there was a sort of sleekness about him. He moved like an athlete – perhaps a sprinter approaching the starting blocks – but there was a sense of danger about him, a feeling that you should leave well alone. He carried three credit cards and a driving licence, issued in Swansea, all with the name Matthew Reddy. A police check would have established that he was a personal trainer, that he worked in a London gym and lived in Brixton. None of this was true. His real name was Yassen Gregorovich. He had been a professional assassin for almost half his life.

The hotel was in King's Cross, an area of London with no attractive shops, few decent restaurants and where nobody really stays any longer than they have to. It was called The Traveller and it was part of a chain; comfortable but not too expensive. It was the sort of place that had no regular clients. Most of the guests were passing through on business and it would be their companies that paid the bill. They drank in the bar. They ate the "full English breakfast" in the brightly lit Beefeater restaurant. But they were too busy to socialize and it was unlikely they would return. Yassen preferred it that way. He could have stayed in central London, in the

Ritz or the Dorchester, but he knew that the receptionists there were trained to remember the faces of the people who passed through the revolving doors. Such personal attention was the last thing he wanted.

A CCTV camera watched him as he approached the lifts. He was aware of it, blinking over his left shoulder. The camera was annoying but inevitable. London has more of these devices than any city in Europe, and the police and secret service have access to all of them. Yassen made sure he didn't look up. If you look at a camera, that is when it sees you. He reached the lifts but ignored them, slipping through a fire door that led to the stairs. He would never think of confining himself in a small space, a metal box with doors that he couldn't open, surrounded by strangers. That would be madness. He would have walked fifteen storeys if it had been necessary – and when he reached the top he wouldn't even have been out of breath. Yassen kept himself in superb condition, spending two hours in the gym every day when that luxury was available to him, working out on his own when it wasn't.

His room was on the second floor. He had thoroughly checked the hotel on the Internet before he made his reservation and number 217 was one of just four rooms that exactly met his demands. It was too high up to be reached from the street but low enough for him to jump out of the window if he had to – after shooting out the glass. It was not overlooked. There were other buildings around but any form of surveillance would be difficult. When Yassen went to bed, he never closed the curtains. He liked to see out, to watch for any movement in the street. Every city has a natural rhythm and anything that breaks it – a man lingering on a corner or a car passing the same way twice – might warn him that it was time to leave at once. And he never slept for more than four hours, not even in the most comfortable bed.

A DO NOT DISTURB sign hung in front of him as he turned the corner and approached the door. Had it been obeyed? Yassen reached into his trouser pocket and took out a small silver device, about the same size and shape as a pen. He pressed one end, covering the handle with a thin spray of diazafluoren – a simple chemical reagent. Quickly, he spun the pen round and pressed the other end, activating a fluorescent light. There were no fingerprints. If anyone had been into the room since he had left, they had wiped the handle clean. He put the pen away, then knelt down and checked the bottom of the door. Earlier in the day, he had placed a single hair across the crack. It was one of the oldest warning signals in the book but that didn't stop it being effective. The hair was still in place. Yassen straightened up and, using his electronic pass key, went in.

It took him less than a minute to ascertain that

everything was exactly as he had left it. His brief-case was 4.6 centimetres from the edge of the desk. His suitcase was positioned at a 95 degree angle from the wall. There were no fingerprints on either of the locks. He removed the digital tape recorder that had been clipped magnetically to the side of his service fridge and glanced at the dial. Nothing had been recorded. Nobody had been in. Many people would have found all these precau-tions annoying and time-consuming but for Yassen they were as much a part of his daily routine as tying his shoelaces or cleaning his teeth.

It was twelve minutes past six when he sat down at the desk and opened his computer, an ordinary Apple MacBook. His password had seventeen digits and he changed it every month. He took off his watch and laid it on the surface beside him. Then he went to eBay, left-clicked on Collectibles and scrolled through Coins. He soon found what he was looking for: a gold coin show-ing the head of the emperor Caligula with the date AD11. There had been no bids for this par-ticular coin because, as any collector would know, it did not in fact exist. In AD11, the mad Roman emperor, Caligula, had not even been born. The entire website was a fake and looked it. The name of the coin dealer – Mintomatic – had been specially chosen to put off any casual purchaser. Mintomatic was supposedly based in Shanghai and did not have Top-rated Seller status. All the coins it advertised were either fake or valueless.

Yassen sat quietly until a quarter past six. At exactly the moment that the second hand passed over the twelve on his watch, he pressed the button to place a bid, then entered his User ID – false, of course – and password. Finally, he entered a bid of £2,518.15. The figures were based on the day's date and the exact time. He pressed ENTER and a window opened that had nothing to do with eBay or with Roman coins. Nobody else could have seen it. It would have been impossible to discover where it had originated. The message had been bounced around a dozen countries, travelling through an anonymity network, before it had reached him. This is known as onion routing because of its many layers. It had also passed through an encrypted tunnel, a secure shell, that ensured that only Yassen could read what had been written. If someone had managed to arrive at the same screen by accident, they would have seen only nonsense and within three seconds a virus would have entered their computer and obliterated the motherboard. The Apple computer, however, had been authorized to receive the message and Yassen saw three words:

### KILL ALEX RIDER

They were exactly what he had expected.

Yassen had known all along that his employers would insist on punishing the agent who had been involved in the disaster that the Stormbreaker operation had become. He even wondered if he himself might not be made to retire ... permanently, of course. It was simple common sense. If people failed, they were eliminated. There were no second chances. Yassen was lucky in that he had been employed as a subcontractor. He didn't have overall responsibility for what had happened and at the end of the day he couldn't be blamed. On the other hand, they would have to make an example of Alex Rider. It didn't matter that he was just fourteen years old. Tomorrow he would have to die.

Yassen looked at the screen for a few seconds more, then closed the computer. He had never killed a child before but the thought did not particularly trouble him. Alex Rider had made his own choices. He should have been at school, but instead, for whatever reason, he had allowed the Special Operations Division of MI6 to recruit him. From schoolboy to spy. It was certainly unusual – but the truth was, he had been remarkably successful. Beginner's luck, maybe, but he had brought an end to an operation that had been several years in the planning. He was responsible for the deaths of two operatives. He had annoyed some extremely powerful people. He very much deserved the death that was coming his way.

And yet...

Yassen sat where he was with the computer in front of him. Nothing had changed in his expression but there was, perhaps, something flickering deep in his eyes. Outside, the sun was beginning to set, the evening sky turning a hard, unforgiving grey. The streets were full of commuters hurrying home. They weren't just on the other side of a hotel window. They were in another world. Yassen knew that he would never be one of them. Briefly, he closed his eyes. He was thinking about what had happened. About Stormbreaker. How had it gone so wrong?

From Yassen's point of view, it had been a fairly routine assignment. A Lebanese businessman by the name of Herod Sayle had wanted to buy two hundred litres of a deadly smallpox virus called R5 and he had approached the one organization that might be able to supply it in such huge quantities. That organization was Scorpia. The letters of the name stood for sabotage, corruption, intelligence and assassination, which were its main activities. R5 was a Chinese product, manufactured illegally in a facility near Guiyang, and by chance one of the members of the executive board of Scorpia was Chinese. Dr Three had extensive contacts in East Asia and had used his influence to organize the purchase. It had been Yassen's job to oversee delivery to the UK.

Six weeks ago, he had flown to Hong Kong a few days ahead of the R5, which had been transported in a private plane, a turboprop Xian MA60, from Guiyang. The plan was to load it into a container ship to Rotterdam – disguised as part of a shipment of Luck of the Dragon Chinese beer. Special barrels had been constructed at a warehouse in Kowloon, with reinforced glass containers holding the R5 suspended inside the liquid. There are more than five thousand container ships at sea at any one time and around seventeen million deliveries are made every year. There isn't a customs service in the world that can keep its eye on every cargo and Yassen was confident that the journey would be trouble-free. He'd been given a false passport and papers that identified him as Erik Olsen, a merchant seaman from Copenhagen, and he would travel with the R5 until it reached its destination.

But, as is so often the way, things had not gone as planned. A few days before the barrels were due to leave, Yassen had become aware that the warehouse was under surveillance. He had been lucky. A cigarette being lit behind a window in a building that should have been empty told him all he needed to know. Slipping through Kowloon under cover of darkness, he had identified a team of three agents of the AIVD – the Algemene Inlichtingen en Veiligheidsdienst – the Dutch secret service. There must have been a tip-off. The agents did not know what they were looking for but they were aware that something was on its way to their country and Yassen had been forced to kill all three of them with a silenced Beretta 92, a pistol he particularly favoured because of its accuracy and reliability. Clearly, the R5 could not leave in a container ship after all. A fallback had to be found.

As it happened, there was a Chinese Han class nuclear submarine in Hong Kong going through final repairs before leaving for exercises in the Northern Atlantic. Yassen met the captain in a private club overlooking the harbour and offered him a bribe of two million American dollars to carry the R5 with him when he left. He had informed Scorpia of this decision and they knew that it would dig into their operational profit but there were at least some advantages. Moving the R5 from Rotterdam to the UK would have been difficult and dangerous. Herod Sayle was based in Cornwall with direct access to the coast, so the new approach would make for a much more secure delivery.

Two weeks later, on a crisp, cloudless night in April, the submarine surfaced off the Cornish coast. Yassen, still using the identity of Erik Olsen, had travelled with it. He had quite enjoyed the experience of cruising silently through the depths of the ocean, sealed in a metal tube. The Chinese crew had been ordered not to speak to him on any account and that suited him too. It was only when he climbed onto dry land that he once again took command, overseeing the transfer of the virus and other supplies that Herod Sayle had ordered. The work had to be done swiftly. The captain of the submarine had insisted that he would wait no more than thirty minutes. He might have two million dollars in a Swiss bank account but he had no wish to provoke an international incident ... which would certainly have been followed by his own court martial and execution.

Thirty guards had helped carry the various boxes to the waiting trucks, scrambling along the shoreline in the light of a perfect half-moon, the submarine looking somehow fantastic and out of place, half submerged in the slate-grey water of the English Channel. And almost from the start, Yassen had known something was wrong. He was being watched. He was sure of it. Some might call it a sort of animal instinct but for Yassen it was simpler than that. He had been active in the field for many years. During that time, he had been in danger almost constantly. It had been necessary to fine-tune all his senses simply to survive. And although he hadn't seen or heard anything, a silent voice was screaming at him that there was someone hiding about twenty metres away, behind a cluster of boulders on the edge of the beach.

He had been on the point of investigating when one of Sayle's men, standing on the wooden jetty, had dropped one of the boxes. The sound of metal hitting wood shattered the calm of the night and Yassen spun on his heel, everything else forgotten. There was limited space on the submarine and so the R5 had been transferred from the beer barrels to less-protective aluminium boxes. Yassen knew that if the glass vial inside had been shattered, if the rubber seal had been compromised, everyone on the beach would be dead before the sun had risen.

He sprinted forward, crouching down to inspect the damage. There was a slight dent in one side of the box. But the seal had held.

The guard looked at him with a sickly smile. He was quite a lot older than Yassen, probably an ex-convict recruited from a local prison. And he was scared. He tried to make light of it. "I won't do that again!" he said.

"No," Yassen replied. "You won't." The Beretta was already in his hand. He shot the man in the chest, propelling him backwards into the darkness and the sea below. It had been necessary to set an example. There would be no further clumsiness that night.

Sitting in the hotel with the computer in front of him, Yassen remembered the moment. He was almost certain now that it had been Alex Rider behind the boulder and if it hadn't been for the accident, he would have been discovered there and then. Alex had infiltrated Sayle Enterprises, pretending to be the winner of a magazine competition. Somehow he had slipped out of his room, evading the guards and the searchlights, and had joined the convoy making its way down to the beach. There could be no other explanation. Later on, Alex had followed Herod Sayle to London. He had already been responsible for the deaths of two of Sayle's associates – Nadia Vole and the disfigured servant Mr Grin – despite little training and no experience. This was his first mission. Even so, he had single-handedly smashed the Stormbreaker operation. Sayle had been lucky to escape, a few steps ahead of the police.

## KILL ALEX RIDER

It was what he deserved. Alex had interfered with a Scorpia assignment and he would have cost the organization at least five million pounds ... the final payment owed by Herod Sayle. Worse than that, he would have damaged their international reputation. The lesson had to be learnt.

There was a knock at the door. Yassen had ordered room service. It wasn't just easier to eat inside the hotel, it was safer. Why make himself a target when he didn't need to?

"Leave it outside," he called out. He spoke English with no trace of a Russian accent. He spoke French, German and Arabic equally well.

The room was almost dark now. Yassen's dinner sat on a tray in the corridor, rapidly getting cold. But still he did not move away from the desk and the computer in front of him. He would kill Alex Rider tomorrow morning. There was no question of his disobeying orders. It didn't matter that the two of them were linked, that they were connected in a way Alex couldn't possibly know.

John Rider. Alex's father.

Their code names. Hunter and Cossack.

Yassen couldn't help himself. He reached into his pocket and took out a car key, the sort that had two remote control buttons to open and close the doors. But this key did not belong to any car. Yassen pressed the OPEN button twice and the CLOSE button three times and a concealed memory stick sprang out onto the palm of his hand. He glanced at it briefly. He knew that it was madness to carry it. He had been tempted to destroy it many times. But every man has his weakness and this was his. He opened the computer again and inserted it.

The file required another password. He keyed it in. And there it was on the screen in front of him, not in English letters but in Cyrillic, the Russian alphabet.

His personal diary. The story of his life.

He sat back and began to read.

READ OTHER GREAT BOOKS BY
ANTHONY HOROWITZ...

ACTION
ADRENALINE
ADVENTURE

Alex Rider – you're
never too young
to die…

Alex Rider has 90
minutes to save
the world.

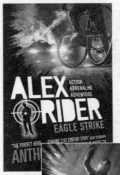

High in the Alps,
death waits for
Alex Rider…

Once stung, twice as
deadly. Alex Rider
wants revenge.

Sharks. Assassins.
Nuclear bombs.
Alex Rider's in
deep water.

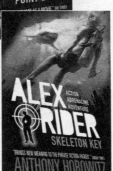

He's back –
and this time
there are no limits.

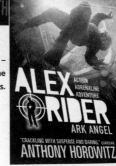

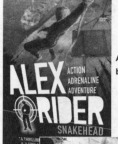
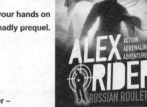
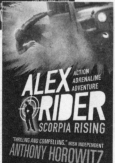

# WELCOME TO THE DARK SIDE OF ANTHONY HOROWITZ

**BOOK ONE**

He always knew he was different. First there were the dreams. Then the deaths began.

**BOOK TWO**

It began with Raven's Gate. But it's not over yet. Once again the enemy is stirring.

# THE POWER OF FIVE

**BOOK THREE**

Darkness covers the earth.
The Old Ones have returned.
The battle must begin.

**BOOK FOUR**

An ancient evil is unleashed.
Five have the power to defeat it.
But one of them has been taken.

**BOOK FIVE**

Five Gatekeepers.
One chance to save mankind.
Chaos beckons. Oblivion awaits.

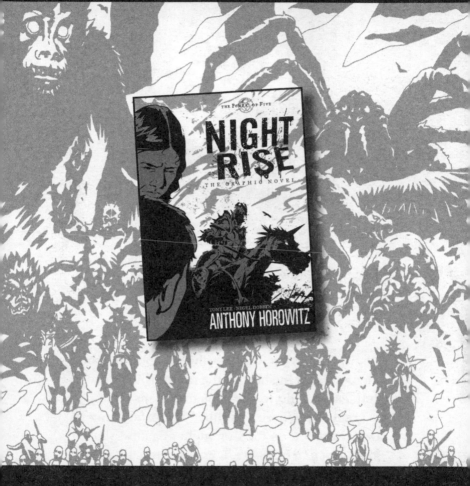

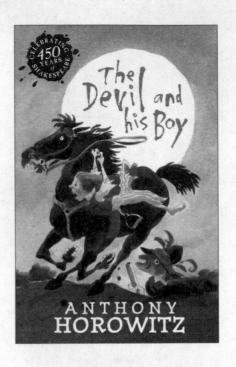

Heading for an exciting new life in London, Tom
Falconer is ambushed by the murderous Ratsey.
Helpless and alone, the orphan gallops towards
the great city, where a number of mortal dangers
await him. But on the first night of a new play –
*The Devil and his Boy* – Tom discovers that the
fate of Elizabethan England rests in his hands.

"A cracking historical adventure... Thrilling." *TES*

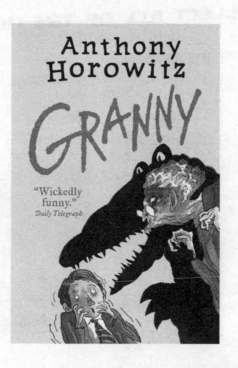

Anthony
Horowitz

GRANNY

"Wickedly
funny."
*Daily Telegraph*

Joe Warden isn't happy. He has rich, uncaring
parents and he's virtually a prisoner in the huge
family mansion, Thattlebee Hall. But his real
problem is his granny. Not only is she physically
repulsive and unbelievably mean, she seems to have
some secret plan – and that plan involves him.

Can Joe thwart Granny's evil scheme before he's
turned into neoplasmic slime?

"Wickedly funny." *Daily Telegraph*

"Hugely popular ... I can hear Horowitz fans
drooling." *The Times*

# COLLECT ALL OF THE HILARIOUS

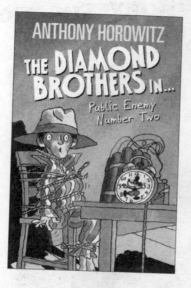

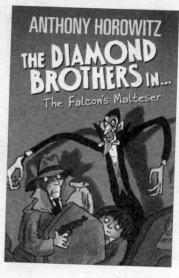

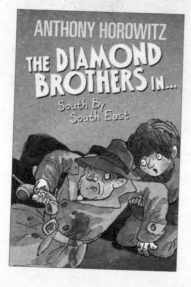

# DIAMOND BROTHERS INVESTIGATIONS

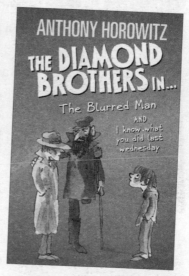

Tim Diamond is the world's worst private detective, and unfortunately for his quick-thinking brother, Nick, the cases keep coming in. What connects them? Murder! And if the Diamond Brothers don't play their cards right, they could be next!

# MORE WICKEDLY FUNNY
# ANTHONY HOROWITZ BOOKS

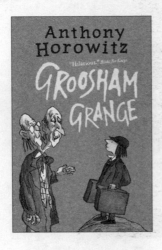

Sent to Groosham Grange as a last resort by his parents, David quickly discovers that his new school is a very chilling place indeed. How on earth can he escape with his life?

One evening Tad Spencer wishes he was someone else. When he wakes up, he is in a cruel and squalid funfair world and soon uncovers a secret that puts his life in danger.

"Move over Roald Dahl, here comes Anthony Horowitz." *Young Telegraph*

"Hugely popular... I can hear Horowitz fans drooling." *The Times*

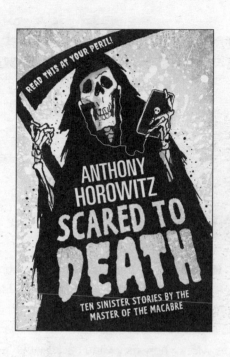

## SOMETIMES
## YOUR NIGHTMARES BECOME REAL...

This terrifically twisted and wickedly funny
collection of spine-tingling short stories is only
recommended for the most fearless of readers.

"A deliciously macabre collection of horror
stories told with lashings of gruesome relish."
## THE BOOKSELLER

Photograph © Jon Cartwright

**Anthony Horowitz** is the author of the number one bestselling Alex Rider books and the Power of Five series. He enjoys huge international acclaim as a writer for both children and adults. After the success of his first James Bond novel, *Trigger Mortis*, he was invited back by the Ian Fleming Estate to write a second, *Forever and a Day*. His latest crime novel, *The Word is Murder*, introducing Detective Daniel Hawthorne, was a bestseller. Anthony has won numerous awards, including the Bookseller Association/Nielsen Author of the Year Award, the Children's Book of the Year Award at the British Book Awards, and the Red House Children's Book Award. He has also created and written many major television series, including *Collision, New Blood* and the BAFTA-winning *Foyle's War*. He lives in London with his wife, two sons and his dog, Boss.

You can find out more about Anthony and his work at:
www.alexrider.com
@AnthonyHorowitz